D1483289

STEVEN FARQUHAR

THE SPANIARD'S DAGGER

ARAGON PUBLISHING
Kennebunk, Maine

Published in the United States by
ARAGON PUBLISHING
65 Old Port Road
Kennebunk, ME 04043

Library of Congress Control Number: 2007900383

ISBN 978-0-9792949-0-7

First Aragon Publishing hardcover edition April 2007

Artwork Copyright © 2007 by Manuela Lorenzi

Visit our website at:
http://www.stevenfarquhar.com

ACKNOWLEDGMENTS

This book would have never been completed without the help of numerous individuals. Their editorial suggestions, logistical support, and many words of encouragement have kept me going. Special thanks go to Andrea Goodwin, Frank Grandone, Marilyn and Richard Kayser, Giovanni and Mimi Lorenzi, and Marcia Powers.

My family has watched me devote hundreds of hours to a word-processor. They have shown a tremendous deal of understanding and patience. Ashley and Sabrina have been wonderful. My utmost gratitude goes to Manuela, copilot from the inception of this novel all the way to her designing its cover.

Finally, I am indebted for inspiration and constant guidance to my teacher, Paramahansa Yogananda.

The law of gravitation worked as efficiently before Newton as after him. The cosmos would be fairly chaotic if its laws could not operate without the sanction of human belief.
 – Sri Yukteswar

~ 1 ~

The woman searched desperately for something firm on the drenched slope, her feet probing gingerly. She had to muster all her will power not to panic and kick blindly for a foothold, as clumps of soil were breaking off all around her. At last, she struck a narrow ledge. Forgetting even to breathe, she tested its strength, feeling her heart thump behind her naked breasts. The coarse sandstone didn't give. She pressed hard. It still held. She locked her knees, straightened out, wiped the water off her face. No time to rest. The cliff became more treacherous with every drop hurtling from the sky. Worse, if she didn't hurry, he'd cut off her escape route.

She looked down, squinting through the downpour. He had already ascended to a point three arm lengths to her right and less than twice her height below. She had to get to the top first. She knew she could outrun him, despite her present state.

She gulped a huge lungful of air, thrust up her hand, and drove five nails deep into the wet dirt. The second hand followed, less aggressively, for she had to protect her belly. The child growing inside had suffered a severe blow when she slipped earlier in the ascent, which left bloody scratches and a throbbing gash by her navel. Her brain tried to block out what this probably meant. She didn't want to think about it. Not now.

The two bodies continued to claw their way up the cliff like two giant insects. Though the man gained, she finally dragged herself over the edge before he did. For some moments she recuperated, her face pressed into the soggy moss, while cold and heavy raindrops pelted her bare back. *Keep moving!* Run!

STEVEN FARQUHAR

But when she pulled herself up, her heart froze. He had already reached the top, kneeling just a few feet away, his dark eyes consuming her glistening torso.

~2~

N aked from the waist up, knees pulled to his chest, Liam Kindayr squatted in the bow of the *Sea Urchin*, his bare back rubbing up against the weathered teak of the cabin. Santa Rosa Island's verdant hills loomed large in the background, though they grew more distant with each leap the vessel made into the wind-swept Channel toward the mainland. Trying to ignore the deafening roar of an ancient diesel, Liam puzzled over the origin of the strange dagger in his hand, contemplating the last few days.

Had it only been a week? Frustrated from his latest battle with an unyielding client, he had traded canvas and paint for the elbow space of Channel Islands National Park. He'd needed to get away from the stress of a hectic civilization, to forget the false promises and wasted time, to feel one with earth and sky and trees, and to meditate and draw closer to God. Last night, watching the sun bleed into the western horizon in screaming scarlet and ocher, the reflection of a light ray grabbed his attention. Lying on the stream bank near the water, he picked up what at first looked like a rusty knife. Closer inspection revealed a dagger, similar to those he'd seen in movies.

How heavy it was! Broken at the end, no longer tapering to a perfect point, a thick veneer of rust covered much of the flame-shaped blade. He again tested its sharpness, where the steel had not yet oxidized, and bloodied his thumb for a second time. The blade's edge nearly matched that of a razor. A round pommel, also coated with rust, topped the beautifully chiseled handle. A chipped, circular piece of ruby-red glass adorned the pommel's center. The guard formed a "T" with the blade, with four more pieces of red glass on the top of the "T," two on either side. Four concave depressions lined the bottom of this guard. Three were empty, but the fourth held another piece of the same red glass.

"What are you doing?" Binh shouted from the helm, startling Liam. He glanced up.

"I found this old piece of junk."

The fisherman gave his trademark throaty chuckle and ran a hand through coal-black hair. "Then why do you act like it's precious? Let me see." Skipper and owner of the *Sea Urchin*, and youngest son of the last Franco-Vietnamese to get out before the Stars and Stripes sank over that infamous Saigon rooftop, Binh Debettencourt's livelihood depended on diving for the critters in whose honor he had baptized the boat. The Japanese had a ravenous appetite for California urchin. He supplemented his income by ferrying people to and from the islands, though he never expected any pay from friends.

Liam didn't want to move back to where Binh stood, but he knew that doing so would beat dealing with the skipper's insatiable curiosity. No way would Binh let him have peace. Any unnecessary conversation promised to tighten the knots in his stomach, the last thing he needed. "It's a dagger some hiker must have lost," he hollered toward the helm, rising and beginning to slowly tip-toe aft. He religiously kept his eyes glued to the horizon to ward off seasickness.

"I found it in a canyon, lying on the stream bank." He slapped it into Binh's outstretched hand and took a deep breath.

Binh's amused smile vanished. Mindfully turning the weapon in his hands, his dark eyes sparkled with fascination. "Hmm, this sure is something. I've never seen one like it. And you found it where?"

"On the island's south side," Liam answered curtly. "By a stream." When a rolling swell lifted the boat, he quickly planted himself on a bench, the well tanned and healthy look of his face incrementally fading to a sickly white. Fool! He chastised himself. Why did he have to move? Staring fixedly

4

toward the shore, he fought to keep calm, exhaling slowly and performing mental acrobatics to ward off the rising nausea.

"You're gonna keep it inside you, right?" Binh suddenly demanded. Liam ignored him, sucking in and tossing out rhythmic breaths.

The skipper laughed uneasily. "Just don't mess up my deck. I sure as hell don't want to be scrubbing up your breakfast."

That did it. Liam's belly stiffened, and he could feel the blood drain from his face. Binh finally shut up and, with a sympathetic glance, quickly turned the helm to change course. The *Sea Urchin* now sliced into the Channel's heavy swell at more of an angle, lessening the boat's vertical motion. Liam kept his stomach's contents and drifted off into a fitful slumber, more optimistic he'd make it to shore without having to feed the fish.

A dilapidated blue Cadillac with scuffed white walls pulled into a parking stall behind the yacht club. The door swung open, and a stunted leg jabbed the air. A blimp of a man got out and somehow managed to slam the door with exquisite flair, belying his slovenly appearance. The man's massive torso covered nearly the full breadth of the door, but his balding head only reached to about flush with the car's roof.

He lumbered into one of the waterfront stores and pushed through a crowd milling around the cash register. He paid for a medium bag of barbecue-flavored potato chips and a pack of bite-size Snickers. Then he exited and took up position by one of the restrooms overlooking the harbor. He assured himself that he would have an unobstructed view of the *Sea Urchin's* mooring and touched the binoculars under his shiny polyester jacket. He sensed impending success and began to attack the chips. Important work awaited him.

Liam woke when the motor wound down and his body registered the vessel decelerate. Five hundred yards separated them from the entrance to Santa Barbara Harbor. Binh kept the *Sea Urchin* clear of a collection of loud-colored sunfish racing each other around a string of buoys. Liam shuffled to his friend, who pointed the bow at the wharf.

"You'll be off the boat soon enough. Feelin' any better?"

"A little. The waves always do me in." He didn't let on that he was happy to get back on land. Once, as a twelve-year-old, he'd fallen into the Colorado during a rafting trip through the Grand Canyon. They finally fished him out a mile downstream, shivering from cold as much as fear. He had acquired a deep respect for water.

A few minutes later, the *Sea Urchin* approached the piers with the diesel puckering and Binh poised to dock. He tossed Liam a rope. "Tie her up," he barked over the noise of the engine before finally turning off the ignition.

Holding the rope, Liam jumped on the pier as the hull made contact. "Have you ever thought about investing in a new motor? That thing's a torture."

Binh raised an eyebrow. "Tell you what. I'll take you on as a deck hand for a couple of weeks, at the end of which you'd be in love with my baby. Might even make a sailor out of you." He rubbed the top of the cabin affectionately.

"I'll consider it, Admiral." Liam loved the ocean, but it also made him nervous. Dark and foreboding, its depths represented a repository of all kinds of critters driven to sting or bite or tear or grab him. He couldn't explain it, but the sea seemed to hold some secret he had yet to uncover. He jumped back on the deck to get his backpack.

"I've got to go."

The skipper flashed the dagger. "Don't you want this?"

Liam shrugged his shoulders. "Toss it. It looks kind of nice, but it's useless. An old knife with glass beads."

Binh stared at him in disbelief. "Glass, my ass!" His face instantly lit up, and he smiled proudly at his poetry. "Your years in college apparently haven't done you any good."

Liam smiled sheepishly, waiting for Binh to illuminate him. "So, what's the story?" he finally asked.

Puffing up his chest and flaring his nostrils in an overblown display of superior intellect, Binh delivered. "I'm not claiming to be an expert, but this is some damn hard 'glass,' if I may say so. I've tried scratching it—which didn't do a thing." He let it sink in, eyeing Liam with increasing bemusement. Then he got serious.

"Listen, my mother used to work for this jeweler. Rich guy! She'd decorate his stores and learn all about precious stones. When I was a kid she sometimes took me along and let me watch. She'd explain how gems form, how they're cut, all that. Now, I admit it's been an awful long time, and I don't remember all she taught me." He scratched the side of his head with the pommel. "But I have no doubt that, um, 'educated people,'" he chuckled, "would know these red sweeties for what they are—rubies."

"Rubies! No way!"

Binh waved him off. "I'd put money on it."

"Give me that dagger!"

Binh handed it to Liam, who examined it with a whole new attitude. *Was this really ruby?* He pulled out a Swiss army knife and tried to scratch the red stone. No effect. So he scraped the chipped corner of the larger stone along the blade of the knife. It cut a groove. He looked up at Binh, who grinned knowingly.

"You believe me now?"

Liam thought back to Geology 101. Ruby, also known as corundum, was the hardest naturally occurring substance, except for diamonds. He felt extremely stupid now for dismissing it as glass. And his friend's annoying laughter didn't help.

Binh boxed him on the shoulder. "So, what are you gonna do with it?"

Liam hesitated. "Well, I suppose that whoever owned this dagger can't be too thrilled. I think I should try to return it."

"Nonsense!" Binh huffed. "Look at the rust on that thing. It's been out in the open for some time, and not even all of the gems remain. Doesn't that tell you something?"

True. The dagger had obviously been lost a while ago, and its owner must have given up on it. "I wonder why anyone would carry a ruby-studded dagger to Santa Rosa."

Binh turned pensive. "Some rich tourist, I bet. The guy camped in the same place you went and lost it. He's probably not from around here."

"And how do you figure all that?" Liam shot back, irritated that Binh's brain seemed to process at twice the speed of his own.

"Rubies aren't cheap. If I had lost that dagger I'd sure as hell come looking for it, unless it wasn't worth my time. Anyone living close enough would have done the same. But they didn't. Or at least they didn't find it. It's yours now."

Liam smiled. "There's nothing left then but to find out what rubies go for these days. I'll sell them and we'll have ourselves a feast."

Binh's face lit up. "You're finally talking sense."

They shook hands. Liam shoved the dagger into his backpack and leapt onto the pier.

"In the meantime, you know where to find me when the sea calls," Binh shouted, giggling with glee. Liam pretended not to hear. He marched past the moored fishing vessels and toward Cabrillo Boulevard, brooding over the mysterious dagger's origin.

The hand holding the binoculars fell to the man's side. He stomped his feet like a disappointed child, bemoaning his bad luck. At his post right on time—he took great pride in his reputation for punctuality—he had observed the *Sea Urchin* make fast and even seen the skipper hand something to the passenger, who now was leaving with that something in his pack.

Two sturdy fishermen suddenly strode up, making pointed remarks about nosy slobs with scopes minding others' business. They stopped in front of him, staring menacingly. It smelled like trouble.

"Hi, nice day, guys, isn't it?" Nothing disarmed like good old-fashioned politeness. But when one of them stepped closer, he knew that these brutes weren't interested in small talk.

"If I thought you were checking *me* out, I'd kick your fat ass. Got it?"

He quivered like jelly. The bag of potato chips slid off his hand, his fingers and mouth glistening with grease. "Please, I would never do such a thing. I was only checking out those hot babes by the store. You can understand that."

The angry chap nodded derisively. "Is that right? Looks to me like those lenses aimed at the boats." He shook his head is disgust, and his eyes held a warning. "Don't let me catch you here again." With that he turned to his friend, and the two left, casting threatening glances over their shoulders. By the time they finally disappeared in the distance, the young guy from the *Sea Urchin* had vanished.

Binoculars bouncing off his chest, he waddled to a bench and let himself fall back on it. He whipped out a cell phone and punched in a number. "It's Dave." He listened. "No," he repeated twice. "I couldn't really tell. He had his back toward me." He listened again. Then more high-pitched, "what was I supposed to do?" He fidgeted with his shirt collar. "No way. I can't follow him anyhow, and I already ran into trouble with a couple of jerks." He breathed heavily. "Good. Yes."

Relieved, he hung up and lost himself in the crowd, pulling a Snickers from his pocket.

The person on the other end of the line, his pallid face taut with fury, straddled a boulder on Santa Rosa. He picked up a rock and flung it savagely.

The Jeep squealed off Cheltenham Road and roared up a driveway ascending to a white stucco villa with a red-tiled roof. Passing through a cedar arbor that strained under a bougainvillea filled with a thousand burgundy blossoms, the vehicle continued past the villa and slid to a stop in front of the guest quarters. Liam admired the lush plantings of the property and inhaled the spicy scents of sage, eucalyptus, and wild fennel. He loved living in Santa Barbara, with its warm days and cool nights. The architectural and physical beauty of the area never grew stale, and Liam couldn't imagine a community where he'd rather spend his life.

Silence enveloped the sprawling main house. Its proud owners, Tim and Elizabeth Ludmon, happily circled the globe aboard a luxury liner. One month into a hundred-day itinerary, they wouldn't disturb Liam for weeks. Tim originally built the guesthouse for his son. When he and his wife at last faced reality after having spent half a lifetime in a materialistic fantasy world, and recognized that Junior's ever-deepening addiction to drugs and promiscuous sex would not go away, they kicked out their only child. Timing couldn't have been more fortuitous. Liam's banquet hall murals so impressed the Ludmons that they asked him to stay and keep an eye on the Spanish mansion during their numerous excursions abroad. To Liam the arrangement came from heaven, with rent a token of market value and limitless space for his canvases.

He went straight for the kitchen and fixed some fresh lemonade. The cold, tart liquid began to relieve the seasickness-induced headache. *So how much are those rubies worth?* He reached for the Yellow Pages. After jotting down an address he kicked his Tevas into a corner and checked the answering machine.

THE SPANIARD'S DAGGER

A call from a woman with a very sexy voice, who "absolutely must have one of your murals to bring light into my four walls," neutralized his migraine's last jabs. Several messages from friends, a reminder of a dentist's appointment, then the voice he'd been waiting for.

"Hey, there's a mob laying siege to my booth, so I won't be long. We got grounded in Sicily. Mechanical problem with the bird. Looks like I'll be stuck here for a day. I'll call again." Static replaced the voice. Then the line went dead, followed by a long beep. The tape rewound.

A sad smile shot across Liam's face. As much as he looked forward to seeing his brother for the first time in two years, Patrick's voice never failed to evoke sad memories. The two of them represented the last functioning remnants of a broken family.

A blood clot in the brain killed their super athletic mother while running the Boston Marathon during Liam's second year as an art student at the Rhode Island School of Design. Father, who ran a thriving law firm in Providence, snapped. Within a few months he lost all but the shirt on his back. Conquering his addiction to alcohol took him another four years. The wound of Mother's death never healed. He worked in a nursery now, having found some solace in the company of his beloved plants. Liam sent money when he could. Patrick diverted a portion of his army salary. It didn't add up to much, but at least it kept the old man in a small apartment in a decent neighborhood. Since Father had never tasted poverty, the brothers could not bear to watch him wither in some dump.

Their sister suffered from no such compunction. Andrea had also struggled to get over Mother's death, but she found it even harder to deal with their Father spiraling out of control. Fifteen at the time, she never forgave him for succumbing to gin just when she needed him most. Eventually she married a handsome pilot and left the Ocean

State. She lived in Chicago now. She rarely made contact. In fact, it had been so long, she might be dead.

The shop façade on the corner of Garden and Anapamu oozed uninhibited commercialism. *Michael's Treasures'* doors stood wide open, covered with colorful, fancifully-shaped ads designed to convince the gullible that opportunity beckoned here. "Gorgeous necklaces," "rarest gemstones," and "razor sharp" cutlery of all sorts "could not be purchased cheaper, or sold for a better price anywhere west of the Rockies." The owner obligingly supplied a crude, hand-drawn map depicting the Pacific coast with San Diego as the southern, Seattle the northern terminus. Santa Barbara sat nestled in the mountains between the remaining two dots on the map, Los Angeles and San Francisco. Only the "SANTA BARBARA" sported heavy underlining, and a fat dollar sign below the name occupied most of the Channel. The mapmaker had scribbled the words "ROCKY MOUNTAINS" near the right edge, leaving blank the thousands of square miles in between. A large sign on the window advertised Native American art from the Southwest.

This guy'd do better on Cabrillo Boulevard, or lower State, Liam thought. But he quickly changed his mind. Though tourists concentrated their purchasing power nearer the waterfront, the stiff rents there kept all but the wealthiest at bay. *Should I get an appraisal at this shack? Or should I go elsewhere?* Liam was not a shopper and hated spending time in stores, any stores, but hey, he'd come this far. If their estimate didn't satisfy him, he could always go elsewhere.

He entered and approached the counter near the back. "Hello," he said, in no particular direction. No response. The smell of cheap sandalwood incense hung heavy in the air. Hunkered over a tiny workbench behind the counter, a fortyish woman with cotton candy hair took no notice of her customer, battling with the innards of a dissected watch. Liam waited respectfully, not wanting to disturb. After a solid minute passed without any acknowledgment of his presence, he scanned the shop's recesses. Was she serving someone else? But he saw no one.

Another thirty seconds transpired, and he felt his temperature creep up a few degrees. What the hell had gotten into this woman? She continued to ignore him. His throat dried. *Okay,* he decided. She asked for it. But just when he opened his mouth to let her have it, she pushed aside the watch and looked up. Thick black gloss covered her lips.

"I'm sorry to make you wait." Her voice rang sweet, but sterile. "Can I help you?" she mollified him. At least she had apologized.

He reached into his canvas bag, with a dull clank placed the dagger on the glass counter, and pointed at the rubies. "I'd like to know how much these are worth."

She cast him an innocuous glance and began to carefully scrutinize the weapon, remaining taciturn for some time. While Liam wondered whether her husband got more than three sentences per day out of her, he caught sight of two sizable breasts glaring at him from beneath her low-cut blouse. He tried to avert his gaze, but a dark spot on that flesh locked his eyes like magnets to a metal plate. Though the store's weak lighting cast long shadows, there could be no doubt. A dense tuft of black hair grew between her breasts. He felt her eyes on his and looked away, coughing to hide his embarrassment.

"So, uh–hum, what do you think?" he said, sensing a major blush traveling from the neck up. When she graced him with an inviting smile, Liam contemplated escape. He hated such situations. They annoyed him to no end.

She took the dagger in her hands and placed it so that her palms supported opposite ends, trying to get a feel for its weight. "How long have you owned this?" she demanded, alternately raising and lowering her hands so that the weapon moved up and down as if controlled by an invisible puppeteer. *If she would just wipe that suggestive smile off her face.*

"A couple of days. I found it on the islands."

13

"Oh," she said, in a drawn-out way. "Which one?"

Liam could have sworn her ears rotated his way, and he instantly regretted his words. Having a powerful sense of being interrogated, his instinct warned him to beware. "Santa Cruz," he lied. All he wanted was an estimate on the rubies. *Does this woman know something about the dagger I don't?*

"Really? Well, it's yours now. And you want to know how much the gemstones are worth. Well, not a fortune," she giggled, "but I can make your trip worth your while." She leaned forward just enough to allow Liam an unobstructed view of her breasts, almost to the nipples.

After some moments of inspecting the rubies, she looked up. "These smaller ones exhibit nice faceting, but they're quite dark. Far too many inclusions for AAA quality. They leave much to be desired."

"Can you translate that? I don't have much experience with gems." He bit his tongue. Why had he raced down here like a schoolboy without reading up on the stuff first? *Amateur!*

"Of course. Rubies can be quite costly, but this depends to a great degree on their color. When they come this dark, they're not nearly as precious as their higher-grade AAA cousins. As you can see, these here are not very striking. In fact, except for the expert cut, their value would be relatively insignificant."

She continued, visibly relishing Liam's ignorance. "I do have a pretty good idea how heavy they are, but even the large one, a quarter karat at best, isn't very valuable." She paused, pensive eyes caressing the dagger. "I would have to give serious thought to how I could resell these stones." She again fell silent, calculating the low price the rubies would fetch.

Liam grew impatient. This woman began to get on his nerves. Finally she finished her additions. "The smaller stones don't count for much, but if you want to sell the dagger I'll give you a good deal." That seductive smile crept into her face again. "I'll pay you $675 cash, or you can have $750 in store credit. You may redeem it anytime in one chunk, or piecemeal if you choose. You do live in town?"

"Yes," he nodded, wondering whether she'd made him a fair offer. He had no clue. But seven crisp hundred-dollar bills made for a pleasant New Year's bonus. Should he take the cash and get it done with, or should he get a second appraisal elsewhere? *What if she's trying to rip me off?*

While he weighed the pros and cons, the woman's subsequent behavior settled the issue. She put down the dagger and reached for what looked like a leather notepad. Her breasts bouncing with each move, she nonchalantly placed it on the counter. A ballpoint pen materialized in her hand. With its tip she flicked open the pad, revealing a receipt book.

"What shall it be, cash or credit?"

Liam couldn't help laughing out loud. "I didn't think we had a deal," he said. "I'm not ready to sell the dagger."

"But that's what you wanted to do," she said sourly, her smile no longer so sugary.

"No, I only asked for an estimate." He gave her his best what-are-you-gonna-say-now? stare.

She raised her hands in an appeasing gesture. "Of course. You just wanted to know how much the rubies are worth. I'm so used to clients coming in here wanting to dump their merchandise to make a quick sale. You give 'em a fair price, they accept, and it's finished. No hassles. No wasting each other's time. I'm so sorry." Her tone had changed again to pure honey.

She got up, her hand firm on the dagger. "Perhaps you'd like to speak to Michael. He's the owner and an expert on gems. He could examine the stones and will happily pay you more, if it's warranted. Please wait a moment."

She was trying to take him for a ride. *The rubies have to be worth more than she'd offered, a lot more.* And she had exhausted

Liam's patience. He pointed at the dagger. "That can stay while you talk to your boss."

A shadow fell over her eyes and her face grew so rigid, Liam feared the black lips would crack. "As you wish." She withdrew her hand and disappeared through a narrow door.

With her gone Liam shoved the dagger in the bag and hustled to get out. The Jeep's engine sprang to life and he pulled across the street in a tight U-turn. Just as he accelerated to make the traffic light, a handsome man with long dark hair and high cheekbones darted from an entrance adjacent to *Michael's Treasures*. With hurried steps he darted into the street behind the moving Jeep. Continuing briskly to the other side, he pulled a pen from his shirt pocket.

Liam had seen the reckless fellow in his rear view mirror. But he did not notice him scribbling on the back of his hand.

Alex Malreaux mustered all mental powers to control his hands from trembling. With enough concentration they would obey him once he began. Less obvious but more unnerving than the trembling, the clammy dampness on his palms and upper back would haunt him for the first couple of lectures. Long experience had taught him that he could do absolutely nothing about the perspiring.

Bringing his head close to the overhead projector, the professor inhaled deeply and inconspicuously, repositioning the syllabus for the tenth time. The pungent metallic odor of the heated motor brought on a feeling of queasiness, and he silently cursed whoever didn't turn off the machine earlier that day. *Okay, Showtime!* He exhaled and nodded at the sea of faces before him.

"Good morning," with a forced vigor that immediately dispelled his trembling and got everyone's attention. A door slammed in the back of the huge hall. Alex seized the opportunity to relieve tension. He grabbed the pointer leaning against the overhead and took a few measured steps until he came to the edge of the stage. His naked toes extending over the side—students loved his trademark barefoot lectures—he cut the air with the stick in a mock warning. "I would like to see that fellow after class," he lisped with an exaggerated Schwarzenegger accent. Those students who'd had him before greeted this with an outburst of laughter. The new ones eyed each other, uncertain what to make of this.

Alex was easily one of the most popular professors at this University of California campus. Well-traveled and full of colorful anecdotes, and enthusiastically telling jokes his colleagues shunned for their politically incorrect overtones, his sections always filled soon after registration commenced. Women took his classes in disproportionate numbers, and many made a point of arriving early in search of a front row seat. At this very moment, as he prepared to introduce the course, one stared at him from less than five yards away, just left of center in the first row.

He had noticed her the instant he stepped on the lecture platform. Reddish hair trailed lavishly about square shoulders, and pronounced cheekbones gave her emerald eyes a vaguely detached look. She wore a pink corduroy miniskirt and a black tank. Golden sandals contrasted beautifully with her dark skin. She sat with her back straight and legs crossed. Truly stunning, and no older than twenty-five, she effortlessly manifested the aura of a much more mature woman. Alex, in love with everything beautiful, struggled to keep his eyes off her. He'd love to meet her. Perhaps she'd show for office hours.

"The syllabus that you see before you," he gestured at the overhead, "lists all the information you need for now. As you can see, it's rather short. The pertinent information will fit into a snug paragraph at the beginning of your notes. I could have run off a few hundred copies, but why waste paper while the rain forests go up in flames?"

"All right!" one young man hollered from the rear. "Tell that to the rest of the faculty!"

This class would be fun. Alex jabbed the air with his pointer. "I have, but I'm afraid they won't take me seriously until I emulate their style of dress." More laughter, this time from the front rows. Students in the back hadn't noticed his naked feet. A few of the more perceptive craned their necks. Alex sensed the emerald eyes studying him, and he stared right at her. Their eyes locked for a fleeting moment. He smelled opportunity. Then he noticed movement in the aisle and recognized the familiar gait of his head teaching assistant.

THE SPANIARD'S DAGGER

Kate Matzak *never* showed up for the beginning of class, and Alex pondered whether the continuation of this tradition amused him. Had she been a man, he would have squared her away a long time ago. He liked her sense of humor and natural flirtatiousness, though, even if she didn't attract him physically. They nodded at each other. He turned and flicked off the overhead, ignoring subdued murmurs of protest. He had no sympathy for sluggishness.

"Copy from your peers what you've missed," he said, and for the next forty minutes he delved into a lecture that focused on the implications Italian and German unification had on the future of Europe. With a few minutes remaining, he called his eight teaching assistants to the lecture platform. He introduced each, identified Kate as the one in charge, and explained the functions of the group as a whole. Then he finally dismissed History 192 A.

Kate cornered him, a disappointed sigh deep in her throat. "Another overflow class. Not enough seats. They're stretching out on the floor again." She winked at him. "Why don't you limit the class size to . . . let's say 250?"

Alex chuckled. "I love a woman who works to live, instead of the other way around. But I fear I can't oblige. The university would wonder, in no uncertain terms I might add, why I requested *eight* TAs."

At least twenty-five students swarmed them and the other teaching assistants. Some wanted to add the class, and others asked the typical dumb questions that a simple glance at the syllabus would answer. He had instructed her beforehand to deal with that. Now he elegantly extricated himself from the group and tried in vain to catch a glimpse of the red-haired chick going for the doors. Kate tried to subdue a rising wave of jealousy. As always, he looked great. God, he could almost pass for a student himself. His youthful smile and stylish dress belied his thirty-two years, and his very pores oozed an irresistible southern charm. She knew that the rumors of an unhappy marriage contained truth. She'd seen him court more than one student. Nevertheless, he had never made a pass at her.

"Kate, I've got to go. A friend of mine is dying to show me some strange artifact he's found." He collected his belongings and rushed out of Campbell Hall.

*　　*　　*

The light of a million stars suffused the tranquil sea. Hissing foam, audible only to those who huddled near the bowsprit, coated the crest of the bow wave. A light breeze ruffled the lateen, and the galleon seemed asleep, like a gorged whale drifting with the lazy currents. Tidbits of subdued conversations, the moans of a man who had smashed his hand earlier that day, and the muffled pumping of bilge water floated on the air. John Waspe, the ship's cook, and his assistant, Richard Argyle, loitered by the galley. They surreptitiously scanned the poop deck, where the short, stout figure of the captain was leaning against the mast, chatting with one of the noblemen.

"Look at them," Waspe muttered through closed teeth. He had the rare ability to speak without moving his mouth and projecting his voice in any direction. "They're surely thinking up another filthy lie." He spat into the sea. "I don't trust that tyrant, not since he told us the fairy tale of sailing for Alexandria. His words are as false as his eyes are mean. He distorts the truth the instant he opens his mouth."

Waspe gently caressed his neck, like a fellow might carefully run his fingers over a precious vase. "Since he cut off Mr. Doughty's unfortunate head I don't suppose there's a seaman aboard who holds much faith in his own. Richard, I swear we won't see any of the gold, no matter how much that Spanish vessel might carry in its hold. Those 'esteemed' gentlemen are growing rich on our sweat and blood. We must take command and throw them and their scoundrel lord overboard." He bowed low in the affected manners of the aristocrats.

Richard pushed a lock of long blond hair from his face. "I've told you I will not take part in a slaughter. Bloodshed will bring terrible luck. The sea herself would turn and devour us in due time. Besides, we will gain nothing from moving in haste. The Papists are searching for us, and we must find their lonesome treasure ship before we can even think of taking our own."

"Why?" Waspe asked, his facial muscles twitching with impatience. "The men are with us now. Even if most of those dim-witted fools weren't fond of Doughty, they haven't trusted the captain since he murdered him. He no longer commands their respect. All of them care for naught but the gold anyhow. And if we wait too long they'll forget and fall prey to new lies. They'll again fancy a fair share of the profits will enter their pockets when we return to Plymouth—if we ever will. You know them. They're the most ignorant collection of vermin I ever had the misfortune to sail with. Idiots! Stupid, rotten idiots!"

Richard tried to fathom the intense dark eyes glowing fiercely below the bulging brow ridge that made Waspe look like a formidable enemy. Over the months, Richard had come to appreciate the normally taciturn cook as the one man among the crew behind whose mask of indifference raged a storm of activity. Waspe was clever, cunning, and always careful in his speech, while quietly making his own plans. Then things had changed. The General, as they often referred to their captain, had executed Thomas Doughty on murky charges of treachery. Many of the men had been incensed, and the stench of mutiny had begun to foul the air. Few believed the flimsy accusations, since all knew Drake's jealous side. Worst of all, Doughty had been the only gentleman who afforded Waspe a measure of respect, while treating the rest of the sailors little better than dogs. Since the execution, Waspe was given to rash thought, possessed by a fiery temperament theretofore unknown. *Must be the hot Latin blood.* A Catalan woman had mothered him. His sudden outbursts, Richard feared, might lead to the discovery of their scheme. He had to do all in his power to control the cook.

"You always say yourself that the men are untrustworthy fools. There's no telling then who'll stand with us, and you know I can name several who'd do anything to thwart a revolt. You would only cause division and weaken us when we must be strong. The Spaniard can't be far off, and no one knows what kind of resistance to expect. Besides, the General has done us no harm, and I still believe he's the sole man who can sail us back to England. We might never see home again without him at the helm."

A cold, measuring look entered into Waspe's eyes. "Richard, I will take this ship. I need you with me."

*   *   *

"Professor, over here!" Liam sat at a corner table, sipping strong mocha. Malreaux maneuvered around a group of students, balancing his own cappuccino. He took a spot across from Liam.

"So, work in full swing again? A fresh quarter, endless brown bag lunches, and many a mind-numbing gathering." Liam grinned. "But I do hope you had a nice Christmas." Amused, he watched Malreaux's face contort as though he'd bitten into a lemon. Liam knew how deeply he hated lunch talks and the usually boring meetings academicians seemed so to cherish.

"You make much money lately?" the professor countered. "Sweating at your canvases day in day out without making a whole lot must really suck." He smiled benevolently, savoring the scent of his dark roast.

They constantly pecked at each other, and Liam expected nothing less than a sharp comeback. Nevertheless, Malreaux had hit a very sensitive nerve, wiping the grin right off Liam's face. His last client dragged ass when it came to parting with the commission, a particularly irksome state of affairs because the scoundrel had all along insisted on exact specifications for an extremely complex mural. In fact, the constant money-haggling over the past several weeks had driven Liam to Santa Rosa in search of some peace. Over the years a number of his clients had failed to pay the agreed-upon price. One had stiffed him outright.

"I get by," he replied. "Besides, I have you to fall back on, though you still haven't told me when to start on your place."

"I'm just about ready, but I have to finish my book first. That done, the house is available for as long as you need it."

They engaged in chitchat, fine-tuning Malreaux's conception of what the spacious home office in his villa should eventually look like. Liam disliked some of the ideas but let it go. Malreaux could be stubborn. Suddenly, in mid-sentence the professor fell silent, focusing on the entrance. Liam spied a gorgeous woman with flowing red hair stroll to the counter.

"Any pretty ones in your classes?"

Malreaux tilted his head. "Judge for yourself." She picked up her salad and found a seat two tables over, flashing a beguiling smile their way. The professor flashed back, which Liam resented.

Theirs made for an enigmatic friendship, if an outsider could properly call it that. They enjoyed long, broad-ranging conversations, had a like sense of humor, and viewed life from a similar perspective. Malreaux loved Liam's art and represented his most loyal and financially rewarding client. But the tension between the two, an unwillingness to let the other be one up, always simmered beneath the surface. Liam easily held his line when their intellects did combat, and neither of them conceded an inch of defensible ground. On the tennis court they squared off with a ferocious tenacity that admitted no defeat till the last ball flew out of bounds. While discussing Liam's work, Malreaux inevitably took great pleasure in pointing out the flaws, subjecting him to harsh criticism, despite paying good cash for it. But worst of all, to Liam's eternal dismay, the professor bedded select students while his beautiful wife faithfully waited for him at home. And since Liam's special attraction for this woman never grew weak, Malreaux's making lover-boy eyes at this college babe only added fuel to the fire. *Time for a fight.*

"You're up for a match?"

"Today?" Malreaux looked at him.

"You're done lecturing, right?"

"Yes, I am. When would you want to play?"

"When you finish your coffee."

"Now?" he squawked, completely surprised. "What about the dagger?"

"That can wait till after. Come on, let's hit a few balls and let me drive you into a corner."

Malreaux's eyes narrowed. Liam knew exactly what he thought. They usually arranged matches at least a day before. The professor was analyzing this anomalous behavior, while at the same time he wouldn't lightly refuse the challenge. He looked at the girl, who was nibbling at her greens. "I've got to attend to a few things."

"Scared?" Liam grinned sardonically. He had no doubts the red-head would have to wait.

"You have your stuff?"

"In the car."

"Alright! You asked for it. I'm going to polish that court today, with your tears." He scratched his face, stealing another glance at the girl. "Give me, ah, thirty minutes."

*   *   *

"Sail! Sail ahead!" the elated man erupted from the crow's nest just as the noon watch started to climb up the mast to replace him. The gold chain promised by the General to the first man to spot the 120-ton *Nuestra Senora de la Conception* now belonged to the happy fellow who, within seconds of being relieved, would have seen the prize disappear into the pockets of his replacement already ascending the rigging far below. The sailors and all the gentlemen aboard the galleon stormed to the bulwark, craning their necks in feverish anticipation.

"Where?" the captain cried.

"At the horizon, just left of those clouds to leeward," the watch echoed from forty feet up.

The captain had waited a long time for this moment, had fantasized about it. If all his calculations proved correct, he would go to bed that night a fabulously rich man. All that he had ever wanted beckoned: a country house, a title, plenty of gold in his coffers. Those slimy aristocrats would never again treat him as anything but an equal. He waved at the boatswain.

"I will not hoist a single additional sail and thus risk the Spaniards correctly interpreting our precise intentions. We will catch them in due time, when darkness affords us maximum disguise. Have the men rig a line with the empty water and wine casks, and have them toss it overboard. When these fill, they will cut our speed by a few knots. I believe our friends from Peru will then find us no more noteworthy that any other merchant sailing these waters."

Eight hours later, with the enemy ship one league off the port bow, the captain barked his final orders. "Arm the men and prepare for boarding."

The gentlemen hastened to grab their helmets and armor while the mate distributed bows and arquebuses to the agitated sailors as fast as his whirling hands permitted. Waspe and Argyle pushed toward the front of the cluster because the officer in charge had a habit of assigning the first fully armed men to the boarding party. Some of them already began transferring to the pinnace.

"She's coming around," a voice boomed from above. "Bearing down right at us." The captain smiled with infectious anticipation. He loved to fight.

The stretch of water separating the two ships narrowed as dusk gave way to night. Stars tickled the sky by the time the treasure ship, which they had hunted for so many anxious hours, finally pulled alongside.

¿"Cual tu nombre y tu puerto de destino"? came the first call from the *Cacafuego*, as the Spanish sailors good-naturedly referred to their galleon.

Drake chuckled quietly. They wanted to know his name and destination. He had a ready answer. The moment had come for a little amusement. He'd see what they'd make of this. "Señor, lower your sails, unless you wish to join the fish."

Hearty laughter drifted across the water. They apparently took this as a joke, a rather funny one. "You humor me," a man replied in surprisingly fluent English. "Come aboard and join me for dinner."

At this the captain replied with a signal to his crew, and a trumpet shattered the tranquility of the encounter. The seamen, ducked low behind the bulwark, showed their faces. Dozens of muzzles and arrows pointed at the Spanish complement. The ear-numbing report of a cannon instantly swept away any vestiges the Spanish commander might entertain of having met a jester. The lead ball slammed into his mizzenmast, which cracked and trembled like a tree struck by lightning. The next second it thundered down on the stern, shredding most of the foremast's rigging. Several men barely escaped the giant hammer from pressing them to mush. The English let go of their shot and arrows, forcing the enemy to scurry for cover at the same time that the boarding party began pulling themselves over the port side of the hapless prize. The pinnace had secretly swung around the *Cacafuego's* bow, the Spaniards completely unprepared for this maneuver. The two cooks were amongst the first to jump on the deck.

"Watch my back," Waspe shouted. "We're going below."

*   *   *

The ball whizzed so close past Alex, it tickled his left ear before striking the ground just inside the bounds. It flew off and jammed into the chain link fence. Muttering curses under his breath, he fought to subdue a violent urge to rain blows upon the net with his racket, as if that would reverse the solid defeat he had just suffered at Liam's well-aimed strokes. He'd lost every game and could hardly get his best serves past the opponent. Yet, Liam kept nailing him. Drenched in sweat, the two men exchanged a blunt handshake and collected the balls. Liam sat down and stretched out his legs. Alex took off his tennis shoe and sock to examine a huge blister on his big toe. They didn't talk for some time.

"Couldn't get the damned thing across the net," Alex finally snorted. "Stupid game." He cut a grimace while popping the blister.

Liam savored his victory and decided to rub it in. "Your best days do seem to have become a thing of the past."

Alex hissed. "There's always a rematch. Don't get cocky."

"Alright, I might let you win the next one. If I foul my serves on purpose, you're bound to score at least some points."

Alex didn't find it funny. "Sure."

Liam got up. "I'm sorry, but I had forgotten an appointment with the dentist. Let's meet for dinner tonight. I'll show you the dagger then, and you can enlighten me."

*   *   *

The pirates swarmed over the Spanish ship, feverishly combing it from back to front to flush out anyone preparing to spring an ambush. Richard and Waspe spilled down the stairs to the 'tween deck, running on toward the bow. Several enemies fled frantically before them, clambering back up to the main deck.

"Alto!" Waspe barked. When they ignored his command to stop he flew into a rage and stormed after them.

"Let them go!" Richard yelled. Waspe was a dreadful runner. "You won't catch them." But he didn't listen, already hastening up the stairs. Richard raced after him, linking up on the main deck in front of the galley.

"What good did that do?" he demanded, his lungs in overdrive. The Spaniards had escaped amidships, where they awaited their fate with the rest of their compañeros.

"I'm just too damn slow," Waspe panted. "Let's examine the galley first."

They burst into the small enclosure lit by a solitary lantern, almost ramming into a Spanish officer and a sailor with greedy hands sunk deep in two chests sparkling with gold, silver, and precious jewels. The sailor stared at them in total horror and froze, crouched over the chest. The officer put on an air of indifference as he turned back to measure the intruders with a haughty expression. Two barrels stood behind the men, each containing a portion of the riches already transferred from the chests. Several more chests, all exactly like the one the sailor still clutched, had been hastily stacked along the wall opposite Argyle.

Waspe took it all in with one glance, his mind processing each detail. Could their captain have ordered these two men to hide part of the precious cargo before the English could seize it? No! The lightning raid had transpired with no forewarning. This officer, he sensed, was looking out for himself, secretly sequestering a chunk of wealth his master would have believed lost to the marauders.

Argyle's elbow interrupted his thoughts. "What do you reckon they're planning?"

He felt elated. "I have a pretty good idea. We'll find out for certain in a moment." *Thank you Lord, for having blessed me with a Spanish mother.* She had raised him in her native tongue, and he spoke the language like a Barcelonan. This was the chance of a lifetime. Never mind Argyle's moral hesitations and aversion to spilling a little blood. Time did not favor them. They had to act now.

He stepped up to the officer, inquiring how his captain would punish such a clandestine undertaking. With a short reply and simple shrug the man demonstrated incredulity at such a preposterous proposition so convincingly, he would have fooled anyone. However, the sailor's face blew the superb performance. His fear spoke volumes. Glancing at his superior in unveiled terror, the man had stopped breathing and quickly looked away. He blushed, his face laden with guilt.

"They're a bunch of stinking liars," Waspe burst out. "I'm gonna slit their throats from ear to ear and bleed 'em like hogs." Furious, he reached for his knife, but Argyle yanked back his arm.

"Don't! I won't bloody my hands with murder."

John hesitated, irritated beyond words. Finally, he tamed his emotions and nodded. "Aye, I'll spare the bastards. But the gold is ours." He turned and bored a finger into the officer's chest, ordering him to finish what he had started.

The man's defeatist posture mirrored surrender to the inevitable, but it was only another of his ruses. With a subtle motion of his hand under cover of the lantern's shadows he drew a bejeweled dagger. One more second and all would be lost. Only Argyle's alert eyes prevented catastrophe. "Watch out!" he yelled.

John reacted on pure instinct and delivered a mighty kick to the Spaniard's hand. The man screeched with pain and, stumbling back, dropped the weapon. John jumped on him like a wildcat and snatched the dagger. Then he put the blade's sharp point to his throat, breaking the skin and bearing down. The beaten man closed his eyes.

"No!" Argyle shouted. "Make him pack the gold and silver! We can't do it ourselves. It's too risky. The others could come barging in here any time."

He was right. If their mates caught them they would end as shark food. This situation called for a different strategy. He knew how much terror his face could instill. He had heard men remark that his heavy brow rendered him fiendish when he entertained a rotten mood.

John relaxed his grip on the dagger and barked his order once more, this time with a voice so brutal and an expression so uncompromising, he felt a chill in his own spine. Then he extracted the blade and watched a thin line of blood snake down the Spaniard's throat and stain the white collar. The man's resistance now evaporated quicker than a puddle of water at high noon. Shooting Argyle a frightened but grateful glance, he dug his hands back into the chest as though nothing in the world could gratify more. His helper emulated him instantly.

With Argyle standing guard outside the door, in case the other boarders came across the galley, John forced his prisoners to pry open two more barrels and dump their contents. Hunks of salted pork and a grainy river of maggot-infested flour poured onto the planks. He directed the men to distribute evenly all treasures throughout the four barrels, layered with the pork and flour. This would prevent the precious cargo from shifting and attracting attention during transfer. Suddenly he heard Argyle's voice, diverting several of their crew away from the galley. He kicked the officer in his back to speed up work. The sailor, easily the most eager packer alive between New Spain and the Orient, required no such reminders. One final layer of meat topped each barrel before he nailed them shut.

The task complete, John grabbed the officer's right ear lobe and pulled it back so hard as though he meant to tear it off. He looked his victim hard in the face. The man winced with pain and stumbled over one of the barrels, John still holding the ear in a crushing grip. Then he stuck the tip of the terrified man's dagger a generous inch into the opening. A sheet of sweat washed his face, and he trembled like a pig dragged to the butcher's blade. His eyes almost popped from their sockets. His accomplice, also fearing his last moment was near, backed into the wall and sank to his knees, folding his hands in desperate prayer. *Perfect!* John bared his teeth in a cruel smile and gave the dagger a gentle twist, just enough to cut the tender flesh of the inner ear.

"Di algo sobre los barriles y te abro tu cabeza de oreja a oreja con mi acero." He leveled his eyes on the sailor. "Y lo mismo va por tu amigo." The threat of splitting their faces from one ear to the other worked wonders.

"Dios mio!" The kneeling sailor's lachrymal glands let loose a veritable deluge. With tears streaming down his face, his prayers became ever more fervent, and he sported the quintessential look of the unwilling martyr. His disgusted superior remained rigid as a corpse.

"Nadie va a oir una palabra sobre esto," the sailor whispered so meekly, John hardly heard. The poor fellow wouldn't tell a soul. Then, with the dagger pricking the officer's spine, he shoved the two men through the door and helped Argyle drive them toward the other prisoners herded near the ship's aft.

Would they, John fretted, keep the secret?

T he patio overlooked the Santa Barbara Channel, with all four northern Channel Islands in stark relief in the crisp, clean January air. The descending sun hovered inches over the razor-sharp horizon, dragging a burgundy tail across the vast sky. Malreaux sipped his South African Chardonnay, savoring its oaken bouquet with an intermittent lip-smacking punctuated by drawn-out "ums." This annoyed the hell out of Liam, who imbibed the heavy but pleasant scents of the lush vegetation. He said nothing, instead watching the tall lanky waitress place a basket filled with hot rolls on their table. Two bowls of steaming lobster bisque followed. Chunks of the sweet pinkish-red meat welled to the surface.

"Enjoy." Glancing at the canvas bag on the empty chair, she refilled their glasses. He noticed her check out Malreaux's lean body before returning to the kitchen. Liam cringed when he smacked his lips again. They tackled the bisque.

"Absolutely delicious," Malreaux volunteered between slurps off his spoon. "As good as any I've had in New England."

Liam reached for the bag. "I've kept you waiting long enough. Here, what do you think?"

Malreaux moved forward while Liam produced a rolled-up towel, placed it on the table, and unwrapped the dagger. "Voilà."

The reaction baffled Liam. The professor's forehead collapsed into a set of fleshy folds. His eyes fleetingly took on a glassy gaze, and he shook his head like people do after a misfired sneeze. "This *is* interesting. And you found this on your camping trip?"

"Yes, on Santa Rosa," Liam said, intrigued. *First the woman in the store and now Alex. Why did this dagger elicit such responses?*

"You went over Christmas break, right?"

Liam nodded. "I came back Sunday."

Malreaux picked up the dagger and subjected it to a thorough examination, his bisque totally forgotten. He thoughtfully caressed the smaller gems.

"Rubies. Too bad for the others," he remarked, pointing at the empty depressions. He took the weapon by its handle and held it close to the candle light, turning it back and forth. He ran a finger across one edge of the rusty blade, then the clean side. Unlike Liam, he avoided cutting himself. To estimate the dagger's weight, he rested it in his palm. "This is definitely no cheap piece. Few artisans have mastered the skill to produce such quality. In fact, if I were to place a bet, I'd say a Spaniard made it back in the Old World."

These statements came out so nonchalantly and so confidently, it exasperated Liam. He accepted Alex was an accomplished historian with a well-developed ego, but since when did he claim to be a weapons expert? He just loved showing off. *Typical. Always an answer for everything.*

"And how did you figure that out, Mr. Professor?" Liam ventured, his mind already racing to construct counter-arguments.

But Malreaux ignored the question. "Where on Santa Rosa did you find it?"

"In one of the canyons in the southwest, hardly a stone's throw from the sea on the stream bank near water's edge. You've been to Santa Rosa, haven't you?"

He shook his head. "Julia and I have sailed around the islands countless times. She has a fascination with them. We've camped on San Miguel and Santa Cruz, twice, but never on Santa Rosa. We always pass it on the way to Point Bennett's seal colonies. For some reason, though, she's never wanted to stop there." He paused, pensively sipping his Chardonnay. "I'll have to ask her about it."

Liam spooned down the bisque now and finished his water, drawing ice cubes into his mouth. He imagined camping with Julia, a recurring pipe dream that would never become reality. She was married, chained to a man who had few compunctions about bedding whomever he pleased. Liam crushed a chunk of ice with such force, the elegantly-clad lady sitting at the next table turned to punish him with a frosty stare. He withstood these withering eyes, trying not to laugh when the tip of her nose ascended several degrees. She finally turned away, visibly loath to share the restaurant with this rude Neanderthal, and he crunched down on the remaining ice. She ignored it but shifted her weight, which made Liam chuckle. Her appalled friend, a stiff chap in a starched suit, whispered something in her ear. Liam put them out of his mind and turned to Malreaux.

"How is it you know so much about this dagger? You hardly looked at it."

He smiled and slid back in his chair, beaming with the happy expression of the professional storyteller called on stage. "As a graduate student at Harvard I once helped my mentor—a military historian and weapons buff—write a chapter on the arms used to conquer the Americas. My work entailed focusing on the demise of the Incas and Aztecs due to superior European weaponry. In addition to muskets and pistols the Spaniards carried the usual assortment of swords and daggers, including some very beautiful pieces. You know how I love art. In fact, that's why I became interested. So I read a great deal more than I really needed to. And this," he lifted the dagger, "especially the double-edged blade, looks an awful lot like those weapons I've researched."

"You're saying this thing is five hundred years old?"

Malreaux shook his head. "Of course not. The elements would have destroyed it long ago."

"Then it's a replica, and some weapons freak like your mentor lost it."

"Probably. I can't think of another explanation either. I do know of several companies specializing in the manufacture of such weapons for collectors. These replicas can be quite costly in their own right, which is why I believe that this one was made by a skilled artisan."

"You're sure those are rubies?" Liam slipped in casually. But it didn't work. He instantly got the 'you're-hopeless-look.'

"You really can't tell?"

"Well . . ." He remembered Binh's lecture. Malreaux would exploit it to the max. Unable to wiggle free, Liam opted for the best way out—honesty. "I do art, and gems aren't one of my hobbies. I never understood why people go nuts about them. Anyway, I had the dagger appraised."

Malreaux processed fast. "And they tried to rip you off, which is why you want my input."

"Right."

"How much were they willing to pay?"

Liam related his experience at *Michael's Treasures*, ending with a graphic description of the breast hair. "I figured you'd enjoy that detail."

Malreaux became very quiet. "Your charming seductress knows her business. She offered you a pittance." He wrapped the dagger in the towel, casting discreet glances around the restaurant. "Put it back. No need attracting any more attention."

Why the sudden concern? He never gets this uptight about anything. Liam tried to make sense of the professor's uncharacteristic reaction when the waitress interrupted, delivering two dishes heaped high with fried seafood. "I can have it appraised elsewhere," he started, but Malreaux cut him off.

"If you don't mind, I'd like to borrow the dagger and study it further."

After dinner Alex had hurried home to his office. The dagger and an open folder containing a fat pack of support materials used to write the Harvard chapter stared at him. A booklet on daggers lay nearby on its spine, an empty mug keeping it open. As a student he had always collected excessive amounts of information as a matter of principle. Those days were over. Spoiled by financial security and the good life, he had little taste for research now. Except tonight. The dagger, he felt more and more, had a history, and he no longer believed it represented a modern replica. He pushed aside a copy of the chapter, whose thick black title read *Carving Out an Empire: Spanish Arms in the Americas in the 1500s.*

Anxiously sorting through the pile while discarding sheet after sheet, he grew increasingly nervous. Had he tossed it? Wait! He stopped. *Ah, finally!* He held a thin pack of neatly stapled pages. They depicted sketches of medieval swords and daggers. Alex relaxed. This felt good. It had been long since he worked with such enthusiasm. He proceeded deliberately, studying each page in detail.

First came the Agincourt, a light sword designed to wield single-handedly. English knights had chopped and hacked their way through French lines in the bloody battle from which the weapon derived its name. The next page showed the Moro Flamberge, another single-hand sword. Moors armed with the Moro had subdued most of Spain. Sporting a handle with a small steel guard to protect the fighter's hand, this sword's blade was fashioned in the shape of a flame, engineered to increase its cutting edge by several centimeters. Kindayr's dagger's blade exhibited a very similar design. Alex compared the two, running his finger over the cold steel, and experienced an uncanny sensation of what it must have felt like to have an African warrior stick one through his ribs.

He shook off the thought and flipped more pages till he hit the fifteenth century Finger-Ring sword. Distinguished by a finger ring attached to the upper portion of the blade and guard, this contraption increased agility and balance while protecting the index finger. A round pommel topped the dagger, almost exactly like the one on Kindayr's trophy. Alex dug into the section on daggers.

There was the Arming Dagger, widespread in fifteenth century Europe. Thirteenth century crusaders fighting their way toward Palestine favored the Hawk Dagger. Then, Alex's pulse quickened—the Toledo. He grabbed Kindayr's dagger and held it above the sketch of the ancient Toledo. But for the blades, they represented an excellent match in shape and proportion.

Both weapons had steel guards that formed a "T" with the blade. While that of the Toledo had stubby ends right-angling back to parallel the blade for roughly an inch, the top of Kindayr's "T" curved slightly at either end. The Toledo also had a knuckle protector, a circular shield mounted on the guard that functioned precisely as its name implied. But the rest of the handles looked alike, up to the pommels. Equidistant lines suggestive of the globe's latitudinal grid ringed that of the Toledo, while a thick layer of rust still coated Kindayr's. Alex drummed his knuckles on the table. This dagger had to be an original. Probably sixteenth century. Spanish. He had no doubts.

Another thought shot through his brain, and he frantically shuffled papers. Did he still have it, the article on the manufacture of Old World swords? Yes! His thumb pointed right at it, a short piece describing how the master sword makers of medieval Spain fashioned their deadly works of art in the city of Toledo on the River Tagus. Making these swords, he recalled, involved a fascinating ritual. He devoured the information.

Convention required the artisan do his work on the darkest of nights, with the sky free of reflected moonlight to let him better observe how the heated metal welded. If the temperature dropped, all work on Toledo blades stopped, for the transfer of a red-hot blade from the glowing coals into cold river water required one of those characteristic evenings when the fragrant breeze blowing across the Strait of Gibraltar filled the Iberian air with Africa's heat. No master who took pride in his craft would ever permit cold air to interfere with the river's work. With each dunking of the blade, his apprentice praised Christ or the Lord, in a rhythmic chant that rang something like "His will be done," or "Thou art almighty." Then, once the master had welded the last veneer of steel to the solid core of high-grade iron, he made his helper coat the blade with goat fat. Finally he set the sword down to cool. By this time it required but the final touches. He polished it to a high luster, put a razor's edge on it, and engraved it if the buyer so commissioned.

Alex thoughtfully raked his palm across the pointy stubble on his unshaven chin. The rust definitely had to go. Steel should not survive centuries exposed to the fury of the elements. Why was this dagger still intact? And how in the hell did it get to Santa Rosa? California's historical record, a long-term fascination of his, made no mention of any Spanish settlements in the relevant period. Unless . . . the navigators!

Juan Rodríguez Cabrillo, the first European to sail past Santa Barbara, had raised his anchor in Portugal sometime around 1540. He had named the Channel Islands on his way up the coast. Returning back south he had actually landed, which led to a bloody quarrel with the natives. Cabrillo died during this tussle. His lieutenants, or so went the legend, later buried him on San Miguel. A monument erected there in his honor before World War II still remained. Alex had seen it. What he did not see was how anyone aboard that vessel would have parted with such a valuable dagger. It could have been lost during fighting. He dismissed this as doubtful. Who else had sailed these coasts?

In the early 1600s the Spanish crown dispatched Sebastián Vizcaíno to reaffirm His Majesty's claim to what would become the Golden State. Vizcaíno spent the lion's share of his time exploring and giving names to countless bays, points, and capes. Without a doubt he too must have had contact with the natives, probably trading for food and water. One of his officers may have lost the dagger at that time. Again this was not likely. Yet Alex knew that the Spaniards ignored the area for the next century and a half. Dagger design by 1769, when Gaspar de Portolá and the Franciscan padres marched from Mexico to colonize Alta California and enslave its peoples, had changed drastically.

There existed one other possibility, however far-fetched— Francis Drake! The British Sea Dog, after robbing the Spaniards of tons of gold, had sailed past this coast. But he stayed far out to sea, making his endlessly debated landfall much farther north near San Francisco. Alex shook his head. Projecting the Briton onto these shores made the least sense.

A gentle creak gave her away. She would never conquer that parquet, no matter how hard she tried. She watched him spin around, spooked like a burglar caught right in the act. "Julia!" he exhaled, panting. "You scared the crap out of me."

"You're working?" she teased cheerfully.

"I want to get this damn book off my back." He quickly turned back to the desk, shoving things into piles.

She covered the remaining steps to his chair, making her hips swing seductively. She pressed a firm thigh into his side. When she sensed a response she pushed harder. No way will he resist, she knew, fantasizing about what they would do five minutes from now. But he surprised her when he only brandished a brief smile. "You look beautiful." And he twisted away so that her thigh no longer made contact.

Her lust evaporated, and her breath returned to normal. Lately he had a way of making her feel unwanted. *Okay. I caught him at a bad time again.* She tried to persuade herself the awkward distance between them would go away and dismissed that nagging voice, which challenged her finally to face reality. Then she spied the dagger under a bunch of loose paper. "What's that?" She reached for the weapon. He made no reply and looked flustered. *How odd.*

"Wow, these are rubies! Where did you get this thing?"

"From the islands." Now he tried to sound bored, but he couldn't fool her.

"Santa Rosa," she said, inexplicably convinced she hit the nail on the head.

He was thunder-struck. "How the hell did you guess that?"

She looked up briefly wondering, no less surprised than he. "A freak hunch. I don't know. Regardless, whoever lost it must be very sorry. I bet it's got sentimental value." She fixed him tight in her sight. "But how did it end up in your hands, unless you snuck out there secretly?"

He withstood her searching gaze, looking her hard in the eyes. "Liam went backpacking over Christmas break. He found it in the dirt."

Now she struggled not to loose the staring contest. A sharp blush stung her from the chest up, and she wanted to kick herself. *You idiot!* She had nothing to feel guilty about, except that whenever Alex mentioned Liam it stirred something deep down. In truth, she couldn't wait for him to start work on the office.

Think. Say something! She could see his brain mull over her embarrassment. She had to throw him into defense, quickly, and she knew how. "Since when are you interested in stuff like this? It's not like you to work evenings anymore, unless you have to."

She'd bugged him many times to use his hours more productively, even if it meant they'd see less of each other. Though he only had to hustle one more year to make tenure, he'd slowed down so much over the past eighteen months that she agonized over him not making it. Five years of work down the drain would be his own problem, but loss of his position would affect her too. The university could choose from a hundred budding genius historians, each willing to kill for his job. She had no intention of leaving her family and Santa Barbara to follow him to some second rate school in a dull town just because he couldn't get his damn act together.

"Back in Cambridge I did a project on medieval weapons, and the shape of this piece brought back memories. So I dug out my work."

"Medieval? You don't think it's that old?"

"Yes. I mean, no. It's a . . . a replica," he stumbled over his words. "Some nerd must have lost it not too long ago." He hesitated. "I've got to get some work done." He turned and began organizing his things.

"Feels funny, doesn't it?"

"Why?" He continued sorting paper, not bothering to look at her.

"I don't know. It just . . . it's weird."

"Yeah. I guess. It's quite heavy." He still kept his back to her, which pissed her off.

She threw the dagger on the desk. "You're right. It *is* heavy." She headed for the door. "I'm going to see my parents."

"Again?" he said, obviously annoyed. "Well, have fun," he added, not even bothering to mask his sarcasm.

A silent office greeted her when she later passed by on her way to the garage. She poked her head in. He sat still, gazing out the window, a million miles away. She fought rising despair. He hadn't been the same in bed for weeks. For the thousandth time she dismissed the nasty rumors and her friends' pitying glances.

Alex listened to the front door slam, shame and relief clashing inside his skull. Julia had always been wonderful, and had done everything to make it work. Even so, over the past year and a half, he had preyed on other women. Today he couldn't even remember some of these fleeting and nameless liaisons. He'd battled it, at first. But one firm body at a conference in

Seattle led to another at a publisher's office in New York, and habits make for resourceful enemies. The voice of conscience whispering from its lonely hideout had grown weak. Soon it would cease to make a ripple.

He flung a pen through the room. The fault lay with her anyway. She couldn't bear him a child, and she'd suspected it even before they married. Damn it. He felt justified for having affairs, especially given Julia's mother's insistence on the ridiculous financial arrangements. At the thought of it, Alex's mood swung again. With a sense of impending doom his eyes caressed his workstation—all this in danger of vanishing. The largest flat panel display money could buy, the high speed color printer, digital telephone, and the fax all smiled at him from a spread of solid cherry valued at many years worth a grad student's grocery bills. Then there were the tailored clothes, cruises aboard his in-laws' motor yacht, *Helen*, lavish European vacations, the villa! Yeah, the villa, which wouldn't become theirs till the day Julia's first child turned five. Except, she never would have a child reach any birthday. Inexorably all these luxuries would evaporate in thin air after the years of hard work and sacrifice. Visions of the past began to crowd in on Alex.

Raised in a depressed area outside Oakhurst, North Carolina, he was the second son of a hardware store owner and a truck stop waitress. The milieu of his childhood had no resemblance at all to the life he'd eventually embrace at Johns Hopkins and Harvard. His father, a high school dropout who never missed a day having sex with Jack Daniels, perpetually hovered near economic ruin. His mother had at least managed to graduate, pregnant and barely literate. They'd pushed her through the system to get rid of her. His brother, Travis, two years up the pecking order, got the lion's share of dad's genes. He left high school in his junior year, headed for California girls and the surf. The junkyard-bound Shark fin Chevy, proudly acquired in a haze of hash and on a belly full of brew, never rolled past Alabama. Travis got stuck hauling shrimp on a trawler out of Mobile, making his home in a trailer park swarming with low class hookers.

Alex had no recollection of family love. Growing up he had one goal. Escape. Getting away from them, from the poverty, from the South. Wealth, ascending the social ladder, mingling with the rich—these obsessions fuelled his drive. When in tenth grade he realized that college presented the sole ticket out, he broke with his circle of friends, except the girls, and focused all energies on school. He graduated second in his class—number one had remained chaste—and entered UNC, Chapel Hill on a full scholarship. The B.A. in history came summa cum laude. Two hectic years at Johns Hopkins resulted in an M.A. and a letter of acceptance to Harvard. He stuffed his meager possessions into the VW Beetle and on a hot and humid July day rolled into Cambridge. He'd arrived.

International Relations at Johns Hopkins had prepared him for Harvard. Research came easy now, almost too easy. He published his first article within five months, then turned his dissertation on the British settlement of North America into a 400-page hard cover that became required reading for grad students across the country. The most elite history departments competed to recruit this rising star. When the University of California began to court him, it was love at first sight. Who could resist the magic of Santa Barbara? Most importantly, the city boasted an adequate number of super rich families whose daughters would inherit.

In the beginning he and Julia doted on each other. Their life consisted of spectacular restaurants, ski weekends at Tahoe and Telluride, and vacations in Rome, Crete, and Sydney. UC loved him, though he increasingly resented the pressure to publish or perish. Then the bomb hit. No matter how hard he tried, and try hard he did, Julia could not get pregnant. The gynecologist confirmed the unthinkable. Strangely indifferent, Julia finally confessed that she had known. He would never have a son. Worse, Julia's mother—oh, how he despised that hag—had stipulated that the villa would remain in her name until the fifth birthday of their first child. She didn't trust him from the start. Since the doctor's report the marriage took a nosedive. His first affair soon led to the next.

Alex shook off the mental torment and picked up the dagger. *This is no damn replica. It can't be!* This weapon held the answer to his problems, and it might yet afford him his last chance. Kindayr had to take him to the canyon, but must not know that the dagger was the real deal. Not yet anyway. Alex smiled. That wouldn't take much. He reached for the phone.

*   *   *

Not until morning, after sailing farther out to sea and away from the Ecuadorian coast, did the captain board the *Cacafuego*. The fabulous wealth awaiting him in the ship's dark hold stunned him. A mountain of coins, heavy gold plates, chests gleaming with precious gems and jewelry, and more than a thousand bars of silver from the Potosí mines sparkled there. He was richer beyond anything he ever imagined possible.

For three days the ships continued to put distance between them and the lethal Spanish squadron sure to hunt them. The Englishmen utilized this time hastily emptying their prize of its cargo. Waspe and Argyle saw to it that the four 'meat' barrels went straight to their galley. Not a man aboard the *Golden Hind* would have dreamed that they contained anything but salted pork.

The powerfully built man didn't move, his head resting against a dead oak on a knoll overlooking the endless sea. Lightning had struck the once massive tree twice in the same storm. It had withered quickly and lost all but one branch about six feet up. Next winter would surely decapitate the trunk itself.

The man had come to seek solitude and feast his eyes on the blue sky and ocean, but warm sun and gentle breeze had worked their universal magic. He had slipped into a slumber. By mid-afternoon, insects buzzing around his face, he stirred. His hand felt for his shin, where a deep abrasion marked a reckless descent into the backcountry's ravines the day before. He rolled over and stretched his sore muscles like a cat. Then he took a long draught from his water pouch.

He scanned the watery expanse from its hazy horizon toward the shore until half way in he spied a bright blotch brake the familiar flatness of the sea. He lost sight of it. Intrigued, he shielded his eyes from the sun. They quickly focused. There, he caught it again. Something strange floated on the water. His gaze grew motionless, his face as rigid as the dead oak. All his superbly-tuned senses fully alert, he could taste the salty air. He could hear the brush by the cliff's edge rustle, which brought about in rapid succession the distinct rattle of a snake warning some careless explorer and the sound of a small animal's scurrying feet. With the passage of time the thumb-sized curiosity on the waves grew larger. It headed straight for the coast.

He could no longer control his excitement and ran off at breakneck speed.

* * *

The air sparkled with such clarity, a person looking due south could, with a bit of imagination, count the canyons on Santa Cruz Island twenty miles across the Channel. Even San Miguel, the island farthest west, and often cowering low behind a wall of marine mist, was clearly visible. With its calcified remains of ancient forest and huge seal colonies, it proudly raised its twin peaks to an azure sky as though it feared to be overlooked.

Liam lazily surveyed the scenery. He could almost feel the miles of sandy beaches shudder under the relentless attack of Pacific breakers that spat wild-haired surfers onto the shore. Running from Gaviota in the west past Montecito and Carpinteria in the east, the majestic Santa Ynez Mountains hugged this entire stretch of coast, their foothills dotted with avocado ranches, lemon orchards, and white stucco villas with red-tiled roofs. Long before the Chumash settled here, raging mountain streams had sliced through the softer strata of these foothills and created natural greenways in their violent journey toward the sea. For the first time this year most of the channels carried water again. The onslaught of powerful winter storms had drenched the land and turned the canyons into death traps.

Potent low pressure cells that marshaled their forces over the limitless Pacific would repeatedly invade and let loose a deluge till the earth itself bled. Runoff washing through the chaparral would strip the land of its skin and choke streambeds with tons of silt and car-sized boulders. Sliding seaward, these ramrods ground to powder everything in their path.

Like the Hindu Goddess Kali, the downpours destroyed as well as created, nursing plants and animals whose survival through the dry season remained tenuous. When the clouds held back, trees withered, wildflowers lay dormant, and animals died. But when the skies broke, life reignited with a vengeance. Ancient oaks reduced to drooping ghosts lifted

46

their arms and grew new flesh. A luxuriant green spread over brown hills, and carpets of poppies paraded their orange faces along roadsides, creeks, and over lush mountain meadows. Fish swarmed the streams, and scattered vernal pools that had not yet fallen victim to bulldozers croaked with a million frantic frogs.

Such beauty in a land where the mercury doesn't stray far from the seventies beckoned movie stars, presidents, and CEOs, all happily spending their wealth. The dollar dwells where life is good. At the American Rivera, life leaves little to be desired, except the dollar.

Which is precisely what I need more of, Liam mused, watching Patrick sprint up the winding road at his brisk army pace. Money! If all his clients paid the agreed price, he could live well and save some for the meager years, or for when his hands grew stiff. Sure, he could take the cheapos to court. But he had no stomach for that. He hated dealing with the law and had no need to poison his system with its venom. Modern life was too complicated. The native Chumash, though, in their time, had it figured out. They respected nature, roamed canyons and plains, took what sustenance they required. Did they sue each other? *Ah, how I would love to live such a life.*

He shrugged his shoulders and went back to halving oranges just as Patrick's shoes ground into the gravel path. His six-foot frame, holding 190 pounds of lean muscle, turned the corner of the deck. He leapt up the four steps and immediately reached for fruit.

Like a mining shovel digging into a coal seam, his teeth scooped out the pulp. "It's still warm from the sun," he mumbled appreciatively.

"You have a good run?" Liam asked, inconspicuously comparing his abs to Patrick's.

He nodded, spitting out a mouthful of seeds. "You're one lucky dude. Santa Barbara is damn nice. It reminds me of Liguria, or the Côte d'Azur, only with English street signs."

He grabbed another orange half. "I've been all over the world, but I've never seen anything like it. This is a first rate botanical garden." Patrick had inherited their father's plant genes.

Liam worked the citrus press. "The old sea captains brought stuff from all corners of the globe. I've heard it said that you can find more plant species here than anywhere else in North America." They fell silent.

"You plan on visiting Dad on your way back?"

Patrick shook his head. "You know how it is. There isn't anything to say, and I think he prefers it that way. Besides, I don't have a whole lot of time."

Liam sighed. "Yeah." He paused. "Any news from Andrea?"

"Not in over a year. She sent a card from some resort in Miami. A two-liner." He sat down on the steps and reclined on his elbows. "I should resign my commission, come live here, sip Margaritas, and run on the beach."

"There are hordes of beautiful girls." Liam immediately regretted this. The other sex remained a touchy subject. Patrick had married the daughter of a famous Murano glass blower. While they vacationed on Mykonos, a van full of beer-guzzling Germans passing a shepherd's donkey cart in a blind curve slammed into Patrick's Kawasaki. He got off with cuts and bruises. Raffaela was thrown twenty feet and landed on her head. She died the following morning in a local hospital. Two years had passed. Patrick had never mentioned her name again.

"I've noticed already," he said without much enthusiasm.

Time to change subjects. "Listen, about spending a week in San Francisco." Liam stopped to let it sink in, handing his brother a glass of thick, pulpy orange juice. Patrick had long wanted to see the city. He'd be disappointed. "I was wondering if we could condense our visit to a few days next week, or postpone it altogether if necessary? Something very unusual has happened."

48

"Come on, we've planned San Francisco for a year." Patrick gave him that crooked glance. He had to return to his base in Italy the following Friday. "Why?"

Liam stayed cheerful. "I was wondering if you'd come camping."

"Camping? You're joking?"

He pointed at the Channel Islands. "No, I want to go to Santa Rosa, the second one from the right."

Of course, Patrick didn't like it. "What the hell for?"

Liam had his lines memorized, and he knew just which buttons to press. "For one, it's beautiful country, chock-full of endemic plants. Santa Rosa is as close as you get to what it looked like before they drained the wetlands and buried the valleys in cement. You can hike for days without crossing another soul and see sunsets that'll knock your socks off." Liam conjured up his most winning smile. "And if you're lucky, you might discover a nice little ruby."

"A ruby?" He hesitated and studied Liam's face. "Go on." Patrick's tone now resembled that of an assassin who had learned of his target's whereabouts. He loved adventure. He flew attack helicopters and hunted tanks. How could he possibly turn down an opportunity to hunt gems? Liam knew he had him hooked.

"This is the story. A couple weeks ago I needed to get away, so I went to the island." He paused for suspense. "One night, at my camp site, I found this dagger with what I first thought were red glass beads set in—"

"Rubies!" Patrick shot.

"Yup . . . set in the handle. Plus, there were three more gems in what are now empty spaces."

"Where is this dagger?"

"A friend of mine has it. He's a history professor at the university."

"How big are these stones?"

"I don't know. The smaller ones maybe the size of a pea. The big one, though, is more like a nickel."

"And?" Patrick's face glowed.

"And what?"

"What are they worth?"

"I'm not sure." Liam wished he had an answer, because Patrick gave him that look again.

"That's the first thing I'd find out."

"I tried to." Liam told of *Michael's Treasures*, leaving out nothing.

"What a sly devil!" Patrick pondered. "Took you for a fool alright."

They sipped their juice, competing to see who could spit seeds higher into the air. One hit a striped lizard basking in the sun. The reptile froze, played dead. A soft breeze carried a hodgepodge of aromas from the fruit trees.

Patrick slammed his glass on the table. "What's your friend got the dagger for?"

"He thinks it's a modern replica, probably made by an outfit that produces stuff like that for wealthy collectors. He wants to try to locate the company."

"I still don't get why you want to go camping on that island."

"Alex—that's his name—wants me to show him where I found the dagger."

"What's the point? Oh, wait. Don't tell me you guys expect to find the missing rubies."

Precisely! What was Alex thinking? Liam had wondered since their dinner and Alex's phone call asking him to go to Santa Rosa. He put his hand on Patrick's arm. "He actually does believe those rubies might still be kicking around. I suppose he fancies himself sort of a treasure hunter, though I'm with you on that account. He's bound to waste a lot of time. The rubies are so small, even if they're still out in the open, there's no way anyone would ever spot one."

"Then why go along? Tell him where to look."

Liam hesitated. That nagging doubt had left him no peace. "To be totally honest, I'm not sure what to think. I only know I *have* to be there."

*   *   *

The galleon sailed along a narrow tongue of land toward the shore of a broad bay. Its crew stared nostalgically at the white cliffs, so evocative of England's southeastern coast. One of the gentlemen had even called out in astonishment at how much they reminded him of the Seven Sisters of Sussex.

Most men had gathered between forecastle and main mast. A handful clung to the rigging of the fighting tops, their bulging muscles flexing with the ship's subtle sways, their weather-beaten faces fixed on the coast. The curious lingered by the stairs leading up to the poop deck, where the captain engaged in heated conversation with the gentlemen. Hoping to catch scraps of officer talk, they craned their necks and pricked up their ears.

Richard stood by the forecastle, his nervous gaze oscillating between shore and the pilot, the only man aboard who cared for naught but the soundings. His skill kept the ship afloat. With lead and line he saw to it that seabed and keel never got too near each other.

He registered under the name of Roger Blacoler. On account of tar-black eyes, framed by the bushiest and most grizzled eyebrows imaginable, and a skin pigmentation that darkened above his twice-broken nose, those before the mast called him 'Blackeye.' With a voice more monotonous than that of a Plymouth fisherman selling his catch, Blackeye announced that seven fathoms separated the hull from disaster. But his calm deceived no one. The men had spent two years on this vessel, and the long voyage forced them to get to know each other better than they wished. Space was precious on a ship so small that a strong-chested man could spit from the starboard bulwark clear across deck into the sea, unless he faced the wind. More than one sailor had on occasion found himself hoping for an annoying bunkmate to get washed overboard.

Blackeye, everyone knew, had become one with his task. When sailing off the Spanish Main, the ship had struck a shoal with such force that all efforts to pull free proved futile. The horizon had then filled with a band of galloping storm clouds, their tops sprouting into evil-looking anvils. Sporadic gusts that whipped new life into the limp sails foreshadowed hell, and when the sea grew choppy, the men took to prayer.

Richard had never been so afraid. He had never had anything to lose. But had he and Waspe become as rich as princes only to have that vicious wind toss them into the waves like nameless paupers? Their bones threatened to litter the sea floor alongside all the gold and silver. Yet, miraculously, the storm became their savior. Its swells lifted the galleon across the treacherous bar. But the memory remained vivid. Richard wiped the sweat off his face when Blackeye brought him back to the present.

"Six fathoms."

Then it came from above, the confirmation of what everyone feared. Dennes Woodd, eyes sharper than an eagle's, leaned from the nook in the mainmast's crow's nest. His whole body arched forward, and his eyes pinched near shut because of the sun's reflection on the water. His right hand clasping a rope, he shouted from his lofty perch.

"Savages! Savages! Down by the water, just below the huge tree with the crooked top."

Still sprinting after two miles, the man's feet pounded sharp rocks and bits of decaying wood, but his brain registered no pain. He vaulted across a rivulet, negotiated a prickly thicket with one arm shielding his face, and raced across a golden meadow. At last he slowed into his village, where a cold silence greeted him. None of the comforting chatter of men and women working, no screaming children darting from hut to hut, but only the smoke of the cooking fires lent the place any semblance of life.

The man felt the hair rising at the nape of his neck. Never before had his village been so quiet, so . . . dead! A thought calmed his heart. They too saw it. He would find them down by the beach, looking, just as he had from the bluffs.

He raced the short distance to the water—where familiar voices soothed his frayed nerves—and, skirting a grass-tufted dune, beheld a wondrous sight. His people were gathered, some alone and others in groups. Some were silent, but most argued. Children ran in circles, screaming like wild beasts. His youngest brother perched in Twisted Tree, with one foot dangling free. Several stones' throw behind them all, too massive to believe possible, drifted the strange men's tree canoe.

On Thursday afternoon, four days after Kindayr found the dagger, Alex ran across the driveway and into his kitchen. After lecturing to his students, he had endured an overdue meeting with the chair and took care of a backlog of administrative chores. Now he wanted to finish cleaning the weapon, to which he had applied a generous coat of potent solvent before leaving for campus.

He tore a towel off its hook and wiped down the dagger. Surprisingly the stuff worked. A smooth, beautifully crafted blade shone through reddish-brown grime. The peculiar flame shape really added a great deal of character. Alex fetched a fresh towel and rubbed down the pommel, his heart thundering in his chest as details began to emerge. Letters! He darted to the sink and shoved the dagger under a stream of water, brushing off the rest of the slush. He dried it and with shaking hands examined the pommel. Thin grooves framed an inscription composed of finely curved letters. It read "St. John of Southampton."

An Englishman? That made no sense. The dagger's design was absolutely not British. Alex stormed to his office and plunked himself down in front of the computer. He ran a search. An hour later he sat back clueless and frustrated. *Who the hell was St. John of Southampton?* A thought occurred to him. Van Haik!

Alfred Van Haik, pride of the department and UC's preeminent medieval historian, enjoyed international fame. A genius, a walking dictionary, he conversed eloquently in five languages. Alfred had the outright eerie ability to analyze complicated sentence structures as though their authors had addressed him personally. Early on in a career that spanned nearly half a century, he had accomplished a feat still talked about by his admiring colleagues. He revised the translation of a manuscript long regarded as official correspondence between a Tuscan monastery and a Venetian countess. The professor recognized it as a cleverly encoded love letter—a fairly graphic one. The Italian press circulated his work widely and would have scandalized the countess' family, had its last surviving heir not died years before. The Order, however, continued very much alive. It had responded with a vitriolic attack aimed at discrediting the young professor.

Alex tried to reach him at the university, without luck. He looked up his home number and got his wife on the second ring. He had always liked the little lady, whose vivacious eyes and passion for surfing masked her sixty-eight years. She still hit the surf several times each week. They exchanged pleasantries. Yes, Alfred was working in his study. If Alex would hold for a minute. A few seconds later Van Haik picked up the phone. His voice had something of a rebuke.

"Alex! I haven't seen much of you. You're not on sabbatical?" The man was also infamous for his bluntness.

Alex hesitated, choosing his words judiciously. He had spent so little time on campus during the previous term, even the medievalist, with an office on a different floor, noticed. "I've been extremely busy," he lied. "Trying to tie up loose ends on my new book and several articles I'm about to fire off. Plus, I'm teaching an upper division course and a seminar this quarter."

"Yes," Van Haik said abruptly. It alarmed Alex. The old Dutchman wielded much power, and he knew how to use it. He had undermined more than one young associate professor's path to tenure. Alex had no intentions of getting on his black list. He took a deep breath and tried to sound as natural as possible.

"Say, Alfred. I came across this name. I think it belongs to an Englishman, but I can't find anything on him. I was wondering if you could help?"

"Oh, my pleasure. Go ahead. What's the name?"

Van Haik's tone had changed completely, and Alex could feel his curiosity ooze through the phone. *He's hooked.* Alex gazed at the dagger's inscription. "St. John of Southampton."

"Ah . . . that's too easy!" Alfred instantly shot from the other end, his voice ringing with disappointment. Van Haik loved few things like a challenge. Strangely, even after Alex has spent an earnest hour on the Net, this didn't qualify.

"St. John was indeed born to an English family, a quite ancient one. As a young man he left Britain and lent his services to Philip II of Spain."

"Sixteenth century!" Alex burst out excitedly.

"Very acute," came the response, dry as the sherry Alfred favored. "A momentous period in British history, as you well know. Tell me, why are you interested in this fellow?"

Alex's mind raced, but he couldn't think of anything good.

"Are you still there?" Van Haik inquired.

"Yes, Alfred. Sorry, I was just wondering about something." He finally knew what to say. "You know I've done work on medieval weapons. Today, while comparing illustrations of daggers, I happened upon the name, and I got curious."

"I don't understand the connection between illustrated daggers and St. John, but it is rather interesting indeed. His brother was convicted of treason, and most of the family was executed. The name has largely been expunged from the historical record." He paused. "Well, give me a call if you have any more questions."

"I sure will. And thanks a bunch, Alfred. You saved me some footwork." *Shit! Why did I have to make that stupid comment?* Van Haik might get the impression he was allergic to work.

"Glad to be of service. I know how busy you are." The curiosity of before had dissipated. Thinly veiled sarcasm now took its place. "Oh, I'm looking forward to that book of yours."

The lump in Alex's throat tightened. His face on fire, he thanked his lucky star they weren't in the same room. *That old shark!* Did he smell blood already? Could he actually sense the truth? "Yes, yes, I'm sure you'll like it. It's going to stimulate much discussion on California's coastal Indians. You'll be one of the first to get the galleys. I'd love your input."

Alfred said nothing for so long, Alex thought he'd lost the connection. "By the way, your interest in medieval Europe has always focused on Spain, has it not?" Van Haik suddenly popped back to life.

"Correct."

"I'm not sure where you're going with this, but it might help to know that your man, St. John, played a particularly fascinating role in his times. I had forgotten, until you mentioned the Indians." Another long silence followed this announcement.

"Go on." Alex finally prodded.

"He was the hapless chap whose treasure ship fell into the hands of Francis Drake."

Alex dropped the phone. Perhaps it wouldn't be such a shot in the dark after all to visit Santa Rosa.

* * *

The captain, who'd been much more quiet than usual, left his favored spot beside the helm and threw his head back. It gave him a good view of the sailor perched fifty feet above the deck. "How many, Woodd? Can you count them?" he bellowed in a commanding voice.

Woodd's arm shot up to shade his eyes from the solar glare. He barely clung to the rigging, his gaping mouth exposing a set of buckteeth so pronounced, even from this distance Richard couldn't help but think of his uncle's horses.

"A few dozen, Sir. Fi'ty or sixty, maybe more."

The master returned to his position and stared at the shore, his cold eyes calculating. He turned to one of the gentlemen and made a subtle remark not meant for all ears. The man in turn sauntered over to the gunnery mate. When both went below deck, Richard felt a bony hand clench his shoulder.

"I'm not liking this. We should search for another anchorage, one without savages," an agitated Waspe whispered.

Richard twisted his shoulder free of the cook's grip. He too feared the impending landfall. Indians on both shores of this vast continent had been thirsty for battle. Attacking twice, and once laying a treacherous ambush that nearly cost the ship its master, the Indians had left each man skittish at the mere thought of going ashore. Few things filled a sailor's thoughts with more dread than having his skull beaten to a pulp on a God-forsaken coast thousands of leagues from home. But Richard knew they would land.

"We have no choice. The leaks must be plugged, and we'll deplete our provisions before long. Besides, it's better now than later. Otherwise, they'd have us open the four barrels." He lowered his voice, afraid of the General's sensitive hearing. "I pray these Indians won't drive us off!"

They had sailed far into the icy northern waters in their hopeful search for the legendary Atlantic passage, which had proved elusive. Going back around Cape Horn would amount to suicide, with the Spaniards sure to lie in heavily armed wait to prevent it. So the General had decided to reach England by way of the immense Pacific, and they had to careen the vessel and fill every nook aboard with fresh water and food. Or they would never return home.

"They're launchin' a boat," Woodd shouted from above. Richard observed the Indians shove a canoe into the surf.

"Strike sail," the General shouted. "Stand by to drop anchor."

THE SPANIARD'S DAGGER

The heavy chain rattled out of its housing and splashed into the shallow sea while the canoe skipped over the waves like a dragonfly, muscled by a single man. Richard exchanged a nervous glance with Waspe. They would both hang if this messenger refused them friendship.

*   *   *

Alex couldn't contain himself. He hadn't felt so exuberant in ages. Kindayr's dagger had belonged to an Englishman in the service of Spain four centuries ago, and by some strange twist of fate it had landed on Santa Rosa. But how, since Drake never did sail close to these shores? Or so everyone thought. The historical record might yet prove incomplete. In fact, the more he thought about it, Alex persuaded himself that the *Golden Hind* could have easily dropped anchor off Santa Rosa. If he showed that beyond reasonable doubt, he'd make the news. Alfred Van Haik would ask no more questions about his book. His career would bounce right back on track, with the university all too happy to dust off the red carpet. He'd be in like Flynn, and tenure would be but a formality.

His mind raced. If Drake really did land here without recording it, he must have had a damn good reason. Alex shivered at the possibilities. *Did the pirate stash part of his Spanish booty for a covert future retrieval? Why not? Columbus had retraced his path.* Alex slapped his legs, laughing with profound joy.

He poured himself a tall gin & tonic, gulping half before the ice had time to chill it. His spirit soaring, he tap-danced out on the deck, which afforded a good view of the neighboring property with its oval swimming pool. Bulky, palm-filled ceramic pots blocked the deep end, but he'd seen movement. *Rachel must be back, doing her lanes.* Rachel Staufen, half Austrian, half Puerto Rican. Stunning. Bends a man's will with one glance. His memory caressed the past as he downed more Beefeater.

Julia had been out of town, and Rachel needed a warm body to fill the boredom between two assignments. Discovering him admiring the property, she invited him to try out the pool. A few laps in the sparkling water earned him a drink. One glass became two, then three. She told him about her work: the photography, the people, the planet's most remote reaches. He had no desire to decline when she asked him to stay for dinner. They ate by the pool, a delicious Sudanese dish of spicy chicken in a creamy tomato sauce laced with peanut butter. They sipped sweet Greek wine for dessert. Her subtle hints met zero resistance. The first time had been wild. He remembered lifting the skimpy cotton dress over her shoulders, smelling the exotic perfume, as though it were yesterday. She wanted him right there, on the table, then on the hard concrete. The sex continued through the night, interrupted only by short rests and more sweet wine.

Alex snapped back to the present when she climbed out of the water and turned. She waved, grabbed a towel, and disappeared into her house. His body shivered with lust. He emptied his glass, letting the alcohol surge through his veins. Julia wouldn't be home for some time, and Rachel could be off again anytime, lost to the world for months.

*   *   *

Fifteen yards short of the galleon the Indian pulled up his paddle to gesticulate wildly with both arms, talking without catching a breath. His torso swung rhythmically from side to side, like a strand of seaweed swaying with the currents. Never stopping to formulate his thoughts, he delivered an interminable monologue, repeatedly nodding at the beach in an obvious invitation. Finally the man fell silent. In an unmistakable show of submission, he cast down his eyes, and, crossing his arms, bowed his head. Then he took up his paddle and returned whence he'd come.

Captain Francis Drake looked for Lawrence Fletcher, one of the moneyed gentlemen who had joined the enterprise soon after its conception. The man had a razor-sharp mind and a keen sense of observation. Drake had great respect for him. "What do you make of it Mr. Fletcher? This savage looked as well-intentioned as any I've seen."

Fletcher squinted. "I doubt he has yet met with the misfortune of coming face to face with the Spaniards. We are in all likelihood the first white men to drop anchor in this bay, and I'd wager ten pounds that his people harbor no hostile intent."

"Mr. Chester, do you agree with this appraisal?"

Frederick Chester, a powerful man with a barrel for a chest and legs like oak trunks had a suspicious nature. Also the most impulsive officer aboard, his temper could flare as quickly as a straw fire. Drake derived great pleasure from soliciting his opinion, for he never agreed with Fletcher. Yet, he kept both men believing that their words counted and that they could influence his decisions.

"Sir," Chester started. "I need not remind you of the horrible end you nearly met in Chile. The savages may bid us welcome today, while tomorrow they may bash our brains. However, since we cannot search for a suitable anchorage forever, I propose we take all necessary precautions and give an account of our strength to impress upon them our resolve to punish any betrayal."

Drake suppressed a smile. He'd expected something of the sort. "Though I share Mr. Fletcher's assessment, we are no strangers to the ways of the savage. There is no certainty that—"

Loud chatter erupted among the crew, cutting him short. The Indian had climbed back in his canoe. Two others stepped into the surf behind him, each placing a bundle into the boat. Then they gave it a push. The emissary again flew

61

over the sea and stopped near the ship, this time only five yards away, and stowed his paddle. He seemed to repeat his entire oration. After making his now familiar though indecipherable signs, he proceeded to tie the bundles to a short stick, and from a sitting position cast the awkward contraption straight into a sailor's arms. The excited man ran for the ladder leading up to the poop deck and passed on the gift. Drake held the bundles moments later and tore them open.

The first one consisted of a bunch of crow feathers, neatly attached to a string and pulled into a tight circle. The individual feathers smelled so fresh, it seemed the birds had been killed that very day. All were flawless, and none longer than the other. Drake marveled at the fine ornament. The second bundle contained a small reed basket filled with fragments of an unknown plant.

"Give this man a token of our gratitude," Drake shouted. "We must not be stingy." At this request the boatswain drove several men to stuff a sack with clothes, mirrors, and a pile of the shiny belt buckles from the market vendors in Plymouth. One of these sailors, the Frisian Jhan Laus, stood out by way of his wide-rimmed black felt hat. He'd taken it from a Spanish prisoner in Peru, and had since grown so fond of it that few of his mates could remember him bare-headed. He even kept it within arm's reach when asleep, which was the cause of much ridicule.

Laus took the sack and nimbly ascended the rigging, where a dangling rope caught his hat's rim and tilted it just enough so that it began to slip. With one hand clinging to the rigging, the other the gift, he had no way of checking the hat's momentum. It fell, bounced off the hull, and sailed into the water.

The ship exploded with laughter, which in itself infuriated Laus. But then he caught sight of the universally despised Tim Smythe. Choking between outbursts of high-pitched giggles and gasping for air, Smythe held his ribs in an apparent attempt to relieve cramping. Laus flew into a rage. He turned crimson and clasped his knife. At that point Drake, who had joined in the laughter, reminded him that he still held the sack.

In the meantime the Indian had used his paddle to fish the hat from the sea and placed it on his head, beaming with pride. With a great sense of importance he looked up at the ship, waiting.

*   *   *

Julia felt great, and her eyes glowed with fiery vivaciousness. She had spent a perfect afternoon galloping Snowflake back and forth along the broad beach. Now she settled in for the last run from Atascadero Creek, past More Mesa, and toward Hendry's Beach.

The tide rarely went out so far, exposing tightly packed low tide terraces that were made for racing. She led the stallion into the swash zone and gave it the spurs. Snowflake let go like a devil, storming into the wind until tears streamed down Julia's cheeks. The hooves pounded sand and water, and she felt a cool mist all over her face. She signaled a "Thank You" at an elderly couple picking up shells, who moved clear of her path.

Before reaching Hendry's Beach, she pulled hard on the reins and brought the horse to a full stop. She slid off its back and handed the reins to Chuck Sartini, who worked at the stables.

"Sure is a perfect day for riding," he said, while she dried her face.

"It's great! He's got such energy." She patted Snowflake on his glistening flank.

"Listen, I've changed my mind and won't come to the stables today. Would you take care of him?"

"No problem."

She knew he'd do everything she'd ask and rewarded him with a bright smile. "See you later, then." She jogged off toward the road, waving good-bye. Feeling the stallion's immense power between her legs, combined with the tangy scent of the sea in her nose, had suddenly stimulated her. She'd make up for the confrontation of last night. A nice surprise awaited Alex.

Fifteen minutes later Julia parked a couple hundred yards from her driveway in a hidden turnout. She walked briskly toward the property and climbed over the gate like a common thief, noticing his car parked in its usual spot. She ducked behind a bush and scanned the windows. No movement. Good. She peeled off her riding boots, made a rush for the front entrance, and gingerly inserted the key. The lock opened with a barely audible click. No way could he resist her today. She closed the door gently and listened to any sounds. She'd check the office first. His work would simply have to wait.

Julia quietly put down the boots and inched upstairs, silent as a shadow. On the last steps she unbuttoned her shirt and unhooked her bra. She placed both softly on the floor. That's when she first heard a faint rustling sound, like papers being shoved across a desk. She snuck along the wall, loving the secrecy. The hum of his computer reached her ears. He had to be sitting at the desk, his back toward the door. *Excellent.*

Julia glanced down at her firm breasts. Her nipples were hard and smooth. Nature had been on her side. She flicked open the button of her tight jeans and pulled down the zipper. Then, holding her breath, she stepped out of her pants. Clad only in a black lace thong, Julia's eyes peeked around the corner into his office.

Papers were spread across the desk, and a stack of books stood precariously near the edge. The illuminated monitor stared at an empty chair. *Where is he?* Again, Julia heard that

64

strange rustling, this time louder and more persistent. She broke into a wide grin. *The walk-in closet!* He'd seen her jump the gate and played along. The outlines of what promised to turn into a wonderful evening made her feverish with desire.

Contemplating whether she should drop the thong or not, she opted to keep it on. She advanced and turned the knob with agonizing deliberateness.

The next instant Julia's head jerked back as if a fist had suddenly punched her. The blood drained from her face.

On the twentieth of June, when the tide attained its highest point, they brought the ship landward until its keel touched bottom. An initial detachment of twenty-four cautious men armed with sword and arquebus transferred to shore. Their first order of business involved collecting stones for a defensive wall while more of their mates landed as quickly as possible. The second wave split into three groups, some setting up tents, others piling up gear, and the rest guarding against attack.

By early evening the Indians, who for most of the day had observed the English from a hilltop, became restive. At least thirty warriors, bows and arrows in hand, split from the group and started running for the encampment.

"They're attacking!" several men shouted at once. The sailors dropped all work and threw themselves into positions behind the half-completed rock wall.

"I will hang anyone who fires without my permission!" the captain's voice roared above the commotion.

Richard looked for Waspe, who hunkered down twenty paces along the line, his barrel aimed at the enemy. The moment of reckoning had come. The welcome had been sufficiently friendly to persuade Drake to make a landing. But there were never any guarantees. If the savages fought, all would be lost. They'd shoot them like birds, hustle all equipment back on board, and set sail for another site. The General would find the gold and execute him and Waspe.

But no fighting broke out that day. Well short of the defensive wall the Indians slowed to a walk, staring in great astonishment at all the things their strange visitors possessed. Knives, swords, firearms, shirts, silver earrings, oak barrels, glass bottles, tarpaulins, woolen blankets, spades, cordage, and a hundred more necessities. Women and children soon joined the men, until upward of two hundred gawked in wonder.

Drake, who seemed to entertain a particularly foul mood despite avoiding bloodshed, bellowed that every third man on the perimeter remain on guard. The cause of his irritation immediately became clear. "Where is our cloth?" he demanded belligerently. "We must convince them to cover their nakedness."

Many of the Indian men wore nothing. A score, those who in build and posture looked most war-like, did wear feather bundles on their heads and deerskins on their bodies. As to the women, long skirts made of bulrushes covered their private parts, while deerskins with the hair still on them hid the shoulders of most. Some were bare-breasted.

"Mr. Fletcher, where in the Lord's name are the cloth and shirts? Entreat these heathen at once to imitate our manner of dress."

Men hurriedly procured the chests, and Drake himself began pulling an armful of breeches from one, beckoning the nearest cluster of Indians to accept his gifts. But all color left his face when two women suddenly stripped naked. They dropped their skirts and handed their deerskins to the bewildered sailors. The Indians saw the entire thing as an exchange.

When Drake's face finally resumed color, it did so by turning bright red. "Don't just stand there like fools! Attend to your tasks! Bestow the items!" he thundered, his voice trembling. The sex-starved pirates sprang to action, each man vying with those around him to see who could pass out the most. A disproportionate share reached the women, though they had no need for either breeches or shirts.

Richard, one of those ordered to watch for a surprise attack, instinctively sensed someone's gaze upon him. Intuitively, he turned left, where fifteen yards away and partly hidden behind a tree, a young woman studied his every move. Their eyes found each other, and when she didn't look away, his throat tightened. The next instant he had a sensation as if he'd been struck, and a powerful urge to know her made him lose all sense of time and place.

The Miwok woman didn't stir, staring at him with such intensity that for a fleeting moment he thought he had done something wrong. *Oh, God!* Had he missed a sign? Were they laying a trap? *I must warn the others.* Just then her mouth widened into a smile that dispelled his fears. She stepped over the tree's huge root system, which coiled all around its base. With two women in tow, she came straight for him, never breaking eye contact.

Almost as tall as he, who topped six feet, her shiny black hair fell past her shoulders without any artificial contraptions to break nature's pattern. A dark complexion enhanced the whiteness of her teeth, which gleamed behind parted lips. Black and uncommonly curious eyes sparkled above pronounced cheekbones. *This woman has spirit—and a will of her own.*

When she stood in front of him, waiting, he didn't know where to start. He yearned to know her name, her age, whether she had a man, and a hundred other things. But their languages differed as do day and night. And so he said nothing, just smiled like a young lad in love. Her companions giggled, as did women everywhere when a mature man is reduced to a nervous boy. The whole scene hummed with the energy of a lightning storm, captivating those of his comrades who stood nearest.

Then, with one curt outburst, an Indian man quashed the moment's magic. Well past his prime and with streaks of gray accenting his long black hair, his muscles still firm, he had the look of one used to enforcing his wishes. The girl bowed her head and stretched her hand toward Richard.

Frantic, he turned toward the mate at his side. "Give me that." Not awaiting an answer he grasped a shirt and placed it in her warm hands. He felt light-headed at the touch, and an inexplicable joy flooded over his entire being. She turned and joined a group of other women busy comparing their new possessions. He shot a shy glance at the Indian. *Did women here take such old men for husbands? Or is he her father?* Richard prayed for the latter and determined that he would find out, no matter what the cost.

*   *   *

Julia's brain spun in neutral. Utter shock paralyzed her. She gaped, uncontrollable twitches racking her body. Was she having a nightmare?

Alex sat on their heavy trunk, the one filled with wedding mementos. With his left side toward her, his head rested against the wall. His eyes still closed, he wore nothing. Their neighbor, Rachel, straddled his waist with long and slender legs wrapped around his lower back. She did have clothes on—Julia observed with an odd clarity of mind—if the colorful bandanna covering her eyes counted. Their ecstasy was so great they didn't hear the closet door, so they went right on with undiminished passion. She thrust her pelvis with such vigor, her left knee scraped against a box. It explained the rustling sound.

After what seemed like an eternity, but was only a nanosecond, Alex saw her. His head twisted, as though an invisible puppeteer had given him a neck-breaking jerk. His gaze met Julia's, and in that instant she knew *all* the rumors were true. Rachel ceased thrusting, her hips suspended in the air.

"What is it?" she panted breathlessly, raising her lips from his glistening throat. "Don't tease me."

When neither his loins nor his voice made reply, she yanked off the bandanna. Her face turned ghastly white.

Excruciating seconds of absolute silence followed, as humiliating for the twosome as for Julia. Almost completely in the nude, her shoulders sagging, she shivered with rage. Try as she might, she could not move. She had come to seduce her husband, who sat there slumped with his chest caved in and his head low to avoid facing her. The temptress, apparently ashamed to get up and fully expose herself and Alex to Julia's view, stayed attached to him, transfixed, her look fixed on some spot on the far wall. Sweat ran down her sides in tiny rivulets.

A spark finally jump-started Julia. She had to get away from here, from this whore who had contaminated her own four walls and forever defaced the trunk that held her wedding dress. She slammed the door so hard the frame vibrated, retraced her steps as fast as she could, and retrieved her clothes in reverse order. At the bottom of the stairs she dressed in record time and bolted into the open. Her mother's prophetic words kept flashing in her mind. "Alex will bring you sorrow."

*　　*　　*

Chewing with delight on a slab of fat seal meat, his gold earrings swaying with each chomp, John surveyed the rock wall that enclosed the camp on three sides. The sea afforded protection in the rear, at least from Indian attack. Chances of the Spaniards sailing into this bay were slim. Besides, with most cannon placed to rake the sea, only fools would try. The Dons could possibly land a few hundred men out of reach of the cannon and then overrun the position.

John shook off the thought in favor of a more optimistic assessment. They'd dwelled here a week already, and the savages had shown no hostility. Instead the Indians showered them with presents of colorful bird feathers, arrow quivers made from the skins of fawns, and shells. Some of the sailors had stuck so many feathers into their shirts and breeches that they seemed more bird than human. Fools, John mused.

He looked at the ship, lying steeply tilted on its port side as near shore as the tide permitted. Heavy ropes connected the masts' tops to trees growing beyond the sandy beach. Men were at work on the hull, scraping it free of several layers of encrusted growth after so many months at sea. They labored with such purpose that the carpenters could soon begin to replace the various rotten timbers. The General would exult.

But not for long, John gloated. The back-breaking drudgery of careening the ship had already begun to take its toll. Prevented from mingling with the women, sailors grumbled in private. *Proper exploitation of these sentiments, and they will belong to me.* John shoved the last scrap of meat into his mouth and rose. *Where the hell was Argyle?*

Richard sat on a sack of flour, poking at his rations with indifference. Since that first encounter he had seen the girl only twice, even though the Indians came to the camp every day. The officers had driven the men like slaves, which made it almost impossible to consort with the women. Not a moment passed without him thinking of her, and as a result he had grown careless with his work. Once he'd nearly gotten a mate crushed while felling a tree.

Richard tried to stay cheerful. He did learn her name— Mónoy. Moreover, the man with the gray in his hair was not her husband. One way or another, Richard had to find a way to see her alone, for if the General didn't relent, he'd lose his mind. Familiar footsteps approached through the grass. He turned.

"Dreaming again, no?" Waspe planted himself on a stump, a scowl on his face.

"It drains me of any purpose," Richard sighed.

Waspe glanced over his shoulder, leaned closer. "I am counting on you. You have got to pull yourself together."

This annoyed Richard. "Don't belittle me. I'm prepared do whatever it takes to get to her."

71

Waspe nodded. "I know you have no stomach for blood, and from the looks of things we will not have to spill any. All is working in our favor. The Spaniards can't find us, and most of the men are with me. We will strike soon. Then, once the carpenters mend the last hole, we sail for England with all of the gold. The General and his lot, they stay with the savages. Everyone has had his fill with him and his pig-headed gentlemen working us to death." He spat. "Besides, you're not the only one who's got fire in his loins."

Richard nodded approval. The galleon still required repairs and provisions to ready her for the long Pacific crossing. Each sailor would then see his fair share of the treasure. The General and his conceited cohorts would not leave this shore. They'd never be heard of again, while the Indians would treat them well. Yet his conscience nagged him. Yes, their master had never shied from pushing them to their limits, and he had Thomas Doughty killed. But did he really deserve abandonment in this land? Could they really risk sailing without use of his skills? And, what really mattered, how about Mónoy?

"John, let's exercise patience. We'll be here for some time. There's no purpose acting before the ship can sail. We'd have to keep the gentlemen under guard until we weigh anchor, and you know how easily the General wins a man to his side. I don't want him to string me up because we moved with premature haste."

Waspe looked him hard in the face. "Few stand with him today. This could change."

"We'd be the better off for it. I want no part in a mutiny unless the men are of one heart."

Frustrated, Waspe rose. "Let's be sure we keep our barrels together."

"You've told me a dozen times."

"No one must touch them."

*   *   *

Julia sobbed uncontrollably, huge tears rolling down her cheeks. Thank God mom and dad had gone out, affording her the chance to use the sauna without them seeing her. The service personnel never came to the main house in the evening, unless called. She couldn't bear even the thought of facing anyone in her present state.

She felt dirty and polluted, as though that slut neighbor had left marks on every thing she possessed. Images kept flashing in her mind. The naked bodies, his ecstatic face, her thrusts, the damn bandanna, the way those perfect thighs embraced his waist. Try as she might, she just couldn't shake that dreadful sound of the knee scraping the box. Julia yearned to kick that knee, no, to smash it with a sledgehammer. As for him, why did she fail at the very least to spit in his face, or punch him till her knuckles blistered? She'd run off like a frightened foal. How lame! She had displayed too much weakness for far too long.

She shivered, despite the cubicle's 100-plus degrees, and threw a quart of water on the red-hot stones. Steam hissed, driving humidity in the tiny body cooker to choking levels. The chill finally went out of her as she began perspiring from every pore, sweat mixing with tears. The light pine around her wet buttocks and soles turned dark brown. With a rough cotton cloth she began to scrub every square inch of her body, stopping only to toss another quart on the stones. The ritual complete, she felt cleansed. The tears had stopped and rationality returned.

She had let him blind her. *But, I'm a Henderson, not a doormat to be trampled. He will never betray me again.* She vowed to make him pay, ignoring the nagging guilt for having deceived him about her infertility.

Julia had felt drawn to him since the day they met. It happened at one of her father's glamourous parties, given in honor of her return home from Stanford. She had earned two degrees in five years, completing graduate school a year ahead of schedule. Her parents were overjoyed that she wanted to step into the family business and help administer the vineyard and rental properties. Her two older sisters had shown no such inclinations and lived in New York and Boulder. Mary nursed stocks, Laurel her three children.

Friends and relatives had mingled freely with the usual assortment of VIPs—movie stars, eminent UCSB professors, renowned physicians, and a select group of key figures in local government and business. Alex, hailed as a rising star in his field, had accompanied the university contingent.

At first she didn't think much of him. Her father had coaxed the young academician into giving a speech, which came off with too much self-confidence. Alex seemed artificial. But he did look good, very good, with more than one hopeful chick demonstrating interest throughout the evening. In fact, Julia had forgotten him over the busy chatter with friends and cousins. Later, while talking to one of the country's most popular actors and long-time family friend about an upcoming film, Alex managed to butt in. Bothered at first, she soon felt an uncanny sense of familiarity. A whirlwind romance followed, and they married that fall.

Her father selfishly disapproved of the way she rushed into it. He'd wanted his girl back for himself. But he liked Alex, as he did all who excelled in honest work. Mom saw the situation differently. While dad prized his son-in-law's ambition, she was suspicious of it. She never let Julia forget that Alex had muscled himself into that conversation. It had been her idea to keep everything in the parents' name.

*   *   *

A month without serious incidents found Drake in a splendid mood. The sky shone brightly, and there was much to be thankful for. The galleon might take to sea within a fortnight, should progress continue at the current pace. He had once again, by heeding the warning signs and easing the pressure, gotten the men to respect him. He still reveled in having taught the hated Spaniards a lesson they'd never forget, and cherished to the utmost that the Pacific's days as an exclusive Spanish trading lake were ending. To top everything off, his ship held a vast treasure. He'd need the Lord's blessings in only one further endeavor—navigate the breadth of two oceans, round the African cape, and sail north through the Atlantic, a feat no Englishman had ever performed.

Deep in his heart Drake knew he was a fair man, a born leader who knew exactly how far he could push the superstitious rabble he commanded. They'd survived stormy seas and skirmishes with the Indians, froze in frigid northern latitudes, and endured weeks of such grueling labor on the hull that the mutinous had again fanned the flames. He'd instructed his officers to extinguish the fire before it flared. Work duties were slashed by two hours per day and wine rations doubled. Likewise, the willingness of the local women appeased his men's irrepressible instincts. With no enemy sail in sight, time now belonged to them. The men stuffed their bellies with deer and fat bear meat, tart roots and berries, fowl and fish, and fresh greens every day. They drank clear, cool water from sparkling creeks and benefited from robust health. Their contentment was complete with access to the village and its pleasures, though one man had lost himself. In fact, the offender had become dangerously careless in his tasks.

Drake decided to resolve this problem once and for all.

"Waspe, I want to speak to you."

John stopped mid-stride, an ominous foreboding taking hold of his heart. "Aye, Sir. How can I be of service?"

"It has come to my attention that your assistant has not been properly discharging his duties. Men are talking."

John felt a noose tightening around his neck. The General had never rebuked him, even indirectly. "Yes, yes, I think it's the girl. He's excessively fond of her."

Eyes of steel gored him. "And what do you propose to do?"

"I've talked to him several times, but it's a difficult affair. Argyle hasn't been himself since we came ashore."

"How do you mean?"

Choose your words with care, John cautioned himself. "Aye, the rest of the men see the women as a, ah, diversion." The General's countenance lost nothing of its rigidity, nor did his inquisitive gaze weaken. John mustered courage.

"It's . . ." he tried to clear his throat, "they're having fun while they can. Nothing more." At this, Drake's face frosted over, and beads of sweat pearled on John's back. "But Argyle is different. He becomes a mere boy in her presence, acting as though she was going to be his, his . . . " he wished he could burrow into the mud like a worm, "his mate." The last words came out in a whisper.

"Waspe!" The General enunciated the name with painstaking clarity, squaring his shoulders. "Do you suggest we return to England with a ship full of heathens?" He bristled with sarcasm. "Perhaps we should all burn our clothes and take to sea in our God-given nakedness? Her Majesty would surely approve."

John would have given anything to end this. Directly responsible for Richard, he was accountable for his actions. "No, Sir," seemed the safest reply. Meekly he added, "I'll have another talk with the lad."

"You'll have 'another talk?'" he replied. "I suggest you inform Argyle of the consequences if he continues to prove stubborn. Waste no more time with it. I should be very ill-humored if this matter comes before me again. Go now."

"Aye, Sir. I'll attend to it at once." *And when the time is ripe, I'll attend to you, too.*

76

He started for the village, when he heard the General's voice call after him. "One more thing, Waspe. I had nearly forgotten." John turned.

"I want to discuss our provisions this evening. It is time to take stock, especially of the Spanish items. Be at my tent after the men are served."

"Aye, Sir." A sharp pounding in his temples, John hurried off. *Bloody bastard. The General must under no circumstances be permitted to stick his nose into the barrels.*

~ 8 ~

No clouds marred the rich sapphire sky, and the crisp air accentuated the characteristic tinging of steel cables beating a forest of masts. Hundreds of boat flags danced in the fresh breeze, whose spicy scent told of the exotic flora carpeting the hills.

A brown pelican sailed effortlessly twenty feet above the water, searching. It abruptly slowed its glide into a steep ascent, its wings churning the air. Tucking them in tightly, the airborne fisherman became a feathery replica of the infamous German STUKA dive bomber and smashed into the sea. By the time the spray settled, the bird had already composed itself, a sizable bulge deforming its pouch. With a pelican's uniquely dreamy-eyed expression, it threw back its head and, with an enormous gulp, swallowed the out-of-luck fish. An uptight seagull, angered by the lack of scraps, emptied its bowels in protest. The slime barely missed its stoic target.

Liam and Patrick navigated the pier toward a gleaming forty-foot yacht moored at the very end. "That's the one," Liam said, as they got closer. The name *Helen* shone in bold black cursive across the bow.

Patrick laughed heartlessly. "She's worth more than you and I will make in our entire lives."

Liam spotted Julia sitting in the captain's swivel chair, her back toward the pier. He couldn't see Alex. "Boat ahoy," Liam hailed. "May we board?"

Julia rose from her seat, welcoming them with a dashing smile. "Come right up," she called, and slid backwards down the ladder to the main deck. She wore a white Tee and frayed denim shorts. A rip on the back exposed a tiny patch of skin where there would have been underwear.

Liam commanded his eyes away. *Don't mess it up*, he admonished himself. *It's all in the timing*. Her tanned body exuded health and the vibrant energy of an outdoor athlete. Even Patrick couldn't hide his surprise at her beauty, mumbling something under his breath. Liam elbowed him sharply in the ribs, torn between relief that Patrick actually showed emotion again toward a female, and fear he'd say something stupid.

"Don't embarrass me," he whispered. Patrick had a tendency to speak his mind. Liam shook himself loose from the moment and led the way up the narrow gangway.

"You can put your packs over there for now," she motioned. "So nice of you to join us again."

She hugged Liam, holding on longer and tighter than usual, or did he imagine this? After another moment he knew he did not. There was something in her sparkling black eyes he could not fathom. God, he was so attracted to her, it hurt. It had been like this from the minute he met her.

He introduced his brother. "This is some cruiser you have here," Patrick marveled. "A real beauty."

"She's my father's pride. He's got to have his toys," she laughed. "Alex will show you around." Her tone had grown cooler at the mention of his name, and a subtle shadow darkened her face.

Great, Liam thought with a sinking feeling. They fought. Hopefully they would keep it to themselves during the crossing.

"Guys, I still have to run some checks, make sure everything is in order." She motioned with her hands at the open sea. "We don't want to get ourselves in hot water."

This reminded Liam, and he cursed himself for having forgotten. He fingered his pocket and retrieved a tube of motion sickness pills. Better late than never. "Doesn't look too bad today," he said, hopeful.

"Three-foot swells. Pretty calm," Julia assured him.

When he shoved two tablets into his mouth, she patted him encouragingly. "Why don't you stay next to me in the copilot's chair? It's the best spot to be."

Alex's head popped from the cabin. A practiced smile on his face and a beer in his hand, he looked the permanent vacationer in his khaki shorts and canvas shoes. Liam got a short "Hey there," and even shorter eye contact. Patrick got a handshake. "Glad you fellows could make it."

The following awkward silence ended with Julia turning away. "Why don't you show Patrick the boat?" Then she ascended the ladder and busied herself with the controls. Liam glanced from her to Alex, who quickly averted his gaze.

*   *   *

"Anyone seen Argyle?" John barked at the group of men handling large coils of ropes. "I saw him with you not long ago."

They chuckled. One, who worked a few yards away by himself, laughed out in a particularly galling manner. John yearned to kick him in the teeth, but the General's words still rang in his ears. The last thing he needed now was to fall from grace. He leveled his gaze on Tim Smythe, whose bloodshot eyes bulged from broadly set sockets. Combined with an abnormally narrow skull, this gave him the distinct look of a swamp ghoul. Tall and lanky, he stood with a slight hunch that signaled perennial untrustworthiness. His hair fell in long, filthy mats onto a crooked back. He was more devil than human and thrived on others' misery. Since the men avoided him whenever possible, he often worked alone.

Persistent rumors told of Smythe murdering a whore when she demanded payment for her services. They told of him stuffing a burning candle into her mouth before slitting her throat. The prostitute's outraged associates incited a local riot, and a magistrate eventually sentenced Smythe to death. The execution was scheduled for the following dawn. With his own throat now pushed onto the stained and grooved executioner's block, the ax rose, and the blood-thirsty crowd surged forth in its greed to watch the head fall. Suddenly, a detachment of armed sailors led by an officer had punched its way through the mob. Smythe had saved the man's life in a raid on coastal smugglers, and the officer had come to pay his debt. Thus went the story.

"What's so funny?" John asked.

Smythe pointed a thumb in the direction of the Indian village. "I reckon the good-for-nothin' is laying' up with that savage maiden, wearin' out his musket." He exploded with more laughter, slapping his thighs like a lunatic. "I'll be damned if she isn't a wreck by now, all split open." He looked from man to man, eager for applause, but got none. Though the pirates made up a rough lot—brutal, fearless, and hard-drinking—they had no love for the demented.

"You're a greasy swine who wouldn't recognize a woman if you saw one, since your paws never touched anything but a sow," John growled. "One for hire at that." *If I could just strangle that rat, twist his neck.*

The laughter dried up and Smythe's face turned purple. The bulging eyes glared from his quivering face, and a small trickle of dark saliva oozed from the corner of his mouth. "The day will come that you regret your words, you stinking half-Spaniard. Act important as long as the General likes your stews. But you dog won't get special attention forever." His voice trembled with rage.

"Is that so? You gobble up everything we cook, scraps and all. Why don't you watch what I put on *your* plate tonight? I might give *it* 'special attention.'" John snickered, hoping this would incense him even more. Then he turned and walked away, relieved to hear the other men laugh. Who could tell what that freak might do?

*   *   *

On the outside, the *Helen* distinguished herself from the other luxury yachts moored in the harbor mostly by size. When Liam descended into the belly of the Henderson family ark, he once again understood a comment Alex had made after a tennis match. "Marrying Julia had forever rescued him from the poverty of his childhood." Liam had seen the yacht before, but it again took his breath away.

His hand gliding over a tropical hardwood railing polished to a perfect luster, he followed Patrick and Alex down a flight of stairs into the main cabin, whose plush carpet swallowed all noise. The common living area consisted of a spacious rectangle divided into a solarium and a kitchen-dining room combination. Lined with low palms in terra cotta pots fastened to bolts in the floor, it exuded the posh aura of a five-star resort. Costly pastel curtains adorned the frames of paneled windows, through which the Californian sun bathed everything in its golden rays. Silver and brass fixtures in every nook and cranny sparkled like a miniature galaxy.

Liam looked for the magnificent table near the center, which always aroused his artistic instincts. He went to touch it. Elaborate carvings of tigers, pandas, and steep mountain scenes imbued its top and the four-inch rim with vivid life. The piece boasted a dozen colors, with white, black, and hues of tan and brown predominant. Color-coordinated, the pandas shared white and black, tigers the intermediate hues, with the remaining tones reserved for the mountains.

"This is amazing!" Patrick said, stepping up to the table.

"It never fails to evoke wonder," Alex said proudly. "This treasure is quite ancient," he continued, "predating Columbus' voyage by several centuries. It once belonged to a Chinese prince, at least until the Opium Wars put an end to that. Some high-ranking naval officer accompanying Sir Henry Pottinger's expeditionary fleet 'obtained' it after the British captured Shanghai in 1842. The chap ordered his detachment to loot the prince's abandoned palace." He paused. "I understand you're army, but I figure you appreciate any military history."

"How did it get to the States?" Patrick wanted to know.

"An eccentric merchant from Boston scoured the French countryside for collectibles after World War One. The table had somehow found its way to a hunting chalet in the Ardennes where, incredibly, it was collecting dust in the attic. The Bostonian, who happened to sire Julia's grandmother, never found out how the piece left Britain for the continent." Alex drummed his knuckles on the table. "Each of the colors you see represents a different type of wood. The thing is priceless."

"It's an odd place for it, I mean, out here on the water," Patrick said. "I'd fear someone breaking in."

Alex nonchalantly gestured at the walls. "The insurance premiums on this yacht are astronomical, and the security system is first rate. The windows are stronger than steel, and you'd need heavy explosives to get in. To top things off, Julia's father knows some high-ups with the local police. The *Helen* is a law enforcement priority."

He popped open the refrigerator, scanned the shelves, and asked if they wanted a beer. Patrick settled for a Sierra Nevada. Liam wanted one, but he knew better. They'd hit that heaving Channel within minutes. An empty stomach couldn't surrender anything, and the thought of Julia watching him bend overboard and fertilize the sea proved decisive.

"Think I'll pass," he said. "Thanks." Patrick ogled him along the length of the beer bottle, taking a long draft. His eyes twinkled maliciously. Liam didn't let it bother him, studying the bar instead. It boasted enough liquor to immobilize an infantry regiment. Many pounds of Waterford crystal hung from a custom rack above this collection of finest spirits.

Alex went on to explain something about the Opium Wars. Liam stopped listening, his attention totally focused on a photo he hadn't seen before. It was a black and white close-up of Julia in her late teens, and she sat in the aft of a sailing boat on what looked like Lake Tahoe. The way she smiled at the camera, with that tiny dimple on her chin and those full lips, it made him dizzy. He forgot where he was.

Silence! No more voices! How much time had passed? He saw them staring. Patrick seemed amused, though a tad embarrassed. But Alex's eyes had grown cold and calculating. A queer electrical impulse jolted Liam, absolutely convincing him the tension which had always characterized their friendship would never go away. A deep gulch opened between them, bridged only by modern civility. What is this? he wondered. *I've never had such a weird experience.*

A distant roar liberated the three men from the situation. Julia had ignited the powerful engine. Alex put down his bottle. "Let's help cast off," his voice flat as day-old soda.

"Yeah," Liam said.

"Good idea," Patrick added.

They emerged onto the deck, where Alex went to untie the rope securing the bow. Liam and Patrick busied themselves with a thick knot that held the aft to the pier.

"So what do you think of my father's yacht?" Julia called down, emphasizing the words, 'my father's.'

"Very nice," Patrick said after a pregnant pause.

She looked askance at him and Liam and turned toward her husband, who was just returning from the bow. He looked pissed. A shadow went over her. "Liam, why don't you come up and take this seat?" She pointed at the copilot's chair. "Tracking the waves lets your body prepare for the motion."

Alex encouraged him. "Go on. I want you to enjoy the crossing," with a hint of sarcasm. Julia threw him a frosty glance and signaled Liam with a hand.

"Come on. I, too, would like to enjoy the crossing."

Patrick made himself small on a bench, pretending not to have heard any of it. Alex only stared, a strange look on his face. Liam contemplated. What could he do? *Screw it!* He climbed the ladder.

*   *   *

Spellbound Indians crowded around Richard as he carved a horse from a smooth piece of driftwood. Having worked the wood for several days, he would finish tonight, tomorrow at the latest. The head needed more detail and the legs a little trimming. Mónoy squatted by his side, following his every move. He loved it. Her attentiveness and physical closeness gave him a satisfaction he'd never known.

Richard heard a familiar panting behind his back. Waspe! *Something had happened.* The cook avoided coming here. Weak lungs kept his voluntary exertions to a minimum. He ran only when absolutely necessary—and never to the village. Waspe rudely cleared a couple of boys in his path and dropped on his butt, his chest heaving.

"What in God's name are you doing?" he demanded between breaths.

His demeanor, his sweaty face, his whole being irked Richard. He wanted to put him in his place for shoving those harmless boys, and he knew just how. Sensing Waspe's growing impatience, he imbued his voice with as much passion as he could and continued with his work. "I could do well as a carver amongst my new friends. I'd trade my products with the other villages." He let it sink in. "And you could cook for visitors."

"You're losing your senses," the cook bristled. "Listen, the General just talked to me. He's not happy with your work. And," he cast about for words, "neither am I. You cannot come here until after you see to your duties. You've been risking our heads to play with wooden horses." Then he added. "Later today I'm to account for our provisions. I got a lousy premonition bad things might happen. We must have a plan."

85

"A plan for what?" Richard found the whole thing tiring. That man would one day get them both killed.

"I suspect he'll open some of the barrels, if for no other reason than to punish us for your laziness. While I loathe him as ever, I can't fault him. No captain worth his salt can afford to leave the galley completely to his cook, especially when preparing to cross the world's largest sea. I know he'll shake us out like a dirty blanket. You remember Quentin, don't you?"

Master carpenter Quentin, a wiry midget, spoke only when asked a direct question. A few months back, the General had wanted some planking replaced in his cabin. Somehow the request never reached Quentin and so went unheeded. The General flew into a rage and paid the carpenter a personal visit. It took Quentin not only a week to get his shop back in order, but even to this day, the crew found him much more willing to complete his tasks.

Richard nodded. How could anyone forget that tempest? "You're right. We better move the gold."

Waspe smiled. "I see your head is still well. We have little time. He wants to see me once the men are fed."

"Tonight then. He won't take stock after dark, but will dine in his tent with the gentlemen as he always does. By morning, if he still wants to stick his nose in the casks, it'll be too late."

"Right." Waspe's eyes glowed with relief. "We'll see to it that everyone eats and drinks like a lord. The hunting party is bound to bring in deer or fowl. When the last man falls asleep, we'll hide the casks in a thicket. That shouldn't take long. After the General satisfies his damn curiosity in the morning, we will return them at our convenience. No one will suspect a thing."

Richard wished he had Waspe's optimism. Instead, he felt a heavy burden pressing on his soul, as though something life-altering was about to happen.

All work on the ship's hull and on land had stopped. Each hand stared as the group inched its way down the grassy slopes toward camp. Eight sailors had gone hunting that day, led by two Indians. They marched slowly, carrying a bounty of duck, quail, and meadowlark strung from sturdy branches. Near two hundred birds dangled from their claws, like bats sleeping before a nocturnal feeding frenzy. The men also brought two deer and a score of ground squirrels. The land was rich beyond comprehension.

An officer detailed two sailors to the galley to help remove the birds' feathers and entrails. Richard then soaked the cleaned birds in red wine pilfered from the Spaniards and rubbed the flesh with salt. Waspe stuffed the carcasses with a tart root the Indians supplied in great quantities. They called it wáyla, which, eaten raw, crunched like an onion and tasted like an early-harvest apple. The first batch of duck soon roasted over open fires, filling the air with a mouth-watering aroma.

"Pollmane, help me lift these," Richard commanded one of the sailors. Four huge kettles heavy with clams from the estuary stood ready. They hung them over the fires next to the birds. Satisfied, Richard placed on the rough makeshift tables wooden bowls heaped high with black raspberries brought by Indian women. These tólpas berries, a favorite with the men, grew in enormous quantities throughout the country. The General had even uprooted ten bushes. Stored for transport back to England, he desired to present any survivors to the sovereign.

The sailors devoured the fruit, played cards, sang, and looked forward as much to the meat as to the sediment-laden Peruvian wine. No matter how much Waspe insisted that they all hated the General, Richard realized by looking into these faces that all but a handful would stand by their master. The voices of discontent had faded. Attempting a mutiny now would constitute suicide.

He glanced at the gentlemen seated around the General's table adorned with silver and crystal. The captain had his head in the charts captured from the Spaniards, listening to his second in command, Gregory Hord. Richard could swear the conversation revolved not around charts, but the inventory. He moved closer to Waspe, who dressed the deer.

"John, I know Hord is up to something. The scoundrel is so obsessed with gaining favor he can't let even the General study in peace."

Waspe innocently studied the officers. When Hord turned his head toward the galley, he quickly looked down and worked his cleaver. "Aye, the bastard is spying on us. He makes me nervous." He chopped at the animal's ribcage. "We better see to it that not one man runs short of wine tonight."

"When's the birds gonna be done roasted?" a rude voice interrupted them. "We been settin' here for an eternity, and you got nothin' better to do than gossip about Argyle's exploits amongst the savages?" Smythe, sitting by himself, searched around to see if anyone would take up his cue. A handful of men impatiently looked toward the fires, but most ignored him, as they would a stubborn, noxious odor.

Richard's skin prickled all over. How he detested Smythe! After a meaningful gaze at an axe on the table, he leveled his eyes on him. "Listen, dirty pig. Don't ever burden yourself with my affairs. You do so again, by God I swear I'll split you like I did these birds."

Smythe snarled like a kicked dog. "You can't speak to me like that. You're nothin' but a helper for that, that . . ." he stared derisively at Waspe, his demented mind struggling to complete the sentence. "You can't even hold your own up in the masts with the rest of us fellers."

This was enough. The pig deserved a beating, with a little bit of terror beforehand. Richard took the axe and slowly walked toward Smythe. "I warned you. Now I'll have to crack your skull." Smythe jumped to his feet, his eyes bulging dangerously, his filthy hair stuck to a sweaty forehead. Suddenly, Hord appeared out of nowhere.

"What is going on?" he demanded.

Richard lowered the axe, trying to speak calmly. "Nothing, Mr. Hord." He pointed at Smythe. "He was only meddling in matters that don't concern him."

"I should know of any 'matters' serious enough to threaten a man with an axe." He paused. "Speak, Argyle."

Do not mention Mónoy! He lifted his hand and looked at the weapon with as much surprise as he could feign. "You mistook my purpose, Mr. Hord. I had been cleaning the fowl when he started."

"He's lying. He's a damn liar, and knows it," Smythe exploded, his face full of hate, bile oozing from the corner of his quivering mouth. "Just 'fore you stepped up, Argyle threatened to split my skull with his hatchet. He was dead serious. I swear it."

Hord's impenetrable countenance revealed nothing. Though all knew him to despise Smythe, the second in command's respect rested in no small measure on his rock-solid impartiality. "Is that true?"

By now several sailors had gathered, one of whom stepped forward. "Mr. Hord, I been here since Smythe ran his big mouth, offending Argyle about a personal matter. Now, the man only told him to shut up, like anyone else would have, but Smythe kept at it. Argyle put him in his place, and so far as I can judge he wasn't threatening no life." The other men nodded in assent.

Hord's icy eyes measured Smythe, whose changed demeanor resembled that of a cornered rat. "I caution you to mind your own affairs, Smythe. Nothing good comes from prying into another man's life." He faced Richard, who sensed that Hord didn't trust him. "Go attend to your duties. The men are hungry, and I will tolerate no more idling." Then he rejoined the officers.

STEVEN FARQUHAR

Abysmal hate distorted Smythe's expression. He spat black bile on the ground and sauntered off with a grunt. Richard nodded thanks at the sailors who had supported him and waited for them to get out of earshot. He knew he could count on those fellows. "We better watch that animal. He'll want to have his revenge, I'm sure."

Waspe rolled his eyes subtly without moving his head at all. Hord was looking their way, as did the General.

The enormous yacht sliced smoothly through the harbor's placid waters. Liam wouldn't have known they moved, if it hadn't been for the boat changing position relative to its surroundings and the hum of the motor. He felt needle pricks all over his back, convinced Alex's eyes hurled a metal storm at him from the deck below. Julia looked professional, the way she hooked her arm to pull down her sunglasses and the other hand draped so comfortably over the helm, her mind on the exit maneuver. The breeze ruffled her hair, and Liam couldn't resist the temptation to study her legs. *I don't care if Alex sees that.*

They cleared the narrow opening, gliding by a catamaran on its way in. A happy couple lifted wine coolers in a raucous salute. The woman sported a few tattoos on her arms and legs and around her navel. Reds, blues, and blacks plastered the man's entire torso. Liam and Julia waved back. The *Helen* rounded the breakwater, and Julia gave her more gas. She went to full speed after the last "No Wake" buoy, steaming head-on into the open Channel. Whitecaps smacked the hull as it cut through the clear green waters, and Liam steadied his gaze at a point far off the bow. The motion sickness pills should kick in anytime.

"What a stench!" Julia complained two or three miles out. "It's not usually this bad." Buried deep below them lay one of the continent's richest oil fields. The black gold constantly seeped through natural fissures in the sea floor, sending the blobs of crude swirling up the water column. The currents tossed the sticky goo ashore, creating Santa Barbara's greatest plight. Liam had ruined more than one pair of shorts by sitting without first looking. He avoided the hardest-hit beaches and shunned Isla Vista all together.

"I hate getting that nasty stuff stuck between my toes," he said. He looked at Julia. "I have often wondered what the Chumash thought of it."

The Indians had made heavy use of the resource, caulking their planked canoes with it. In fact, the town of Carpinteria fifteen miles south derived its name from the Spanish word for carpenter. The conquistadors had thus immortalized the natives' sophisticated boat-building skills, unique in pre-European America.

"I always imagine how the mainland and island tribes crossed the Channel to trade furs and shell bead money and stories. But that's all long gone now, shattered by time." Sadness spread over her face. "Everything ends, doesn't it?"

They made it in little over an hour to the Santa Cruz Channel, which separated the two largest islands. To the left rose the ragged cliffs of 100-square-mile Santa Cruz, while Santa Rosa's East Point poked a stubborn nose into the sea starboard ahead. The vast, untamed Pacific, unbroken by land straight to the icy shores of Antarctica, extended to the south.

"Thank God the islands are tough to get to," Liam said. "But for the Channel, I'm sure they would have ruined them like so many other places."

An ironic grin spread over Julia's face. "Don't let appearances fool you. The grasses brought in by the ranchers have long since wiped out what grew here before, and the cattle have crushed and stomped and uprooted pretty much whatever original flora survived that."

He shrugged this off. To him the environmental argument had limited perspective. "I've heard that. But does it really matter? Survival of the fittest is always at work, with or without human interference. The plant and animal world are as much in a state of permanent warfare as we humans. It's lush and green and healthy. That's what counts." He remembered his six months at Mt. Shasta. After high school he'd wanted to learn more about Native American spiritualism. He'd joined a commune that included seven

Modoc Indians. Bill Shatuc, their most eloquent speaker, had lectured him on the same subject.

"That's one way of looking at it. The lush grasses sure beat concrete freeways and tract homes." She opened her arms at the landmasses towering to their sides, as if to embrace them. "These islands have always fascinated me. I can't count how many times I've come. Strangely, I've never been to Santa Rosa. And I don't know why." She fell silent as they rounded East Point. "No, not true. For some odd reason the island makes me . . . ill at ease."

Liam looked at her in surprise. Now that she verbalized it, he realized that he, too, had ambivalent feelings about Santa Rosa. On the one hand he loved it, but he was always glad to get off it as well. They continued in silence.

Twenty minutes later Julia turned to the two men on the main deck, where Patrick struggled to pull something from his backpack, arms sunk up to their pits. Alex leaned over the railing, methodically scanning the shoreline with binoculars.

"Okay," she called out. "It's time for the zodiac. I'm not familiar with this shore, and I don't want to get too close. My father would disown me if I added his pride to the wrecks that litter these waters." Alex stuffed away his lenses and got busy.

"You should be getting ready," Julia reminded Liam.

He rose. "Thanks for the ride," he said, thinking how much he wanted to kiss those full lips. He descended the stairs to the main deck instead. Their day would come, he hoped. Then he heard a loud gasp and looked up. Julia had jumped to her feet, craning her neck overboard, her expression changing from shock to dread. In an instant the engine roared and the props thrashed the sea into a foaming chaos, like a school of piranhas fighting over scraps of flesh.

*   *   *

Their stomachs bursting with meat and berries, and the Spanish red coursing through their veins, the men did what they liked best when the night is young and the wine plentiful. They clamored for more, and Waspe obliged them. The lucky ones, those whose faces were without scars from pockmarks and whose teeth resisted the rot, stole off to the Indian village to indulge appetites of a different nature. They sought the warm bodies of willing Indian women. This sultry night was bound to, in the generations to come, betray the presence of the British in the shape of Indians with green or blue eyes and red or blonde hair.

Lust, the greatest leveler of society, convinced most of the gentlemen to set aside their privileged status and become comrades in arms with the men before the mast. Noble birth accounted for nothing when competing for women completely ignorant of such European distinctions. Disregarding the captain's sensibilities, and fully aware that he toiled with the thought of forbidding the drunk sailors to go to the village and risk trouble, they dutifully reminded him that doing so would earn him unceasing hatred. They even alluded to the unspeakable—mutiny. If he could just maintain the present goodwill, they agreed unanimously, then the only thing that could possibly stop him from returning home a hero, a very wealthy hero, would be the elements. Of course, no one doubted that he could handle any storm, short of a tempest of vengeful sailors crazed with lust.

Only two gentlemen stayed behind, rather ugly chaps on whom no self-respecting woman anywhere would waste a second glance. Dowsing the flames of their frustrated desires with the captain's brandy, they accepted his invitation and drank hard until a deep stupor overtook them one by one. By midnight the camp fell silent, but for the chorus of snores.

Richard gazed at Waspe, fearing the momentous and irreversible step they were poised to take. Already they had stolen gold from the Spaniards, behind their master's back. Discovery meant certain and severe punishment, but not necessarily death. Tonight this would change. The treasure casks had become part of the General's most vital calculations. Nothing concerned him as much as securing food supplies sufficient for the interminable voyage across the Pacific. Had he known that four barrels held but a token few layers of salted meat, and that these barrels would be removed, he would cry for blood. Richard entertained no illusions about his or Waspe's possible fate. The General had executed a nobleman of much higher social standing without holding a royal commission authorizing it.

The white surrounding Waspe's pupils contrasted starkly with his dark Latin complexion. When he rose to his feet, Richard knew the time had come. "Let us take to it," Waspe hissed, his hoarse voice trembling with an odd mixture of trepidation and excitement.

"Wait," Richard whispered, a finger on his lips. He listened to the night, his heart pounding. He thought he'd heard an odd thump. But only the sea lapping the shore and the sailors' snoring broke the silence. *I must be imagining things.* "It's nothing."

The two surreptitiously tip-toed to where the provisions stood in neat rows, three or four barrels high, near a kink in the stone wall raised for defense. They pulled out the casks containing the stolen gold and replaced them with four from the stack of wine casks. Since all eight barrels were of similar size and design, no one would notice the rearrangement. The dent made by the four missing 'wine' barrels could be explained with the night's feast. Hopefully neither the General nor Hord would detect the net loss of casks on first inspection. Two heads depended on it. They worked with haste, propelled by the horror of discovery.

The Spaniards preferred a heavy wood for their wine casks. Richard cursed them for it under his breath. The hard work, combined with the night's warmth, had turned his breeches into a soggy rag pasted to his legs. With the last barrel finally positioned where they wanted it, they dropped to their knees, resting before transport of the gold. Waspe's throat whistled like a windpipe, which drowned out the faint rustle coming from the brush.

"Are you ready?" Richard demanded, exasperated. Waspe had less endurance than any man he knew.

Waspe coughed, struggling valiantly to keep it quiet. Still out of breath, he got to his feet. "Give me a minute."

"Heavens!" Richard burst out. *Why haven't I thought of it before?* "Wait for me." He slipped away, leaving Waspe happy to give his lungs some time. Richard soon returned with a long coil of rope dangling from his shoulder and began to cut it into six equal strips. He tossed the rest aside.

"Here, wrap this around your hips and make a triple knot. Then push the knot to your back. It will carry the weight."

Each man wove a rope over and under his belt, then tied secure triple knots the size of fists. Richard finished first, rotated the rope, and checked the fit. Perfect! Tough and snug, it would hold a cask.

Waspe completed his own contraption. "What are the other strips for?"

Richard threw him a piece. "Watch!" He worked a length of rope under the one hugging his hips. Then he led it over his shoulder and brought it back down to tie to the other end. Satisfied, he tugged at the first of a set of straps for a carrying frame. He bade Waspe emulate him, and in a few moments they tested each other's work, ready to move the gold. Richard listened attentively to the night. Hopefully none of the men would have a mind to leave the warmth of his woman before dawn.

"I'm going," Waspe said, backing into one of the barrels. Richard helped him slide the heavy load off its platform and position it on the make-shift harness. Then he went for his cask, stacked precariously on top of another, and hooked its base onto the knot. Together they trudged off.

They had covered hardly a hundred paces when a strange sound, like the slashing of air, shattered the silence.

*　　*　　*

"Hold tight!" Julia screeched over the roar of the engine.

Patrick reacted lightning-fast. Arms exploding from the pack, he dove to the deck to brace for impact. Alex, less elegant, slammed his knee into the railing and groaned. His frantic hands finally latched onto the metal, which he clasped like a drowning man. In spite of the situation Liam, his arms embracing the vertical bars of the rail and his fists clenching the steps, found all this hilarious. Alex must have read his mind, for he shot him an angry glance.

The next moment, with increasing momentum, the *Helen* backed off the shallows. Julia turned with a sheepish look on her face. Liam slid down the last few steps like a monkey, joining the other men bending overboard to scan the surface.

"It's all right," Julia called out. "We're back in the deeps." They had narrowly missed ramming into a submerged reef. The charts even showed it. Uncharacteristically careless, she had almost paid a terrible price.

Patrick nodded. "That counts for fast thinking, Julia. Most people would have panicked."

She shook her head. "No, I'm an idiot, a fool! Especially because I actually saw the reef on the chart. I know how treacherous these waters are. I wouldn't have been the first to lose my boat."

"And surely not the last," Alex chimed in. "Last summer a crabber wrecked off San Miguel. Two men went down. The Coast Guard never found the bodies."

Liam remembered. The local news had covered it extensively. One of the guys left behind a wife and five children. "Let's hope our stay on the island will be less eventful," he said, sensing it would not.

*   *   *

His heart pounding in his throat, Richard strained to make sense of the sudden commotion, suggestive of an animal stomping into dense brush. But strangely, no noise trailed off in the distance to indicate further movement. Calm settled over the forest, except for a gentle sea breeze rustling the grasses. *A wolf, or one of those huge bears the Indians hunted might lurch at them!* Still as a statue, he narrowed his eyes, hoping to pierce the mysterious dark. But they found only Waspe, who had the look of a man stepping up to the gallows.

"What was it?" he whispered, his voice breaking.

Richard tried to sound more confident than he felt. "I don't know. A bird. An owl. Something on wings must have startled a bigger creature." He paused. "Let's go on."

The hunched shadow waited till his quarry left the field of view before allowing himself to stir. He cursed his stupidity. Fascinated by the two cooks' private enterprise and oblivious to all else, he had lashed out instinctively when something brushed his hair. Damn bats! Fluttering so near his face that he felt the air of their beating wings, he swung his sword overhead. The unexpected motion caused him to stumble into a bush.

Fear now poisoned his veins. Exposure would result in a fight for his life. He could still go back to his blanket, but then he'd never learn the destination of that mysterious cargo. It had to be gold stolen from the ship's hold. But how did it get inside those casks? All of the Spanish treasures were stored in chests and never left the gentlemen's tents. Besides, those thieving bastard cooks had no way of getting the gold back to England and off the ship. No one could deceive the General for long, and every man knew the consequences of pilfering the provisions.

Curiosity prevailed, and an evil grin stole over the shadow's face. He'd find answers soon enough, much sooner than those two scoundrels sneaking through the wood could imagine. He cast aside his fears and resumed the hunt.

*   *   *

The *Helen* had anchored a hundred yards off the beach, its bow kissing the rolling surf. Two rocky points enclosed this stretch of sand, sheltering it from the frontal Pacific assault. A fast-flowing creek tumbled down rugged cliffs, the only break in otherwise steep terrain.

This slice of the island made a fine place to camp, Liam thought. It had a wild feel, in contrast to the more scenic character of the canyon where he found the dagger. Alex, paranoid about drawing attention to the site, had insisted they avoid landing there. His excessive precautions made no sense—unless he knew something he hadn't been willing to share. Few people visited Santa Rosa this time of year. Fewer ever made their way to that part of the island.

The inflatable's small outboarder sprang to life with a whine, interrupting his musings. Patrick took his seat next to Liam, and Alex started for the mouth of the creek, skirting a sand bank. Upon arrival Liam jumped ashore right behind Patrick, and they dumped their backpacks on the ground. Alex turned back for his gear and Julia. When they returned she steered the zodiac.

As soon as Alex got himself and his equipment on the beach, she hailed them all. "I'll return Sunday, with the second high tide, around four." She looked at the hills. "Good luck."

Everyone waved, watching her speed back to the yacht. She climbed aboard and raised the inflatable with a winch. A few moments later the *Helen's* engine roared to life and her hull swung sharply to starboard. Julia waved once more and off she was, flying across the water. Liam couldn't help but feel abandoned. He shot a glance at Alex, whose whole being struck him as remote. *Fine. Let him stew in his broth.* The men shouldered their packs and, Liam taking the lead, turned upstream. No one talked.

Liam mentally reviewed their simple plan. Get to where he found the dagger without delay, and next search the area for other potential artifacts, to use Alex's terminology. The path would take them around a narrow headland and across a ridge before descending into Kindayr's Canyon, as Alex liked to call it. They'd make it there in a couple of hours. They would then explore the canyon till dark, all of Saturday, and the first half of Sunday, reserving sufficient time to rendesvouz with Julia.

Marching in silence, Liam reminisced about the chain of events that had gotten them here. He didn't expect to find anything, but who could tell? Patrick, after his initial reaction, had warmed to the idea of finding a ruby. He had always been a hopeless romantic. But the odds of stumbling across one of the missing gems were literally infinitesimal. Alex's behavior, though, left him no peace. The professor, driving force behind the entire venture, had virtually begged Liam to lead him to the canyon. His eyes had taken on a feverish, almost glassy sheen since the landing. He seemed in another world. Clearly, he would leave Santa Rosa extremely disappointed should this excursion prove fruitless. *And what about the peculiar incident aboard the Helen?* Since then, Alex sulked, but in a serious way that only deepened the chasm Liam felt had opened between them.

The trio came to a steep incline, a talus slope strewn with the debris of eons of weathering. The loose rock fragments made a doubly tough climb, affording few places for a strong foothold. Each man inched his way up by making a path for himself, losing much ground to slippery soil. The heavy packs only worsened things, and Liam tried to keep the bitching to a minimum. Then the unexpected happened about fifty yards below the top.

Patrick, on all fours, was crawling up a stretch that sloped at least forty-five degrees from the horizontal. An arm's length short of a boulder as big as a family-sized ice chest, he flung himself forward with one arm to grab hold of the rock and pull himself up. But he never got a solid grasp. The moment his hand latched on, the boulder took on a life of its own. Patrick rolled over on his side, sliding down ten feet of slope before digging in his heels. The rock swept right past him until it crossed a shallow depression. Thereafter it rolled, picking up speed with each rotation.

Liam observed all this well clear of the projectile's path and grinned. *That's what you get for that stupid grin back on the yacht.* Then the boulder slammed into a protruding ledge, bounced off, and took a new bearing. The rock now headed in a direct line to the spot where Liam stood, still grinning. Within a second of impact he realized that the joke now was on him. His smile vanished. Tucking his head, he exploded sideways. He got a powerful kick in his back, which completed his body's 180-degree turn, and hit the ground like a sack of potatoes. It felt like a 275-pound tight end had tackled him.

"Shit!" he heard Patrick shout. A spray of gravel all over Liam's body announced his brother's arrival. "Are you okay?" he bellowed.

"I guess." Liam pushed himself up on his hands and spat out a pebble. He rolled over to loosen the straps of his backpack.

Patrick gave him a hand. "You're damn lucky you have that thing on." The top of the aluminum frame, extending to just below the base of the skull, bore long scratches. One of the pockets, torn wide open, dangled from the few shreds of nylon still attached to it. A dented can of corn lay on the ground. "If you had waited one instant, you might have had it."

Liam picked up the corn. "This wouldn't even have happened but for Alex insisting on this ridiculous detour."

Patrick grinned sarcastically. "There's a reason for everything, right? Used to be your favorite mantra, you will recall."

"Hey, everything okay down there?" Alex called from above. "Let's get on with it. We're wasting time." He made no effort to descend, nor seemed in the least bit concerned.

Patrick raised his eyebrows. "He's got to be kidding. And now that I have a chance to ask, what the hell was that all about on the yacht?"

Liam got to his feet. "We're on our way," he hollered.

"Good." Alex resumed the climb with no further ado.

"Hey, just a minute!" Patrick protested, his eyes filling with disbelief. "That boulder almost crushed your skull. I know he saw what happened. He was climbing just to my right." He kept staring after Alex. "I sure as hell don't want to be around that asshole when a situation gets sticky."

"Yeah, I'm beginning to think so myself," Liam uttered slowly. "We had a good thing going, but the way he ogled me back on the boat when I checked out that picture . . . it gave me the creeps." He stooped for his pack, shouldering it as they resumed the ascent. Patrick recovered his gear on the way. Alex had disappeared from sight, having already crossed over the ridge.

"This is not good," Patrick exclaimed when they traversed the peak. The professor had almost reached the bottom. "No one would act like that just because you made love to a stupid photo. Besides, with such a knockout in tow he should have gotten used to men drooling all over themselves."

"Hmm," Liam replied, only half-listening to his brother. *What had gotten into Alex?* He no longer recognized him. They had shared so many good times—the tennis, the soccer team, the coffees on campus, the work he'd done for him, the many conversations.

"Listen," Patrick cut short his musings, putting a hand on his arm. "You better watch your butt. I don't know what the hell is going on, but the guy has got one up his sleeve. I can smell it. You're sure he's told you everything about that dagger?"

"What do you want me to say? If he hasn't, how would I know? He's the expert. So far he's never lied to me, I think. What *is* clear is that he's talked of nothing but this dagger ever since I brought it to him."

Patrick kept pushing. "We've got to find out what he's up to. The guy has money to burn, so why such a production for a few little bitty rubies that most likely will never surface?"

Liam shook his head. "I'm not so sure he's got all that much to his name. From comments he's made, it seems he might not be so well off, at least not on paper. He may have married into wealth, but lots of rich folks minimize the temptations of a greedy in-law, lest their hard-earned dollars vanish in thin air."

They caught up with Alex at the base of the slope, his legs stretched out and a canteen at his side. "I'm glad you're okay," he said, his tone indifferent as they sank to the ground. "Looked like a close call." A talking doll would have easily voiced more genuine sympathy.

Patrick spoke his mind. "Yes, very close. Perhaps you didn't get a clear picture from your vantage point, but that qualified as a pretty mean boulder. Point is, it damn near shattered his back and crushed his skull. My brother is still with us because of inches, a spit on a yardstick. I figure you might have condescended to offer your assistance. Just in case, you know?" He glared at him. Patrick had flown Apache attack helicopters into battle. His life depended on precision teamwork that forgave no mistakes. People whom he could not trust 100% counted for worse than useless. They represented a lethal liability.

Alex, not accustomed to such a talk-down, shrank visibly. No match for the ice in Patrick's eyes, he averted his own. He cleared his throat and actually made a rare concession. "Sorry, I've been a bit absent-minded. I guess I didn't appreciate the gravity of the situation."

"It's no big deal," Liam jumped in. "I'm okay, so who cares? Let's forget about it and continue with what we came for. We've still got to cross that hill. Night will be upon us before long."

* * *

The two pirates had covered five hundred yards, winding their way north through thick grassland and thorny brush before swinging back east to one of the long, narrow bays that fanned from the main estuary as do fingers from a hand.

Richard lifted his feet circumspectly. He hated even the idea of briars entangling his ankles, sending him crashing to the ground with the barrel on his back. Waspe trudged on close behind, breathing hard and cursing. When Richard finally emerged from the thicket onto a beach littered with driftwood he stopped abruptly. In some spots the surf had packed the piles of debris so tight, it reminded him of discarded timber in a shipyard.

The cook ran into him, almost knocking him down and banging his own forehead on the barrel. "Hell, why can't you warn me? I almost busted open my face."

Richard ignored this. "We've come far enough. This beach is ideal."

"That's alright by me," Waspe grunted, bathed in sweat, and rubbed his bruised head. He looked miserable, his shoulders sagging under the heavy weight.

"Let's leave the casks here and rest before we get the others." Richard sank into a squatting position. When he couldn't get any lower, he arched his back and let the barrel fall off. It landed with a soft thud. Waspe didn't hesitate for a moment and dumped his own without even taking the time to squat or checking the ground behind him. It hit a sharp rock broadside, and Richard thought he heard the wood crack. Waspe must have too, for he rolled it over to check for damage.

"It's fine."

"Couldn't you look first?" Richard burst out. At times the cook had a way of exasperating him. "The last thing we need is a broken barrel."

"I did," Waspe shot back defensively, "but I must've missed that bloody rock."

Richard knew he lied. The crooked look on Waspe's face spoke volumes. "We better go for the casks immediately. There'll be time to rest later."

On their return to the camp they passed a gnarly pine. A crouching shadow silently circled around, always keeping the thick trunk between his two antagonists on one side, and himself on the other.

The shadow let them go, let them march right out of earshot. He waited a little longer, then dropped all precautions and made a dash for the barrels. The two thieving cooks would be gone a while.

He dropped on his knees to inspect the casks, especially the one Waspe dropped. The man's fingers explored the smooth wood for a rent seam, but found nothing. He made a second pass, more slowly, putting his whole mind into his fingertips. He knew he'd heard the wood split. There! His thumb struck a crack where a stave joint met the central rivet, little more than a rough line where the oak had given. He needed to move fast before those scoundrels returned.

The stalker frantically scoured his surroundings, searching for a suitable tool. He selected a heavy rock the size of a cannon ball and ran back to the barrels, stumbling when his scabbard caught between his legs. Pulling himself up, he unfastened his belt and stuck the sword under his armpit.

Only the faint humming of insects and the distant call of an owl greeted him when he got back to the casks. He still had plenty of time. He laid his sword on the ground, turned the barrel till its damaged side faced up, and lifted the rock high over his head. It came down with all the power he could muster, smashing the wood upon impact. He grinned wildly, oblivious to all but the cask's mysterious contents.

Twice more he pounded, till his victim finally surrendered with a wooden squeal. A greedy hand immediately forced its way into the fracture. The man chuckled, gloated, spurts of frothy saliva running over an unshaven chin. Something soft inside the barrel compressed when he pushed. Dried meat! he realized, dumbfounded. A seaman for over twenty years, he'd eaten enough of the stuff for ten life times. He'd recognize a hunk of salted pork in his grave. But these two bastards wouldn't make off in the dark of night with four barrels full of pork.

He reached to the side. More meat, but this slab he could work around. His middle finger met something cool, solid. He pushed so hard that the barrel's jagged edges shaved the skin off his wrist. "Slimy thieves," he hissed like a snake. "Got themselves a mountain of bullion."

"Wrong, you swine!" answered a disembodied voice.

It had to come from a nearby bush! The shadow suddenly shivered. He'd paid attention to nothing but the barrel. The predator had turned prey.

He carefully pulled his hand from the barrel, sat back on his heels, and went for the sword. But his hand only groped at his empty waist. Hell on Earth! He'd put it down. The hair on his neck rose, and goose bumps crawled up his back. The owner of the voice, that rotten cook, was not in yonder bush. Waspe had that devilish ability of speaking with lips half shut, making his voice come from any corner. He could smell his sweat now. He must stand right behind him. The shadow gingerly felt for his knife, but he never had a chance. The unmistakable unsheathing of a sword promised imminent disaster. He heard the weapon descend, part the air above him.

THE SPANIARD'S DAGGER

The moonlight reflected off the steel. Smythe tried falling to the side, ironically out of his own sword's menacing reach, but he lacked momentum. Waspe struck the face below the temple. The blade severed the ear, carved a slice of skin off the cheek, mangled the lower jaw, and sank deep into where the shoulder meets the neck. The impact knocked Smythe over like an inconsequential lump of nothing, forcing a long sigh from his throat.

~ 10 ~

It took Richard some time to collect his thoughts. "Why did you kill him?" he stuttered aghast, cold sweat on his brow. Waspe's spontaneous action filled him with unspeakable horror. "It wasn't necessary." Smythe lay stock-still, dark blood oozing from the gory wound.

Waspe's face had turned into a mask disfigured by hate. "Maybe not. But if he is still breathing, I'll finish him off just the same."

Richard grabbed his wrist. "Wait! We must think this over. It's dangerous enough to steal. For killing, the General will have us keelhauled."

"What do you propose we do?" Waspe snarled. "Ask him to keep his filthy mouth shut? We have no choice. He must never talk again."

Richard wanted to make all this go away, but he couldn't. His parched throat itched. This night was evolving ever more into a visit to hell. Waspe's chilling words rang true. They could not afford to let Smythe live.

"Instead of feeling sorry for that swine you ought to thank the stars I trapped him." On the way back to fetch the second set of barrels, Waspe had marched unflinchingly, stopping Richard only after a safe distance to tell of a man hiding behind a tree.

"What about the body?"

"We're gonna leave the casks here, right? There's plenty of space for him too," Waspe replied. "Besides, we don't have all night."

Richard fought the urge to vomit. The corpse would lie next to their gold, and by the time they'd return for the booty the rotting carcass would crawl with worms. He shivered despite the warmth of the night. Things had gone terribly wrong. He didn't want to see *anyone* murdered, even Smythe. He never spilled unnecessary blood, including that of the Spaniards. Dispatching a helpless man with blood streaming from his neck utterly repulsed him. He would have never gone to sea if he'd had any inkling events would take this turn. He'd roast in hell for this. How he wished now he could turn back time, arguing with his father about the decision to go to the coast and sign on aboard a vessel bound for exotic shores. Why didn't he stay home and make an honest living as a sculptor? He should have listened to the old man. *But then I would have never met Mónoy.*

Reality put a brutal end to Richard's pathetic self-pity, for Waspe bent down and with one fierce twist tore free the blade. Blood started gushing as he threw down the sword and kneeled, a huge knife in hand. He took hold of a thick tuft of Smythe's hair and pulled the head up and back. The swift motion forced open the throat, air streaming as from an obstructed pipe. Richard wanted to stop him, but he had lost command of his limbs. With a steady motion Waspe pulled the blade across the throat, severing the vital tissues. Thick dark blood washed over the chest of the dying body, which quivered spasmodically. A horrible gargling that froze Richard's heart drowned those lungs' desperate gasps for air. At last, Smythe's nerves ceased their ghastly dance. The body twisted and jerked once more, and the gargling ceased.

Richard had never witnessed the cold-blooded butcher of another human. Infinitely worse, the killer, his own friend, to all appearances seemed unshaken by his actions. Clasping the dripping knife, Waspe stood over the lifeless shell with a peculiar expression of curiosity. Rattled after watching a friend kill so effortlessly, Richard had an epiphany. He and the cook really had nothing in common, had absolutely no emotional ties at all. Only chance had flung them together.

"Help me bury him," Waspe ordered, pointing to an oval depression. "That looks like a good spot." He cleaned the blade on Smythe's shirt and stuck it in his belt. With an impatient glance at Richard he put his hands under the corpse's armpits and began lifting the torso.

Richard grabbed the legs below the knees, still warm to the touch. He fought down nausea. They half carried, half dragged the contorted body to the ditch and dumped it unceremoniously. Then, with their hands and feet, they shoveled and kicked sand over the corpse. They piled up driftwood and rocks, and Waspe finally destroyed all traces of their bloody deed by smoothing out the disturbed ground, scattering more debris.

He wiped his hands on his trousers. "Let's get the gold. But for that bastard we'd be long sleeping by now." Richard had nothing to say. *Waspe must lead us through this. I can't.*

The camp was still quiet, except for the drunken men's snoring and coughing. None of those who left for the village had returned. So Richard and Waspe transferred the last two barrels with no further incident. They buried the gold much the same way they had buried Smythe.

Waspe nodded with satisfaction. "I'll be damned if anyone would suspect a thing. I almost fear I might not find the exact spot myself, come morning."

Richard mulled over the future. Try as he might, he could not see a way out of their predicament. "John, the men had rest, wholesome fare for weeks, and more wine than water. Women sweeten their nights, and all talk centers on returning home with a sack of gold. For days now, that's all I hear. What will they say about his disappearance? No one of sound mind would think of jumping ship now, especially Smythe, especially in this wilderness."

Waspe managed both to spit on the ground and look sagacious doing so. "I figure there isn't a single man, including the General himself, that's gonna feel overly sorry about Smythe. No one hardly talked to him, and they won't give a damn what happened. He simply vanished the night of the feast, which couldn't have come at a better time. Think! Not one lousy soul back there didn't fall over drunk. In the morning, men will tumble all over the camp, their heads poundin' like a cannon ball exploding out the bore of a twelve pounder. And they'll say Smythe drank himself to death."

"What about the body?" Richard asked. "Dead men don't *vanish*. With no corpse to account for, questions will arise."

Waspe pondered this for some time. "He could have walked off, gotten himself lost, and transpired in the brush."

"The General will form search parties. Drunk, Smythe wouldn't get far. The sea surrounds us on three sides, and there are few places he—" Richard stopped. A clear picture took shape in his head. *I know what we'll say.* "Wait! He could have collapsed while pissing in the sea. The tide would have taken him in the morning, and there'd be no need for a search."

Waspe laughed with glee. "There you are! A fitting end for him. Good! Excellent! I'll tell the men I saw him last with a pint of wine sitting by the water."

Richard shook his head. "That's stupid."

"Why?"

"Hord surely told the General how Smythe insulted me. If either of us says anything, he'll get suspicious and put us under close observation."

Waspe looked toward the grave, tapping his foot on the ground. "Let's get some sleep. We can talk in the morning, when our minds are sharp." Only three hours remained before the sun's first rays would crawl over the horizon.

Arriving at the make-shift galley, its rows of barrels arranged like a wall of silent sentinels, Waspe stalled in mid-stride. He pointed at a small cask standing by itself.

"I could have sworn we returned each to its place. Do you remember this one?"

Richard frowned. They *had* put everything in order, he thought. But then, with all the excitement they had possibly overlooked a barrel. "We must have forgotten. Let's get it done."

Waspe mumbled incomprehensively. They lifted the cask and started carrying it when a sudden clapping of hands shattered the peace. Waspe flinched and let go of the load. The barrel fell to the ground. A sharp voice rang unpleasantly in their ears.

"Perhaps you can explain your business at this early hour!"

*   *   *

By the time the three men descended into the valley, the late afternoon sun hung low in the sky. "Where did you find the dagger?" Alex queried the moment Liam halted the group near a patch of sandy soil adjacent to the creek.

"You're virtually standing on the spot. Right over there, on the bank."

They dumped their gear. Patrick helped Liam pull up their tent, whereas Alex set off without delay. Liam, fascinated by such single-mindedness, couldn't keep from watching how he scoured the stream bank, exuding the air of a real treasure hunter. Alex looked behind bushes, turned over rocks and driftwood, and finally took off his boots to wade into the current. He crossed to the other side, the crystal-clear water reaching to his waist near the center, and then returned upstream without bothering to put his boots back on. All the wooden debris and sharp stones cluttering the ground didn't seem to affect him.

Approaching the camp, he turned abruptly and retraced his steps, oblivious to the world. This time he went more slowly, his focus on the creek itself. When he again crossed over, Liam lost his interest. His empty stomach suggested that a hot meal promised much more satisfaction than following Alex's aimless wanderings. A few minutes later came a loud splash, and Liam turned just in time to see Alex thrust an arm into the air, screaming with wild elation.

"Yes, yes, yes! I knew it!"

*   *   *

The Indian girl had taken good care of his needs. So Gregory Hord, terribly thirsty, made his way back to camp. Drake, should he still be awake, liked to take stock of how long his officers stayed in the village. Hord hoped to return before the others.

Passing by the galley, he immediately noticed the lone Spanish wine barrel. This irked him a great deal, especially after having spent such pleasant hours away from this rabble. Couldn't he enjoy just one day free of trouble? Responsible to Drake for the provisions, he had expressly told Waspe that the General expected all casks to stay in the galley. And now this! Unholy sloppiness! Damn, the cook had need of some firm words. Men too quickly grew accustomed to idling. To run a sharp ship, one had to keep tight reigns.

So Hord gave himself to thoughts of how he would ruin Waspe's Sunday when a pair of footsteps startled him. He slipped behind a cluster of bushes.

Aha! What a surprise! Waspe himself, accompanied by his dull assistant, Kindayr, had come upon the barrel. Hord strained to hear their words, but he had the breeze at his back. Finally, the two night birds lifted the cask and started for the galley. That was when he stepped into the open, clapping his hands for effect, and demanding to know their business.

Waspe regained his composure first, imbuing his voice with a righteous tone calculated to feign self-confidence. "We were collecting the casks, just as you ordered." It stank sky high, but the greatest falsehood always stands a better chance than its silent twin—silence. Hesitation inevitably invites suspicion, causing far more damage.

"At this hour?" Hord replied. "Explain yourselves."

Richard had recovered from the initial shock. They needed a story fast, for their entire future rested on the next few moments. Hord, no doubt, wouldn't think twice of putting them in chains if he suspected them of stealing wine. Ostensibly he knew nothing of the four missing barrels, or Smythe. Perhaps all wasn't lost.

"Sir, a little while ago I rose to help myself to some water"—this strand of his yarn saved their lives, since Hord had been thirsty after all the wine and sex himself—"and chanced upon a man poking around the galley." He flung an arm at the rows of barrels for emphasis. The gesture had the added benefit of relieving anxiety. "At first I thought it must be Waspe. Then I recalled that he, too, had gone to sleep. I feared an Indian had come to pilfer, but I soon recognized Smythe, his hands on a cask of Spanish red." A shudder went through him at the memory of the split throat and the windpipe's final susurrus. He hoped Hord didn't notice or misinterpret it.

Richard continued spinning his web. "Smythe didn't see me, and I ran for Waspe. I've never trusted Smythe and didn't know what he would do if he discovered me, especially after this evening. You were there, Sir, when he started trouble. So Waspe and I hurried back, but he dashed into the night. We tried to follow, but the dark swallowed him. Then we turned back to see what damage had been done. That's when you surprised us." He caught his breath, so pleased with his tale he almost forgot the gravity of their situation. He had never before dreamed up a lie so effortlessly.

When Hord stepped closer and looked him deep in the eyes, Richard knew he had him hooked. The officer wanted to believe the account, which had the ring of truth and had been delivered with such conviction. Hord considered him a dumb country lad who couldn't handle the rigging, and whose mental capacity permitted little more than boiling a tasty stew.

"You're certain it was Smythe?"

"Why, Sir! I wouldn't forget his face if I lived to see the end of the world. If that stinking thief can prove me wrong my name isn't Richard Argyle, and I'll sail our ship back to England single-handed." He tried to sound as simple-minded as he could. As long as they stuck to their story they need not fear.

"Why didn't you alert one of the officers?" Hord probed.

"I went for Waspe, he being master of the galley. As for the officers, most left . . . ah . . . for the village, I believe."

Hord shifted his weight. He suddenly looked uncomfortable, a tad vulnerable even.

Waspe finally found his voice again. "I would have done likewise had I discovered the scoundrel meddling with our rations. Too much commotion might have scared him off, and we would have never known his identity. It would be his word against that of another man. As it is, he knows he's in trouble, and I'm damn curious as to what he'll say."

Hord pouted his lips, as always when he had to weigh information before making an important decision. The men had witnessed this all too often when the General went below deck, leaving him in command of the ship. He massaged his throat with the tips of his fingers and licked his lips.

"Get some rest, and be watchful. Should Smythe return before dawn, he might pay you a visit. I shall post a few men around the perimeter."

The first officer stared after them until the night swallowed their shapes, his fingers still massaging the throat. What a tale! His first instinct had warned him they were up to no good, and they appeared startled and nervous as sheep when he cornered them. But Argyle's story made good sense, and it explained their surprise. Besides, that bumpkin didn't have the brains to concoct such a fable. However, he looked forward to Smythe's version of the events. The morning might prove very interesting and a splendid opportunity to impress Drake with the competence of his second in command.

* * *

Alex ignored Patrick's repeated "What-have-you-got's?" and savored the awe with which Liam looked him over. They had secretly scoffed at this entire outing, he knew. Now the moment belonged to him. *Simpletons!*

A heavy golden cross bearing the raised figure of Christ shone in his palm. No inscriptions, no design of any kind graced this otherwise rather nondescript artifact. But its color allowed for only two possibilities. Either it sank to the bottom of the creek a very short time ago, or its golden luster derived from purity. Of course, the odds eliminated the former.

Alex pulled out a pocketknife and scratched both front and back of the cross. Any lingering doubts evaporated. Neither scratch revealed an inferior sub-stratum. "It's gold!" he called out. "I knew it. There had to be more."

He watched them exchange silent glances. *They don't have a clue.*

"I don't get this," Patrick finally said.

Alex loved it. Nothing beat center stage. For the moment, he ruled triumphantly. With a gesture calculated for its theatrical impact, he lifted the cross toward the sky. "You found that dagger. How could there not be more?"

"You make no sense," Liam retorted angrily. "Someone could have lost the dagger. Haven't you ever lost a watch or a wallet?"

The professor smiled to himself, reveling in the superiority of his intellect. They seemed like amateurs by comparison, struggling to solve a particularly tough riddle. His expression must have betrayed his thoughts because Patrick snapped at him.

"Alex, is there something we should know about?" Nose to chin he resembled a Doberman ready to pounce.

Alex, his cheerfulness torpedoed, suddenly felt unsure. *Tread lightly. And choose your words judiciously.* "One doesn't just *lose* a bejeweled dagger. Therefore, I presumed that whoever owned it carried other valuables as well. That's all."

This should get them off his back. Besides, now that the initial excitement began to fade, the freezing cold made itself known. With his shorts and tee still dripping water and plastered to his body, he picked up his boots. "I better get into some dry clothes before I get chilled."

He left them standing. When he looked back, Liam crouched on the bank, staring at the water. Patrick had actually stripped and climbed into the stream, walking small circles while scanning the current.

Night fell as the last sliver of orange slipped from the sky and the hemisphere called it a day. The first stars twinkled high above. The three men huddled around a cozy fire, satisfying ravenous appetites. After all the physical exertion hearty vegetable soup, tortillas smeared with mayonnaise and stuffed with lettuce and tuna, and crisp carrots composed a dinner fit for royalty. Power bars lay in wait for dessert.

"Damn lucky strike," Patrick observed between bites, turning the cross in his hands.

Alex downed a mouthful of Cabernet. "I still can't believe it myself. I'm dying for what morning may bring."

"What do you think we'll find?" Liam probed.

Alex had had enough time to strategize. He didn't want to alienate them any further and showed his most sociable side. So this time he didn't hesitate. Cherishing the professor's role, he savored their curiosity. "Well, this is how I see it. The dagger is anywhere from three and a half to five centuries old. Its style is typical of that period, and I'm sure of my dates. We could do tests to narrow it down, but at this point that's unnecessary because they take time."

Liam's jaw dropped. "Wait a minute. I had no idea. This is the first time you've told me its age."

Alex opened his hands wide. *Be cool!* "It's no big secret. I didn't think it mattered so much, and it took me some time to arrive at this conclusion. In any case, the cross has changed the situation, and I'm informing you, am I not?" He smiled disarmingly before continuing.

"No sensible person would hike this island with such an ancient weapon. If you owned it," he looked at Patrick, "would you bring it out here?"

He shook his head with conviction. "Of course not."

"We still have to determine how the dagger got to this remote location," Alex led them on.

"It must have been here for all those years, based on your belief about its longevity," Liam offered.

"Precisely. And today I retrieved this cross in the same spot."

"I discovered the dagger on the bank, not in the water."

"Yes, but I'm certain it also came from the creek."

"This cross is licked clean," Patrick interceded. "Centuries of water will do a serious job on anything."

"Not *anything*. Pure gold doesn't oxidize. Divers in Florida have recovered piles of Spanish bullion from the sea. Some of the ships transporting those went down in the early 1500s, and many of those coins look much as they did when the Spaniards stashed them aboard their treasure galleons."

Liam laughed out loud. "You don't expect to find a Spanish treasure here? We're just a bit off the beaten path. You're obviously the authority, and correct me if I'm mistaken, but from what I remember, the Spaniards shipped all their gold across the Atlantic. We're on the wrong side of the continent."

"I know that," Alex said, faking impatience. "Of course there's no treasure buried on this island. It would contradict the historical record. Spanish explorers did, however, land in this area. I assume one of them, perhaps a deserter, never left.

He eventually lost his dagger and cross. Perhaps, there is more."

"But," Patrick interrupted. "If I understood correctly, only a light coat of rust covered the dagger. No way in hell will steel survive that long under water."

Alex nodded. "It must have been buried. Then the river eroded its bank and flushed it out. In fact, that's the spot we're looking for."

"What do you expect to get out of this?" Liam wanted to know. "Even if we find a couple more pieces, you've turned into a bloodhound ever since I showed you the dagger. I don't get it."

Good, Alex mused with satisfaction. They had marched straight into his trap and had swallowed the bait. "To tell you the truth, I don't care a whole lot whether there are any more artifacts. Based on what we already have, I can write a wonderful article, the first one in a long time on this subject. It's great stuff and couldn't have come at a better time. Gold evokes such a powerful response that it's bound to make it from a scholarly article straight into the news headlines. That, in turn, will assure my tenure."

"So what's next?" Liam asked. His face did not hide the hostility, but Alex didn't give a damn.

Patrick brimmed with excitement. "Tomorrow we'll sweep this entire stretch of stream and adjacent banks. I'll divide it into three sections with overlap at each end. Whatever may still remain below the surface, we'll find it next time we come out here. We'll have to bring a metal detector."

The fire began to die down, the last embers splitting with crackling pops and spraying sparks into a star-studded sky. Each man saw to his needs and crawled into his sleeping bag. The stream's waters flowed inexorably toward the sea, moaning where sunken debris caused a ripple, or where a channel obstruction straitjacketed the current.

STEVEN FARQUHAR

The little creek, still draining winter's first severe rains from its basin, continued to chew away at an ancient cave-in.

Heavy, horn-rimmed glasses covered the man's eyes. A thick scar running from temple to lips made his face look strangely stunted on his otherwise tall and rugged body. The most visible vestige of a botched legal career, it attested to a society that left more and more children to fend for themselves starting at an early age. The scar marked the results of the immature urges and evil cravings of a middle class teenage punk whose character development ceased in ninth grade. The adult world, however, proved unforgiving.

Cob Rash had entered dangerous terrain when he took advantage of an attractive woman's misplaced trust in the course of a divorce case that promised a juicy reward. Exorbitant fees, followed by the discovery that Rash and his client maintained a motel room, enraged the husband. Bursting into his office, he slashed Rash with a hunting knife.

The episode destroyed Rash's already suspect reputation, irrevocably forcing him into a new line of work. He became an English teacher in a small town, with disastrous results. Abhorred by students and colleagues alike, the incurable alcoholic lasted exactly one semester. But he did learn how much power a principal wielded. Several years later, with an administrative credential, he secured the principal's position in a high school. Making a far cry from what he had as a lawyer, principal's pay still put to shame the miserable salary teachers got. Who could tell? A few years of clever manipulation might find him drawing a superintendent's salary. More power. More money. In the meantime, to recover his former lifestyle, he'd have to find a way of supplementing his income without putting in too much time. He'd found that without even having to look. Last summer, after a year without contact, his brother waddled back into his life with an irresistible proposition.

THE SPANIARD'S DAGGER

Leaving his incompetent, sycophantic vice principal in charge at Oak Grove High, Cob Rash skipped town for Santa Rosa Island whenever he could. His brother, Dave, expert at not making an honest living, now cowered at his side near the edge of a cliff overlooking the canyon. He was grazing on a candy bar, his huge belly making for a comfortable pad on the rocky ground.

"Just what the hell did they find in the river?" Cob mumbled. "I can't believe we forgot the fucking binoculars."

Dave spat over the ledge, watching in fascination as his chocolaty saliva dropped a hundred feet. "It's got to be another bone. The guy in the middle is the one you saw camping here last week, and now he's brought his buddies. We gotta do something before the competition gets too strong. We've gotta really switch work to *this* canyon."

Cob only half-listened. "I never heard of anyone taking bones from the water. It's weird."

"Maybe it's gold nuggets," Dave volunteered with a dumb smile on his face. "They act like it was."

Cob swallowed his irritation. Dave's stupidity had a way of rubbing him wrong. If his brother hadn't let those fishermen intimidate him, they wouldn't be stabbing in the dark. "Don't talk nonsense. Why would there be an ounce of gold on this crappy island? They're artifacts, probably bones, just like the ones we took from across the ridge. But I need an explanation what they're doing in that creek."

"It was only a way of saying," Dave said crossly.

Cob ignored this entirely. "Just cause we've never dug this close to water doesn't mean anything. I suppose the stream eroded its banks and washed out a site." He reflected. "I'm positive now the guy who made the find is a history professor at the university. He did a guest lecture for one of my AP teachers once. Anyone who likes history, I suppose, would love to find himself a Chumash artifact." He got up on his elbow. "Well, since the other dude has led him here, I'd say it's high time to make a move."

"That's what I just told you," Dave snorted, twirling the edges of his new mustache. "What's the plan?"

Cob cackled with glee, his scar coming to life under the shaking cheeks. "Easy. First of all, I want you to stay out here. No more trips to the mainland for a few days. Second, we must find a way to take the canyon away from these sorry losers. Any suggestions?"

~ 11 ~

E arly in the morning, before the sun suffused the calm blue sea in its sparkling light, the thick fog bank advanced. It had hovered offshore for two days, even at night. Since the men had sailed into the estuary more than a month ago, the fog stayed with them every night, drifting inland in the evening and retreating by mid-morning.

Thickening mists smothered the shore once again, hiding all stars and hugging a narrow strip of coastline in their moist embrace. Everything they touched turned damp and clammy, chilling to the bone every man without a cover. Sailors clasped their blankets, pulled them back up over their faces. Snoring soon filled the camp again. No one rose on that Sunday morning, because it was probably the last restful day before the ship would continue its voyage around the globe. Work on the hull neared completion.

Richard hadn't slept at all, tossing back and forth restlessly. For the hundredth time, the night's most vivid scenes flashed through his brain. Smythe prying open the barrel. Moonlight reflecting off the blade. The thick, dark blood gushing from the slashed throat. Waspe and he burying the limp, still warm corpse. Worst of all, the writhing body's desperate fight for air and the throat's horrid gargling kept reverberating in his ears. He threw off his woolskin and rolled over on his knees. His mouth tasted like rotten meat, a flavor so noxious he feared if he did not get to a water cask he'd vomit.

Richard scooped out several ladles of the clean, cool liquid, gulping them greedily. He emptied his bursting bladder, then got back under his cover, grateful for its warmth. Waspe didn't move, but Richard knew he was awake. They needed to talk, as they would shortly have to face the General and his lieutenants.

"What will we say?" he whispered at the rigid body. "Hord must suspect us."

Waspe half opened his eyes, raised his head an inch or two. "I've pondered it all night, and I keep coming to the same conclusion." His lids slid back down and he coughed.

"So what is it?"

Waspe turned on his side. "With Smythe dead, Hord can't get the explanation he undoubtedly craves. Therefore, the General will send scouts. Should they find the body, he'll string us up like dogs. Should they find nothing, he'll put us in chains. And you know what that means." Waspe measured him with an iron stare. "We have to take the boat and leave."

Richard gasped. Had he heard right? "Take the boat? The crew never had it so good in their lives. We won't convince a single man to risk the consequences after last night's feast."

"That's not what I meant. I said *boat*."

Richard didn't understand. What *did* Waspe mean?

"The General will raise anchor within the week. Our skins will loose their value by the end of two days. We must take the ship's boat and sail for Panama."

"Panama? In that shell? Have you lost your sens—?" Richard burst out, but Waspe quickly pressed a callused hand on his mouth.

"Panama is fifteen hundred leagues away," he muttered. "It's certain suicide. And even if by God's grace we somehow survived, what do you want me to do there? I don't speak a word of Spanish. They'd quarter me after what we've done to their settlements."

"Keep your voice low. We're not alone."

The whole idea so appalled Richard, he wanted to smack the cook on the head. "Besides, what next? What do you plan to do in Panama?"

Waspe brought his face so close, Richard smelled the stale breath. "It's not as daunting a task as you might think.

Oxenham crossed the isthmus with his men, starting on the Atlantic side. We will make our way from the Pacific. That's what the Spaniards do. The gold and silver mined on the Spanish Main travels by ship to Panama's Pacific coast. From there, most goes to the port of Nombre de Dios, where they load galleons bound for Spain. We can follow the same trail and pay for passage back to Europe on a ship out of Nombre de Dios."

"And what of me? I told you I don't—"

"Calm down! The Don merchants don't care who comes aboard, so long as we pay handsomely. You will never open your mouth. You can't, since you never spoke since birth."

Thunderstruck, Richard didn't know what to say. *Waspe has thought this through.* It actually made sense, which scared him. Waspe grabbed his wrist.

"Hear me. It's a new day. Hord will reconsider each word we told him. He won't buy Smythe's absence for long." The man lying closest mumbled unintelligibly in his sleep and rolled over on his back. For a moment it looked as though he would wake, but his breathing became steady again and his chin dropped. Waspe waited another minute before continuing. "Don't forget, Smythe had no place to go. He hated the Indians, and they never made much of him."

It finally sank in. They didn't have a choice. Richard capitulated. But he swore not to abandon her. "John. I won't go without Mónoy."

He saw a dark cloud settle over Waspe, who stiffened like a sail stung by a squall. "*You* have gone mad. What in the devil's name do you want with her? It's one thing to take your pleasures on this forsaken shore, but she's a savage. She can never live in England. And how do you expect we explain her to the Spaniards? She'll spell our ruin."

"*Ruin?* How do you reckon? God knows how often we'll have to go ashore for water and victuals and to avoid storms before reaching Panama, and you know damned well that our lives will hang in the balance each time. We don't understand

125

the customs of the people, nor their language. Mónoy would be worth ten times her weight in gold."

Waspe's face softened. The cook couldn't deny it. Sailing down the coast in a tiny open boat presented enough of a risk in itself. If the sea didn't claim them, the Indians probably would. Only Mónoy could get them through. Richard didn't want to give him too much time to think.

"I meant what I said. If she doesn't come I'll stay and live here."

"You're a damned fool!" Waspe fumed. "You can't become a savage. You don't belong here."

"Then she'll sail with us. Alone you can't risk it."

Waspe couldn't hide his disdain. "If you must take her, so be it. But under these conditions."

"Speak," Richard prodded anxiously.

"We sail without delays. No landfalls, except to replenish our stores, or if the weather forces us. I've no mind to spend the rest of my years with savages, nor will I rot on a desolate coast with my skull chopped in half for landing where we shouldn't. If she loses heart we set her ashore where there are people she can join." Waspe stuck a finger into Richard's chest. "Once in Panama I will plan how to proceed and explain what you want with a savage woman, or why she wants a man who can't speak. Lastly, the command is mine."

Richard nodded. "I can live with that." He didn't make an issue of setting Mónoy ashore alone. Of course, he would go with her and send Waspe to hell.

"I have no doubts the Spaniards will understand. Mónoy carries my child."

*   *   *

They had started scouring the stream at the crack of dawn, after wolfing down a coarse breakfast of plain oatmeal and scalding coffee. The day had proved disappointing, though, with no gold in sight. Yet their spirits remained high. The descending sun would end their work in the next hour, and Liam waded into the creek for a final run.

He hated the cold but couldn't let Alex, a bundle of pure energy, outdo him. The chilly water had no discernible effect on the professor, and his contagious optimism never waned. In fact, it was he who kept them going, systematically turning over every rock and scrap of wood on the bank, poking through brush growing in the flood zone, and even diving to ensure that no pool would go untouched.

Liam, his section smaller than Alex's, had battled much denser vegetation. Thick tangles of roots clung tenaciously to the debris-studded banks. By early afternoon, for the first time in his life, he began to hate greenery. How much easier the search went in the stream. Now free of the hassle of messing with the thorny brush, he tried to ignore the cold. The sight of Alex sniffing around downstream like a hunting dog energized his sore muscles. With clattering teeth, he charged into the swift current, blocking out memories of the dreadful fall into the muddy Colorado that had almost cost him his life.

Almost immediately, at a section of the streambed where a waterlogged stump had created a dam that impounded a shallow and tranquil pool, Liam spied a sparkle through the placid surface. His heart beat faster as his fingertips worked the silt to retrieve the object. He finally touched something metallic and yanked it free. His cheeks spread into a huge grin.

Patrick, who had taken unofficial control of the mission, hailed him from the opposite bank. "What is it? You got something?"

Liam finally managed to lend voice to his ecstasy. "I found a coin, a golden coin!" he yelled.

Patrick tossed his probing stick and rushed along the bank till he reached Liam's height, then leapt into the water.

"It's a golden coin!" Liam repeated child-like. "Look, there's an inscription."

They scaled the side and found a clearing in the brush. "What do you have?" Alex shouted as he ran toward them, glaring at Liam's protectively closed fist.

Patrick had no patience. "Come on," he pressed. "Let's have a look." Liam opened his palm, exposing a coin roughly the size of a silver dollar. Three sets of eyes focused.

A head in profile attached to an upper torso clad in uniform took up the center. Its stern chin and severe stare commanded a measure of respect. Remnants of letters marked the rim, though the degree of abrasion suffered by the coin rendered most illegible. An "II" on one side and the combination "AG" below the head made up the exceptions. Liam flipped the coin. The backside bore a square, subdivided into four smaller ones, all with rounded corners. Each seemed to contain a unique symbol. One resembled a lion standing on its rear paws. The others were too disfigured. The coin seemed to have suffered a great deal of punishment, completely unlike the dagger or cross.

"Turn it over again!" Patrick said. "What does the 'II' mean? And what about the 'AG'? It's got to be an abbreviation, or initials."

Liam looked at Alex, studying his expression, scrutinizing his body language. He didn't want to miss a single detail.

But the professor betrayed nothing and seemed genuinely frustrated. "I don't know. Of course it's part of a longer word, but I can't think of what that might be. I am convinced, however, that we're dealing with the 1500s, the same age as the dagger's."

"Can I have it?" Patrick took it, scratching the coin with a sharp rock. "Pure gold, and five hundred years old!" He beamed. "We're on Treasure Island! First the dagger, then the cross, and now this!" He handed it to the professor.

"But why here?" Liam wondered. Something didn't click. *Alex still knows something we don't.*

Alex thoughtfully turned the coin in his hands. "I told you last night. Remember, it never rains in southern California, except during winter." He looked up. "I'm positive the two December storms washed out these artifacts. The first storm especially. It dumped ten inches on La Cumbre Peak by noon. Already, they say, we've had some of the most severe erosion on record. And winter has hardly begun. The town is dredging like the devil, trying to clear Atascadero Creek from Fairview all the way to Goleta Beach."

Liam nodded. "You're probably right. The question is, where exactly is the stuff coming from? It looks like we stumbled onto some sort of cache, and I pray these are not just the leftovers."

Patrick stayed optimistic. "I can't imagine anyone would be that unlucky to find only the last scraps." He shook his head. "No, let's search this entire canyon, or divert the whole damn stream. With high-powered metal detectors we'd sweep it clean as a whistle."

"That's not a viable option. This land is not ours to work, and I doubt the Corps of Engineers would approve," Alex fired back.

Liam found the vehemence in Alex's tone odd. *He wants zero outside interference.*

They fell silent. Liam began to shiver and started rubbing his arms and legs. The sun had already sunk behind the cliffs. "We're running out of light. Let's call it a day and plan for tomorrow. We won't have as much time with Julia picking us up."

Alex shot him a cold glance at the mention of her name. "Yes, we must devise a strategy."

They went to change into dry clothes and then cooked dinner. Patrick squatted down near Liam, who watched the steam rise from a pot of black beans and rice. Crusty bread, a slab of cheddar, and a bottle of Napa Cabernet rounded out their fare. The brothers chatted between bites, but Alex volunteered nothing, save for an occasional mumble. Liam examined his behavior carefully. Alex, he knew beyond any doubt, concocted some sort of scheme he had no desire of sharing. Liam also knew that he would not stand by idly.

The Rash duo had watched all day. They watched an elated Liam pull a small object out of the water, watched his comrades rush to him, and then all three huddle and inspect the mysterious treasure. But try as they might, from their distance the Rashes could not guess what caused so much excitement. It could frustrate a saint.

Patience! Cob practiced his silent mantra. Those arrogant interlopers had to pack their bags eventually. But so did he, scheduled for meetings at the Sup's office early Monday morning. These appointments he could hardly afford to miss.

"Our time will come," he snarled maliciously. "You better make damn sure if those assholes come back they'll be disappointed."

Dave grinned. "I've some ideas already."

*   *   *

The captain, his first officer, and Earl George Folsom, a surly fellow who made no secret of considering himself a breed apart, sat in a semicircle. The two officers maintained stern-faced, impenetrable expressions, though neither man would strike a casual observer as ill humored. Only Folsom put on presumptuous airs, convinced he presided in a matter of gravest concern. With his razor-thin eyebrows arched high above a bulbous beak of a nose, and a punishing gaze leveled at the two "defendants," he seemed more vulture than human. Though shaking with desire to commence the inquiry, and visibly eager to pass sentence, the earl kept his sharp tongue in check. In matters such as this, the captain reserved the right to speak first, and all aboard respected his privileges. The memory of Thomas Doughty's fate cast long shadows.

"I am informed you two prevented Smythe from stealing a cask of wine this night. Is that correct?" The General's stare penetrated, but his cordial tone assured.

They had agreed on letting Richard do most of the talking. "Yes, Sir," he started. "On my way to fetch some water, I surprised him rolling a barrel across the field." Then he recounted the story as he had told it to Hord, a story ten times rehearsed. He narrated so convincingly, he almost believed it himself. With what ease he perverted the truth. It both thrilled and disgusted him.

"What would one man want with a cask full of wine?" the captain probed. "I don't suppose he expected to consume it before morning, or even before our departure."

"I have thought about this myself, and the only explanation I have is that he meant to instigate trouble. He's threatened me and Waspe, as Mr. Hord well knows, and probably figured the absence of a barrel would pit you against the galley. Especially," he lowered his head slightly in apologetic deference, "because I must confess to not having properly discharged my duties these days." The General acknowledged this with a slight nod.

"How deep did you follow him into the brush?" Folsom's beak squawked. Incapable of controlling himself any longer, his red eyes gored Waspe.

"Not far. In the dark we soon lost him."

"You feared to go on?"

Waspe surveyed him with thinly veiled derision. "The scoundrel knew we caught him. He could have lain in ambush in a dozen spots. I had no intention of Smythe running me through. Besides, most of the officers had gone to the village, and I did not want to cause a commotion." This came out well. They had prepared for a similar question. Both Hord and Folsom shifted on their seats.

The earl, though, didn't relent. "Then you lacked sufficient courage to corner the thief?"

Waspe's face grew pallid with suppressed rage. "I thought it foolish to sacrifice my life."

Now Folsom cackled like a hen, looking around the semicircle. Richard burned with a passion to choke that swollen neck, to wipe that haughty smile off his puffy face and extinguish the nerve-grating cackle. He didn't need to, thanks to Waspe's next remark.

"Earl Folsom, I don't reckon *you* would have charged after Smythe, or would you?" The beak turned burgundy, and his cheeks quivered from this unexpected impudence. The earl frantically searched for a retort, which eluded him.

The General visibly restrained himself from grinning. He had never seriously concealed his dislike for the nobleman. Clearing his throat, he turned to his first officer. "Mr. Hord, the fact of the matter is, Smythe has deserted my command. In light of these men's account, I have no choice but to dispatch a search party without further delay. I want that chap brought in, today! God be my witness, as long as I'm master of this vessel I will tolerate no thief."

He stared at Waspe, and Richard knew he'd be next. "Justice comes swiftly to the guilty. Smythe will answer for his deeds."

Richard fought a mighty urge to swallow, but feared someone might notice. He must appear calm and confident and took several deep breaths to beat down his agitated nerves.

"Go see to your duties," the General barked, rising from his chair. But Folsom had not yet finished.

"Send them along on the search," he demanded. "They're the ones who discovered Smythe. Perhaps they have a gift for it."

The captain measured Folsom frostily. Nothing poisoned his mood like unsolicited advice, and he seemed on the verge of losing his temper. "We need the cooks here. I've no desire of starving my good men on the Sabbath. Unless, my dear earl, you feel inclined to serve the crew their rations." His voice rang thick with mockery.

Folsom shook with controlled fury. He rose from his chair utterly appalled, as though a noxious odor had given offense. "I'm absolutely not inclined to." The blood colored his nose for a second time that morning.

"Good," the master ended the discussion. "Mr. Hord, please arrange at once for the search party." He paused, contemplating. "Oh, Earl Folsom will join you."

Then he leveled his eyes again on Waspe and Richard, gazing at them with such intensity, Richard felt his heart flutter and stomach lurch. Would he and Waspe survive the day?

*   *   *

Alex stirred first. He'd spent the night in the open, and when the sun's rays tickled his nose he unzipped the sleeping bag and rubbed his face. The other two still slept. He could see them, for they had left their tent open. He wiggled his way out of his Marmot and relieved his bladder's pressure against a manzanita. Watching, he had an idea, which matured into a clear plan by the time he finished.

He called gently. "Let's go guys. Get off your butts. We got another day ahead of us."

Neither movement nor sound confirmed they'd heard him. He smiled, satisfied. An auspicious beginning for the day. He stepped into his boots and left the camp in an upstream direction, making sure not to hurry or betray a specific aim. As soon as he turned the first bend, though, he abandoned all pretense and sped up.

The sun, still low in the sky, kept most of the path in the shade by the time he passed the previous day's farthest advance. He slowed and focused his attention on the creek banks and canyon walls. Scattered piles of driftwood and boulders of all sizes and shapes cluttered the valley floor. After fifteen minutes of fruitless searching he crossed a narrow channel so shallow, he didn't even wet his boots. Only a tiny trickle flowed in it now, but chunks of debris lining this rivulet suggested much greater volume when rain saturated the land. Alex stopped to scan the slope.

The trickle spilled off a ledge that protruded from the cliff about seven feet up, then tumbled down to ground level and emerged from beneath the bleached trunk of a huge tree that must have fallen long ago. A cone-shaped swath of hillside above the ledge looked damp. Totally devoid of vegetation, this scar of a recent slide would mar the cliff for many years. *Just a spring. Too bad.* He yearned to go on, but ticking off the others again, served no purpose. He checked his watch and turned back.

Alex regretted his conduct back on the ridge when the boulder almost hit Liam. The brothers must suspect him, which complicated his plans. But he couldn't help it. A peculiar indifference toward Liam had grown from the boat ride. No! Much more than indifference, he actually wished him gone, out of town, somewhere he'd never have to see him again. Alex understood that Julia's beauty was the ultimate cause of these emotions. All men loved her. *Everyone* stared. He'd gotten used to that long ago, until yesterday. Liam would court her in a nanosecond if he had a chance, and she'd probably go for it. *The bastard! I won't let him!* No, Liam and he had issues. Come to think of it, they always had, but only now had these issues exploded fully.

Alex approached the final kink in the stream before coming within full view of the camp. He pulled down his fly and ruffled his hair in an attempt to pass off as someone who had just risen. If they were still asleep, he'd sneak back unnoticed. Otherwise he'd pretend he'd taken a leak. Rounding the bend, he put on a bear's yawn, fingering his pant's zipper. Neither man moved. *Splendid!*

He shook their tent's frame. "Get up guys, it's late."

Patrick's eyes opened first, staring blankly at the sky. Then he sneezed. Liam didn't stir.

"Come on, let's put something into our stomachs," Alex quipped. "We have work to do."

Liam's lids finally fluttered. Alex turned away, smiling with satisfaction. *If there is a treasure on this island, it belongs to me.* He'd tell Julia's mother to beat it. The old hag. Let her gag on her cash.

Alex never did notice Liam's fully alert eyes, so fiery they'd sear a man's heart.

~12~

E ons before humans drew their first breath, when a spit of water bound to become the Atlantic divided the New World and Old, shallow seas covered much land. Australia and a lush Antarctica broke off from each other, and mountain ranges began to thrust skyward. Ancient rivers watered valleys long since buried below ever-shifting desert sands. Land carnivores returned to the sea and evolved into ferocious marine predators. Bats took to night skies, elephants with stunted trunks combed swamps, and huge birds of prey battled primeval dogs. Vast grasslands spread over Earth, and the first roses displayed their sweetly scented petals.

Water and wind and fire and quake never relented, grinding mountain ranges into grains of sand. Floods washed these out to sea where waves and currents tossed them back ashore to make beaches. Atmospheric changes then wreaked havoc with climate, and when rivers dried up, the sand stopped moving. Time and tectonics cemented the beaches into solid rock formations. One of these, the gray Matilija Sandstone, became the backbone of Santa Rosa Island.

Over uncounted millennia the bowels of the planet, in league with the elements, attacked the Matilija. Quakes busted the sandstone, pounding surf stripped it bare, and streams carved rugged canyons into it. One such stream exploited a fault line, digging deep into the cleft and cutting a subterranean channel through the strata.

Over time, Earth's forces twisted and bent these strata, squeezing out the water. A long, narrow cave lay dry for a few thousand years, isolated from the hydrologic cycle—until the El Niño of 1983. The same tectonic burps that had originally created the cave changed the system's plumbing once again. Ground water trickled in, and with more heavy rains the intruder probed, searched, and got a feel for the cave. Then a drought cut off sufficient reinforcements for the remainder of the decade. The arid years passed, and tremendous amounts of winter precipitation soaked the earth once more. The water seeped through the soil, reconstituted the ancient underground stream, and slammed like a ramrod through the cave.

A massive mound of debris in the largest chamber bore the brunt of the onslaught. Several wet years reduced it. The water dug through soil and rock, showing no more respect for the human remains than for those of the Matilija. It swept away an oddly arranged collection of bones and a skull. The ruby-studded dagger buried among the ribs of one of the skeletons followed. The stream spread out, exposing the glittering edge of the first of four distinct piles of gold and precious gems. Fragments of oak, almost perfectly preserved by lack of oxygen protruded from these heaps. The water carried off pieces of the treasure, washing them through the narrow crevice in the cliff and dumping them where the underground stream rejoined its larger brother on its seaward journey.

One more severe storm, and the entire treasure might disappear before anyone had a chance to claim it.

*   *   *

Richard instantly knew Mónoy was there, not because he saw her, but because her best friend scampered off with a subtle smirk as he entered the village. Weyala, a woman with large eyes and a winning smile, could bewitch any man. Richard had introduced the first daughter of the chief's advisor to Waspe soon after landing. Unfortunately, the cook's charms had been lost on her. His bulging brow ridge proved too unsightly, a defect his shoddy manners did little to mitigate. She avoided him as best as she could, an easy task since he shunned the Indians all together and came to the village only to talk to Richard.

She slipped into a tule-covered hut, and popped back out from the conical structure with Mónoy in tow. Richard's heart beat faster, as always when he saw her. He tried to smile, but the gravity of his mission ruined the attempt. The women's light-hearted laughter died abruptly, and they glanced at each other. Then Weyala left, squeezing her friend's arm encouragingly.

Mónoy pointed toward the creek, grabbed his hand, and pulled him along. She decided to say nothing on the path to the stream, where an old woman fetching water winked knowingly before she disappeared with her heavy load. They jumped into the cool water and sloshed the few yards upstream to the small clearing. Barely large enough for two adults to lie and surrounded by an impenetrable thicket of anise and scrub pine, they had spent many hours here trying to learn each other's language and making love.

They sat on the fine sand, their feet soaking in the clear water. Suddenly the tranquil surface stirred and a large trout sailed through the air with its mouth agape. The colorful dragonfly never knew what hit it when the fish swallowed it in one grotesque gulp before falling back into the stream. Mónoy put her hands on his shoulders and pressed her lips against his, hiding her tongue in the back of the mouth to entice him. He had taught her this game, a favorite, so when he didn't play, her heart grew fearful. *What had happened? Did he want another woman? Why could he not even smile?*

"We must go," he said gravely, pointing from him to her and nodding in the direction of the sea. He made a paddling motion with both arms, repeating a phrase several times.

She caught the word "boat" and felt the blood surge to her head. *He would leave!* She picked up a stick and tossed it into the current. "Bot," she said, struggling with the English pronunciation. She pointed at the stick, which made a full turn as it passed over a ripple, and stuck a finger in his chest. "Bot take yu?"

"Yes," he said, embracing and holding her tight. "And you. I want you to come with me. Tonight."

Her brain reeled with mixed emotions, and her heart pounded in her chest. If she understood correctly, he wanted to bring her on the big tree canoe and take her to his home. But why didn't he seem happy? It didn't matter. He still wanted her, and she could leave this place that had not witnessed her birth, that had never been her real home. She pulled her knees up to her breasts, crossed her arms around them, and stared into the creek from which she had drawn water for so long.

A ferocious forest fire had leveled Mónoy's village, killing her parents and most of the people. She had wandered for some time with the survivors, passing through several villages until a man whose hunting accident destroyed his ability to have any more children gave in to his wife's pleas to adopt her. Before her journey she had never seen how others lived. One tribe, which she always remembered, had a woman chief.

In her new life they expected her obedience, working her for much of each day. All women had to, while the men did as they pleased. She resisted at first, but her adopted father beat her more severely with each attempt, and cursed her for being more burden than use. So she'd always felt like an outsider, except with her few friends. Then Richard came. He never hurt her, never demanded anything, and even helped with some of the chores. Perhaps, she hoped, his people would welcome and treat her as well as he did. She would miss Weyala. But she couldn't change that. Weyala loved her world and would never leave.

Mónoy rose to her feet. Her only chance to get away had come. "What take?"

He smiled in a strange way, pulling her back down. He seemed uncomfortable, and she sensed he had something to say she wouldn't like.

"Listen, my captain doesn't want me to go away. He must not know." He laid a finger across his lips. "You can't tell anyone."

She struggled to make sense of this flood of words. *His chief must keep a secret? Her people should not know the tree canoe would leave?*

* * *

Liam had been awake for a while, unable to go back to sleep. Staying inside the warm bag, he later heard Alex get up and empty his bladder. Liam debated whether or not to get dressed until Alex told them to get off their butts. Not in the mood to have to make conversation with him, he had decided to stay put and kept his eyes closed. When the professor's footsteps grew distant, he raised his head to peek out, startled to find him heading upstream. Liam quickly climbed into his pants and threw on a sweater. It took a minute to find the Tevas. He hit the trail running.

When he finally spotted Alex fifty yards upstream, he stalked in silence, and took cover behind trees and bushes. Once, Alex halted and turned sideways so that Liam swore he'd seen him. Though standing in a large depression in the stream bank where he could lie down flat, he didn't want to duck for fear of moving. He might hail Alex, pretending he wanted to catch up. Or he could stay stock-still. Thankfully, Alex never turned his head but resumed his survey.

For the rest of the way, Liam took no more chances, never exposing his position. Finally Alex reached a small spring gurgling from the cliff face and glanced at his watch. Liam's instincts told him that the hunter would momentarily become the hunted, so he hastened back as quickly as his feet carried him, jumped over rocks, and dodged branches until he reached the tent. Patrick was still snoring up a storm. Liam dove into his bag, feigning the sleep of the innocent, trying to figure out precisely what mysterious scheme Alex engineered in that clever mind.

*   *   *

They couldn't have hoped for a better day to escape. Their greatest fear had revolved around preparing everything under Hord's watchful eyes. Yet, soon after concluding the interrogation, the General had dispatched him with eight men to scour the countryside for Smythe. That arrogant slime bag of an earl was forced to join them. Then, beyond Richard's wildest expectations, the General spent the bulk of the afternoon inspecting the galleon's hull, never alluding to the inventory. He probably wanted to wait for Hord, who normally assisted him. Whatever the reason, fate had dealt them a stupendous hand.

The sailors divided their hours into playing cards, sleeping, and telling tall tales of grandiose exploits that grew more fantastic as the age of the narrators increased. Few Indians visited that day. Relative quiet pervaded the camp, and the cooks alone brimmed with constant activity, though they strove to mask it by pretending to attend to their regular chores.

They worked feverishly, organizing their getaway around cooking supper. Richard inconspicuously passed by the ship's pinnace a dozen times. He took measure of how much sailcloth and lines it held, scrutinized the mast for cracks, checked whether oars and tholepins remained in good repair, and looked at the sea anchor. What he found satisfied him on all accounts. Richard also secured several blankets, small casks of tar and oakum for caulking, and two pairs of oars. He stored all aboard beneath a heavy tarpaulin.

In the meantime, Waspe moved provisions from the galley closer to the water. These included a cask filled with salted seal and fish, a fat wheel of Dutch cheese taken from the Spaniards, ship's biscuit, a hogshead of rock-hard bread, rice, and a box of Spanish sugar. In addition, he collected an assortment of knives and spoons, parcels of twine and thread, a lump of beeswax to make candles, more blankets, muskets, fuzees filled with powder and shot, shirts, breeches, and fishing hooks. He stuffed everything into sacks and scattered these in unobtrusive piles near the boat where they wouldn't cause suspicion. At least he didn't think they would.

* * *

Sunday morning had proved utterly unsuccessful for the treasure hunters. Hours of searching yielded only blisters, cuts, and chilled bones. The men vented their disappointment back at the campsite, each giving his best to turn it into a veritable dump and hopefully keep others out of the area. Any hikers chancing into this canyon might pick the same area to bed down. Who could resist level and soft ground near a source of clear water, unless heaps of trash marked the spot? Nothing deterred more effectively in such a pristine location on a protected island.

Patrick beat the fire pit like a berserk with a thick branch, making it rain ash and half-burned chunks of wood from where they had slept all the way down to the creek's edge. Liam and Alex dumped empty cans, power bar wrappers, knots of toilet paper, glass bottles, and a spent propane cartridge. It looked repugnant. No one with any self-respect would stay in a place so desecrated, or dream of sleeping near this filth, or dip into the stream to wash off a day's sweat. Satisfied, they shouldered their packs and broke camp.

The march back transpired with no incidents. They made good time, arriving early at the rendezvous site. So had the *Helen*. The yacht anchored off shore with Julia waving from the main deck, the wind whipping up her long hair. She climbed into the waiting zodiac, and soon the high-pitched whine of the outboarder blew across the water. She rode the inflatable's nose right up on the beach and jumped on the sand. Patrick grabbed a line to prevent the surf from claiming the boat.

"Well, any luck?" she asked, her voice betraying low expectations. She looked from man to man, neither hugging nor kissing her husband. In turn, he seemed totally indifferent to her distance, Liam noticed. *Strange!*

"Yes, our little excursion paid off. Check it out." Alex pulled the cross from his pocket, his face glowing with pride. "It appears that a European set foot in Kindayr's Canyon a long time ago. Unfortunately, we were neither equipped nor had sufficient time to explore the entire area." He glanced quickly at his two companions. "But it was a great start."

It riled Liam. *'Sufficient time,' yeah!* He smiled politely. He'd have his chance to play his own suit.

Julia took the cross with both hands, as though it were a piece of rare porcelain. "This is pure gold, right? It's incredible," she whispered, turning it over. "Where did you find it?"

"In the stream, close to where Liam discovered the dagger." He paused. "Why don't you show her the coin?"

She stared at Liam, who pulled a sock from his pack and shook out the coin. He placed it in her palm, and her eyes widened. "I can't believe it. What do these letters mean?"

"I haven't determined that yet," Alex said. "But I think the coin dates from the sixteenth century."

Her eyes moved between the two pieces, and her face became radiant. "It's amazing. In graduate school I read dozens of articles and books by archeologists who dug up stuff in all corners of the globe. Now here we are, in our own backyard, with a five-century-old coin, cross, and dagger."

She gazed dreamily at the mountains. "I'd give a fortune to know who last owned these, how he lived, where he came from, how he died." She handed the coin back to Liam. "Funny, just touching it connects me to the past. Wouldn't you have loved to sail the seas in search of exotic shores and peoples?"

"You bet. I'd take with me an adventurous woman afraid of nothing and willing to sink roots in an unspoiled land." She looked into his eyes, and he read an unmistakable like-mindedness. He couldn't help but smile. No one stirred until Patrick casually kicked a stone. It ricocheted off a rock and rolled into the surf. Tension hung heavy in the air.

"You're a hopeless romantic," Alex broke the icy silence, his face a shade darker with otherwise well-concealed misgivings. "We better get going. The tide is going out, and I don't want to risk another shoal." He picked up his gear and carelessly threw it in the zodiac.

Patrick cast an admonishing glance at Liam, who checked his watch. *Actually, the tide will rise for another half hour.*

They transferred everything in two trips. Julia fired the *Helen's* engines and turned the bow toward the Santa Cruz Channel. The sky had turned unusually dark from a heavy cloud cover by the time they navigated the sea wall and cruised into the harbor. In view of the gloomy atmosphere restaurants on the long wharf were already bathed in a sea of cheerful lights. Clusters of tourists mingled with locals. Slim women sped down the bike path on slick rollerblades, and a tight formation of triathlon trainees swept past Shoreline Park toward the Mesa. A lonesome couple, oblivious to approaching boats, had claimed the narrow sand spit curving back into the harbor.

The *Helen* docked. Liam and Patrick helped tie her up and took leave. Liam looked back once. Alex was talking to Julia, using his arms in animated gestures. They obviously had a serious argument. She turned her head and scanned the pier till her gaze met Liam's. Was she smiling? He couldn't tell, but he did know that events had irreversibly upset the status quo. What he did not know was where this was leading?

"Those nasty, stinking dirt bags!" Cob Rash raged, the fury coloring his scar crimson. "I don't believe they live like this, especially the professor. Not like this! Wouldn't you expect a bit more of a damn university professor?"

"Hmm," Dave offered. He didn't esteem academia as highly as did his brother.

"I wish his students could see what a pig he is." The thought never occurred to him that the boys and girls at Oak Grove High would absolutely loathe him if they had any knowledge of his doings.

"I mean, come on, we've left trash all over these islands," Dave mumbled. "What're you so upset about?"

Cob ignored this. "Let's get on with it. I've got to go back today, which means you'll be on your own for a few days." He kicked an empty can. "Two or three hours. That's all we got."

*   *   *

"This is it," Richard said to Waspe. "Pray they didn't find him."

The scouting party clambered down the ridge that separated the camp from the long and narrow bay, which pierced the backcountry like a lance. As they got closer, Richard saw two men carrying Hord, who seemed to be hurt. This promised trouble, since the General would likely have a fit. Besides, every hour that passed with Smythe gone would heighten suspicion. He had no place to go in this wilderness without food, shelter, weapons, or the knowledge of land and Indians. Barring his resurrection and speedy return, the General would summon them before nightfall for a second interrogation. They had to expect pointed questions. Richard wiped his brow. Only a miracle stood between them and heavy chains.

Waspe interrupted his thoughts, offering little encouragement. "I have ugly premonitions. I care nothing for

Hord, but I hope he's not in a bad way. The General can ill afford to have him sit idle now, so soon before sailing. He'll vent his worries on someone, and since the scouts come empty-handed, I fear that means you and me."

"Let's keep as calm as possible. He's a fair man, and I don't reckon he'll blame Hord's clumsiness on us. Smythe can't talk, and that is our strongest card. As long as we stick to our story, they might leave us in peace."

The scouts entered camp. Those who had stayed behind began quickly to crowd around them to learn what happened. One sailor darted off to fetch the General. "Let me down," the first officer barked impatiently.

"Aye, Mr. Hord." The two stout fellows relieved themselves of his weight by slipping his arms off their shoulders and easing him into a chair.

The first officer looked terrible. Torn open from shoulder to elbow, his right shirtsleeve dangled in frayed scraps. Blood and dirt caked his arm. A smear of hair, blood, and grime spread from his right ear to the top of his head, and a monstrous bruise stained much of his cheek dark purple. Hord's left foot, no longer clad in a shoe, had swollen to twice its normal size.

"Has anyone gone to tell Captain Drake?" he demanded.

"Grepe left jus' as soon as you got here, Sir," a voice hollered from the group. "I see 'em both over there by the ship. They're coming."

The crew, its excitement palpable, made the craziest conjectures in the interim. They spun wild tales of what had caused Hord's nasty injury, where the scouts had picked up Smythe's trail, how he cleverly evaded his pursuers, and that he must have eventually run into the arms of hostile Indians and meet a cruel end. No sailor gladly suffered a thief. This longest of voyages required they count on each other. Raiding the stores, especially the wine, was an unforgivable sin. The men speculated vociferously how the Indians would kill him, and not one seemed willing to put an end to this baseless palaver. They loved to let their imagination run wild.

The scouts volunteered nothing, doubtless on Hord's orders. At first he ignored the chatter, perhaps not wanting to spoil the fun. But his expression grew increasingly morose, and his annoyance reached the breaking point. "Shut up, you fools!" he shouted. All fell silent, and he took to studying his throbbing foot with silent stoicism.

When Grepe finally returned with the ship's master, the sailors parted to make a path. Not one man in the encampment talked. All wanted to hear the truth.

~ 13 ~

The chiseled man with long dark hair and angular cheekbones had an acquaintance on the police force. When he handed her a slip of paper with the Jeep's license plate number, she retrieved the information within seconds. He jotted down where Liam lived. She didn't care what his reasons were. He paid for her services with an after-dark visit. She'd take out the "tools," which he handled effectively. They did this every other month, though if she had her way, he'd show up every other day. He never shied away from inflicting pain with those tools, a quality she bemoaned as increasingly difficult to find in most men. She never allowed her mind to dwell on the possibility that her utter dearth of redeeming physical qualities kept all but the hardiest souls at bay.

By two-thirty, he hit US 101 South. He got off in Ventura, parked his Firebird near a fast food outlet in a busy shopping center, and strolled around the plaza to familiarize himself with its layout. Pleased, he called for a cab, which arrived shortly. He got in and without any verbal greeting showed the man behind the wheel a piece of paper with a local address.

"That's no problem," the taxi driver said courteously in a heavily accented British English, which, with his cropped black hair and olive skin, revealed his South Asian heritage. Fortunately, he took the cue and kept his mouth shut till they got to their destination.

"Eleven even," he finally broke the silence. The passenger handed him a ten and three ones, slammed the door, and looked up at a dilapidated building ripe for demolition.

He entered a tiny office that reeked of stale coffee and a synthetic something. Plaster peeled off the walls, collecting on the edges of a threadbare carpet. A tacky 1960s plastic chair hogged the corner. The once white counter had turned dark yellow and sported a galaxy of stains. The mindless babble of an asinine TV talk show blared from a room in the back.

"Be right out," came a raspy old voice. Feet shuffled and a crooked man in his seventies filled the doorframe. He smiled, exposing two rows of brown teeth that had traded the soft caresses of a toothbrush for a lifetime's corrosion by fibrous chewing tobacco. His eyes, though, had lost none of their luster. Sapphire blue and clear as a mountain lake, they belied his age.

"Well, whatcha lookin' for?"

"I want to take the family camping."

"Camping! Wonderful!" The old man nodded approval. "Done plenty of that myself out in the desert, even though it don't look it." He chuckled. "You come to the right place. Got a '78 Chevy Van in damnedest good shape. Prior owner converted it into a bona fide bedroom on wheels."

"How much is it?"

"How long you gonna keep it?"

"Depends. A week. Maybe two."

He clicked his tongue, making a quick mental calculation. "Goin' rate is $30 a day, or $180 a week. But since you gonna show your kids a good time, I'll let you have it fourteen days for three 'n a quarter."

"Can I check it out?"

The model's inconspicuous silver-gray was perfect. The paint looked good enough, despite a few patches of rust. No one would waste a second glance on this van. "All right, it's a deal."

The owner didn't do credit cards. He received cash and a fake ID.

At three-thirty the van rolled into the shopping plaza, stopping in the loading zone behind the nondescript cement blocks that constituted the anchor stores. The man pulled a license plate from his bag and exchanged it with the one on the Chevy. Five minutes later the van merged with northbound traffic on US 101.

Every day, for the next few days, the gray vehicle climbed Cheltenham Road past the Ludmons driveway and parked thirty yards further up the street. This ideal spot on the shoulder overlooked most of the driveway, the villa, and the guesthouse. Beneath the sprawling canopy of an immense eucalyptus, the Chevy seemed little more than a forgotten toy. It would not attract undue attention.

The first night Kindayr had someone over. The lights in the guesthouse didn't go off until well past two in the morning and not until midnight the next day. The main residence was quiet. Not one bulb dispelled its solemn loneliness. On the third night, a Friday, both stayed dark. Kindayr and Co. probably had gone out to party. By three-fifteen the man in the van had enough and left, but he returned before eight. Still no sign of anyone, and the Jeep hadn't made it back. Unless they didn't sleep much, they must have spent the night elsewhere. So he stayed on and observed the house through the day, but no one showed up. By six he reluctantly called it quits. The policewoman demanded action.

On Sunday he manned his post at four in the morning, still sore and hung over from an evening of abandon. Soon after sunrise several people took to the road walking their dogs. Some passed close by the van, and he quickly ducked out of sight. Once, someone caught him by surprise. He barely had time to pull his baseball cap lower and turn his head. Around eleven he started the engine and departed, looking forward to a bite and a break.

He reoccupied his post by one. Still, nothing. Had they left town? Of course! They went away for the weekend, which meant they'd probably come back today. Damned! He'd missed a perfect opportunity. Should he go in now? No, he decided. Too risky while it was light. Barring their return, though, he would enter that night. Six o'clock arrived. Nine. Ten. At ten-thirty, his patience exhausted, he reached under the seat for the gun and silencer. He screwed it on, shoved the weapon into his jacket, and got out of the van, softly pushing the door shut without locking it. Hopefully, nothing would go wrong. Hopefully, they wouldn't roll in from a long drive just now. Waiting a few more hours would make perfect sense, but he just couldn't stand sitting idle another minute. Besides, he had a strong hunch they wouldn't be back tonight.

He stepped off the pavement and descended through lush greenery down a steep slope to the guesthouse. Circling around it, he looked for signs of an alarm system, but found none. With all windows shut, he'd have to use the gun. Good thing he brought it. He returned to the back entrance and pulled a pair of latex gloves from his pocket. The Beretta came out, and he stepped away from the house one last time to make sure no one watched. Then he leveled the weapon at a spot between the handle and the doorframe. A muffled sound accompanied the flash as the 9mm smashed the lock. He picked up the cartridge and pushed the door gently, shutting it behind him.

Pointing a tiny flashlight, he began the search in the living room. He tore out the desk's drawers and dumped their contents on the carpet. He pulled cushions off the couch, felt the underside of chairs, and swept clean the shelves. Nothing! After a quick glance through the windows he stepped into a studio that smelled of fresh paint and turpentine. Easels cluttered the room, supporting canvases in various stages of completion. He checked drawers and cabinets, throwing everything on the floor. Again, no luck. Irritated, he punched one of the easels, watching the painting crash on the hardwood floor. Then he ran upstairs into a bedroom. He went through another closet, a chest, some boxes, and yanked the mattress off the bed. Zero. Now he went for the second bedroom and ravaged it too, again in vain. In a fit of anger he kicked a hole in the wall.

The man looked out the window, where no living thing stirred. He made a mess of the bathroom then raced back downstairs and into the kitchen. He started with the cabinets, pulled out drawer after drawer, and emptied them onto a growing pile near the sink. The first three held nothing of interest. "Fuck!" he screamed, dashing one against the wall. He yanked out the fourth and . . . froze. Bingo! There, on top of a stack of place mats twinkled the object of his mission. The dagger shone in the beam of the flashlight, just as Jeanine had described its flame-shaped blade and faceted rubies. Only, Kindayr must have cleaned the weapon. Jeanine had mentioned a coat of rust. It didn't matter. One glance convinced him of the dagger's authenticity. He quickly put it in his bag.

A broad grin stretched Michael Kuyam's face as he inspected the open fridge and selected a Corona. He could afford another minute. He guzzled two thirds without a breather and strolled into the living room for a final look at the chaos. An air photo of the Channel Islands hung on the east wall. Kindayr had told Jeanine he found the dagger on Santa Cruz, which fit into the old legend. The possibilities gave Kuyam the chills. He felt light-headed. He only had to get the exact location from Kindayr. He'd think of a way for that, but first he'd let a week or two pass.

Suddenly, powerful beams sliced through the living room, for a moment suffusing everything in an otherworldly glow. Startled, he flicked off the flashlight, recognizing the Jeep sitting a short distance down the driveway. Then its motor and headlights died. "Shit!" He tossed the beer and ran for the back entrance.

The two brothers had gone from the harbor directly to the Acapulco on lower State Street, where they had run into a handful of Liam's friends. Limey Margaritas washed down the spicy enchiladas, and all agreed to extend the evening at the Santa Barbara Brewing Company. Patrick had actually tried hitting on one of the girls, a gorgeous brunette, till she told him she preferred women. Liam almost felt sorry for him when he saw his expression. At least his brother seemed to be getting over Raffaela.

The Jeep negotiated a sharp turn as it ascended the hill, the bumper missing an ivy-covered stonewall by an inch. They were dissecting Malreaux's morning excursion at length.

"He really is a nasty back stabber," Patrick said.

"It seems so," Liam sighed. "And we've been friends for over three years."

"I started having serious doubts about him the instant that damn boulder almost knocked you dead. He isn't genuine." He grimaced. "What bugs me most is the thought that he might have found more stuff on his little trip and didn't tell us."

"No way," Liam shook his head with conviction. "He returned to camp too soon after I did. Another piece of gold would have kept him occupied, and he has never been good at hiding his emotions."

"We've got to find out what the hell he's after."

"I'm gonna get on the Net and see if I can dig up something on the dagger and the coin." He tapped his knuckles on the stick shift. "Let's hope you can extend your leave."

"I'll call first thing when we get back. It's already morning in Italy, and I'll get my man on the line quick enough."

Liam turned into his driveway. "I'm looking forward to fin—" he stopped in mid-sentence. "What in God's name?" he burst out, stepping on the breaks so hard the vehicle skid on the gravel.

"What the hell are you doing?"

Liam pointed. "A light! In the house!" he shouted.

Patrick looked at him askance. "I don't see a thing."

"There! Someone flicked off a flashlight in my living room." He turned off the engine and threw open the door. "I've got a damn thief in my house. Hurry!"

Patrick switched to military mode. "Wait!" He reached behind and pulled the machete he'd used on the island to cut his way through the brush and a SEAL knife from his backpack, shoving the knife into Liam's hands. "Don't be afraid to use it. There's no telling what kind of scum we're gonna run into."

They snuck up on the handsome stucco building, halting under a pepper tree twenty feet from the front door.

Liam whispered. "I'm going around to check the kitchen entrance. Then I'll complete the loop. Wait exactly two minutes. If I'm not back in time come after me. For now, block the driveway and look for broken windows. Got it?"

Patrick clasped the machete. He checked his watch and nodded.

"Two minutes counting. Go!"

*   *   *

The General looked his officer over with a curious expression that mixed sympathy with displeasure. "Mr. Hord! Tell me the cause of this hideous injury and why Smythe remains unaccounted for."

Hord sagged as he tried valiantly to get on his feet. He looked sheepishly at his commander, like a boy having to face his father after getting pummeled in a fistfight with a wimp.

The captain placed a reassuring hand on his shoulder. "No need aggravating the swelling. What happened?"

When Hord cleared his throat, every man held his breath. "We ascended the ridge in a northeasterly direction until we entered the forest, an ideal place for anyone wishing to hide. For the most part we stayed on the Indian trails because the forest is too dense and often impenetrable. Regrettably, a man hoping to drop from view has a thousand choices. We found no evidence at all that Smythe had gone that way. The ground is hard and retained no footprints.

"By mid-morning we reached a large meadow, and I ordered the men to sweep in a broad line ten paces apart. We looked into thickets, several caves, even inspected the crowns of trees. As before, we found no hint of his presence."

Chrystopher Haylston, the ship's surgeon, arrived with water, rags, bandages, and a poultice the Indians prepared from the kawátcho plant. They applied it to cuts and bruises with astonishing effect, and a number of sailors swore by it. Haylston got busy and attended to the foot as unobtrusively as possible. Earl Folsom took this opportunity to force his pompous self upon the stage and pick up the thread.

"Let me say that"—but before he could get out another word Drake lifted his hand to shut him up. Folsom took a step back, pouting, his neck swollen from restricted blood vessels. Hord resumed his account.

"After the meadow we turned west, following the second leg of our triangle. We soon came to that treacherous region where deep gullies and steep ravines make for hideouts almost as good as the forest itself. There I stumbled over a patch of briars and down a ravine, even though 'cliff' is a more fitting term. I'm grateful the Lord spared my life." He coughed vehemently, grimacing from the pain this caused, and Haylston kept his hands off the throbbing limb until Hord's breath went smooth again.

"As you should," the captain commented. "From the looks of it, you are a fortunate man to be making this report." He paused. "I suppose you abandoned the search after your mishap?"

"Yes, Sir. I thought it best to return." He looked embarrassed. The poor fellow had marched off leading the scouts only to have them carry him back like a helpless babe.

Drake rubbed the back of his head, gazing thoughtfully at his men. *What would he say?* Richard had feared this moment. His whole body stiffened in apprehension of the General's decision.

*   *   *

Liam moved with stealth, knees bent and torso leaning forward. The knife rested in his right palm, the long blade pointing down. He shivered, but not from fear. A fierce rage eliminated all other emotions. He could not stomach the prospect of anyone violating the very place where he created his beloved art. He cringed at the mere idea of a thieving scumbag polluting his personal possessions with his filthy fingers. *But why the guesthouse, instead of the villa?* The Ludmons owned much more valuable stuff than he did. Perhaps the scoundrel had already cleaned out the main house. He would have had an easy time, with no alarm system.

He looked at the knife, and a very sobering thought entered his mind. He might kill someone in a few moments. Did the guy have a gun? What if several of them waited to attack him? Considering theses possibilities, Liam no longer felt so fearless.

He saw nothing suspicious as he rounded the corner of the house, keeping fifteen feet from the wall as a precaution. Taking up position behind a thick juniper, he scrutinized every square inch of the building but discerned no movement, heard no noise, and detected no open or shattered windows. The back door seemed shut. He considered investigating whether anyone had tampered with the lock, but decided not to expose himself. No matter how solid the steel of his blade, it did not match a pistol or a sawed-off shotgun. He checked his watch. Sixty-five seconds since they split up.

Liam left the juniper's cover and continued on his path around the house. He stopped short of the corner and ducked to take a peek. Then he made for the front of the building, using the hedge between it and himself as cover. The next instant, he heard a faint rustling and sensed danger from behind. He spun around and lifted his blade, but it was too late.

*   *   *

"What has happened to Smythe?" the captain hollered, leveling his gaze on the sailors. A shuffling in the ranks announced one man shoving aside those who blocked his path. The front line parted, spitting out the infamous Harold 'The Hound' Hogges, a loathsome and brutal rabble-rouser who thrived on others' misery like a born scavenger.

Terribly adept at wind-milling his massive arms, The Hound not only loved to incite men, but to throw himself into any frays that his loose tongue instigated. He long ago stopped growing hair, and to make up for this shortcoming he had paid for two huge tattoos on his scalp while his ship docked at Antwerp. A greenish sea snake with its toothy head held high was ready to strike at anyone from above The Hound's right temple. The serpent stretched alongside his skull past the ear, its tail curving down to the neck. The ruffian's fondness for animals that slithered and crawled found further expression in the black spider that covered the left side of his head. A bright yellow anchor glowed in the center of its plump belly, and eight hairy legs reached across Hogges' taut scalp.

"Way I see it, Sir, it don't matter. There isn't many amongst us who care. No one here'd miss Smythe. So I say we leave him behind and let the savages knock his sick brain to a pulp. They know his type, and once we set sail he's good as a carcass. That's if he's not dead already, his throat sliced open by one of the cleverer chaps." 'The Hound' exploded into thunderous laughter. Many of the sailors joined in, and even some of the gentlemen could not hide the hint of a smile. Smythe had few friends.

157

Richard laughed with the others, though he forced it. He didn't find Hogges' allusion to a cut throat funny, but strove to look just like the sailors standing closest. Comradely, he slapped the back of one man who could not contain his mirth over Hogges' amusing comments. Waspe played a similar game, laughing without restraint and wagging his head like a dog.

Renold Brewar, a tall and lanky fellow who spoke little since traitorous Indians clubbed to death his best friend on the island of Mocha off the Chilean coast, finally got all of them to shut up.

"I don't like Smythe any more than you. But that doesn't mean I'd wish him at the mercy of the savages. We all know that none of us is more at home in the rigging. Truth is, I can name two of you who'd be at the bottom of the sea, were it not for him." Brewar was right. Smythe had saved the lives of two sailors. Nimble as a monkey, he elicited the awe of all when working above deck, especially in foul weather.

Drake nodded at Brewar. "Well said. However, Smythe tried to steal from us, and no matter how valuable a hand he is, I shall suffer no thief on my ship."

Lofty words from the lips of a man who has just stuffed his hold with the bounty pirated off a Spanish galleon, Richard marveled. Though the queen might sanction his raids, the Spaniards undoubtedly and rightfully yearned to strap him across the muzzle of a cannon.

The General raised his voice. "In any event, since Smythe knows that every hour which prolongs his absence must add to his punishment, I am convinced he has come to hurt."

He had spoken with such grave conviction, Richard felt a dampness on his forehead and chest. Drops of sweat seeped through his eyebrows, and he tried not to blink when the salty liquid stung his eyes. He wanted to look at Waspe, but feared to do so, for any instant the General would turn and gore him with those icy eyes. He'd order him and Waspe to step forth and level his accusation. All the men would stare, even those with whom he'd formed friendships. They'd explode in curses and furious gestures.

Richard saw a hawk circle high in the sky, so free, perhaps having spotted its next meal. The raptor reminded him of the General, drawing ever-tighter curves around his prey. *God! Why did I let Waspe draw me into all this? I should have never listened to him! I wish I'd never met him.* Richard would happily exchange all of the gold for the ability to join the soaring hawk. He looked at the thick forest, measured the distance to the tree line. He could outrun anyone aboard. *This might be my last chance.*

*   *   *

The characteristic chirping of scattered crickets filled the air with a soothing melody. Patrick glanced at his watch. One minute, fifty-four seconds. Something had slowed Liam down. And whoever broke in must have seen their arrival, for the house stayed dark. Moreover, Patrick had detected no movement behind the windows. He checked the time again. Two minutes one. Okay. Action!

Crouching low, he followed in his brother's footsteps, going as quietly as possible. He rounded the corner, heading for the same juniper Liam had used for cover. Patrick studied the house, but saw no traces of a forced entry. The back door, the windows, all seemed in perfect order. Where the hell was Liam?

In his parched mouth his tongue tasted like a clot of mud, earthy, primeval—the flavor of combat. A familiar taste, it brought back memories of firing on Iraqi tanks. Something felt wrong. Something *was* wrong. He strengthened his grip on the machete and moved out.

He came to the corner of the house. Still, there was no hint of human life, no voices, no footsteps, nothing but the hum of the crickets. The muddy taste in his mouth intensified. Shit! This didn't look good! He squatted and peeked around the corner, where a hedge blocked most of his view. Then his heart skipped a beat. The compact shape of a body was sprawled on the ground. Liam!

Patrick ran without thinking, the huge blade shining in the scattered light of the stars. Two concentrated flashes were the last light he saw. The silencer spared him the insidious pops.

A tremendous double punch tore through his chest. One bullet traversed a lung. The other smashed muscle tissue and passed near the heart before it lodged by the spine.

*   *   *

Hord put an end to Richard's fantasies of taking to the sky. "How do you mean, Sir? Do you suppose the Indians killed Smythe?"

The General shook his head. "No, with what kindness and generosity they have shown, it makes no sense."

Richard felt cold and hollow inside. He resigned himself to the inevitable, his brain incapable of concocting a credible defense against the storm about to hit. Through this confusion he heard the General as through a mist.

"Smythe is injured or dead. Under the circumstances only a fool would fail to return. Judging by your own hard fortune, I bet he got himself into similar trouble. He must have entered unfamiliar and what you call 'treacherous' terrain in the dark. Wouldn't you agree, Mr. Fletcher?"

"Yes, Sir, I would."

Drake's eyes searched. "Mr. Chester?"

"Possible, but I would not swear on it. We can never trust the savages. I, for one, don't ever turn my back on them."

The General nodded. "I want a second party to leave at once. Those men joining it should prepare to spend the night in the forest."

· Richard saw the storm clouds part. A ray of hope energized him. The General gave him and Waspe one final reprieve. Then Brewar had to run his big mouth again.

"Sir, Smythe is too sure-footed to fall off a cliff. He's never missed a step in the rigging."

Richard's heart resumed its wild dance. A morbid desire to wrap his hands around the man's throat and slowly crush his vocal cords took possession of him.

The General beckoned Brewar come closer, which the sailor did with eyes full of apprehension. "I see. Smythe is 'too sure-footed' to fall, while my first officer, at least in your opinion, is not. How interesting."

Brewar lost his pep, shriveling under his master's gaze. "Sir, I didn't mean it like that. I, I—"

"Then *what* do you mean?" Hord cut in. "Choose your words with care, or you will come to regret them."

Brewar's rather dark complexion now underwent a memorable metamorphosis. He paled to such ghostly pallor that it seemed someone had pulled a plug and drained his face. He looked to his mates for help, but they all averted their eyes. The first officer could drive a man without mercy.

"No, Mr. Hord. No," he muttered, his voice hoarse, the words barely audible. "I don't believe there's anything wrong with you. It, it can happen to the best man. One bad step, and . . ." he gulped for air. "Smythe could have fallen." He nodded vigorously. "Yes, Smythe must have, just like you. Yes."

Richard wanted to shout with joy and controlled an impulse to dance. He had one more chance.

* * *

Michael Kuyam had not come to kill, having brought the gun only to get in, but when Kindayr's stupid-ass friend charged with that elephant knife in his hand, he squeezed the trigger by reflex. What was he supposed to do?

161

In semi shock he stared at the prostrate bodies for a long time. Eventually, he sank to his knees and walked his hands through the thick blades of grass. They quickly found the cartridges, which disappeared into his pocket. He glanced once more at the two motionless shapes before running off.

A thick fog ate up most of the moonlight, preventing all but an intermittent twinkle when drifting swaths of the vapor parted to reveal distant stars. This night, the world lost its familiar shape, dissolved into an amorphous blob of dark gloom. Sky and sea became one. Brush and scattered piles of gear flowed into each other like swirls of wet ink on parchment. Tree trunks merged with briars, grasses, and soil into an indefinable whole that made each step a risk.

An owl hooted from its high perch, while languid puffs of air caressed the foliage. Small mammals scurried over the ground, their nimble legs kicking through dry leaves and snapping twigs. A hapless creature somewhere near the camp perimeter issued brief yet desperate shrieks, the only dissonant notes to disturb this nighttime symphony. The outcry died abruptly. A carnivore's jaws completed their lethal task with swift efficiency.

Drake had ordered sixteen men to hunt Smythe, two groups of eight that combed the upland forests in a pincer movement. With so many sailors gone, none of those left behind had leave to go to the Indian village. And most of those men already slept. A lonely guard made his periodic rounds, though the interval between patrols increased as the night grew darker, especially since after Waspe had pressed a third mug of wine into his hands. The chap would not return for a while, and the two cooks made their final preparations in peace.

They had worked fast and inconspicuously right through serving the evening meal. With the dazed guard effectively neutralized, they could begin to load all the previously positioned equipment aboard the ship's boat. Four muskets, two large bags of shot, and several small sacks of powder went in first. Then came the provisions and the rest of the gear. Richard stood broad-legged in the pinnace and unceremoniously dumped a stack of canvas and sail cloth, a chest filled with tools and nails, spikes and hatchets, several long ropes, and a score of other necessities. With time so precious, they would delay putting order into the chaos until far out at sea.

Waspe wiped the sweat off his face, his chest heaving from all the exertions of an exhausting day. "That's it."

Richard swung over the gunwale. "I'm going for Mónoy." He hesitated. "If Milles realizes the boat is gone before we clear the mouth of the estuary, only God can save us. See if you can get another pint into him."

They looked at each other, two utterly disparate men whom fate had tossed together, poised to desert in this remote corner of the earth and sail to far away Panama along an uncharted and wild continent in an open boat better suited to a tame inland sea. They would either survive as one, or perish as one. Their destinies had inextricably cast them for this act of the mysterious cosmic drama.

Waspe cleared his dripping nose. "Go! I'll keep that fool's throat as wet as a bilge. I guarantee he will not discover our disappearance."

"You reckon they'll find the rogue?" Milles asked for the fourth time that evening as he strolled by the galley.

Waspe snorted. "I told you. He'll come back in a day or two, unless the savages already cut him to pieces. To tell you my honest feelings on the matter, either way I don't care a damn. Could never stand him. Wait." He handed the sailor another mug filled to the rim. "Here, keep you warm and in good spirits. As for myself, I'm dead tired. Need to get some rest."

Milles sighed with jealousy, his eyes drooping from fatigue. "Aye. I'll be on my way." And he drifted off, sipping the red wine. Waspe let him drop from sight and sat on a barrel.

"It's me," said a quiet voice a few minutes later. "Mónoy came from the village. Says she missed me." They had rehearsed this in case someone overheard them, not knowing whether Hord kept them under secret observation. It was probably redundant, since a spy would have overseen their preparations and ruined everything from the beginning. But last night's shock was still fresh.

"What in hell . . ." Waspe then replied with righteous indignation. "You know it's forbidden. Send her back before you cause us both trouble."

Though Mónoy could make little of this exchange, she intuitively sensed Richard hadn't told her the truth. *Why this secrecy? And why had so many of the other men gone into the forest?* She thought the English wanted to sail away, not sneak around at night.

Since no one challenged them, Waspe put an end to the show. He lifted a small chest that contained several crude maps and an astrolabe. He had, through a huge stroke of luck, gotten his hands on this precious instrument and a magnetic compass when a Portuguese trader ran aground off Normandy. He had taught himself how to use both by observing the various masters under whom he'd sailed. Without the astrolabe, they had no way of determining latitude.

The three briskly covered the few steps to the water where Waspe unlashed the ropes tying the boat to shore. Richard climbed aboard, signaling Mónoy to follow. But she stayed rooted to the ground, staring toward the galleon riding peacefully at anchor without a man in sight. He said they must sail tonight, *but what were they doing with this boat?*

Waspe had already pulled himself over the side before the vessel drifted too far. Richard waved to her, frantically. Without another thought she ignored her doubts and ran into the cold water. Richard grabbed her arm and hoisted her aboard. Then he took his place on the forward thwart as Waspe moved astern. Each man lifted a set of oars and they began to pull away, Waspe adjusting his movements to synchronize with Richard's. Mónoy huddled on top of a pile of cordage amidships, wrestling with the urge to confront her lover. To calm her nerves, she watched them handle the oars instead.

The four blades dipped into the water, pulled through, and rose in unison like the spindly legs of an exotic ocean creature crawling on the surface. The pinnace moved in complete silence, but for the squeaking of wood where the oars rubbed the tholepins, and the soft splashes of water spilling off the rising blades. They quickly lost sight of shore, except for the faint glow of several low fires still burning behind the mists. This was good, since it meant that no one could see them from land either. As long as Milles kept his mouth to the mug they owned the night.

The estuary into which they had sailed six weeks before covered the land like the imprint of a hand. Its main channels fanned like five fingers off the bay, the shape of which resembled the hand's palm. The General had careened the *Golden Hind* in the westernmost of these, the thumb, in water as placid as a pond's. The index finger pointed due north. Richard and Waspe had buried the gold near its tip.

Their boat just now turned into this narrow sliver of water, five hundred yards in length. The shore seemed dead, the fog absorbing all sound. When the hull finally touched bottom, Richard raised his oars, letting the bow ride up on the sandy beach. Waspe leapt into the water even before they stopped moving, holding two spades in his hands. Richard motioned Mónoy to wait.

Waspe found the spot immediately. He had excellent vision, especially at night. They quickly removed the thin cover of soil, exposing the dull wood of the barrels.

Richard turned up his nose. "This dirt smells foul, almost like rotten pork."

Both men looked at each other. Their breeches dripped seawater, and their sweat-soaked shirts stuck to their skin like wet rags from the exertion of rowing and digging.

"It's us. We're ranker than polecats," Waspe snickered. "It's been days since I washed."

Richard was disgusted with himself and ashamed at what Mónoy must think. The Indians bathed daily and took pride in keeping clean. He swore he'd scrub himself head to toe before getting back in the pinnace. "Let's get this done," he barked, using the spade's handle as a lever to position the first barrel.

He rolled it from its temporary grave all the way to the boat, Waspe following with a second cask. Mónoy only stared at them with a puzzled look. Richard avoided her eyes and turned back for the remaining casks. He stopped before pulling the third barrel out of the hole, burying his nose in his armpit. But the smell was not too bad, so he grabbed hold of his shirt and pressed it to his nose.

"Listen, I don't deny I could use a bath, but there's a stench about this place that's not us." Then it clicked. Richard turned to Waspe, who must have concluded the same.

"How could it be?" Waspe wondered. "He's covered with plenty of dirt, and it's much too soon."

"What does it matter? Let's take the gold and get away from here."

"Wait, we better have a look."

As they approached Smythe's grave, the offensive smell became intolerable, forcing them to cover their faces. Animals had scraped much of the sand off the mound, exhuming Smythe's corpse from the knees up. His own mother would not have recognized him. With most of his face gnawed off, a lonely eye condemned the murderers from its raw socket. Scattered shreds of flesh still hung from the cheeks and forehead, but the bare skull bone predominated. His chest

167

cavity was torn open, and a jumble of organs, tendons, sinews, and ribs poked through layers of flayed skin. The hip bone was stripped clean, his groin entirely removed. Rotting flesh, animal scents, and a skunk's pungent excretions caused the overpowering odors emanating from the carcass.

"What fiendish creature . . ." Richard coughed, feeling he'd have to vomit.

Waspe spat at Smythe's remains. "It's a deserved end. And we're damn lucky the scouts haven't passed this way."

Richard walked away. "I've seen enough."

They rolled the last two barrels to shore, and Mónoy helped lift them aboard. The men stored the four casks. Then Richard pulled off his shirt and breeches and dove into the sea. He rubbed down his body, worked his hair with savage ferocity, and washed out his clothes.

Waspe fiddled impatiently with his belt buckle. "It's stupid to do this now. What if Milles discovers the boat missing?" But when Richard ignored him he got in the water and started to splash his face and head. By the time they finally pushed the vessel farther out and climbed in, the mists had begun to lift.

A night breeze ripped apart the clouds, allowing the moon to wash land and water in its light. Already the mastheads of the *Golden Hind* pierced the top of the fog bank, which meant that a sharp pair of eyes ashore might see the pinnace. So they crossed to the far edge of the estuary, directly away from the camp. They hugged the shore until the ship's hull moved to their aft, then drew back a little toward the center, and finally aimed at the narrow gap that divided the estuary and the open sea one mile due south. Safety beckoned from beyond that bottleneck. This side of it, the General could still intercept them. Less than two hundred yards of water lay between the two points guarding the entrance to the estuary, and a group of strong swimmers sent from either point to stop them could cover that stretch in little time.

They rowed in silence. Fifteen hundred yards! Thirteen hundred! A thousand! The fog had dissolved to the point that the sailors' tents emerged from the dark. At nine hundred yards loud shouting shattered the silence. Someone discharged a musket.

*   *   *

When the sun's warm rays caressed Liam's face, he finally came to. He wiggled his feet and made fists, overjoyed that he still could, but a sharp jab in his head gave notice all was not well. He felt the right side of his face, raw from the temple to above the ear. *What had happened? Why the blood and dirt on his hands?*

He rolled over on his hip and sat up. The throbbing intensified, and he made a point of breathing slowly, filling his lungs to maximum capacity with the fresh morning air before expelling it. A horrible taste pervaded his mouth and he spat, even though his tongue and throat ached for lack of moisture. Liam tried orienting himself, and only now remembered the previous night. They had surprised a burglar. *Patrick! Where is he?*

He looked around and immediately saw the prostrate body near the hedge by the corner of the house. Belly up, its left arm stuck out, its legs stretched straight. The right hand still clenched the machete, stabbing the lawn at an oblique angle. With a sinking heart, Liam crawled there on all fours. A dark band discolored Patrick's shirt from chest to belt line. Liam started to tremble and with shaking fingers touched his brother's throat. "God!" he exclaimed. It felt warm! Patrick lived!

Liam gathered his strength and scrambled to his feet. In his present condition he couldn't possibly move Patrick. So he stumbled toward the front door, fishing for keys in his pocket.

The living room resembled a combat zone. Drawers were pulled out, his stuff dumped on the floor, chairs knocked over, and the shelves wiped clean. The place reeked of stale beer. When Liam got to the kitchen he finally understood. *The dagger! Of course! You idiot!* He grew weak again, his stomach churning, and slumped to the floor. The pounding in his head worsened. He dragged himself toward the wall, thinking Patrick's life depended on speedy medical attention. He reached for the phone, in a haze dialed what he hoped was 911, and gabbled something into the mouthpiece before collapsing.

* * *

"Row!" Richard yelled. "Row!" They leaned into the oars like chained galley slaves desperate to outrun an enemy ship that was poised to gore them below the waterline. Mónoy stayed on her stomach, her face lifted just enough to peek over the gunwale. The shore had exploded with activity. Sailors yelled in confusion, and the wild dance of flaming torches immersed the beach in an eerie light as men ran for their muskets. The voices of officers shouting orders rose above the commotion, and bits and pieces of their words drifted across the water. Eight hundred yards!

A second musket went off, followed by several more. Two of the leaden balls passed over the boat with an evil whiz. Five hundred yards! The two oarsmen strained to the breaking point, their muscles taut as rope.

"Almost," Waspe gasped. "They can't catch us. We're too far out." But he spoke too soon.

Two hundred yards shy of the estuary's mouth, Richard heard a muffled cough not far off the bow. He stood on the thwart and searched the water. Suddenly, he spied a half dozen heads on the surface, blocking their path. The men sent to stop them were making themselves as small as possible, keeping their entire bodies below the surface, and quietly treading water.

"They're there!" he screamed, pointing. "Fifteen yards ahead!"

Now Mónoy got up and furiously vented in her native tongue. Then she jumped to her feet and shoved a musket into Waspe's hands. Richard had never seen her like this. She awed him. When Waspe finally shook off his paralysis, she took his oars and started sculling.

"We have plenty of fire power, and I'm itching to use it," he shouted. For emphasis he fired, aiming a foot above the swimmers' heads. "Make way or die," he warned through the acrid smoke, as he reached for a second gun.

One of the men bent on retaking the boat roared. "It's the cooks. Waspe and Argyle, and the girl, too." That voice belonged to the instigator, Hogges, 'The Hound.'

Waspe greeted the outburst with a second discharge, this time pointing the muzzle at a point between the heads. The bullet smashed into the sea inches short of The Hound's chest, which made for a far more profound impression than the first shot. The would-be boarders now began thrashing the surface as though the devil gave chase. Frantically getting out of the way of the approaching boat, they scattered, and their arms lashed the surface like whips. Not one man looked back.

"Let her stay on the oars," Richard yelled over his shoulders. "There may be more of them waiting for us."

He and Mónoy swiftly propelled the craft over the last stretch of water separating them from the open sea. They cleared the passage without any further boarding attempts. Leaving the confines of the estuary behind them, Waspe threw down his musket and reached for the mast.

"The sail. Now!" he commanded.

Richard pulled up his oars, signaling Mónoy to continue. Then he helped Waspe step the mast and hoist the sail. It unfurled and caught the same northwesterly breeze that had shredded the clouds.

The wind pushed them steadily out into the bay. The three were irrevocably on their own now, one woman and two men sharing a tiny and heavily laden boat sailing into an immense ocean. The shores of Panama seemed as distant as the stars—and no easier to reach.

*   *   *

Spaniards decimated the tribes of southern California. Microbes annihilated whole villages, and the missionaries enslaved thousands. Gunpowder and settlers did the rest. Few Indians survived. Most of their ancient traditions swept away by the tempests of time, the remnants of the Chumash were eventually pushed onto a tiny sliver of land north of the Santa Ynez Mountains. With the deaths of the elders, even the stories that used to pass from parent to child through countless generations began to fade, except for one. This particular tale only persisted because of one man's fondness for it. He liked telling it to the Chumash children during tribal meetings. Keeping the oral tradition alive, he saw as his duty, his one heart-felt contribution to humanity.

Many seasons past, long before the white men marched from the south, but after the first of their great ships sailed into the Channel to visit and trade with the Chumash, two of these white men came ashore on one of the islands. They brought with them a woman from the north. No one saw how the three arrived, for they were put ashore by Sky Coyote, the Chumash name for the North Star. The two strangers differed from those who later came up the coast. They did not destroy the land, they did not covet the women, and they did not take what belonged to the people. The woman followed ways like those of the Chumash, though she did not speak their language.

They lived with the people, who welcomed them to stay, but after some time the white men began to quarrel. No one

172

knew the ultimate cause, but the Chumash thought it must have to do with the woman and the mysterious cargo they had brought with them. The men ended up killing each other on the day the earth shook. Their actions, the Chumash believed, had angered the spirits.

Kuyam never thought much about the legend, other then when he told it to the kids. Then, one day, Jeanine burst into his office, red-faced from excitement, telling of a guy waiting up front with an antique dagger in his hands—a dagger bejeweled with rubies and found on Santa Cruz. *Of course,* she knew an original from a fake. Why would Michael even ask her such a thing? The piece *was* unique, which the dim-wit out there had no clue of, she insisted.

An ancient dagger! Adorned with rubies! From the islands! It had overwhelmed Kuyam. The old legend. The two white men. Could it really be true? The elders always maintained that the stories represented more than just fables. If so, then the two whites must have deserted their Spanish masters, for which only one explanation made sense. The mysterious cargo! Gold! They died in a fight, right?

Unfortunately, Kindayr had left the shop by the time Kuyam hurried from his office. Fortunately, he had managed to rush outside in time to get the license plate number before the Jeep sped off. Now he almost regretted it, but he couldn't change the past. He couldn't undo the shooting. Damned, if he had just taken the old tale seriously. It had never crossed his mind that the story could be true. He might even have found the gold a long time ago, before shooting a man in cold blood.

Heavy, frayed curtains blocked out the sunlight in the sparsely furnished room, its wallpaper grimy from age. A dark painting that depicted a roiling sea on a drizzly winter day hung crooked by the window. The brown carpet did nothing to alleviate the bleak sense of gloom pervading the apartment. A knocked-over glass lay near the edge of a

173

cracked coffee table. A chair, with loose stitching and armrests coated with sweat and body oil, hovered in the corner. Slouched in this chair, Kuyam pondered his situation, lifting a half empty bottle of Bourbon to his mouth.

Not that he shunned violence. As a teenager he had rarely passed a week without a fight during his three years in South Los Angeles. His father worked in construction and helped raise two skyscrapers, while Michael and his brother joined a local gang. A few times he had used his switchblade, but never unprovoked. The most serious wound he'd ever inflicted consisted of stabbing a big-mouthed pimp deep in the buttocks.

Kuyam didn't finish high school and, after the death of an uncle, returned to Santa Barbara to save the run-down family shop on Anapamu. A fresh coat of paint, an ad in the Yellow Pages, and *Michael's Treasures* began turning a profit. He lived a comfortable yet boring life. Until last week. Everything had changed since Kindayr appeared on the scene.

He took another long draft of whiskey, cursing his use of the gun. Then he got up and spread out the map of the islands.

* * *

The steady northwesterly blew unabated, pushing the boat through the night. Except for Richard's rhythmic breaths, silence reigned aboard. The tension of the murder, the fear of being exposed, the intense preparations for escaping had all taken their toll. John battled to keep his eyes open.

With terribly drooping eyes, he watched Richard sleep like a corpse, stretched out with his head at Mónoy's feet. She gazed into the night, her face one huge question. John contemplated striking up a conversation but hesitated. He could count on his fingers how many words of her language he knew, and even those few he couldn't pronounce properly.

Now, for the first time, this annoyed him. Not that he lacked a gift for languages. *Hell, I can switch from English to Spanish and back without giving it a thought, and if I give it a month I'll pass for a Portuguese.* But the speech patterns of the savages, that strange intonation, mystified him. Besides, his dislike of them preempted any efforts he might have made to learn.

However, out at sea, things had changed. Mónoy was quite impressive. She hadn't let the gunfire intimidate her and rowed steady as a man. She didn't seem to need much sleep either. Sitting so erect by Richard, she reminded John of the proud women of Iberia and Italy with their shiny black hair and olive skin. He'd had his fair share of them after running away from his violent mother and drifting around the Mediterranean. For the first time John envied Richard. Lucky bastard, that fellow. But, lucky or not, he'd slept enough.

John clambered toward the bow and shook him. He got no response and shook harder. Richard, still only half-conscious, smacked hard at his hand. This irritated John a great deal. He knelt, unintentionally brushing Mónoy's leg with his arm. Her warm skin felt so smooth, he shivered. Suddenly seething with temptation, he had to remind himself that they weren't alone. Slapping Richard's cheeks helped let off steam. Aha, this worked. The first rap stopped the breath, and the second made him sit up, a startled look on his face.

"Come to," John pressed. "You've had plenty of rest. I can't sail her forever." He smiled at Mónoy.

"Show me sail. I do," she surprised him.

He didn't know whether to laugh or get mad. "You can't," he finally said and started making a bed for himself.

Richard laid a hand on his shoulder. "Why not? We both could use the extra help."

John shoved away the hand, his eyes glowing like coals. "I am in command, remember?" The expression on his face did not bode well.

175

~15~

The wind stayed steady the next day and night and into the second morning, still blowing from the northwest. The men, trying to ignore each other, for the most part kept quiet or took turns sleeping. Mónoy rested at night, but only when Richard slept. During the day she also kept silent, keenly observing the sea and how the boat rode it.

During the previous night they had followed the coast in a south, southeasterly direction. Now, just before sunrise, Richard saw that the land had bent to the east, which an increasingly thick fog had obscured. He needed to turn to port and get much closer to shore, for in such a small craft they had to avoid the high swell of the open sea. Moreover, their voyage would end abruptly, should a Spaniard chance upon them so far out.

He warned Mónoy. "Watch! We're going to port." He motioned her to stay low before performing the simple maneuver. The bow turned left as the boom swung right, gliding over her head. Their new bearing led due east. She could sail the boat herself, he thought, as long as the wind remained steady and the sea calm. Waspe resisted it, but he'd come around. Richard would make sure.

First light forced the night to flee seaward while the sun's flat disk ascended over the rugged coast. Oranges and yellows and pale pinks streamed from the sky, dabbing steep and forested mountains that ringed the shore. Several leagues ahead, the land curved south and then back west. The new day thus revealed a bay shaped like a half-circle, its tips separated by seven or eight leagues of water.

Richard pointed the bow at the bay's central coast, much lower in elevation than its sides and blessed with long, cream-colored beaches. A broad and tranquil river cut through grass-tufted dunes that extended along much of the shore. Richard drank in the sights and scents of the wild land and wondered about the future. One day fishing villages might sprout on this bay, with people making a living off the riches the cold waters harbored.

He studied Mónoy, who was so withdrawn and must feel terribly disappointed and bewildered. She had expected to sail on the *Golden Hind*, not to make off like mean thieves in this glorified raft. Thank heavens she'd not complained or asked to go back. He knew she loved him. She'd come through.

After Richard had sailed for five hours, he climbed over equipment to where Waspe snored peacefully and reached out to tap him on the ankle. Then he remembered the first night's rude awakening. Why not finally even the score? Waspe got a firm kick to the shins.

He jerked up as if stung by a bee, staring with a blank expression. "How are we doing?" He caressed his leg and ogled his companions suspiciously.

Richard motioned at the ocean, white caps dotting its surface. "Look for yourself."

"How far have we come?" Waspe rubbed his arms and reached for a water pouch.

"I reckon we've logged thirty leagues since the estuary. We're safe."

"Yes, yes. I know that. The canoes of the savages aren't seaworthy anyhow. But we mustn't cross paths with a Spaniard."

"I doubt we will. They probably won't patrol this far north. For all the Spaniards can tell, we disappeared into the Pacific weeks ago. Or they expect us to navigate the southern tip of the Main. Either way, it doesn't matter." He paused. "Listen, I see no signs of Indians. No smoke, no huts, nothing. I say we land and reload the pinnace."

Waspe shook his head. "Those dogs are probably watching us right now. And I don't suppose they'll give us the same welcome her people have." He looked Mónoy over. "Besides, I don't like this place. The forest in all likelihood swarms with savages. We shall wait for terrain where we can defend ourselves."

"How can we ever replenish provisions if you're so worried?"

Instead of answering, Waspe stared at two casks stored by the mast. "How many of the large barrels did we bring?"

Richard swallowed his rising wrath. He hated when Waspe didn't listen. "Three. Those two have water, and there's the smaller one with rum under the tarpaulin."

"Those casks by the mast," Waspe said haltingly, "they don't hold any water. They're filled with Spanish wine."

It jolted Richard. "They can't. You're wrong." Yet in the same breath he realized their mistake. The water casks had a smoother and darker wood, unlike these two. "Why didn't you see this?"

"I don't know. I had other concerns." Waspe cursed ferociously and kicked the gunwale with abandon. "Damned! What fools we are! But we have no choice. As much as I hate to dump the wine, we do need water."

They looked quietly at each other. Landing, no matter how necessary, could easily get them surrounded and slaughtered. Now they were forced to risk it.

*   *   *

Sheriff Trevor Quint, running the investigation, found Kindayr a disconcerting subject. So he would have him repeat his story a third time, even if the hospital staff disapproved.

So far he learned that the Kindayrs had arrived home late. They'd seen a light in the house and split up to trap the thieves. Liam had gone around the back and next found himself the following morning, lying in the grass with his skull pounding like a jackhammer. He then discovered Patrick, the chaos inside, and called for help. Quint detected no discrepancies in the story, but he sensed he didn't get the whole scoop. He tried again, this time watching the body language.

"But what did they want? You must own *something* of considerable value."

Aha! He'd hit it. Kindayr suddenly looked unsure and scratched the back of his hand—clear signs of nervousness. "No, I don't even keep a hundred bucks in my desk. There's a TV and a stereo, nothing fancy. Unfinished canvases. That mostly sums it up."

"Tell me about your work," Quint probed. "Are you known in the art world? For example, how much do people pay for your paintings?"

Kindayr smirked. "Once I made $7,000 on a mural, a large one. But that took over a month of very intense work. Most pieces fetch much less, the canvases one or two grand." He hesitated, scratching his knees. "Regardless, the stuff remains worthless until completion. I work on commission. Finished projects go to the buyer the day after they're done, if possible, and nothing in the studio is even near that stage."

Quint processed this, searching for an angle. "Why would anyone go as far as dumping kitchen drawers, unless they were looking for something much smaller than a canvas?"

Kindayr threw up his hands. "That's what you're here for to find out, right? Obviously they wanted cash, expensive jewelry, electronics, I don't know. It's an upbeat neighborhood. The bastards simply picked the wrong place."

Quint massaged his broad forehead, striving to imitate a befuddled man. Then he tried to nail him to the wall. "It just doesn't make sense, a random entry into the guesthouse. If I wanted to hit your part of town I'd go for the heart. The robbers left the main residence untouched. Moreover, not counting your own head injury, we've got a man in critical condition." He fixed his gaze squarely on Kindayr.

"Look, I don't get why you're so surprised about the damn shooting," he replied defensively. "If *you* broke into a house, you'd bring a gun, wouldn't you? I sure as hell would. There's plenty of homeowners who maintain full-fledged arsenals. One friend of mine owns at least a dozen rifles and pistols. Only an idiot wouldn't carry a gun to a robbery. Patrick ran into the guy, maybe even cornered him. And he pulled the trigger. Seems logical to me."

Quint nodded pensively and yawned. "What keeps bothering me is that you didn't have anything worth going to such extremes for. Your brother almost died. They wrecked your place, but ignored the main house. Doesn't that strike you as odd? I haven't seen such a thing in all my years on the force."

Kindayr tried to brush this off with a wave of his hand, but he looked away. "You're the expert. I've told you all I know. And my headache isn't getting any better."

"Alright." Quint slapped his hands on his thighs and got up. "I've taken enough of your time. You need to rest. Perhaps you'll think of something else in a day or two." He left the room.

I'm going to trip up that fellow, he thought. *One thing I hate is people taking me for a fool.*

*   *   *

"Fresh water!" Richard hollered. "Finally! Let's risk it."

A forbidding mountain range towered over the coast, its peaks dotting an ice-blue sky like a string of bejeweled crowns. The ocean's deep turquoise rivaled the vibrant hues more commonly found in the southern seas. A stream had cut the sole indentation in the coastline, completing what had to be a wild tumble down those slopes by splitting the short beach in two.

There was no telling the distance to the next river, and judging by the formidable landscape, this area didn't support many people. If they did make contact with a small band looking for a fight, they would have to subdue them with their firepower.

"Aye, we will land," Waspe agreed, scanning the gap in the range through squinted eyes. "If any of the dirty savages mean war, we'll greet them appropriately."

Richard looked at Mónoy. She sat stoically in the bow, ignoring them. Waspe's comments were beginning to have the effect of a sharp-beaked bird pecking at his skin. Before the *Golden Hind* sailed into the estuary for repairs and provisions, he also had thought of the natives as little better than upright beasts, as had most of the sailors. But Mónoy's people excelled in kindness and generosity. They had brought game and greens, feathers and arrows, and shells and baskets. The unmarried women had shown little restraint with the Englishmen, and no bad blood had come of it. The Indians took pride in honesty and led cheerful lives. There had been no fights, no theft, and no word spoken in ill temper.

"Have you already forgotten the last weeks?" he demanded of Waspe. "You have much to be grateful for. The Indians gave us mountains of meat and presents. What the Spaniards will do to us, should they catch us with their gold, and what you did to Smythe, *that* is savage. Mónoy's people treated us like their own, which I have not experienced since leaving my family. So where does this unwarranted hate come from?"

Waspe rolled his eyes as if this bored him, though he couldn't hide his shame when he stole a glance at her. But he said nothing and made no attempt at an apology. Instead he reached for his musket and studied it like some rare treasure.

Richard ignored it—for now. They'd have to settle this eventually. In no way would he listen to the cook's ravings for months on end. He pulled two muskets from beneath the pile of sailcloth that had served him as pillow.

The boat rapidly approached a shore sheltered from the open sea by a huge sea stack that had once formed part of the mainland. The oval base of the stack measured over a hundred yards in circumference. Its protruding granite ledges could cut into flotsam any hapless ship that dared come near them. The top of this massive monolith could easily support a manor house. A scattering of gnarled evergreens sunk their twisted roots into the granite's jagged crannies, which disfigured the rock's sides like the pox scar a man's face. Colonies of brown and black seabirds, whose droppings smeared the sheer walls in great drapes of white, occupied the larger of these nooks.

Though a mere forty yards lay between the sea stack and shore, the tight gap made for a perilous crossing. A heaving mass of water surged through this opening, swirling back and forth over submerged reefs and slamming into the base of the islet with a deafening thunder. To sail straight into the river's mouth would have required traversing the choppy passage. Instead, they aimed for the near side of the river, where the beach sloped toward a high berm. Timing it right, they might ride a wave up the beach face.

"You two jump when we touch bottom. Let's take her high," Waspe barked.

Richard explained the impending maneuver to Mónoy, using a combination of English, her language, and lots of arm and hand gestures. She understood and moved aft, since they needed to let the bow rise as high as possible. He joined her, taking his place on the starboard gunwale while she straddled the port side. Waspe waited a little longer. Then he foiled the sail and launched his oars, pulling the blades through the hissing waters the same moment a broad wave lifted them shoreward. The hull scraped over sandy bottom.

"Now! Get off!" he shouted.

Mónoy and Richard dropped into the frigid sea. She seemed unaffected and quickly waded the short distance before the next breaker came roaring in. Richard caught his breath, his chest feeling as though caught in a vise. "Cold!" he shouted, raising his arms and shoulders as high as possible to keep them above water.

Waspe jumped onto the beach. All three pooled their strength to pull the boat farther up, but it already rested securely on the sand. Waspe quickly climbed back in, reaching for the muskets. He handed one to Richard, placed two within easy reach by the thwart, and sprang back down toting the fourth.

"Let's take a look before we get to work. She stays."

"Wait!" Richard protested. "Why should she? We can't leave her alone. She doesn't know how to fire these."

"They're loaded. All she has to do is aim the damn thing and pull the trigger. That'll make any savage run like a rabbit."

"We don't know this place. They could surprise her."

"It looks to me the only way to reach this beach is either the way we came, or out of that canyon." He pointed at the gap in the hills. "I haven't seen any canoes. So any stinking thief interested in the boat must first cross our path. I want someone watching, and it's best she does. I'd rather have you at my side. Besides," he sniggered, "I thought you trusted the savages."

Mónoy grabbed one of the muskets. "I do. It's good." Since her expression made clear she meant it, Richard resigned himself.

*   *   *

Patrick's steadily rising and falling chest boded well for his recovery. A healthy color had begun to conquer his previously ashen cheeks. In fact, he looked shockingly good in view of the events. No signs of the battle raging within, the cellular fight to outwit death, manifested on the exterior. But one could not ignore the needles stuck in his arms and the maze of tubes snaking beneath the blanket. A scary array of instruments hummed not far from his head. Liam had to remind himself that he wasn't watching a science fiction flick, that his helpless brother was no movie actor. The doctors seemed optimistic but stressed not to take anything for granted. A fifty-fifty chance. It all depended on Patrick's constitution and inner will.

Liam stared in silence. *Why did this happen?* Little more than a week ago he had anxiously awaited his brother's arrival after so many months apart. The trip to the Bay area, planned for almost as long, promised a lot of fun. Then he canceled the whole thing to go to that damned island. *And look at us now.* Both could have been killed. If Dad knew, he'd have a stroke. And all of this happened because of a stupid, rusty dagger. He half-wished he'd never found it, but that line of thought led nowhere. On the contrary, he needed to find out who shot Patrick.

*   *   *

With muskets pointing ahead, they were most likely the first whites ever to go into this lush land. They followed the stream around a right-angle bend in the cliff. The beach widened here, protected from the open sea by a kink and the towering sea stack. Richard looked back at Mónoy. She sat in the bow, a weapon resting on her knees, her long legs dangling over the side. When she waved he felt a lump in his throat. God! He hated leaving her like this. Waspe should have stayed behind instead of her. Richard repressed nagging doubts.

The shallow creek meandered through layers of well-sorted sand and emerged from the box canyon about two hundred yards from the shoreline. Finally leaving the beach, they stepped into the shade of a dense, vibrant canopy. With no trail, no indications at all of a human presence, the thick brush made an effective barrier to penetration.

Waspe stopped and took bearings. "I'm crossing to the other bank. Perhaps there's a path over there." He hobbled into the water and worked his way through the waist-deep current. Alighting on the opposite bank, he disappeared into the greenery, but he soon burst in the open. He pointed upstream.

"It's no better. Go on. I'll stay on this side."

They marched over roots and fallen branches, stomped through tangles of briars, and skirted countless boulders. Richard tried to keep Waspe in sight, which proved difficult, but he heard him cursing and crashing through the brush. Finally, the men broke free from the forest into a welcoming meadow richly speckled with ocher poppies. They kept moving, and soon Richard heard something at odds with the rest of the forest's sounds. Reminiscent of the wind caressing the tree crowns, it struck him as queer because there was no wind.

"You hear that?" he called across the stream.

Waspe shook his head. "Nothing out of the ordinary. There's lizards everywhere," he added in a low tone, "and plenty of birds hopping through the undergrowth. Let's stop at the end of the meadow. It's far enough. The water runs clear here, and I've seen no harmful debris at all."

Richard hadn't covered another five yards when a violent cracking made him jump straight up. Still airborne, with legs kicking as though he were running, he slid sideways toward the stream and closer to Waspe. For an instant he was surprised at this athletic feat, but then he forgot about it. Only one thought animated his mind. *Enemies!* Richard realized he trembled all over.

"John, get over here!" he cried. "The Indians are setting an ambush!"

Waspe, who'd gotten down on a knee, stared at a spot on Richard's side of the stream, thirty feet ahead and just before the meadow gave way to the tree line.

"Shut up!" he mouthed, then pointed. "Look over there, by that big bush? You see?"

Richard moved his head slowly, until the object came in full view. A dead buck, part of its antlers broken off close to the skull, glared from lifeless eyes. The strange shape of the body made Richard jumpy, and it took him only a few moments to figure out why. *The back!* The ugly curvature of the animal's back betrayed a broken spine. He looked around for a ledge, some high ground from which the deer might have fallen, but he saw no sign of any.

Suddenly a vicious, dreadful growl shattered the peace. Hundreds of birds fluttered in panic from their high perches, exploding into the blue sky in an ear-numbing cacophony.

"Where is it?" Waspe yelled.

Whatever beast had warned them off, the shouting human voice infuriated it. A deep, incessant roar that curdled Richard's blood and raised his hair issued from the woods. Primeval dread, the horror of having a raging carnivore tear him to shreds, paralyzed him.

"I can't see anything," he finally found his voice. "Let's get awa—!"

But before he could finish, a nearby cluster of bushes took on a frenzied life of its own. Overcoming his paralysis, he instinctively backed toward the stream. When his feet reached the sandy edge of the bank, it crumbled under his weight and he fell into shallow water. Lying on his back, he beheld something terrible. A brown bear the size of a young cow, its enormous paws endowed with finger-length claws, broke through the brush.

It was coming for him.

The bear's shaggy, mottled brown fur and the large hump behind the neck lent it a doubly aggressive appearance. Stout legs inexorably propelled the huge animal toward its victim. Hypnotized, Richard watched glistening lips draw back and reveal two rows of teeth that would momentarily finish him. Another growl pierced the air, and he had an acute sense of man's total inability to confront such power, except with firearms.

He finally got up and swung his musket, when the explosion of Waspe's weapon from the other side of the creek forever destroyed the valley's innocence. Richard felt the ball whiz by his cheek like a giant bee. The bear, hit in its great chest just below the throat, roared in blind rage.

The wound Waspe inflicted might have festered and caused an infection, in time even killed the beast. At that moment, though, it had little useful effect. To the contrary, the bear kept coming. An all-consuming fury now glowed in its eyes, an unbridled desire to rip apart this two-legged, miserable creature. The enraged grizzly had closed to within a few feet, where Richard could distinctly smell its musky dander. He backed deeper into the stream with his musket aimed at the animal. Already resigned to dying, he felt a strange peacefulness envelop his soul. He pulled the trigger.

The lead exited the barrel and entered the grizzly's gaping jaws on a rising trajectory. Richard saw the tongue explode in a mass of blood and tissue as the beast jerked its huge head upward, its menacing growls expiring in its throat. A lucky shot, the ball must have smashed into the brain. The bear's momentum continued to carry it forward, and it crashed into the water with an enormous splash. Richard threw himself to the side just in time to avoid the descending mountain of flesh pinning him flat to the creek bed and drowning him like a rat.

He heard a second splash. Waspe had jumped in and was wading across. In a moment Richard felt himself pulled up and dragged to the bank, his own legs failing to obey him. When they reached dry ground, he shook like a twig. Waspe eased him down.

In awed silence they stared at the dead grizzly. No such beasts roamed the English forests. Immense, it nearly dammed the narrow stream. Measuring from its hind legs to the head, the carcass sprawled over seven feet. The enormous torso protruded well above the surface, forcing the water around it.

Waspe cleared his throat and whistled. "What a shot! I'd given up hope."

Richard looked up, feeling light-headed. The trembling had subsided to irregular twitching. "Have you ever seen such a creature? It's got to weigh a thousand pounds."

Waspe shook his head. "Only in this forsaken land can such things thrive. I know of men who saw huge bears in the mountains of Spain and Italy, but what I've heard, they're not half the size of this demon."

Richard pointed at the deer carcass. "The beast must have crushed its back. Then we came along. No wonder it charged. It feared for its meal."

A sudden ruckus in the brush on the edge of the meadow made them whirl. "Another one!" Waspe screeched, frantically reaching for his musket.

Richard, his heart racing, dropped to his knees and pulled a powder flask and ball from his pouch. He grabbed his musket and rammed the charge down the barrel. "Hurry!" he yelled.

* * *

Sheriff Quint returned the morning of Kindayr's scheduled release. Barging into the room as though it were an annex to his office, he planted himself in a chair. Kindayr, who was flipping through a *Time*, tossed the magazine on the table, and it sailed off the edge.

"Morning to you, too. Please come in."

The Sheriff had no time for pleasantries. He'd come to try his best and trip up Kindayr. "Hope you're feelin' better now that you'll be out of here in a couple of hours. Three nights is enough, isn't it?" When Kindayr leaned far back, Quint suppressed a smile. He knew just how toxic the coffee and nicotine vapors spewing from his pre-breakfast mouth could get.

"I don't understand why they've kept me so long in the first place. I'm fine."

Quint acknowledged with a short nod and got down to business. "Mr. Kindayr, we've examined your place very carefully and haven't come up with anything. No fingerprints. No foreign fabric. No spent cartridges. And whoever drank your beer even took the precaution not to touch his mouth to the bottle. We are not dealing with fools."

"What about the yard? That's where they got Patrick."

"That's the good news. We found fresh footprints on the slope leading up to the road."

"And? Whose are they?"

"That's one of the reasons I'm back. We don't know yet. But perhaps we've got at least *something* tangible. A size thirteen shoe made those prints, which rules out most women. Not that I'm surprised. But if we do identify a suspect, this information obviously could prove of great value." He leaned forward a tad, like a man really striving to make sense of simple facts. Lending his voice an innocuous tone, he continued, closely watching Kindayr's expression.

"Since neither you nor your brother have such large feet, I need to know whether anyone has been clambering around your backyard in the last few days. For example, any professional landscapers, a recent party, neighbors dropping in?"

Kindayr shook his head. "No, the property owner pays a commercial crew for seasonal clean-ups, but the winter prep is long done. They won't be back for a while, probably not till March. I help out here and there myself, but I haven't been on that slope in a long time. In regard to parties, I don't throw any. No one should have been out there."

Quint pulled a pad from his pocket and pretended to jot down a few notes. "We have questioned your immediate neighbors."

"You've talked to my neighbors?"

"Mr. Kindayr, we've got two men assaulted, with one still in serious condition. Your home is a mess. In such cases it is common practice to interrogate potential witnesses."

"Ah. Well, were you successful?"

Quint turned his chair so it faced Kindayr directly. "We do have two witnesses. The lady living across the street with her two children noticed a van parked on the shoulder three different times. Saturday morning and late that afternoon, and again Sunday morning, the day they hit you. She thinks she might have seen it on Friday, too, but wasn't sure. When she saw the van Sunday, while walking her dogs, a man was in the driver's seat. He wore a dark cap pulled deep down his face and looked the other way. Unfortunately, she has nothing concrete on age, size, hair, eye color, or anything else. At least she's convinced it was a male."

Kindayr seemed fascinated. "Who was the other witness?"

"A man who lives farther up the hill remembers seeing the van several times, always parked in the same spot. He thought it was someone's friend visiting."

"Sure wasn't mine," Kindayr said.

"Well, it's clear the guy was familiarizing himself with your routine before making his move. From where he parked, he had an excellent view of the driveway and could tell when you were coming and going. He simply waited for the right moment."

"How about the license plate? Anybody get that?"

"The woman actually did. We've already checked on it. Our friend stole it off a Toyota Camry, registered in Thousand Oaks, two days before the break-in. He is very clever."

Quint decided to catch him off balance and applied his hardest stare. "Mr. Kindayr, do you really have no idea why anyone would want to rob you?"

Liam's mind raced. Should he tell the truth? After all, the police wanted to find the bastard who shot Patrick and ravaged his house, and he might require their protection. Though the guy had the dagger, he didn't know where it came from. Therefore, one thing was certain. He'd make another move. One more thing was certain. If he told Quint of the dagger, he might as well announce it on the news. The police would never keep quiet about such a thing. One of the cops, guaranteed, would spill the beans. Before long half the town would trample all over Santa Rosa, ushering in California's next gold rush.

Liam didn't like Quint's intense gaze. *The Sheriff doesn't trust me.* "Rob me? This is what I think," he said. "A lot of wealthy people live on Cheltenham Road, mostly families with kids. I live alone. No children roam my back yard. So if I were a burglar and targeted a particular neighborhood, I'd love to find someone like myself. As you said, from the road you overlook most of the property. All you gotta do is wait for the right moment and—bingo! You clean out."

"Again, what do you think he wanted?"

An unexpected knock on the door saved Liam, who jumped up, grateful for the distraction. He felt Quint's penetrating eyes drill into his back, hoping Nicole, his favorite nurse, had come to chat. "Come in," he said.

The door swung open before he reached it. The view stopped him dead in his tracks. It was not petite Nicole with the million-dollar smile and Barbie breasts. *Shit! This is bad timing!* He started weaving a plethora of explanations, hoping he wouldn't have to use any, and praying that Alex would just keep his mouth shut.

*   *   *

No second bear came, only a trim Indian woman running across the short stretch of meadow.

When Mónoy saw them ogle her like two scared dogs, she let out a huge sigh of relief. Upon hearing the shots, she'd abandoned the boat and ran like an antelope, her heart skipping beats in horror of what she might find. Then she saw the grizzly and understood. She put down her musket and embraced Richard for the first time since they'd left her village. Seeing him alive was all that mattered. She no longer cared that he'd made her believe they would sail with the big ship. They were still together. Hadn't he promised to take her to his home? She trusted him.

Waspe ruined the moment. "If any savages happened through this valley, they're likely long gone. The beast's growls and the shots will have scattered them."

Richard looked at him. "Curiosity is stronger than fear. Let's get the casks filled and sail as soon as possible."

They picked up their weapons and cast a final glance at the scene. The brown mass of the bear didn't move, except where the breeze tugged at the fur. The carcass had constricted the stream to its right side, where the current already began to carve clumps of soil out of the bank. Once the dead animal began to rot, it would poison the water.

They found their way through the brush and back toward the beach, with Mónoy leading. When they exited from the narrow confines of the canyon and left the thick vegetation behind, Waspe, who'd marched in the rear, overtook them running. "I don't like the boat left without a guard," he shouted over his shoulder.

"He strange man," she said. "I no like him much."

Richard looked at her, and she could tell he was worried. But he said nothing. When they rounded the nose of the cliff, they could see Waspe already climbing aboard.

"Come on, give me a hand with these," he hollered when they approached. He lifted one of the casks and passed it to Richard, who placed the heavy weight on the ground by carefully squatting and then getting down on his knees. The second cask followed.

Waspe grumbled, staring sullenly at the barrels. "Sure amounts to an awful sin to dump this wine. I never thought I'd do such a crazy thing." He swore. "Go ahead. Do it."

Richard drained the first of the casks, and they all watched the red wine collect into a small puddle. The porous sand absorbed this rare treat within seconds. He emptied the second barrel. Again, the greedy ground sucked up every last drop until only a rich red stain remained.

"It's a pity. A terrible injustice." A dark cloud hovered over Waspe's face. "You two get the water, and I'll see to properly loading the boat." With that he turned away, attending to the mast.

Richard and Mónoy each took one cask and began rolling them across the smooth white sand. After some time Mónoy sensed that he was staring at her. When she looked back and saw his face flushed with excitement, she knew he had a pressing desire. Feeling hot surges coursing through her body, she pushed the empty barrel toward the headland with twice the effort. The moment she rounded it and reached a spot out of Waspe's sight, she abandoned the load and waited impatiently for him to catch up.

*   *   *

"Hello, I hope I'm not interrupting?" Malreaux asked, smiling congenially. On a more somber note he put a sympathetic hand on Liam's arm. "I apologize for not coming earlier. I've been extremely busy, working to meet a manuscript deadline. But tell me, how is Patrick doing? The whole affair is shocking, especially after having met him only so recently."

Liam bit his lips. *This won't go over well.*

"You know his brother?" shot the ever-watchful cop. Malreaux turned to the police officer, who rose to his feet and offered a hand. "Sheriff Quint. I'm investigating this case."

The professor shook his hand solemnly. "I am Alex Malreaux, and I certainly hope you will find those responsible. I'd hate to see this town turn into just another crime-ridden city." He ignored Quint's question, and Liam exhaled relief.

"We will do everything in our power."

Malreaux nodded. "The newspaper alluded to the possibility of more than one suspect. Do you know how many people were involved?"

"Initially, I believed two," Quint admitted. "But I no longer think that. One of them would have stayed in the van to keep an eye on the road, which would have let him warn anyone inside the house of Mr. Kindayr's return. The kind of thug we're dealing with probably worked alone."

"Yes, yes, I see." Malreaux said. "Well, I do hope you nail the guy."

"In due time," Quint replied with confidence. "You mentioned you just recently met Patrick Kindayr?"

Liam's mouth tasted acrid.

"Yes, I have," Malreaux started playing with a shirt button. "We met only days before the shooting."

Sweat started running down Liam's back. He felt dampness on his temples, too, and brushed back his hair to wipe it off as innocently as he could. *Damned! If Alex gives it up now, I'll kill him.*

"What occasioned this meeting?"

Malreaux looked at Liam and back at the officer. "Why these questions?" he asked with a crooked smile.

"Well, Mr. Malreaux," Quint uttered with a hint of irritation. "I am only trying to put together this puzzle. And whatever information I can gather to help me is vital."

"Of course. I'm sorry," Malreaux yielded, scratching his hand. "Well, I own a yacht, and Liam joined me and my wife for our last Channel cruise. He brought along Patrick. That is how we met."

"You and Mr. Kindayr are good friends then, I presume?"

Malreaux hesitated. "You could say so." It came out awkwardly. "Sheriff, you referred to this case as a puzzle. May I ask what is so puzzling about an armed entry into a home?"

Quint's eyes narrowed. He had the look of a lynx, ready to pounce. "An unidentified person fires his way through Mr. Kindayr's back door, then takes apart the house rather systematically. Later he smacks one man over the skull, sending him to the hospital. Before taking off he shoots another man, nearly killing him. Yet nothing is stolen. Add to all this that Mr. Kindayr apparently owns little worth taking, and I'm left without much of a motive. Lastly, based on all the evidence, the suspect is no common thief. I'm convinced he came for a reason."

Malreaux took this in pensively. "Hmm, I would agree with that. What do *you* think, Liam?" They looked at each other. A subtle exchange occurred, lasting but a nanosecond.

Liam turned up his hands. "The only explanation I have is that the guy chose my place because it seemed safe. It's a quiet property. The owners are out of town, and I live alone. It's easy enough to keep tabs on one person. The moment he sees me leave he knows the house is empty."

"You're probably right," Malreaux said. "That makes good sense. But what was he looking for? One of your paintings? And why did he ignore the main house? It's pretty odd, to say the least."

The professor's face beamed such genuine confusion Liam couldn't help but admire him. It also struck him like a hammer, for the first time in all these years, that Alex could deceive very convincingly.

"You know me. I don't collect stuff. There's little anyone would want. Like I said, the bastard targeted an expensive neighborhood but picked the wrong place. He pulled the trigger when Patrick cornered him, which doesn't surprise me. You've seen Patrick's physique, and he was wielding that machete."

They fell silent. After a moment Quint jumped to his feet. "I need to go. I'll keep you posted on any new development. If either of you should think of anything that might prove useful in our search for the suspect, please call me." He fished in his jacket. "Pleasure to have met you, Mr. Malreaux. You can reach me at either of those numbers." He handed him a card, nodded at Liam, and left the room.

The echoes of his steel-tacked soles faded down the hallway. They were alone for the first time since returning from the island, but Liam had bad vibes that Malreaux's game of deception required more victims than the sheriff.

*   *   *

Before Richard reached her, she dashed off toward the base of the cliff, hooked right, and bolted for the canyon. Mónoy savored the moment she'd let him overtake her. She was a very fast runner, putting to shame most men. Her friend, Weyala, had always said she could outrun the birds. It amazed her when Richard suddenly caught hold of her near the mouth of the canyon. He must have made a silent sprint, for she had just heard him at least ten paces behind her.

She let him pull her to the ground. The panic caused by the bear attack and the residual excitement of their escape

196

had transformed into a deep need for closeness. She tasted his lips and smelled his skin as he pushed her against a half-buried outcrop. With impatient fingers she undid the loop holding her deerskin skirt and reclined against the cool rock, shivering with anticipation. He stripped in an instant and flung himself across her.

Their skin soon glistened with perspiration. Without separating they tumbled over the beach, the fine white sand coating their wet bodies like intricate beadwork. She felt the rising wave, and when it washed over them she sank forward and collapsed on Richard's chest.

Relishing the warm currents tingling inside her, she suddenly sensed a foreign presence. She looked up, startled to see Waspe glaring at her, his eyes consuming her body. She got up and ran into the stream, feeling Waspe devour her all the way to the water. She immersed herself up to her neck.

"Leave us alone!" Richard thundered. He hadn't noticed Waspe until Mónoy disengaged so prematurely.

"We're not on *your* time, are we?" the cook barked.

"Stop staring like a mad dog! She isn't for sale."

"Ah! No, unfortunately not. She's all yours to take your damn pleasure whenever you itch. What a blessed lad you are." His voice was full of derision. "Now, do you think that you could fill those casks so we can leave? After all, it's why we came, isn't it? You were so anxious not to waste time." He cast another glance at Mónoy before he wheeled around and stomped back to the boat.

Richard had enough. They had formed a friendship soon after the *Golden Hind* left England. They had fought the Spaniards side by side. They had become accomplices in murder. They had betrayed the General. Today, though, Waspe had snapped a thread.

Mónoy finished bathing and dressed. She squatted at his feet. "Waspe no happy," she said. "I afraid with he."

He stared at her for a long moment, lost in random thoughts. "Hmm." Then he got into the stream to wash off. He put his clothes back on his wet skin and ushered Mónoy toward the casks. They filled them in a deep pool where the water ran crystal clear. Then they rolled the barrels back over the sand in the direction of the pinnace. When they rounded the headland Richard caught his breath. "God, no!" Like idiots, they had stumbled into a trap.

*　　*　　*

"Am I glad you didn't tell him," Liam said. "At one point I was sure you would."

Malreaux fell into a chair like a man relieved of a heavy burden. "I don't want the cops sniffing around the canyon any more than you do. It would mean the end of our little adventure." He got very serious. "Did they take it?"

Liam nodded dejectedly. "The bastard knew what he was looking for. It's the only thing missing."

Malreaux trained hard eyes on him. "We must get back out there and find exactly where the gold is coming from. Whoever is on to us is not afraid to go to extremes. You could have both been killed. In fact, I wonder why — "

Liam slapped his cheek. "Of course! How stupid I've been. What a total moron! I've been so dazed, it didn't even occur to me."

"What?" Malreaux sat up straight.

"The pawn shop! She acted oddly at the time, and I had completely forgotten about it." He shook his fist. "I've spent hours trying to figure out who could have known. When Quint told me his men discovered size thirteen footprints in the dirt, probably a male, it just didn't cross my mind. The only people who have seen the dagger are Patrick, you, that woman, and Debettencourt, the guy who ferried me to the island. But he's a friend, and the last man who'd do such a thing. Besides, he doesn't have large feet, which puts the spotlight on the shop. I remember she wanted to show her boss the dagger and went to the back of the store to get him."

"What's the name of the shop again?"

"*Treasure Master*, or some such silly thing." Liam threw back his head and clasped his temples, searching his memory. "No, *Michael's Treasures*. That's it! The place is down on Garden Street, I think. Or Anapamu. Tacky as hell. I didn't like it the second I entered. In retrospect, I should have followed my instincts."

Malreaux looked out the window, brooding. "Well, there isn't much we can do about those scoundrels. We certainly can't ask Quint for help. If we do, the word'll be out. But most importantly, you didn't tell that gal where you got the dagger, correct?"

Liam puckered his lips. "Unfortunately she knows about the islands. But she thinks it's Santa Cruz. The way she asked made me wary, and I lied just in time."

"Which means they need you."

"The owner of that crummy hole, it has got to be him. I've never seen the guy, but there's an easy way to find out."

"How?"

Liam smiled maliciously. "How many people have size thirteen?"

Eight Indians huddled by the base of the cliff, fifty yards from the boat. How they had gotten there, with no canoes in sight, Richard had no idea. Each man carried a bow and a quiver filled with arrows on his back. Even from this distance, he saw that all of them were of strong build, young, and trim. Hunters! Warriors!

The Indians made no attempts to move closer. Waspe sat behind the gunwale with one musket in his arms and the other three by his legs. The cook and he might kill three of the braves. Mónoy could fire one weapon but would miss her target. Of course, he couldn't let her waste a crucial shot. He'd discharge her musket in addition to his own. Still, that eliminated only four of the Indians, at best. In reality, they could not survive a determined and orchestrated rush.

Richard dwelled on no false hopes of beating back the braves. A child could see that those men made the forest their home and spent their lives stalking game all over this rugged terrain. They'd probably tracked that gigantic bear, and their endurance and strength probably matched that of the hunters he'd met among Mónoy's people. God help us! Not sure what to do, he peered at Waspe, who sat in stoic silence. *He doesn't want to provoke an attack by making a wrong gesture.* Mónoy finally put an end to the awkward standoff.

Accepting the presence of the Indians as the most normal thing, she stooped and resumed rolling her barrel toward the shore. Richard reacted without thinking and fell in step behind her, pushing his cask while whistling up a carefree tune. Pretending to ignore the eight men, he strained never to lose sight of them.

The distance to the boat shrunk fast, but the Indians made no threatening moves. The spectacle of the strangely-clad, pale man, and the woman moving these odd barrels over the ground, kept them spellbound. Ten yards short of the boat, Richard hailed Waspe through clenched teeth.

"They're all loaded?"

"Uh huh," Waspe muttered.

Mónoy and Richard reached the boat. Though he detected no sign of an impending charge, he heard two of the Indians begin an animated conversation. "Stay aboard and cover the port side. If they attack we might get lucky and dispatch four by the time they're upon us. We may stand a chance against the rest if we keep clear heads and God sides with us."

Waspe's face hardened. "Hell, I'm glad you're back. I already imagined myself cut to pieces. Now everything changes. We can put holes through 'em before they get half way across this beach. It'll teach those dirty dogs a lesson they'll not forget."

"Let's just get out of here and sail while we can."

"Is that so?" Waspe turned on him like a viper. "We would have been on our way long before those hideous toads crept from their hideouts." He threw up his hands. "Oh, I almost forgot. You had to get under Mónoy's deerskin before fetching the water. In case you didn't know, *I was* hustling to ready the pinnace."

Richard fumed, but realized Waspe had a point. "Let's get these aboard," he said, pointing at the barrels, and he squatted to lift the first one. Waspe put aside his weapon and grabbed hold of the heavy load. Mónoy stepped in to help Richard balance it. Then, with the second cask safely in the boat, she pulled herself over the gunwale and helped store the water amidships while Richard focused his attention on the visitors. The moment had come for the real test. Would the Indians stand by idly as they pushed the boat back into the sea?

"I'm thirsting to put those savages out of their misery," Waspe volunteered.

An icy fury swept through Richard like a North wind. He wanted to clasp Waspe's neck and snap it. "They haven't done a damn thing. You'll end up getting us all killed. Now get down here and help."

Waspe hesitated but then unwillingly shoved his musket into Mónoy's hands and jumped on the beach. The two men anchored their feet deep in the sand and leaned into the bow. The hull resisted at first, until it suddenly dislodged and slid into the sea. Waspe quickly grabbed the gunwale and pulled himself up. Richard, still running along, felt his left knee give when his foot banged into a rock. The eruption of loud shouting in his rear startled him just as he regained his footing, and he turned his head reflexively. The Indians were growing restive, their harsh gestures leaving no doubt about their intentions.

"Richard!" Her shout brought him back to the task at hand as he saw the boat drifting farther out. He waded into deeper water and dove through a curling breaker to avoid getting shoved back to shore. The frigid sea sharpened his senses, and he bolted for the gunwale. Then the unthinkable happened. His hand slipped off the smooth wood, sole link to the world he knew and the safety line that separated him from those eight men. That instant his heart and soul hit bottom.

"Here!" Waspe yelled, dangling an oar in front of Richard's nose. "Take hold!" But he had to duck to stay clear of a huge breaker smacking the oar into his face. Down he went, into the cold, gurgling foam of a wall of water.

*   *   *

At five thirty in the afternoon, the heavy brass street lamps began to cast their cozy light on white adobe houses framed with dark timbers. Three teenagers with shaved heads and baggy jeans precariously balanced on their butt cheeks sauntered along Anapamu Street. As they approached their target, the skinniest of the trio, a beanpole of a boy hardly five feet tall, imbued his gait with real purpose and crossed the street. He surveyed the handful of pedestrians, all too far off to interfere with what was about to happen. A few cars sped by, even a Testa Rossa, which turned the boy's head in total admiration. But the drivers paid no attention. The beams of their headlights barely grazed the sidewalk.

The kid pulled two five-pound bags of flour from inside his jacket, and a straight-edge razor from a back pouch. The blade cut the paper like butter. With one last glance at his surroundings, he sprinkled the fine powder on the pavement at the store's entrance, his arms swinging like the pendulum of a cuckoos' clock. When he finished, the front entrance resembled a patch of fresh snow. The boy crumpled the empty bags and flung them into the street. It was the sign his companions had been waiting for. A bombardment of the windows commenced. Fragile paper sacks filled with more flour pelted the glass, bursting on impact and leaving puffy white blobs.

The good-for-nothings delighted in their little prank, squealing and hooting with wild joy, while the skinny one moved to a spot that allowed him to monitor the inside. A woman came into view, peeking out the windows from a safe distance. The next instant a big man swooped past her. Skinny put his nimble legs in motion and bolted down the sidewalk faster than a champion greyhound.

Kuyam sprang into the street like some diabolic apparition, his black eyes spewing flames. He started after his prey just as a bag of flour hit him full in the ribs. He stopped in mid-stride, trying to locate the new quarry. But the two bigger boys, sprinting after their brother-in-arms, already melted into a dark alley. Kuyam gave chase, almost knocking down an old man with long silvery hair and thick glasses shaded by a broad-rimmed hat.

"My gosh, what is this all about?" the man demanded with a raspy voice. "What's with these kids?"

203

"They're animals!" Kuyam shouted without slowing.

The old man looked at Kuyam for a moment before he resumed his slow shuffle, shaking his head in dismay. When he reached the front of *Michael's Treasures*, he looked through the windows. A woman he immediately recognized was on the phone. She seemed agitated. *Probably calling the cops.* He scanned the street. The store's owner too had disappeared down the alley.

The old man suddenly held a measuring tape and bent low with a dexterity that stood in stark contrast to his previous stiff movements. He chose the closest of the footprints in the flour and read the numbers off his tape twice to make sure he hadn't made a mistake. Then he bounced back up and strode away with a newfound vigor, his feet no longer dragging. He crossed the street and dove into the passenger's side of a rented Ford. The idling automobile sped off before the door shut.

"Clockwork," Malreaux observed with cold satisfaction. "I'm beginning to like this." He turned. "So?"

Liam smiled. "They're thirteens. He's got to be the one."

Malreaux made a sharp right. "I'm impressed. Such a primitive plan." He shook his head. "My compliments." He turned left and coasted into an abandoned lot where thick weeds pried apart what remained of the pavement. The Ford's headlights skimmed a skinny silhouette, which strutted up to the car with the exaggerated self-confidence of a never-been-caught teenage crook.

Liam pulled the hat deeper over his face. Malreaux adjusted his baseball cap and turned the other way. "Where are your friends?" Liam asked.

Skinny checked the dark around them as though he had a hidden audience of awed fans, bopping his head in a cocky way. "Yeah, they be here."

Liam gave him a double nod, like an understanding conspirator. "You did well." He waved a hundred dollars in twenties. "We're in a hurry. Don't forget to share."

The kid grinned. "Don't worry." He finally got the bopping under control. "Mister, you need us again, come look me up. You know where I hang."

"You bet." Liam hit the window's power button as Malreaux accelerated.

They stopped at the deserted lot of a city park a couple of blocks away. Malreaux slipped on a pair of rubber gloves and exchanged the license plate for the proper one. He wrapped the other in a plastic bag and threw it into a dumpster. The Ford melted into the city.

* * *

Richard shot to the surface, a thick strand of seaweed plastered to his face. Waspe screamed at the top of his lungs.

"Get on! They're attacking!"

Then Richard heard the Indians shout. Something hard hit him in the chest. *The oar!* Half-blinded by the seaweed, he clenched it with all his strength. The hull rose right in front of him. He flung up an arm, which Waspe grabbed with an iron grip. With a painful tug he felt himself raked over the gunwale. He had no time to catch his breath. Mónoy pressed a musket into his hands just as the report of Waspe's gun stifled the Indians' war cries.

"Ha!" he yelled. "Take that!"

He must have scored a hit. Richard couldn't see a thing because he still had his back toward the Indians. Mónoy handed Waspe another musket, an arrow whooshing by only inches from her neck. That got Richard's attention. He scrambled to his knees and swung his musket around like a sword. He took aim, but hesitated.

Waspe's bullet had found its mark. One of the Indians squirmed on the sand, a crimson hand pressed to his side. His motions were slowing as death made its claim. The other Indians seemed rooted to the ground, paralyzed by the thunderous boom that had magically made their comrade collapse like a sack.

A second shot shattered the air, and the Indian closest to the boat dropped with his face bathed in blood. He must have been dead before his body hit the ground, for he never stirred. Waspe had razed the skull from the forehead up.

A horrid howl arose from the shore and chilled Richard to his core. Goose bumps prickled his entire body. The furious Indians screamed like madmen and pounded the ground with their bare soles. Several shook their arms in blind rage. Their fierce display made Richard shiver. This day could end only in one of two possible ways. *Either we get away, or our hacked-up bodies will litter this beach.*

An arrow zinged past his face, burrowing into something with a dull thud. He turned. The still quivering projectile protruded from the mast two feet behind his head. He finally brought up his musket and fired at an Indian about to let loose another arrow. Waspe discharged a third musket. Richard's bullet snapped the enemy's bow in half and hit him in the stomach. The man slumped to the ground. Waspe had downed a fourth attacker, who wiggled in the dirt like a mangled snake. Richard couldn't see where he had been hit.

"Reload!" Waspe shouted, pointing at the sea stack. "I must hoist the sail."

Swirling eddies drove them rapidly toward the sea stack's sharp edges. If they rammed them, they'd be lucky if the rocks broke their bodies. It would make for an easier end than if those Indians got hold of them. Waspe worked like a possessed man. When the steady breeze finally inflated the fluttering canvas, he raced astern to take the tiller from Mónoy. The bow turned just in time, and they sailed clear of the submerged reef into deep water.

Three more arrows streaked through the air before Richard could reload. One plunged into the sea to starboard.

Another passed well overhead. The third, however, found its way into Waspe's thigh. He grunted with pain and slid off the thwart. Richard immediately threw down his musket and hurried to his side.

"I'll steer her," he shouted, pushing him away. "Stay down. We're almost out of range."

*   *   *

Kuyam bounded down the alley like a tiger. He could see them climbing a fence at the end of the narrow way. It took him seven seconds to reach the chain link barrier and pull himself to the top. He dropped to the other side and crouched, his eyes straining to penetrate the long shadows of an empty parking lot open to three sides. The boys were nowhere to be seen.

"Don't let me catch you, or I'll beat you to pulp," he growled with such menace, had the kids heard him, they would have pissed their pants. For lack of a body he drove his boot into a flowering bush so hard, it broke in two. Then he crossed back to the other side of the fence. Arriving at the shop, he surveyed the mess on the sidewalk. What was the meaning of this?

The door opened and pale-faced Jeanine stepped out. "This is disgusting! Outrageous! I called the police."

"What do you think the fucking cops are gonna do? It's too late. Those little punks are long gone." He ran a hand over the soiled windows. "But I tell you one thing. They better pray I never cross their path, cause I'll kick the shit out of their little asses."

"Oh, you know what?" she burst out with a sense of importance. "Just after you took off, a man walked up and squatted right where you're standing. At first I thought he dropped something, but he stayed down an awful long time. I couldn't see what he was doing."

Kuyam knitted his brows. "Old? Gray hair?"

"Yeah, I think so." She nodded zealously. "He wore a hat and glasses."

"What did he do next?"

"He crossed the street real fast and got into a car. It left right away. Someone else was driving."

Kuyam looked at the passing traffic. "You didn't see the driver?"

Jeanine shook her head. "It was too dark." She hesitated. "Why, is something wrong?"

He turned abruptly, a crooked grin contorting his thin lips. "No, nothing to worry about. It seems some old buddies played a little joke on me. And I think I know exactly who." He scraped his feet over the sidewalk. "Why don't you get a broom?"

As she went back in he worked his fingers through the flour. Perhaps the guy *had* dropped something, and it just took him a while to get up? He did look pretty old. He could have been shopping while his wife waited in the car. But then how come he left in such a hurry?

Kuyam studied the pavement that was covered with flour and a bunch of footprints. His stuck out from the other much smaller ones. It made him smile, but not for long. By the time Jeanine returned and began sweeping, he had regained his composure and forced a grin.

"Was it a Jeep?" he asked casually.

*   *   *

A few more arrows rose from the beach, but all fell short and splashed into the water. The Indians had shrunk in size to small figurines and shook their arms impotently. Richard took the boat to the open sea, reckoned they were already making seven knots, and hoped the Indians wouldn't give chase in canoes to avenge the deaths of their brothers. He signaled Mónoy to take the tiller and helped Waspe amidships.

"Did it hit the bone?" he asked, hunkering down next to him.

"I don't think so," he moaned, making a weak effort at turning his leg to allow for a better look.

Richard examined the wound. The arrow had entered the inner thigh, sliced through thick muscle, and punched through the back. The head and two inches of shaft protruded from the ruptured flesh. Both holes oozed blood.

"Looks uglier than it is. The shaft went through intact, no splintering. It didn't touch the bone, it seems. We'll have you patched up in no time, but it has got to come out immediately."

Waspe scowled. "If you'd fired more than once, this wouldn't have happened," he accused.

"Was I supposed to know which one of them had you in his sights? It's not my fault they hit you," Richard defended himself.

Waspe shook his head in disgust. "Just get the damn thing out before I bleed to death."

Richard turned to look at Mónoy. She smiled encouragingly, keeping firm hold of the rudder. *Thank God I'm not alone with him.*

"Raise your leg so it's supported on the thwart. Then turn till the shaft lies flat against it. It'll give me the angle I need. I'll hack off the head and pull the rest out."

"Alright, alright, I'm not an idiot," Waspe snarled as he pushed himself backwards and positioned the wounded leg as directed. "Just get it over with."

Richard cut the breeches below the groin and reached for a hatchet. He made sure the arrow's shaft pressed firmly against the wood. One swift blow would sever the tip. "Are you ready?"

Waspe closed his eyes, his hair wet with perspiration. With clenched jaws he gave a nod. Richard had no room for error. An unsteady hand could drive the blade into the leg, with disastrous results.

"It won't be bad." Richard lifted the hatchet, taking deliberate aim. He watched the sweat streaming down Waspe's face, dripping on the collar of his shirt. The cook made tight fists and held his breath. *Now!* The blade came down and bit its way through the shaft, digging into the thwart two fingers' width shy of the thigh. The arrowhead flew off sideways. Waspe, who had permitted himself only a subdued grunt, maintained his composure. The dangerous portion of the extraction was over, but not the painful one.

Richard tugged gently on the arrow. It made a sucking sound like a stick stuck in mud. "Bite down on your teeth!" He closed his fingers around the broken shaft and, with one quick motion, drew it from its fleshy nest.

Waspe's head jerked up. He exploded in vicious curses and punched the gunwale before getting hold of himself. "Stop the bleeding!" he ordered.

Richard's patience approached exhaustion. He only nodded, reaching for a piece of canvas. He cut a long strip and worked it around the leg above the wound. The blood flow slowed to a trickle of red as he tied the fabric into a knot. "We haven't anything to clean it."

"Richard!" Mónoy pointed at herself, then the bloody leg, and motioned him to take the tiller. Then she moved toward the bow, where she kept her meager possessions. She retrieved a small leather pouch and then grabbed one of the copper cooking pots. She leaned overboard to dip it into the sea and placed the full container on the thwart by Waspe's leg. She cut several more strips of canvas and submerged one of these in the pot. After wringing it out, she began cleaning the leg with small circular strokes.

When Waspe squirmed at the first touch, she readied herself for another outburst. *He behaves like an old woman.* To her surprise, he stayed quiet, sitting rigid throughout most of the procedure. She rinsed the blood-soaked canvas three times before the healthy part of the leg was clean. Then she dumped the soiled water into the sea and refilled the pot. The wounds came next.

The instant the salty liquid made contact with the raw flesh, Waspe contorted his face but said nothing. Mónoy held the leg firm with one arm and focused on the small entry hole. The combination of salt and pressure, however, proved too much. He cursed loudly.

After washing out the exit wound in the same fashion, the leg looked almost normal again. Two holes, the smaller surrounded with a ring of purple caused by the high velocity impact, were the only telltale signs of the fight. They still bled. She exchanged the dirty water in the pot with fresh water from one of the casks. Then she untied her pouch and pulled a small leather bag from it. She fished out several slender, dry leaves.

"What are these?" Waspe demanded, his eyes suspicious. Ignoring him, she crushed the leaves in her fist and ground them into tiny fragments. Her skin turned greenish-blue. She submerged her hand in the pot, mixing the crushed leaves with the water.

Mónoy let this concoction steep for some time and periodically stirred it. At last she put two clean strips of canvas in the pot. The fabric turned blue. Satisfied, she wrung it out and placed the cloth on the bleeding holes.

"Ah, this feels good," Waspe admitted. "It's numbing the pain." After a few minutes, Mónoy lifted the canvas to check the wounds.

"Look!" Waspe exclaimed. "The bleeding stopped."

Richard looked at her proudly as she secured the patches with long strips. "Get some rest now," he called. "We need that leg well as soon as possible. The Indians may try to catch us."

~18~

Northwest winds sweeping across the vast Pacific, with no large landmass breaking the flow, had driven the craft and its crew southeastward along the coastline. Fifty leagues lay between them and the beach that had almost become a death trap. The Indians had not followed. Perhaps they could not. Waspe said little in these hours, indifferent to everything but the arrow wound. Fortunately, his leg showed no sign of infection, and with a bit of luck and Mónoy's care, the flesh might soon heal.

They had agreed not to stray farther than a mile from shore, magnificent in its untamed beauty. Sailing north, the *Golden Hind* had shunned this lee coast, and Richard never imagined how spectacular the land was. Steep mountains towered five or six thousand feet above the ocean, their slopes cloaked in dense forests. The uninterrupted succession of jagged peaks did have a serious drawback, though. There wasn't a single cove affording real protection from the fury of the open sea.

By late afternoon they entered into a light fog, which thickened over the next hour. Though the vapors had not yet condensed to where they permanently veiled the shore, they had a way of obscuring large swaths of it from one moment to the next. The fog also put a damper on their spirits. They talked little until dusk, when Mónoy came astern to ask Richard all kinds of questions about sailing.

Around midnight the coastline curved until it ran due south. A million brilliant stars and a glowing moon illuminated a ghostly white shore composed of interminable beaches. The fog had dissipated and exposed a mountain range of much lower elevations than those they had passed farther north.

THE SPANIARD'S DAGGER

The next day found the boat making little headway because the breeze was finally spent. The air had a fresh bite to it, and after the sun's disk dipped out of view in the evening, the temperature tumbled. Mists began rising from the surface once again. The sea's inexhaustible supply of moisture, combined with the cooling air, soon thickened into a formidable fog. Its dripping fingers turned everything sodden. Waspe crawled for shelter under a cushy stack of blankets and lay immobile at the foot of the mast. Richard and Mónoy huddled by the stern, wrapped in several blankets, trying to keep each other warm.

"This is meant to be the hottest season," Waspe sniveled, with pounds of wool muffling his voice. "I've fished off the Isle of Wight on rainy November nights, but I swear this forsaken sea is more miserable even in summer."

"Let's strike sail and turn in," Richard said. "It's not wise to go on like blind men."

Waspe pushed back the blankets, lifting his head just enough to peek at the couple. "It's anyone's guess when this damn fog will clear. We're well off the coast, and at two knots we're safe as long as we keep taking soundings. I recall from sailing north to search for that dream passage around the continent that the coast here runs south. Besides, I'm in no mood to fight off savages, even if I wouldn't mind killing me a few more on account of my leg."

"As you wish, Captain." Sarcasm marked Richard's voice.

But the land did not run south much longer and instead turned ninety degrees to the east. Drake, having stayed far out to sea, never encountered this particular kink in the shoreline. The surrounding treacherous waters could prove unforgiving.

*

In early September 1923, fourteen commanders stood on their bridges as the sleek ships of Squadron 11 weighed anchors in San Francisco. The nearly new Clemson-class destroyers cast off and, in perfect battle line, slipped through the narrow gap in the coast that divided the placid bay from the Pacific. Turning to port, and following virtually the same route taken by Mónoy and Richard and Waspe three and a half centuries before, the warships began steaming for San Diego. The lead and flagship, *Delphy*, after passing Points Arguello and Conception, had orders to turn ninety degrees east and lead into the Santa Barbara Channel. The other thirteen destroyers would follow in the flagship's wake, only a few seconds apart from each other in their tight battle line. With Captain Edward Watson commanding, the *Delphy* guided the other vessels.

When the squadron finally neared the two Points, and ran into a thickening nighttime fog, Watson misjudged the latest radio bearings and therefore his position. He mistakenly imagined himself well south of Point Conception in the open waters of the Channel's western end. He issued the fateful command to turn to port, a maneuver the other thirteen ships immediately mimicked.

The fog soon eliminated visibility, but the battle-ready squadron steamed on without deck illumination, fourteen ghost ships cutting through the mist. Minutes later, its heavy hull slicing the sea at twenty knots, the *Delphy* impaled herself on the seabed off Point Arguello. Then, in quick succession, six more destroyers smashed into the razor-sharp offshore reef. The last seven ships, thanks to alert officers, escaped the disaster. Twenty-three men died.

*

So the three people aboard the tiny boat continued through the mists toward the south. Unlike Squadron 11, they navigated Point Arguello without incident. Like Squadron 11, however, they too misjudged the bend in the coastline, instead limping for the open sea at two knots. At the same time, the prevailing drift carried them east into the Santa Barbara Channel toward clusters of sharp, volcanic rocks that lurked below the surface. Mónoy suddenly raised an arm and pointed into the night, screeching at the men.

"What the hell does she want?" Waspe quipped, shaking off his blankets.

Richard strained to make sense of her words. "I can't say. Maybe—"

Waspe cut him off. "Hear that queer sound, like the wailing of dying men?"

Richard turned his head. *There!* He heard it too, a muffled howling in the distance. *No, it's not far off!* Now it seemed to be coming from all directions. When Mónoy unexpectedly erupted in high-pitched shouts, Richard felt chills coursing up his spine.

"Damned, what is it?" Waspe cried fearfully, reaching for a musket. For an instant Richard forgot his own terror and pitied him. Under the circumstances there was absolutely nothing pleasurable about sitting in this miserable raft with one leg wrapped in bandages.

The wailing became louder and more numerous. Waspe took up a second musket and threw it into Richard's hands. Then Mónoy shouted, "Rok! Rok!" and gestured hysterically. When neither of the men reacted, she grabbed the tiller with such force that Richard feared she'd break it. Finally he understood.

"The shore!" he yelled. "We're running aground!"

*   *   *

Sheriff Quint felt like rice inside a pressure cooker ready to blow its lid. "How could you possibly lose those two unsuspecting amateurs riding into town? Ridiculous!" He bellowed.

Deputy Keller kept his back straight. "I'm sorry, Sir. It was beyond our control. That fellow, Malreaux, knows how to move. He cut corners like a pro and kept his foot on the gas. They were maybe twenty yards ahead when he accelerated to make the light at State and Mission. He flew through red and almost caused an accident. I was burning to nail him, but we would have blown our cover."

It took more to mollify Quint. "Next time nail his ass regardless." He flung his pen across the desk. "I want to find out what the hell they're up to. ASAP! They wouldn't get a rental, not when both Kindayr's and Malreaux's cars seem to be in perfect shape."

He fell silent, thinking things over. The deputy stood awkwardly before the sheriff's desk, anxious to leave the room. Quint finally leaned forward in his chair. "Okay, Keller. That's all for now."

"Yes, Sir."

Quint watched him slink to the door, careful to maintain his poise. "By the way."

Keller froze. "Sir?"

"I should have assigned more men. My fault."

"Yes. I mean, ah, thank you, Sir," Keller stumbled over his words. He closed the door as softly as possible.

The sheriff leaned back in his chair and gave his forehead the routine massage. Kindayr and that university professor were playing some game. He'd sensed it the minute Malreaux stepped into the room at the hospital, not to mention that Kindayr never told him the whole story. Whoever broke into his house had done so with good reason. But what did he come for? Quint could swear it had to do with their little excursion into the Channel. Malreaux had taken both Kindayrs aboard his yacht, ostensibly for a pleasure cruise. Bullshit! Quint's instincts never let him down. Well, if they wanted to play, he'd give them a match they wouldn't easily forget.

He reached for the phone and began barking orders.

*   *   *

Waspe threw himself into the sail, even though it hung limply. He foiled it as the pinnace turned around and Richard paddled frantically with one oar. They braced for the catastrophe. Richard looked out for the rocky shore, hoping he would spy it in time to turn away and avoid the sharp rock splitting open the hull.

But Mónoy's warning saved them. As the men continued paddling, slowly backtracking, they thought the thunder of the breakers grew less threatening. Then, suddenly, raspy gulps of air erupted all around them. Everyone aboard froze, their faces reflecting horror. Finally the fog parted and revealed several smooth, shiny heads with curious eyes that studied the humans.

Richard exploded in uncontrollable laughter, feeling a huge burden lift from his shoulders. "The wailing we've heard all along is seals!"

They had chanced upon a great natural spectacle. Disoriented by the dense fog, the three voyagers had missed the coast's eastward turn, unwittingly sailing south on a collision course with an island realm home to seals and sea lions numbering in the tens of thousands.

They worked the oars for the remainder of the night, and listened to the low rumble of breakers rolling onto sandy beaches off to port. Waspe twice tried to estimate their position with the astrolabe, but the fog still obscured the stars. When the sun finally lit up the early morning sky, patches of undulating uplands appeared sporadically through the scattering mists. They caught sight of a hilltop and glimpses of the coastline, as though a giant's fingers poked the fog and parted the moist air for a few moments. Soon the vapors pooled in the spaces left by the retracting hand.

"The land points dead east," Richard observed, checking their magnetic sea compass. Waspe hoisted the canvas, which gave them the same speed as using the oars, but without the labor.

They sailed on, keeping at least two hundred yards between the shore and themselves. A second, lower hill moved into view. It pierced the dissipating upper-level mists a thousand feet up in the sky. Nearer sea level, the haze persisted, still choking most of the shoreline. Later, when it seemed that the sun would finally break through, the swaths again coalesced into solid patches fed by a gaining breeze. And so it went on for the entire morning, as the boat negotiated the whole south side of the island and the narrow passage which separated it from its much larger neighbor.

"I haven't seen the coast for a long time," Richard finally complained.

"Hold her steady," Waspe answered. "Just keep your ears open. We'll stay this course."

Mónoy, who hadn't opened her mouth since they almost wrecked, came astern. She looked spooked. "Good we stop."

Waspe ogled her like a man who has been slapped in the face. "You want to go ashore, don't you?" he thundered, his brow ridge crinkled.

"Is better. Sail not good. We go land."

Richard suddenly felt extremely vulnerable. Unlike most sailors, he never let superstition poison his mind. But Mónoy's tone had an unpleasant quality. She didn't make empty statements, and she had a sixth sense, an uncanny ability to look into the future. Besides . . . she had been so quiet.

Waspe bristled. "I never thought I'd live to see the day a savage woman, who understands not the damnedest thing of sailing or the sea, has the gall to tell me when and where to go ashore." He turned to Richard. "If you remember, it's I who commands this boat, and when I need anyone's bloody advice I'll ask it." He glowered. "Now, if either of you doesn't like it, get off. I'd just as soon go on alone."

Richard got up and let go off the tiller. "You're in command? Then you steer her." But he couldn't fight down an ugly premonition that something bad lay in wait for them.

*   *   *

Patrick still couldn't move much with all the instruments and tubes, but he talked again. He'd come through.

"Does it hurt?" Liam asked.

His brother wiggled a finger in negation. "Not bad. Reckon they pumped me full of painkillers." He sighed.

Liam smiled. "Doctors say you're doing great. You're definitely over the hump."

"Do you know who did it?"

Liam looked around the room, almost fearing Quint might enter. "I think so, but I can't yet go to the police. The bastard has the dagger, and if I turn him in, Santa Rosa will suffer an invasion of gold diggers. Trust me, once all this is over, he'll go to prison."

"When are you going back to the island?"

"Tomorrow."

Patrick looked at him long and hard. Finally he said: "Don't be rash." He tilted his head at the life support system. "You don't need this crap."

*   *   *

Julia entered the garage from the kitchen, lugging Alex's oversized sports bag stuffed with warm clothes, food, a sleeping bag, and diverse camping gear. She dumped it in the trunk of her car. He had called from campus, and begged her to do him this favor. He'd been held up at a meeting, and Liam's fisherman friend supposedly ran a tight ship and hated delays. Alex asked her to park near MSI, the Marine Science Institute, where his meeting took place. They would

219

exchange cars so he wouldn't have to walk to where he normally parked, saving the fisherman ten minutes.

At first she'd been tempted to hang up on him. *What nerve, to make requests after that dirty escapade.* Actually, she did it for Liam's sake. Besides, the time to mess up whatever Alex must be secretly scheming had not yet come. She wanted to slam dunk him, present him with divorce papers *and* frustrate his present plans all at once.

Julia pressed the button on the remote and watched the door rise as the garage was flooded with sunshine. *What business had Alex at MSI anyway?* He had nothing to do with oceanographers. She pondered it. The past couple of years had seen more interdisciplinary work, but not with the life sciences. She had a hunch it somehow related to the gold from the island. *Just you wait! You're not half as smart as you think.* The black Maserati rolled down the driveway.

"She's leaving now," the voice spoke into a radio.

"Is she alone?" it came back through the static.

"Yes, her mother is still inside."

"Okay. Follow the vehicle. And don't lose her, or Quint'll go ballistic."

The man in the unmarked sedan tossed his crossword puzzle on the passenger's seat and turned on the ignition.

*   *   *

Richard was trimming his fingernails when a sudden sloshing of water broke the monotony. A five-foot long seal shot through the air and smacked into the gunwale. The crazed animal, howling wretchedly, flapped its short fore limbs, desperate to get aboard. Unfortunately, either the boat cleared too much water, or the smooth planking prevented it from gaining a firm hold. Richard, his heart pounding, dropped his knife and jumped to his feet. He stared at the animal, not knowing what else to do.

As the seal continued its valiant effort to pass over the hull, the water immediately behind it parted, and an enormous gray head that was white on the underside emerged. This glistening head opened into a gaping and cavernous hole, exposing jaws equipped with jagged rows of triangular teeth. With water dripping off its sides, this dreadful apparition somehow hinged its jaws outward, past the stunted nose.

Immobile, they all stared at the pinkish and white maw, and at a narrow rim of mouth surrounding the circle of teeth. Frigid black eyes that seemed almost lifeless rolled back into their sockets an instant before the jaws crushed the seal, tearing through the small body like through a hunk of lard. A distinctive cracking told of severed bones. Vibrations running the length of the boat told of powerful teeth striking into its planking.

The sea's surface closed above the terrible creature as it slid back into the mysterious depths whence it had risen. Scattered specks of blood on the gunwale and an inconsequential scrap of seal head floated nearby. A big round eye gazed inquisitively at the voyagers, as though wondering why these fellow air breathers hadn't intervened. Thankfully the ocean drift whisked the fragment away.

No one spoke. Mónoy, who after the cold night had been soaking up the warm sun in the bow, trembled like a small child. Waspe, his mouth agape and twitching, looked outright despondent. Richard backed as far away from the water as possible, to the exact middle of the boat, and latched low onto the mast with an iron grip. If the situation were not so serious, it might pass for being comical. He found his voice first.

"I want to go ashore, and I don't give a damn whether you agree or not. I'm going. And so is she."

He waited a few moments before rising from his squat, but maintained such a low center of gravity that he looked more dwarf than man. Gingerly he waddled toward Mónoy.

He tried pulling her up and out of the boat's narrow nose. But she proved such a deadweight that he sat down beside her and took great pains to keep his back toward the mast and away from either of the boat's sides.

Mónoy finally shook off her lethargy and picked up an oar. She thrust it at two triangular teeth stuck in the top of the gunwale until they broke free and fell into the sea. Then Richard mustered the courage to stand up and take down the sail. *We will turn and row straight for shore.* Waspe still didn't stir.

It paid off now that Richard had spent so many months at sea, for he had developed a balance those who made their living on land could only envy. Working on a ship when the wind whistled through the rigging and the deck below one's callused soles rose like an obstinate horse made a man as sure-footed aboard a galleon as a foot soldier on the field of battle. Just before Richard reached the mast, the inevitable happened. The boat's hull touched bottom.

They came to a complete stop as a powerful shudder traveled from bow to stern. A sheepherder, or peddler, or blacksmith would have flown off his feet, or perhaps sailed overboard. But Richard's sea legs absorbed the jolt, and he threw his arms around the mast.

"Hold on!" he shouted at Mónoy, bracing for the bottom planks to split open and reveal the dripping, barnacle-encrusted surface of the submerged reef. *This is it. We end here.*

"Save the gold!" Waspe shouted like a Caesar entering Rome, though he sat there impotently.

Richard sensed motion. They must have slipped off the reef. "We're moving!" He dropped on all fours, running his hands over the bottom planks. To his astonishment, they felt dry and the hull remained intact. He crawled toward the bow to check for damage, but only got half way. His peripheral vision had detected movement. *No! This cannot be true!* The sheer enormity of it paralyzed him.

~19~

A gigantic fin one yard across at its base cut through the water fifty feet off and was closing fast. *The monster!* Richard got a real sense of the beast's great size because its mass disrupted the normal pattern of the small surface waves. The creature measured at least seventeen or eighteen feet. But he had little time to muse because the fish's mighty mouth already opened.

The upper jaw rose an arm's length above the surface and chomped down on the gunwale with shattering force. For a dreadful moment, the shark hung on, just like the seal, as though *it* had now become the prey and something even more powerful ascended from below to tear it apart.

The bright pink tissue of its bony jaws, with shreds of the hapless seal still dangling from serrated teeth, filled Richard with terror. The animal's eyes, their covers pulled back, resembled disks of wet charcoal. Such an abysmal void! He believed in his heart this fiend was incapable of even the basest animal emotions, incapable of making any distinctions between grabbing prey, mating, just gliding through the immense ocean, or engaging in mortal combat with its enemies. And he yearned to kill it.

Then the shark pumped its head sideways and tore a chunk of planking with tholepin right off the hull. It slipped back into the sea as Waspe, shouting unintelligible gibberish, fired a musket into the water. An ugly hole gaped in the side of the pinnace. Luckily, the damage didn't reach to the waterline.

At least it didn't seem so.

* * *

As Julia piloted the Italian sports car onto the freeway, she let it fly, watching everything fall behind. She didn't notice the Mustang trailing her by a hundred yards, or the dark blue sedan racing down the on-ramp.

At the university gate she turned left and coasted toward where the Marine Science Institute overlooked Campus Point. She pulled into a stall near a group of surfers peeling skin-tight wet suits off their bodies. The moment her legs emerged from the slick roadster, four sets of admiring eyes traveled from the car's frame to hers. The students flashed her friendly smiles, but when she faced them they respectfully looked away and got on with their business. She grinned. They were boys, the oldest hardly twenty. She remembered periods in her life when the constant ogling had annoyed her, but she learned to deal with it. Now she appreciated the attention as a compliment. Some day the ravages of time would stalk her, and then she'd mourn those stares. *It won't last forever.*

She headed for the bluffs and was thrilled to discover a large pod of dolphins gorging on corralled fish a stone's throw from shore. Should she jump in and swim out to them? No, she'd freeze her butt off in the frigid January water. She waited till the pod moved on and hiked around the lagoon to the University Center. With the afternoon to kill, she purchased a newspaper and cappuccino, and made herself comfortable at a secluded table.

A man with close-cropped hair seated himself in the far corner, sipping black coffee. He placed a crossword puzzle on the table.

* * *

They'd been scanning the surface in expectation of another assault for ten minutes when something cold touched Richard's heel. He yanked his leg back and saw water pooling among their equipment, with a pile of sailcloth already submerged. "I'll be damned," he exclaimed. *The reef did cut us open!*

He put down the musket and grabbed a set of oars. "We're taking on water! We must get to shore immediately!" he yelled. No chance in hell would he let the boat sink from under his feet, not in this infested sea. Not for anything in the world could he see himself swimming with that shark. In the meantime the fog had thinned, affording frequent glimpses of the coast. The last mists would soon burn off.

Waspe flung a cooking pot at Mónoy, motioning her to start bailing. "Go ahead. Throw out the water." He tied the tiller to keep them on course. Then he took up his oars and joined Richard, both sculling furiously. The shore came up fast. They only needed to find a safe landing site.

Mónoy, kneeling between the bow and the forward thwart, kept baling without missing a beat. For every pot she poured overboard, two flowed in. "Water not stop," she finally cried out.

Richard and Waspe exchanged glances and threw themselves into the oars, rowing that the tholepins creaked. Richard thought his arms would snap, and the fire in his muscles became intolerable. He only had one oar in a tholepin, having lost the other to the fish, and keeping the oar steady on the splintered remains of the gunwale proved excruciatingly difficult.

"We're almost there!" Waspe yelped.

Steep rock outcrops hemmed in a gently sloping beach. It looked like the only spot they could even pull the boat ashore. Nothing but cliffs lined the entire stretch of coast to either side of these towering barriers. White sand and mounds covered with sea grass divided the promontories, one of which rose a hundred feet from the sea. A lateral kink tapering to a point near the top gave this landform the shape of a roughly hewn horse head. *If we can only reach that beach*, Richard silently prayed.

But the water kept rising with undiminished force.

STEVEN FARQUHAR

* * *

The elevator jolted to a stop on the UC library's fourth floor. Alex let the blonde out first. *Why not enjoy the view of that firm body right to the end of South Wing?* She quickly hooked right, vanishing in the dim aisles in search of some dusty volume. *Too bad!* Those narrow, dark aisles made for interesting possibilities. What a pity he wasn't a student anymore.

Kindayr had hogged a corner with his back toward the windows, pretending to read a book. A gym bag straddled the table, and the handle of a tennis racket protruded from it. Alex pulled out a chair.

"When did you get here?"

The artist looked at the clock. "Ten minutes ago."

"Did anyone follow you?" Alex said in a hushed voice.

"Not here, I think. But they watched me drop off the Jeep. I took the back entrance and lingered in Map and Imagery. Since none of those who entered after me looked even remotely suspicious, I slipped into an empty elevator and rode straight to the top, from where I snuck back down here by stairway. From this spot I can catch anyone coming in."

"Good." Alex nodded with satisfaction. He too had arrived on the fourth floor in a roundabout way, confident that no one had followed. "So they saw you at the mechanic's?"

"Yup. They parked in front of the IV Theater and tried to act cool. Two of them, in a dark sedan. I'm almost positive they're with Quint. They look just like in the movies." He laughed.

Under different circumstances Alex might have found this amusing, but Kindayr seemed to take this all as a big game. Someone was shadowing them, beyond any doubt. First the car trailing them the night they hit the store, and now the two guys at the theater.

226

"Listen, we still can't be certain they're cops, even—"

Kindayr cut him off. "Trust me, they are. I read Quint's suspicions in his face. He doesn't believe me. And those fellows in the sedan, they're 100% cops. Besides, this Treasure Michael guy has nothing to gain from stalking us."

"Perhaps." Alex didn't want to admit Kindayr was right. "Julia is already here. I called her on the cell. We better keep moving." He checked his watch. "Meet me behind Geology in precisely fifteen minutes, at the cactus garden."

"By the loading ramp?"

Alex nodded. "Who is behind me?" He'd heard some footsteps on the carpet.

"A couple of kids. Just chill out. We're not criminals."

"Alright. Keep the time. I'll see you in fifteen."

Alex went to pull two random books from a shelf and jogged down the stairs to ground level. He made for the circulation desk, dumped the books in a drop-off box, and left the building behind a campus tour group. He circuitously set out for the MSI, cutting through a dorm and along an inconspicuous path past the lagoon.

The Maserati gleamed in the sun a hundred yards ahead. He turned for the tenth time. *No one on my tail?* This was kind of fun. He hopped in the car and slammed the door. With less than a minute to spare he rolled into the lot behind Geological Sciences. Kindayr emerged from the building's back entrance and climbed in with the vehicle already moving.

"Anyone follow you?" Alex inquired.

"I'm afraid they're stuck watching our cars."

Alex chuckled. "They'll have a little surprise when Julia shows up about an hour from now. We'll be halfway across the Channel."

They swung onto Ward Memorial, where Alex showed off the Maserati's power. The needle on the odometer rocketed to ninety, and they pulled into a Santa Barbara City College lot in record time. Kindayr got out swinging his bag, looking impeccably the part of a man on his way to a tennis match. Alex continued down Cabrillo Boulevard and parked in a quaint residential area behind a palm-lined motel. He shouldered his gear and ran across the street to the beach, while keeping his eyes on the sidewalks and moving traffic. Nothing aroused his suspicion.

They linked up at the harbor. "See any cops?" Alex asked, still studying the boulevard.

Kindayr shook his head. "No, but it's too crowded to be sure. I'm not gonna sweat it. Besides, Binh is waiting."

"Okay. Let's go."

They didn't see two men climb out of a white Mustang, hustle along the sidewalk, and take up a spot that overlooked the piers.

*   *   *

A few more strokes and the low-lying vessel finally ground to a halt. The water had stopped rising as quickly, and Mónoy's persistent bailing had even kept pace with it. *Something must have shifted and blocked the hole,* Richard thought. He jumped out.

"Come on, let's see if we can move her." But they tried in vain. Too much water weighed down the craft. The long night and the struggle against losing their boat and all possessions had exhausted them.

"Should we tie her up?" Richard asked Waspe.

The cook, his tired eyes red and beady, shook his head. "The tide is in and the sea is calm. She isn't going anywhere."

Though Richard didn't like it, he didn't care. Waspe knew the ocean like the back of his hand. He trusted his judgment. "Alright, you know best."

He took a musket and two leather pouches, one holding powder flasks, the other shot. He stuck a large knife in his belt and led Mónoy to a sheltered spot higher up on the beach. The warm sand felt wonderful, and the heat of the sun brought on an overpowering urge to lie down. "I need to sleep," he called out to Waspe. "I haven't an ounce of strength left in me."

"What about the savages? We must keep watch over the boat."

Richard was already reclining. "The Lord will protect us."

"What? Your Lord didn't hold back those murderous devils lusting after our blood, did he? Pah! I'm gonna stay right here." He climbed back aboard, collected the three muskets and brought them astern, then made a seat with the last dry blankets.

Richard didn't want to bicker. He took Mónoy's hand and tried to pull her down next to him, but she resisted. His eyelids, heavy and sore, fluttered. He couldn't keep them open. Fatigue shut off his brain and he let go of her.

"I like boat no in sea," she said.

*   *   *

Having absorbed most of the international news and the comics, Julia rose and left the University Center through the front entrance. Her covert escort waited till she was outside the building before following her. When she turned left toward the mountains and the opposite direction from where she left the Maserati, he got on the radio.

"She's heading north, toward Cheadle Hall."

"Where are you?" it came back.

"I'm passing the library on my right. She's thirty yards ahead."

A short pause. "Just as we expected. Stay with her till we're sure."

Julia had no business in Cheadle Hall, or any other place on campus. She passed the university's administrative headquarters and crossed the bike path toward the parking lot.

The man got on the radio again. "She's all yours."

* * *

Lying abreast, they pointed their muskets at a dense thicket. The narrow crescent of sand in front, and the sea in back, trapped them. There was no escaping. Muffled voices in the thicket grew into a chorus until Richard realized they were not Indians. The drooping vegetation parted, and a dozen men clad in brilliantly colored Spanish uniforms spilled over tangles of roots and stumps.

"I told you we shouldn't have come ashore! Where is this god of yours?" Waspe hissed.

"We had no choice. You know that," Richard fired back.

Fitful shouts reached him from a different direction, and he raised his head. The pinnace drifted on the waves. He rubbed his grainy eyes, still dead tired and trying to remember what happened. His whole body felt sweaty. The distant voice grew more intense and desperate. It didn't relent. He squinted his eyes against the sun's glare. *Damned!* The boat *was* drifting, at least three hundred feet out and sitting so low, it should have already sunk. With Waspe screaming and furiously waving his arms, Richard finally understood his dream had come to an end.

He vaulted to his feet and dashed for the surf, tearing off his shirt as he went. At water's edge he hesitated. Monstrous sharks patrolled these coasts. They'd rip him apart. Yet, if they lost their stuff, they would never leave here. All would have been in vain! The long voyage with the General, the gold, Smythe, desertion, everything! Richard clenched his jaws, pummeled his thighs, and sucked in volumes of air to sum up courage. Then he ran in.

By the time he paddled alongside the boat, the hull was almost flush with the surface, and he had to back off for fear of swamping it. Waspe, pale as chalk, still baled, oblivious to the inevitable. Richard started treading water, laboring to keep his head above the waves. His calves already stiffened up with cramps, and he fought off all thoughts . . . "What happened?"

Waspe looked ready to burst into tears. "I don't know," he cried. "The tide must have lifted her off the sand. I woke up with my breeches soaked."

Richard tried to rest his legs, shifting the burden of remaining afloat to his arms. "What can we do? If I come aboard it'll sink. And I don't want to be here any longer than I have to." He felt compelled to gaze into the water. Countless creatures lurked below.

Waspe let go of the kettle, dejected. "It's too damn late."

His words rang true. Anyone could see that the vessel would shortly slip beneath the surface, as would Richard if he stayed much longer. Though an exceptional runner, he swam with the grace of a log and the buoyancy of an anchor.

"I must go back. Get off. Now!"

"Wait!" Waspe looked like a miserable convict facing his executioner. "I dread that shark. I have seen what even small ones can do. Once, my ship sank off the coast of France. We beat them off with knives and killed some of the beasts before a Genovese merchant pulled us out. Still, the boatswain lost both legs and four sailors later died from infection." He shivered. Those hungry devils were hardly the size of a boy. That giant we saw, you can't fight it."

Richard's limbs turned to lead, his heart to stone. "I'm freezing." In the seventy-one degree water he shouldn't have, but panic tricked his nerves.

He rolled over and struggled back as fast as he could, his breath short and hollow. Never before had he known such fear. Waspe called out after him, but Richard didn't listen to a word he said. Ten yards shy of the beach, his right foot kicked into a firm object. He thought he would vomit. *The shark!* He tried shouting for help, barely managed a hoarse rattle, and then tasted the salty sea going into his lungs. He coughed it up and, exploiting his final reserves, thrashed the water like a cat. When at last his knee made contact with the bottom, he almost cried with joy. He stood up in less than two feet of water, not a little embarrassed. Mercifully, Mónoy was still asleep.

He turned, losing all hope when faced with the devastating image. Behind Waspe's swimming body the top of their mast poked through the surface. It tilted a trifle and quickly vanished without trace. Water casks, wooden containers, blankets and tarpaulins, and a scattering of other items had become flotsam. As though this were not enough of a blow, the retreating tide already began to claim it all. Everything else had gone to the bottom. Their provisions, three of their muskets, most gun powder, tools, the astrolabe, compass, and the whole treasure had been swallowed by the sea.

Waspe, even though he had something in tow, covered the distance to shore without effort. Stumbling onto the beach with the Spanish officer's dagger and two hatchets stuck in his belt, he tossed Richard the end of a thick rope.

"You can take in the rest," his said with contempt, lying down to massage his injured leg.

Richard pulled in the heavy rope. Its forty feet slithered ashore like a limp sea serpent. He dropped to the ground, despondent. *They were finished.* "So you blame the tide for all this?"

"I told you." Waspe made an obscene gesture. "I woke up wet to my knees and with such a vicious urge to piss, I could hardly move. Then I almost killed myself trying to get your ear. You know the rest."

Richard couldn't keep it in. "You insisted the tide had reached its high point, did you not? Now we're stranded. We will never get home. Do you understand? We will die here."

* * *

Binh scowled at them, anxious to cruise. "Guys, time is money."

"I'm sorry we're running a little late," Liam apologized, dumping his bag on the deck. "You pull in some big fish today?"

"That's why I want to get out there. The day before yesterday I didn't even catch enough to pay for fuel." Binh shrugged his shoulders. "There are too many boats to compete anymore. It's just a question of time and we'll all be done, unless Uncle Sam steps in to keep the populations from collapsing."

Liam could think of no words to encourage him. The writing had been on the wall for years. In one generation, some of the Channel's species had gone from teeming to near depletion. Friends who'd grown up in Santa Barbara remembered how much fish they used to see and how abalone had literally plastered the bottom. It was a global trend. The Europeans were doing their best to ignore the Canadian experience and their own scientists' warnings, and thus wipe out their cod. And just recently he'd read a terrifying article that suggested the end of wild ocean fish for commercial consumption in as little as fifty years!

He introduced Alex as Binh cast off with a small dinghy in tow. Five minutes later they passed the breakwater, oblivious to the men observing them from shore.

Sheriff Quint had spent the entire morning in meetings with the mayor, a pushy developer, and three greedy business leaders. Then a punk at one of the high schools had come to class with a revolver, and, the frosting on the cake, two prisoners escaped from the county jail. Fortunately his officers had almost immediately caught the scoundrels hiding in a ditch. So far it had been a shitty day, and he consoled himself that retirement beckoned three years down the road. Getting up late, golfing every day . . . the phone rang.

"Quint," he growled.

"They just left aboard the *Sea Urchin*, owned and operated by a local fisherman."

"Excellent!" Quint exploded into the mouthpiece. Finally some good news. His mood improved already. "This time we got them. Who is the owner of the boat?"

"Binh Debettencourt. Lives in Carpinteria. We're running a check on him."

"Good. As soon as you find out where they're headed, I want to know."

"We're on it, Sheriff. Is there anything else?"

Quint drummed his knuckles on the desk. They'd probably hit one of the islands. What the hell else do you need a boat for? Unless they—

"It looks like they set course for Santa Rosa," the officer reported.

Quint leaned back. Things were coming together. He better contact the fellows at the Park Service. "Alright. When those sea birds get to their destination, back off. We don't want to arouse their suspicion. Not yet."

He hung up, content for the first time in days. His men had finally pulled their heads out of their asses. He'd chewed them out after the last screw-up, despite the fact that retirements and transfers had left him with an inexperienced police force. Some of the boys were fresh from the Academy. Beginning their career in quaint Santa Barbara, they simply didn't get the exposure. When he started patrolling the roads of Oakland as a rookie, he'd had a twenty-two day honeymoon before a dirt bag took a shot at his cruiser.

Quint pressed a button. "Get me a line to the Superintendent of National Parks." He had a little surprise in store for those guys.

～20～

Richard slumped to the ground. He felt lost, drained of hope and energy. With no food, stranded in what may turn out hostile territory, they couldn't survive long. "Why the damn rope? You could have chosen a bag of flour, a sack of rice, or some of the dried meat."

Waspe rubbed his leg. "Hungry, huh? Where is your trust in the Almighty? I thought you had faith?" When Richard said nothing, his tone became conciliatory.

"This is how I figure. We'll find something to eat. There's plenty of fish and clams, and though the boat is gone, the gold is not. *That's* why I saved this rope."

Richard wasn't sure if he'd heard right. "The gold lies on the bottom of the sea with everything else."

"That's not going to stop us." He started whistling. "And you want to know why?"

"Is this another of your bright ideas?" Richard asked, wondering what the cook planned.

"I dumped the barrels overboard, just before you finally woke up. They're less than a hundred yards from the shore."

Now Richard couldn't help but grin. The release raised his spirit, though only momentarily. *But, how can we ever get out of here?* "Listen, even if we should recover those casks without feeling the inside of a shark's stomach, I don't see the use. We're trapped, unless you can build a boat."

Waspe turned dead serious. "I never have. But that doesn't mean I won't try."

He was right. Nothing prevented them from fashioning a simple boat. Richard's mind raced. *The Indians make canoes, good ones, from the trunk of a single tree.* It looked easy enough. Mónoy could collect roots and berries, and make water pouches. They had plenty of time, unless the local people would make things difficult.

"There's got to be Indians here. They may try to kill us," he said with a worried look.

Waspe patted him on the back. "Then we better see if that rope will do us any good. With a bit of luck we can reach the pinnace, too."

"Where is bot?" Mónoy's clear voice startled Richard. She had come up behind them, looking rested and refreshed. He got up and put his arm around her. Waspe left them, scouring the beach.

"It sank." He pointed at the last of their possessions still dancing on the surface a thousand yards away. They might have retrieved some, but no sane man would venture that far, especially after the morning's events.

"How happen?" she said, her tone betraying a mixture of rising frustration and hopelessness.

"The tide. It pulled the boat out."

She stood very rigid, shifting her shoulder out of reach of his touch. Beneath her proud face, he read tremendous disappointment. He explained as best as he could that they would recover some of the equipment, but didn't mention the gold. Finally he realized, *she doesn't want to hear this.* Nothing would comfort her this moment. It was best to leave her alone. He turned away.

Waspe already waited at water's edge, with the rope tied to his waist and a five-foot piece of driftwood lying at his feet. "Take this. It'll conserve your strength."

Richard pointed at the cook's leg. "I can't believe how fast it's healing."

Waspe gestured at Mónoy, who was coming their way. "I don't know what she brewed up, but you'd make a fortune selling it to kings."

Richard rolled the wood into the surf. "She will watch the musket."

"Why?" she shot back, her eyes on fire.

He hesitated. "Ah, I don't think you're suited for this," he stumbled over his words. She'd never used that tone. "The casks are heavy." Yet, as he spoke, he recognized his folly. The people of her tribe, young and old, swam like fish. He'd seen the men race each other, sometimes going a mile up the coast. The women too would throw off their clothes and take to the cold sea.

"You not strong . . ." but not finding the words, she mimicked swimming motions with her arms. "Better I go."

This stung. He felt himself blush. "What do you mean? I can—"

Waspe cut him short. "She's right. You're no match for her. Besides, raising the barrels is not yet important. Locating them is. We can use her eyes. Think about it." With that he hesitantly waded into the water till it reached his navel. He looked back longingly.

"Sharks like where it's deep. Let's hope we don't have to go there." Then he kicked off.

Once glance at Mónoy, and Richard gave in, swallowing his pride. "Alright. I'll wait till you find them."

She quickly caught up with Waspe, and they continued side by side until they reached the general area where the pinnace sank. He stared at the beach, swam ten yards west, and stopped. *Here. This must be it.* The boat had to be somewhere within a fifty-foot radius. He'd put money on it.

He dipped his head below the surface, threw his legs in the air, and shot toward the bottom. The water was clear, though he had difficulty distinguishing shapes. He didn't make it all the way to the seabed, but only to where he could brush the tops of broad-leafed grasses swaying in the current. He went up for oxygen. Mónoy was still down.

"You see anything?" Richard shouted from the beach.

Waspe ignored him, saving his air, and tried again a little closer to shore. This time he hit it. Descending in a diagonal he could see the hull's outline deep down. There! It rested perfectly level in a bed of sea grass. But the pain in his lungs reminded him that he'd reached his limit, brutally dashing his hopes. No one could dive that deep. He popped back to the top, his chest burning. Mónoy, catching her own breath, looked at him from twenty yards away. The gold! Waspe shivered. What if it too lay so deep that—no he didn't even want to think it.

*   *   *

The *Sea Urchin's* engine puckered in the cool afternoon air. Binh stood at the helm munching on a BLT, Liam at his side. Alex was slouched on the rear bench, flipping through a *National Geographic.*

"You know," Binh said after washing down the last of his sandwich with a ginger ale. "I still feel like shit about your brother getting shot."

"Don't be foolish. I told you why the gunman came."

The skipper made a face. "Well, that's the point. When we returned from the island and you wanted to toss the dagger overboard, I shouldn't have stopped you. Now your brother is in the hospital, and you are chasing a wild fantasy." He put his hand on Liam's back. "There's no treasure on Santa Rosa. The only thing you and your buddy will find there is trouble with the law. Just let the cops focus on bringing in the bastard who shot your brother."

Liam waved it off. "Forget about the dagger. You've done nothing to regret, and Patrick is getting better as we speak. Besides, once we're done with the island, I'll put that scum behind bars. Not before. He'd spill his guts to the police, which would end our search."

"Okay." Binh studied him. "You call the shots."

Half an hour later the vessel decelerated and turned its nose at its destination. Towering headlands enclosed the sandy beach. The rocky outcrop on the right reminded of a horse's head, with a deformity eighty feet above the sea and twenty feet below the top that was suggestive of a neck. Liam had never seen the odd formation from this angle, he thought. *Or did I cruise past here before, during that island tour? It sure looks familiar.*

*   *   *

Mónoy found the two dark brown barrels lying on their sides. As she got closer she saw two more, fifteen to twenty feet apart and with one standing upright.

She shot to the surface just as Waspe fixed to dive. "Look!" She waved her arm.

He raced to her side and dove. She went with him till they reached ten feet from the bottom, but he ran out of air and climbed back up through the water column. Mónoy decided to go on and ran her hand over one of the barrels. When her lungs started aching, she kicked off from the seabed. Looking up, she saw Waspe treading water.

Back at the surface she watched him work a loop at one end of the rope. He tugged at it, tightened the knot, and turned to flash her a brilliant smile. His eyes pleaded. "It's too deep. I can't get at it." He held out the loop.

He wants me to attach it, she understood. Then she turned and waited for Richard, who sat astride a log and paddled with both hands to reach them.

"What is she doing?" he asked Waspe.

"She found the barrels, and I asked her to tie on the rope. I can't go that deep."

Mónoy, with a pride she'd never known, realized they depended on her. *Their lungs are weak.* She took the rope from Waspe's hands, filled her chest with air, and descended to the bottom.

It took but a moment to attach the loop and pull it taut. She popped back to the surface, where Waspe impatiently grabbed the rope. He pulled up the slack and started for the shore. But he didn't get far. The cask seemed stuck.

Richard slid off the log and swam to Waspe. Mónoy joined in and together they held the rope while thrashing the water with their legs and free arms. The barrel moved, slowly at first, but gave up all resistance once the swimmers gained momentum. Reaching the shallows first, Mónoy planted her feet and dropped the rope, waiting for the men to haul their catch from the sea. While they caught their breath, she pulled the loop off the cask and ran back in.

She went for the closest barrel, the one that stood upright. Descending to the bottom, she scattered a huge school of sardines passing beneath her. The silvery cloud split in half to let her through. Thousands of fish sparkled like underwater stars in the scattered late afternoon light filtering through the water. Then, as if following the impulse of a single brain, the entire swarm made a lightning-fast turn toward the open sea and melted into the blue. *Were they fleeing a predator?* Mónoy pushed away the thought and sank to the bottom to wiggle the loop over the cask, though she couldn't help looking over her shoulders.

Her task completed, she kicked off and shot to the surface like a cork. On her way up she saw Waspe's body cutting through the water, with Richard not far behind. Their closeness reassured her, and she felt huge relief when she broke through the waves and sucked in the fresh air. She immediately started for shore, letting them latch onto the rope behind her.

By the time they dragged this cask ashore, Mónoy had grown impatient to get the others. The salvage operation had become routine, and she ran back out the moment Waspe handed her the dangling loop. Later, when the fourth barrel rested safe on the beach, the men fell down in exhaustion.

"It's a good sign," Waspe said. "We'll build a boat and leave in due time, perhaps much sooner than we thought." Spread-eagled, and panting heavily, he was squinting his eyes.

Richard said nothing and just wiped his face. For the first time in her life, Mónoy knew in her heart that woman was equal to man. She could succeed in things for which men lacked the strength. She could easily do things that her father had always she and the other women could not. When suddenly she noticed movement nearby, she could not know that her resolution would soon face its first test.

*   *   *

They had explored the stream banks until dark, picking up from where they had left off during the last visit, but nothing came of it. No more gold, nothing. Worst of all, the canyon clung tenaciously to its biggest secret—the ultimate source of the artifacts. They needed more rain. Another serious storm would drench the land, and hopefully force it to surrender the truth. *Hell,* Alex thought. *No use in letting it spoil dinner.*

He always made a point of eating in style, no matter what the circumstances. Chewing salmon jerky, he popped a handful of Greek olives into his mouth. Then he tore a slice of crisp baguette in half, broke off a generous hunk of Parmesan, and poured himself another cup of Chilean merlot.

Have I made the right decision to come out here with Kindayr again? he wondered between sips. On the one hand the artist served a valuable purpose. Four eyes saw more than two. But the moment they discovered the gold's source, his presence became superfluous. What if these mountains really did hold a sizable treasure? Kindayr would want his share, and perhaps even claim the whole thing. After all, he had discovered the dagger, and he didn't have a lot of money.

"There is something I want to tell you," Alex interrupted his meal.

Kindayr took his eyes off the fire. "What?"

"You know, I'm real sorry for the way I behaved last time out here. It's a lousy excuse, but . . . well, I've got a few major problems. There is this deadline on my new book, and things aren't exactly great at the university. A lot of departmental friction is souring relationships, and I always seem to get caught in the middle." He fell silent. *No need delving into the Julia situation. That is none of Kindayr's business.*

"I'm not one to hold grudges. I figured you must have things on your mind." He threw another piece of wood in the fire. "Forget about it."

Alex suppressed a smile of relief. Kindayr was in the dark.

Later, after they had both downed a scalding mug of strong and flavorful Kona, Malreaux excused himself to jot down a few notes. Liam retreated to the cozy warmth of his sleeping bag, for the damp air chilled right to the bone. Watching the professor writing in a large notebook by the glow of a lantern, Liam observed a sly smile on his face. *Behind those innocent eyes the chap is concocting some scheme.* Liam chuckled. *He thinks I'm stupid. Okay, I'll play along, but just for a while.*

* * *

Two men, measuring well over six feet, had materialized from nowhere. Walking abreast, they fortunately made no threatening gestures, and neither of them brandished a weapon.

The fellow on the left wore a loosely fitted otter skin skirt down to his ankles. Split open on the sides, it allowed for glimpses of powerful legs. A buckskin belt adorned with colorful shell fragments clung to his waist. It held two chert knives, their wooden handles decorated with beads and pieces of shell. Strong muscle groups supported his torso from abdomen to neck, but his shoulders in particular evoked an acute sense of inferiority. This man, Richard meekly realized, could crush his rib cage. Thankfully, the Indian's face expressed no enmity.

Intelligent eyes peered out over angular cheekbones, a somewhat diminutive nose, and the hint of a smile. Long bits of bleached wood dangled from the man's ear lobes. Fine strings traversed his head in symmetric lines, keeping his long coal-black hair neatly in place. Circular bone fragments with holes in their center and wood chips kept these strings attached to the hair. Above his brow he wore a triangular piece of abalone shell that shone in silvery-pink hues.

The second and much younger man was dressed like the first, though his skirt seemed made from rabbit skin. He, too, would make a formidable opponent. Yet, for all of their imposing appearance, the most striking aspect about both Indians was the similarity of their faces. The elder looked thirty-something, the younger no more than sixteen or seventeen. Beyond doubt, here came father and son.

The Indians halted five paces short of Mónoy. At least as curious as those they beheld, they gazed at the strangers and the four barrels in unconcealed amazement. Both men focused intently on Waspe. The cook had picked up their sole remaining musket, which he now leveled at the Indians.

"For God's sake, put that down!" Richard said firmly when he saw this. "Can't you see they come unarmed?" Rage filled him. "I doubt they're alone. If you make trouble, we'll all die before nightfall."

"You never know with the savages. They could be upon us quicker than a cat," Waspe muttered under his breath, keeping the muzzle aimed at the young man's chest.

Richard, by now seething with violent anger, tried his best not to let it show. With an obliging expression he managed to muster for the benefit of the Indians, he spoke forcefully. "Stop pointing the musket, or I swear you'll taste my knife before either of them gets his hands on you. Now!"

Waspe looked at him in surprise, like a father who realizes his full-grown and wayward son will no longer take orders. His eyes turned hateful, but he obeyed and lowered the weapon. His left hand, though, came to rest on his dagger.

The older of the Indians stabbed a finger past them at the ocean, saying something to Richard. *What did he want?* Richard turned, but made sure to keep the Indians in view. He shrugged his shoulders in an exaggerated way. "I don't understand."

This made them both chortle, apparently amused by his strange speech. They exchanged some words before the son lifted his arm. He too pointed at the sea, but also the sky. He asked a question, judging by the tone of his voice.

Richard looked at Waspe, whose face remained blank. "You don't think *I* can make sense of those grunts."

Now Mónoy stepped forward and began to address the men. They listened intently but said nothing. Undeterred, she started making a paddling motion with her arms, repeating the same word several times. This brought a response. The son imitated her gestures and then asked another question. Richard finally understood. *They want to know how we got here, with no boat in sight.*

Using a combination of signs and words, Mónoy explained that it had sunk. The men had a brief exchange during which the father studied them and their meager possessions with renewed interest. Finally he stretched out his arm and beckoned them.

"He want us come," Mónoy said.

This was a blessing. Richard trusted these two men. Excited, he turned to Waspe. "What do you figure? We've nothing to lose."

The cook showed little enthusiasm. "No? How about the gold?"

Richard glanced at the barrels, then at Mónoy. "Should we go?"

She nodded. "They friend. Give us eat, place of sleep."

"Listen," Richard said, hoping Waspe would stop being so stubborn. "Our prospects are not favorable. The Indians know we're trapped. If they had a mind to kill us, they could do so at will."

"What about the gold?" he repeated.

No way could they take the barrels. "We'll come back later. Let's get them up on the beach past the waves' reach for the time being. They'll be safe."

"Safe? Pah! You've lost your wits. A hundred of those thieving dogs will bury their greedy paws in our barrels in the turn of a day. There won't be a single gold real left."

"Why would they? These people have no use for it. The bullion means nothing to them."

"Gold shines mighty pretty when you clip it to your ears and stuff it in your hair. Look at 'em. Hell, even the men wear enough scraps of wood and shells that it makes them pass for palace ornaments. I reckon the glitter of the gold and jewels would craze their women as soon as they get their eyes on it. I swear to you"—and he babbled himself into a squall of hysteria—"once the savages find what's inside those barrels, it'll be the last *we'll* see of it. Except for when they go strutting through their miserable hamlets with pieces of eight swinging from their filthy faces and rubies stuck to their belts. No, I won't have it. I can't bear even the thought." He was shaking.

"Then what in God's name do you want to do? Guard the gold with one musket, while building a boat and stalking game with bare hands in the meantime?" Richard lost his patience. "They've already seen the casks. Why arouse their suspicion? If we don't like where they take us, we can always return."

"If they let us." Waspe would not be swayed.

Mónoy interrupted them. "I go." She took a few steps toward the Indians, who curiously eyed both men.

This settled it. *The hell with that pig-headed fool.* "Okay, let's go." Richard signaled the Indians that Waspe would stay with the barrels, while he would come with Mónoy.

The father hesitated then nodded. He briefly addressed his son and turned abruptly, starting into the narrow canyon. Mónoy and Richard fell in behind, and then came the son, who left a now pale and tight-lipped Waspe to fend for himself. Richard glanced over his shoulder once.

Would they meet again? God knew what the cook would do if other Indians chanced onto this beach.

* * *

They rose before first light, scoffed down hot cream of oats and steaming coffee, and hit the trail with the enthusiasm of those who expect great things.

This part of the canyon proved the most difficult to date. Though the banks lacked dense vegetation, the debris cluttering the area made for tough going and slow progress. By mid-morning, Liam, working the left bank, noticed movement farther up the canyon. He stopped, training his eyes on a cluster of wild fennel.

Through the green he caught glimpses of a man's huge upper torso, his head bent low. In an instant the stranger disappeared from view. Stunned, Liam tried to make sense of it. What was this guy doing here? A bolt of energy shot through him. *The shop owner!* No, impossible! The bastard didn't even know which island to search, let alone the exact location. *He could have followed us out of the harbor.* But no one could have passed them unnoticed in this tight canyon, except at night when they slept. Very unlikely. No, this man had come here before them.

Alex's voice drifted across the stream. "What are you doing?"

Liam frantically pressed a finger across his lips, making eye contact and tilting his head upstream. The professor craned his neck, but an outcrop blocked his line of sight. Liam waved him across the stream, signaling to stay low. Alex took his boots and socks off and waded through the knee-deep water just in time to avoid detection, for the mysterious man's upper body had reappeared. Liam pushed Alex behind a clump of sedges from where they could spy unobserved.

"He's digging a hole," Liam whispered. "That must be a shovel."

Alex went pale. "The gold! Shit! He must have found its source." Visibly shaking and without bothering to clean his muddy feet, he pulled his socks back on and rammed his feet into his boots. "We've got to think of something this fucking moment."

Liam had never seen him so agitated. "Let's not assume the worst."

"Don't be so damn naive! What the hell else would he be doing here, in this canyon? Collecting rare butterflies? He found the treasure. I know it."

Liam felt uneasy. "He might have a gun."

"I understand that, but we've got to somehow find out what he's up to."

Liam had an idea. "Let's pretend we're with the Park Service. All this is federal land. Even if the guy really did find gold, I seriously doubt he'd take out two park rangers."

"We have neither uniforms nor badges. He'll ask for IDs."

Liam brushed this aside. "We're off-duty, camping. What can he say? The thing that counts is to send him packing."

Alex finally agreed. "Okay, let's do it."

They pulled their hats deep over their faces and quietly snuck up on the unwelcome visitor. He was a very short man with dark hair, a bushy mustache, and a bulging belly. Sweating profusely, he knelt in a low depression, methodically scraping away the sandy soil with a trowel. A pickax, spade, couple of hammers, and an assortment of other tools littered the ground. Coming closer, Liam spotted a half-buried object resembling a rock or lump of bleached wood. Then, as the sweaty digger swished off more of the sand, Liam recognized it was neither.

Unable to take his eyes off the grisly object, he felt something very eerie and totally novel, something akin to a gust of air sweeping through his mind. Liam experienced the oddest sensation of his life as a jumble of confused images started floating across his mind.

~21~

Their path took them along a dry creek bed, its channel so choked with grasses and overgrown bushes that it seemed years had passed since water flowed here. A narrow trail paralleled the sandy creek bottom, winding through thickets, around boulders, and over decomposing tree trunks.

The small party followed this wilderness road to a dense stand of scrubby pines, where it rose into a steep ascent up the canyon wall. The path soon turned more worn and narrowed so much that Richard had to stop. He grabbed hold of a cranny in the cliff with one hand and avoided looking over the edge. The two Indian men continued unflinchingly, as did Mónoy. Richard tried to control his anxiety, imagining himself out of this death trap. Left without a choice, he bit his lips, kept his mind off the airy abyss gaping only inches away, and forced one foot in front of the other. Sweat stung his eyes, but he didn't dare dry his forehead for fear of losing balance. Finally, the torture came to an end as the narrow trail fanned onto a rolling plateau. He wiped his face and sent out a quick prayer of gratitude.

They climbed higher until the Indians halted, waiting for him to catch up. A breathtaking view of undulating slopes in three directions greeted him. Tall grasses swaying in the breeze predominated, broken here and there by dense groves of trees that slithered down from the highlands like serpents crawling towards the sea. The dark-blue ocean and a creamy sky merged at the far horizon. An island floated on the sea in a second direction. On the third side another immense and mountainous island towered across a channel. This struck him as odd, and he felt disoriented.

He looked at Mónoy, who drank in the panorama spread before them, and that's when it hit him. He spun around. The sea surrounded *them!* Everywhere! But how could it? He turned once more. No doubt. That huge hunk of land across the channel, extending eastward into the mists, *was* the mainland. The fog had played a trick. They had unwittingly sailed for the open sea and, through God's grace, escaped disaster and landed here instead of losing themselves in the vast ocean.

Richard pondered the new reality. Should the Spaniards explore this shore and learn from the Indians that other whites had come, they would hunt him and Waspe like wild dogs. On the other hand, isolation from the mainland and its greater uncertainties might prove a blessing. With a bit of luck, the people who inhabited this island would shelter them.

The group descended a grassy slope and marched another two miles into a wooded glen that echoed with light-hearted chatter. There they came across women collecting acorns amid clusters of thick oaks. These women ceased all work and gaped in great astonishment. The leader of Richard's band said something to a young girl, who bounded off like an antelope.

Like the men of their tribe, the women burst with robust health. Land and sea obviously provided all necessities. Though their faces appeared of average beauty, their mode of dress pleased the eye. Each wore a skirt-like piece of deerskin that hung to above the knees, with long fringes trailing on the sides. A variety of white, pink, black, and orange seashells adorned these skirts in patterns of lines and circles. They went naked above the waist. The women's hair, cropped short on top, draped loosely about their shoulders. Meticulously trimmed bangs fell over the forehead, while shiny earrings and necklaces made of bone and colorful shells contrasted with their dark hair and skin. Richard had an inexplicable sense of belonging. England seemed a million leagues away.

Their eyes devoured him, especially his straw-colored hair and blue eyes. Two of the women stared with such intensity that Richard couldn't help but feel uncomfortable. He breathed more easily when they resumed the march. The women picked up their baskets and followed behind.

The group crossed through the woodland and alighted upon a vast meadow brilliant with wildflowers. This lush carpet stretched to a small village built within a few hundred yards of an estuary, which was connected to it by a narrow stream. They approached several dozen dome-shaped thatched houses sprouting from the near bank of the stream like mushrooms from a forest floor. These dwellings measured about sixteen feet across the base, except one at the center, which was twice as large.

The girl who had run off must have alerted the villagers. Yelling children scampered toward the strangers, women abandoned their cooking fires, and men interrupted whatever work they had attended to. Throngs of people surrounded them and led the band into the village toward the large hut at the center.

We will meet the chief. Richard struggled to keep calm. The future depended wholly upon the goodwill of whomever they would encounter on the inside.

*　　*　　*

Dave Rash dropped the trowel and jerked around. Even his deep tan couldn't disguise the blood draining from his face. Nevertheless, he collected himself with astonishing speed, and nothing but a subtle twitch at the corners of his mouth betrayed anxiety.

"What the fuck do you want? You got no right to sneak up on people like that."

"You're trespassing on National Park land," Liam replied authoritatively. "I'd like to know exactly what you are doing."

The man strove to appear totally unimpressed, though his eyes' shiftiness was as good as a confession. He coughed. "So what if it is Park land? That's not trespassing. It's public domain." He paused and, when no answer came, conceded some ground. "Come on, tell me if I'm mistaken. Hell, I don't know the boundaries. You guys with the ranch? Is that it? This ain't private land, is it?"

"You're not answering the question," Alex cut in. "My colleague asked what you were doing."

The man glanced at the ground where a human skull lay half exposed. "Well, I . . . I came across this thing, and figured I'd dig it up. I mean . . . some museum might be interested. Would be a shame to let it go to waste."

"The rules are clear," Liam shot back. "It's illegal to remove artifacts from the Park. Disturbing an archeological site is a federal crime."

Rash's whole being oozed guilt, and he took to scratching his face with a crusty index finger. Then, in a lightening-fast move one wouldn't expect from such a heavy man, he bent low to get a better look at Liam's face, which was still half hidden by the hat. With renewed cockiness he straightened his back. "Hey, I know you."

This jolted Liam. He shook his head. "I don't think so." He didn't sound very convincing.

Rash stared at Alex now, the previously twitching corners of his mouth sliding into a broad grin. He nodded vigorously. "Yeah, yeah, I know your face, too. Both of you ain't no strangers to this canyon, huh?"

Alex echoed Liam. "I've never seen you before today."

He laughed derisively. "No, you sure haven't. But that don't mean I ain't seen you. By the way, you ain't introduced yourselves. Got some tags, some identification shit?"

Liam's mind raced. *This scumbag must have seen us during our last stay.* "We like to camp in this area when off-duty. And today we caught you in the act."

"Camping? Right!" He spat the words. "That's the biggest bunch of crap I ever heard. And don't give me no shit about 'illegal' digging, cause you're doin' the same damn thing. I seen you two, snooping all over the creek like a pack of bloodhounds with that other pal of yours. You ask me, that's pretty odd, ain't it? But I reckon you nature birds are searching for rare toads."

He calmed down, sporting a glib smile. "Now, I say we oughta be good Christians, share the wealth. That way we stay off each others' backs. You do your thing and I do mine." He folded his arms across his massive chest.

Liam and Alex exchanged a mutual glance. Liam knew the expression on the professor's face from their tennis matches. Below those serene eyes glowed a fiery rage. He was seething with anger but still kept his cool. Liam turned back to the stranger.

"I'm not sure what the hell is going on in your mind, but you're dead wrong. We were here first, and we come because it's remote. In fact, we like to think of the canyon as ours."

"You just got done telling me this land belongs to the Park Service. So it ain't yours. There's plenty of space for us all. Stay where you been, and we'll work right up here."

'We?' So the guy isn't alone! Liam quickly scanned the surrounding landscape but saw no one. "So what's next?" he demanded, nodding at the skull.

"What do you mean?" Rash snorted.

"What are you going to do with it?"

He chortled like a pig. "I sure ain't settin' Big Johnny on my TV. He's going the same way all the bones do, same as yours. This boy will fetch me a nice price."

The global demand for ancient artifacts had gone through the roof in recent years, as the public learned when many of Iraq's irreplaceable treasures disappeared in the wake of Saddam's collapse. Scumbag dealers on all continents paid handsomely to tear up archeological sites wherever people found them. An army of unscrupulous thieves was robbing humanity of its heritage. Perhaps even worse than taking the artifacts, by hacking their way through a burial mound or a ruin, these looters erased the contextual clues that allowed scientists to piece together lifestyles of lost civilizations. For the first time Liam realized he and Alex had become looters themselves. They might end up disturbing a site of real historic significance.

"Tell you what. We'll think this over." He pulled Alex with him, determined to find a way to rid themselves of this smug interloper.

*   *   *

When they got near the entrance of the central dwelling and halted, the entire village became silent. No one stirred. The older Indian lifted his arm and pointed in the direction whence they had come. He started quietly, then raised his voice and delivered a short speech punctuated by frequent gestures. When he was done, the villagers, who had maintained a respectful distance, surged forward and erupted in loud patter. They were obviously fascinated by Richard's pale skin and eyes and manner of dress.

Mónoy took his hand. "He is hioh. They friends people. We ask eat."

Richard understood. 'Hioh.' *That's what Mónoy's tribe called their chief.* The man who had led them from the beach was the village leader.

The hioh disappeared into the hut, and his son motioned Richard and Mónoy to follow. She pulled him through an arched doorway supported by bleached whale ribs. It took a few moments for the eyes to adjust, even though sunlight filtering in through a circular smoke hole in the roof's center helped bathe everything in soft light. Wide mats made of rushes hung near the back, separating the hut into two rooms. Wooden bowls, baskets filled with various fresh and dried foods, and stone tools cluttered small platforms around the hut's perimeter. Several bows and quivers filled with arrows leaned against the wall. The dwelling's owners kept everything neat and in order. Mónoy felt quite at home.

The hioh signaled them to sit on the dirt floor. They sat around a fire pit dug directly below the hole in the roof. He began to ask her all kinds of questions, but as hard as she tried to understand, most words made no sense. In consequence the man attempted a different course, speaking more slowly and using a stick to draw in the dirt. This time she recognized some of the sounds and intonations. *He wants to know where we live.*

Mónoy struggled to explain that they had come from far to the north, in a strange boat powered by wind rather than men. She also made drawings on the floor, but her hosts made nothing of the sail and mast. She related their encounter with the hostile Indians, which displeased but didn't surprise her listeners. Their people apparently occupied an area stretching along the mainland coast, and those villages farthest north often fought their neighbors. These war-like and ill-meaning tribes were of no intelligence and fond of stealing.

The hioh and his son, who went by the names of Wi'yapak and Tuqan, listened intently when she told of the shark. Wi'yapak explained that sharks sometimes attacked canoes, and when he was still a small boy, the village had lost its best hunter while diving for shellfish. At least that's what Mónoy thought she understood. Tuqan wanted to know why Waspe had stayed behind. She shrugged and said he'd soon join them.

The delicious scent of roasting meat pervaded the air. Mónoy, her head hurting from the tremendous effort and her stomach empty, could hardly contain her joy when Wi'yapak finally rose and motioned everyone outside and toward a huge fire pit. They sat on the ground as several women brought wooden bowls heaped high with steamed fish, roasted rabbit, fresh greens and berries, and a thick acorn mush. Two women spread grass mats on the ground on which the others placed all the food. Tuqan, very serious now, slid some of the bowls toward her and Richard. She needed no more prodding and reached for salmon. Richard fished for a fat hunk of rabbit and ripped off a large chunk. The Indians grinned.

Mónoy knew she and Richard had passed their first test, but she could only guess at what Waspe currently did, or how it might affect their continued welcome.

*   *   *

"That scumbag thinks we, too, are bone hunters. He must have seen us last time, but knows nothing of the gold," Liam vented his fury.

Alex looked like he'd swallowed acid. "I'm already envisioning this canyon swarming with a horde of treasure seekers."

"No. Even if he knew what we've discovered, he'd be a fool to make it public. He's a grave robber. It's what he does, and you can bet your ass he won't run his mouth. Those guys can pull in some very decent cash."

They ogled the unwanted intruder, who reclined against a boulder, casually puffing on a cigarette and blowing smoke rings as though he contemplated the future of the universe.

"How are we going to get rid of him?" Alex pondered. "He doesn't seem like the type you can bully."

"We must keep threatening with the Park Service."

"But he could retaliate and put *us* in hot water."

"What's he got to say? He saw us search the stream. Big deal. As I said, he can't afford to blow his cover. The fact is he has no proof of anything."

256

"Neither do we. He'll deny everything we say."

"He'd be hard pressed to deny the skull," Liam countered, increasingly irritated with Alex's arguments. *Why was he so damn timid?*

Alex looked uncomfortable. "You're planning on taking it from him? You said yourself he might carry a weapon."

Liam threw up his arms. "Come on, there is no need for a gun out here, unless you're willing to use it. He sure doesn't strike me as someone willing to shoot a federal ranger. If he does pull a pistol, I'll back down. It's definitely worth a try."

Alex finally gave in. "Okay, let's get it over with."

The man stroked his mustache, watching the smoke rings rise and expand till they melted into the surrounding air. He took a last draw and, with a mocking smile, flicked the filter into the creek. Next he searched his pockets and retrieved some candy, his expression saying loud and clear, "you twits amuse me."

"This is one hell of a big island," Liam began, "and there's no need to be crowding each other. Since we've been coming here for a long time, I suggest we maintain the status quo and you find another spot."

He looked as though he'd been slapped and retorted angrily. "Status quo, or queer, or whatever the hell language you're speaking. Fuck off! You think you own this island? You two assholes 'been taking bones all along, and now you've got the nerve to be telling me to leave. Bullshit!" He cut an ugly grimace for emphasis.

"Look, no matter what you think we're doing here, personally I don't give a hoot about the Chumash sites. The Indians are long gone, and I couldn't care less for scattered arrowheads and shell fragments. And I sure didn't join the Park Service to guard a bunch of rotting skeletons. Now, I'm certain you're well aware that the Chumash lived all over Santa Rosa, especially in the northwest. Why don't you try it out there? In the meantime we can have this canyon as kind of an off-limits wilderness retreat for campers like us."

Rash's confidence faltered once again. His eyes became shifty, and the corners of his mouth danced. He put on an air of apology. "Come on man, as of today all I care about is this location. You can do with the rest of the canyon as you please."

Alex jumped in. "You still don't get it. We've been here first, and we will keep it that way. It's your best deal. Take it, or go to jail." Liam cringed. This was *too* pushy. Alex's temper would ruin it for them. And it did.

"Go to hell! You ain't got nothin' on me. I swear I'll ask the Park Service big shots what business you two have here." He laughed like a hyena.

Liam started for the skull, but Alex unexpectedly pulled him back. "We'll talk again," the professor said.

The man snorted. "Stay away from me. I don't like being threatened."

*　*　*

When Waspe first swam along the cliff in search of mussels clinging to an offshore rock, he had missed the dark spot below the surface. Now, with his sight fixed on the beach and towing a shirt filled with scores of mussels, he almost overlooked it again. At the last moment, he sensed something and scrutinized the sheer wall before him. He didn't notice anything unusual, until the heaving surface of the sea pulled back to reveal a tiny cleft. An instant later the surf surged in and submerged the hole. But he had seen it.

Waspe maneuvered to within an arm's length of the cliff, keeping an eye on the open sea. Even with this gentle swell, a freak wave might roil in at any time. It only took one such surge to push a careless man against the unforgiving rock. He dove.

The dark crack in the wall represented the uppermost extension of the entrance to what appeared to be a mysterious grotto. Over six feet high and three across, the crevasse extended from its narrow top down to the sandy bottom. Waspe ached to explore, but the shirt full of shellfish encumbered him. Besides, a ravenous hunger had gnawed at him for hours, and he needed to replenish his strength. The harvesting of the shellfish had tired him. The sun would soon set too, so when the pain in his lungs forced him to the surface, he made for shore.

Back on dry land, he placed his shirt on top of one of the barrels. A healthy pile of food glistened in the light. Without the means to start a fire, or even a pot for boiling, he pried open the hard shells with his dagger. With the blade's tip he scraped the tender mussels right onto his tongue and swallowed with delight. Raw as it was, the meat tasted delectable.

With nothing left but a heap of empty shells, he pushed each barrel on its side to create a wall between him and the canyon, with the opening toward the sea. This illusion of a fortified camp soothed his nerves. He leveled the sand, but piled up small mounds where his head and feet would rest. Finally, he pulled his breeches on and made himself as comfortable as a half-naked man without blankets can on the bare ground. He hugged his musket and kissed the muzzle. It would protect him. He closed his eyes, wondering what he might find behind that dark cleft in the cliff.

~22~

L iam and Alex, having decided to postpone their mission, had spent the remainder of the previous day and the morning soaking up sun, going for short hikes, swimming, and lounging about like two real campers. Sitting by the water with their backs leaning into their gear, they listened to the familiar puckering of the *Sea Urchin* as it rounded a point.

Liam still resented Alex preventing him from grabbing the skull. "I just can't get it off my mind. We should have forced him to give it up and then placed an *anonymous* call with the Park Service. They'd kick his ass out, which would give us the space we need."

Alex gave him the 'not-again' glare. "We've beaten this horse. Stop worrying. We'll turn in the guy, but the proper way. My name is known, and the fact that I do research on the coastal Indians will help explain our presence out here."

Liam didn't trust him. Alex had emphasized speed ever since they found gold and always reminded him that the gunman already possessed the dagger. *Now he preaches caution—with the grave robber digging right under our noses! It just doesn't square.* The only sensible course of action called for removing the competition immediately.

"Here she comes." Binh's boat steamed toward the beach, several hours ahead of schedule. Liam had called him on the cell phone to arrange an earlier pickup.

They pushed the dinghy in the water, tossed their gear aboard, and started heading toward the *Sea Urchin*. "If he finds a coin, it's your fault," Liam grunted.

"Why don't you just let it go, have some faith? You're the religious one, I thought. I told you I'd contact the Park Service when we get back. If their men move quickly, and I think they will, they'll nail him by nightfall."

They climbed aboard. "I sure hope you're right. Then we can return this weekend."

Alex didn't say anything for a moment. "No one would like that better than myself. However, it depends entirely on what exactly the Park Service will do, and when. I'm beginning to doubt the wisdom of coming back too soon. I have no idea how long the area may remain under observation. A couple of weeks might be a more reasonable time frame. After all, we've got nothing to lose. The gold has been here for centuries. It won't disappear in fourteen days."

Have I heard right? Alex's last words demolished any doubts Liam may have still entertained. The professor definitely had his own agenda!

*   *   *

During a breakfast of acorn mush, scalding sage tea, and a healthy serving of cold rabbit chunks, Richard was brooding over whether he should go and induce Waspe to come to the village, when Wi'yapak strode up and took a seat beside him and Mónoy. The two Indians wrestled with each other's vernacular until Mónoy placed a hand on Richard's knee.

"Hioh want show you fish. He much happy."

Richard didn't know what she meant and realized he must have struck them as confused, for Wi'yapak got up and beckoned him to follow. Richard quickly shoved the last of the meat into his mouth and accompanied him to the river, where eleven men readied two canoes at water's edge. Painted a rich red and tastefully decorated with a plethora of shells, these slick vessels resembled giant sea serpents. They measured about twenty feet in length, with one slightly larger. He understood. They wanted him to come fishing. His mind was made up instantly. This might help build

261

friendships, and he would have a chance to see how seaworthy their canoes were. Waspe could wait.

The Indians split in two groups, and Wi'yapak motioned Richard to stay with him, Tuqan, and four others. They went for the larger canoe while the rest surrounded the other. Suddenly all the Indians raised their voices after the hioh, who, judging by the men's supplicating intonation, had commenced some form of chant. They're invoking divine help for a bountiful hunt or protection, Richard thought.

Hoping his hosts would take no offense at his failure to join in, he glimpsed Mónoy looking at him from the upper bank. When the chanting finally ceased and the men pushed their canoes into the stream, she ran to him.

"Waspe hungry, and no like Indian. Is bad."

Richard considered it. "Don't worry. He'll keep out of trouble, and I'm sure he's found something to eat." Nevertheless, a nagging concern persisted. But he brushed it aside, for the Indians began climbing into the canoes, Wi'yapak stared their way, and it just felt good to join the men on this excursion. He gave Mónoy a peck on the cheek and hurried into the creek.

Tuqan, kneeling in the bow, directed Richard to board near Wi'yapak, who commanded the stern. At the chief's signal the man still in the water, a stout fellow with an enormous neck and shoulders, gave the canoe a powerful shove before swinging himself over the side with the ease of a cat. He landed right in front of Richard, spraying him with water. At that very moment the air filled with numerous voices.

The entire village had gathered on the bank, shouting and laughing and waving. Mónoy stood next to Wi'yapak's wife, Umasikh, a tall woman with broad hips and the longest legs Richard had ever seen. They shook their arms as vigorously as the rest of the people. Richard started raising his in return when he realized that not a single man in either canoe paid any attention to the commotion ashore. He stopped his salute midway and inconspicuously drew in his arm. The fishermen shot swiftly downstream.

He studied the canoe. Made of planks over one inch thick and much more similar in design to an English pinnace than the dugouts used by Mónoy's people, the seams' tight fit derived from a combination of a thick seal of tar and a clever technique. The Indians had worked a tough rope through holes drilled all around the planks' edges, tying each so firmly to the next that water could not possibly seep through. The wood used in construction was so extremely smooth that it seemed polished. Thick, sturdy ropes tied the starboard to the port side, and rounded ends at stern and bow prevented their sliding off.

He turned his attention on the Indians. Wi'yapak stood behind him in the stern, silent except when barking an occasional direction. The man who had pushed the canoe into deeper water took up the spot in front of Richard. He wielded a double-bladed paddle, its two ends tapering to a spade-like point. The next three men all handled similar paddles. Tuqan occupied the bow, concentrating on their route. Except for Wi'yapak, each Indian kneeled on the hard planks, and Richard contemplated whether he should imitate them. But as masterfully as the planks had been worked, they already felt like stone under his buttocks. No! He had no idea how long they'd be gone, and he refused to subject his knees to such torture.

The canoes passed a tear-shaped rocky islet that split the stream in two channels. A forlorn pine sapling had made its lonely home on this raw speck, alone but for a scattering of scraggly bushes clinging to the lower ground. They entered into a confusing maze of waterways they would have to negotiate before reaching the silvery sliver of open sea sparkling in the distance. The boats rounded dozens of small mud islands, some covered with low bushes, others with thick stands of rushes. Richard began to grasp why the village lay so far from the sea. The marshy spits of land couldn't support clusters of permanent dwellings.

When the brackish and murky water of the marsh began to give way to the clear blue of the sea, Tuqan struck the hull three times with the palm of his hand. On the third thud, all Indians joined into a song. Their individual voices resonated harshly, but the combined sounds merged into an energetic rhythm. The rowers, released now from the narrow confines of the channels, stabbed their paddles into the sea that the foam flew. The canoes shot for the open waters.

Their speed dumbfounded Richard. The shore fell back so rapidly that he had to keep looking up to remember they bore no sail. They soon rounded the island's westernmost tip and plowed head-on into the broad channel separating them from the mainland. Almost immediately after leaving the island's shelter, the sea changed its mood. Before, the swell had topped out at two feet. Now chaotic whitecaps swooshed in from all directions. They threatened to overwhelm them one moment, only to collapse the next and suck the canoes deep into troughs where water towered all around them. If it weren't for the cool confidence of the Indians, who sang without interruption, Richard would have feared for his life. But they steered clear of the biggest breakers, undeterred, like birds banking into a storm squall. If he and Waspe could have a canoe like this, and rig it with mast and sail, they might yet reach the shores of Panama.

Their northeasterly course into the channel led them into a zone where the waves sorted themselves into a predictable pattern. The sea, no longer so turbulent, turned dark blue, and the team split up when the other canoe abruptly veered off. Wi'yapak continued on his course for a while, patrolling a swath of ocean until Tuqan's impetuous voice rang out. The Indian pointed with his arm, shouting quick commands.

All singing stopped as he picked up a harpoon, its head fitted with a fist-sized stone chiseled to a sharp point. Taut cord secured this head and a finger-thick bone barb to the shaft. A rope tied around the harpoon's fore shaft ran over Tuqan's left palm, past his arm and shoulder, and into a neat coil on the canoe's floor. With the three rowers working just enough to keep the canoe on course, he lifted the spear high above his head, carefully balancing his body against the rearing sea. When the canoe shot into another trough, he hurled the weapon with all his strength.

* * *

Alex took leave minutes after the *Sea Urchin* docked. "There's a lot of stuff I have to take care of. I'll be in touch." He didn't thank Binh for the ride.

"A fine fellow," the fisherman said. "Just the kind of guy you want for a friend."

Liam felt embarrassed. "I'm sorry. It's not like him. Something is going on. In fact, I need to talk to you."

"What's up?" Binh came closer as though he feared someone could eavesdrop.

"The professor is keeping stuff from me, and I'm convinced he's making private plans."

Binh nodded slowly. "I've known you for long enough. Your hunches usually are right. But where do I come in?"

Liam put a hand on his shoulder. "There may come the time when I need your boat on real short notice."

"You bet," Binh replied without hesitation. "Count on it."

"There's one more thing. I'm not sure anymore what I'm up against. With my brother in the hospital, I'm alone. I could use not only your boat, but you to cover my back, just in case."

Binh tilted his head on the side, looking at him with mock pity. "You didn't really believe the *Sea Urchin* comes without me, did you?"

* * *

The harpoon's shaft poked straight up, then tilted away from the canoe as the quarry rolled over on its side. They came alongside the most extraordinary fish Richard had ever seen.

The animal's dark blue back faded on the side into a shimmering bluish-purple stripe that ran from behind the eye all the way to the tail. A long pectoral fin extended between this stripe and a silver-gray belly. The back fin was huge, at least two feet high, but the most impressive part of this fish protruded from its head. With the creature almost as long as the canoe, the sword-like growth alone accounted for a quarter of that. As the majestic fish lolled dead in the water, with the expressionless eye gazing skyward, Richard actually regretted its destruction. Though the body's shape and coloring reminded him of a shark, its broad sword and slick head commanded appreciation and respect.

Wi'yapak put an end to the noisy chatter of the crew and snapped several short commands. Tuqan took up a squatting position and fed the end of the harpoon's rope to the man behind him, who handed it back until it reached Wi'yapak. In the meantime, the three rowers maneuvered the canoe to close the gap separating it from the fish's tail. When the large fin was within arm's reach, Wi'yapak, waiting for another breaker to pass beneath them, bent as far overboard as he could. His son mirrored his movements at the other end of the canoe and leaned to the opposite side to balance the weight. The hioh now reached out with surprising speed and twice wrapped the rope around the glistening fish before the agitated sea forced him to withdraw. Another man pulled a chert knife from his belt and hacked through the rope just above where the shaft's sharp point had entered the flesh. Obviously the Indians feared competition. Tearing the harpoon from the body would have ripped the flesh wide open and spilled a river of blood, lighting an irresistible beacon for sharks. With the fish's head moving off while the tail remained tied to the hull, the Indians lifted their paddles and headed back for the island with the catch in perfect tow.

The sun had already passed its zenith by the time the hunters crossed from the clear sea to the brackish, marshy labyrinth. The men slowed the pace of the canoe to a crawl, deliberately trying to prevent the fish from getting snagged in a knot of submerged roots, or from dragging it across the bottom. When they finally caught sight of the village, children started running toward them, and jubilant adults shouted excitedly right behind them.

Tuqan and two of the crew slid into the stream and worked their way aft as Wi'yapak untied the rope. The three men in the water began to pull the fish toward shore, and half a dozen villagers helped out. The bank was lined with people, most of whom cast curious glances at Richard. Wi'yapak motioned him to get out of the canoe, and they both waded ashore.

"All say you give luck." He hadn't noticed Mónoy, outfitted with new buckskins in the style of her hosts, standing behind Umasikh.

"What?" Richard didn't get her meaning.

"They think you give fish."

He squirmed from all the attention. "I didn't do anything."

They watched a score of Indians lift, roll, and drag the carcass onto a makeshift platform of mats hastily arranged at water's edge. When they finally had the fish where they wanted it, its powerful sword extending past the mats, Wi'yapak raised his arm to silence everyone. He then delivered an animated speech and repeatedly looked at Richard. When he finished, he signaled his son. Tuqan started cutting, hacking, and slicing until he could finally break the fish's sword off its head. Then he carried the blood-streaked prize to Richard.

267

All eyes fixed on him. His mouth felt dry as he searched for words, his mind racing. He didn't contribute in any way and hadn't even touched a paddle. Tuqan threw the harpoon. The sword should go to him. But Richard remembered his time with Mónoy's people. *No one ever refuses a gift.* So with his best possible smile, he took the sword. Cool to the touch, it easily outweighed a musket. He turned it for all to see, placed it on the ground, and motioned the Indians to come and take a look. The children immediately surged forward, and Richard used the opportunity to extricate himself from the crowd and latch onto Mónoy.

"I must get Waspe. We shouldn't leave him without word for a second night." Richard pointed at the canoes. "He needs to see these."

*   *   *

When the first rays of the rising sun tickled Waspe's heavy lids, he blinked and sat up. He'd slept like a dead man. The fresh morning air, pervaded with the characteristic scent of a tangy summer sea, called him to action. He ignored the pangs of hunger. He'd eat later.

He peeled off his breeches and started rubbing the sand out of his crotch, but the finer grains clung to his sweaty thighs. He rushed into a sea sparkling like precious pearls and swam to the hole in the rock. The tide, lower than in the evening, had left the uppermost reaches of the crevasse exposed. He pumped his lungs full of air and shot to the bottom, hovering before the entrance. Though the sun still hung low in the sky, his powerful eyes penetrated the glass-like water. Two fat orange fish languidly drifted out of the hole. Fortunately they ignored him and faded into the ocean's blue.

Waspe felt at ease in the sea. He'd grown up on and in it. But facing this sunken hole, he hesitated. What unknown creatures might lurk in those recesses? *Is that my heart beating?*

268

A sensible man would concentrate on gathering mussels. Curiosity, though, proved an unyielding opponent. He braced himself and inched into the cavity.

Shielding his face with one arm, he propelled his body with the other. Oddly, as he moved deeper into the grotto, the dark seemed to retreat. This made no sense. The light had to be playing tricks on his eyes. He kicked his feet just enough to go two or three yards and turned on his side to look up. He hadn't imagined things. Somewhere above the surface, dull light filtered into what had to be a cave. Since he had plenty of air left, he slowly ascended. A moment later he broke through the surface.

Waspe wiped the water off his face and made for a narrow rock ledge. While trying to pull himself up, he lost hold on the slippery shale and fell back. He looked around and worked his way along the ledge until his feet touched bottom. He continued till the water level dropped to his knees, and he finally stepped right onto the ledge. Intrigued, he surveyed his strange new surroundings.

An oval hole, large enough for a skinny man to squeeze through sideways, split the forty-foot-high roof. Light streaming in through this opening illuminated the tranquil pool and cast long shadows in the cave's corners. The walls rose steeply, except for a recess in the far left. Waspe inched toward it, running his hands along the cold, damp rock for balance. He ducked his head and probed a few feet into what looked like a tunnel. It probably ended just ahead, he thought. Then the hint of a draft chilled his wet skin, and he shivered. *What am I doing in this desolate hole?* He backed out.

He snickered at his childishness, and the sound of his voice calmed his raw nerves. How could he act so foolishly? No monsters roamed this cave. In fact, nothing or no one had likely ever set foot—another thought shot through his mind. Of course! Excited, he dove off the ledge into the water.

Waspe crossed to the open sea and hastened to shore, his hunger all but forgotten. He grabbed the rope and wrapped it around one of the barrels. Then he tied the loose end around his waist. He trudged back into the surf with the heavy load in tow, dragging it until the water reached his chest. From there he worked his way hand over hand along the rough cliff, hauling the cask over the sandy bottom a foot at a time. When he could no longer keep his mouth above the waterline, he went below, coming up for air at regular intervals.

Upon reaching the cave, he pulled in the slack till the barrel rested at his side. He surfaced to get a lungful of fresh air. Then he dove back down to work the loose rope around his forearm to prevent it from getting hung up on his way in. He rolled the cask through the opening to the approximate center of the pool, ascended, and made for the edge. Soon the gold stood safely on the ledge.

Barrels two, three, and four followed until they all faced the pool like silent sentries guarding the entrance to a forbidden place. No one would suspect this hideout in a thousand years. The savages wouldn't have a clue. Neither would Argyle. Waspe snorted. The lad seemed a good man in the beginning, but had grown tiresome. Worse, he would pose a serious problem once they reached the Spanish settlements. Waspe had fooled himself thinking he could talk their way onto a Spanish ship. *My mute brother? No, the Dons aren't idiots.* Besides, Argyle's blue eyes and fair hair stood out like a weathervane. And then he had insisted on bringing the girl along. Waspe cringed. The Governor's soldiers would quarter them. But he had plenty of time to think about that.

One after another he rolled the four barrels away from the ledge and lined them up on the bone-dry tunnel floor beyond reach of the highest tides. He screamed with wild joy, which echoed off the walls and through the crack in the ceiling to the outside. Two terrified pelicans escaped from their rocky perch above the Pacific.

With tremendous relief Waspe realized that he no longer had to worry about the gold.

*   *   *

The trade winds normally blowing toward the west and Indonesia had weakened. This had caused an enormous low-pressure cell to start building off Tahiti since the previous year. These weather anomalies stopped the warm surface layer of the equatorial Pacific from flowing west, reversing its direction toward the Americas and piling up against the coast a pool of hot water larger than the entire U.S. This vast heat engine then released billions of tons of moisture into the upper atmosphere, forming a vast mass of clouds soon to unload on the western fringes of the New World with torrential rains.

One such El Niño-fueled storm system brewed offshore, poised to blow its lid, and on course to smash into southern California.

~23~

The Jeep sped along US 101 amidst the lush plantings of beautiful Montecito. Stately cypress and eucalyptus trees, the latter with long strips of bark peeling off their trunks, shaded the road. They still held at bay the rising tide of strip malls and freeway interchanges that smothered ever more of the rich farmland to the south. Liam switched lanes, pushed the accelerator to the floor, and glanced at the droves of surfers straddling their boards.

He hadn't been able to take his mind off that skull. Its shape reminded him of something he'd seen before. *But where? The anatomy lab?* The teacher of one of his favorite college classes had delighted in placing skeletons in the most awkward positions, in sticking pipes in their jaws, or attaching bracelets. *Or maybe something I've seen on TV, or in a magazine?* Damned, no matter how he tried, he couldn't make the connection.

Traffic thickened where the freeway leaves the coast and begins its long dip into Ventura. Liam let up on the pedal, not noticing one of the cars behind him immediately adjust its speed to that of the Jeep. He drove on through Ventura and Oxnard, past automobile dealerships, mega stores, and cookie-cutter developments, all telltale signs of the spreading Los Angles cancer.

Getting off the freeway at Las Posas, he hammered it to Point Mugu, where he merged again onto the Pacific Coast Highway. On it went, hemmed in by the ocean and the brittle Santa Monica Mountains and past a chain of sandy beaches—Zuma, Malibu, Topanga—his anticipation growing as he got closer to his destination. Where Sunset Boulevard makes a dead stop on the PCH, he turned left and climbed into the hills. Finally he took a sharp right into the Lake Shrine's secluded parking lot.

Liam went into the rustic windmill chapel and sat by an open window. The relaxing environment, with bird songs, and the sound of falling water drifting off the lake, relieved his tension. The muffled chatter of ducks added to the serene ambiance. A young woman and a gray-haired man sat immobile in perfect meditation posture near the front of the chapel. Liam straightened his back and forgot the world around him.

One hour later he rose, brimming with calm energy, the morning's tension gone. He quietly headed for the exit, surprised to see the man and woman still there. *Hadn't the door opened and closed?* He cast a final glance at the gold-framed images of Yogananda and the other masters and left.

When he came here he always walked the path around the lake, stopping at intervals to stick his nose into a fragrant blossom or just admiring the exotic plants. He reached the tiny pier jutting into the lake near the houseboat. Huge multi-hued koi glided aimlessly at the surface, poking their big-lipped mouths into the air in hope of some morsels. Footsteps approached from behind, and a squeaking indicated someone took a seat on the wooden bench.

Mesmerized, Liam lost himself in the never-ending procession of fish and soaked up the sun's warmth until he felt a sudden chill. He rubbed his arms, astonished to find them covered with goose bumps, and looked up. The sun still shone from a blue sky, without a cloud in sight. There was no wind either. He shrugged it off, but when the goose bumps crawled up to the neck and he experienced light-headedness, Liam realized something was wrong. This had never happened before. *Is this what you feel before you get a stroke?*

He turned and found himself staring at a black pistol. A dark-haired man held the gun in his lap, pointing the muzzle at Liam's chest. High cheekbones betrayed Asian or Native

American blood. Liam stole a quick glance at the feet, which were very large.

Two Blackhawk helicopters hugged the tarmac like giant insects ready to take off, their wings anxiously churning the air. Twelve National Park Service rangers filed out of the hangar and ran toward the choppers, each man holding an arm before his face for protection from the dust the whirling blades kicked up. All carried M-16 assault rifles. None spoke because the roaring engines rendered speech impossible.

The rangers split into two groups of six, one for each Blackhawk. They jumped into their seats and strapped themselves in, two airmen slamming the doors behind them. A third soldier standing in front of and between the intimidating war machines threw up his arms and signaled the pilots. The Blackhawks lifted off without delay and swept over the airfield toward the mountains. By the time the dust settled over the tarmac at Vandenberg Air Force Base, they had become two dark specks in the southeasterly sky.

The man commanding the operation, Glen Lerario, scrutinized the rangers in his bird. None had been involved in this type of operation before, at least not for the Park Service. That was no surprise, since it happened very rarely that they received assistance from the military. Four of his eleven men had spent time in the military. Two had actually seen combat. Chip "Rat" Valenzano, the younger, had raced a battle tank across the Iraqi desert. Norman "Gator" Kelly had parachuted into Grenada back in '83. The remaining seven had found their way into the Park Service after a string of other jobs. All good men, he'd handpicked them. Lerario never got caught short, especially not with his oldest son on the other Blackhawk. Besides, the low-lives they were after probably had no weapons at all. And if they *did*, they'd be fools to even think of using them.

Looking down at the calm Pacific spreading from the Santa Ynez Mountains to the horizon, the commander recalled the highlights of his nineteen years with the Service. During that time he had brought in poachers on five different occasions and in three disparate locations a continent apart. In Yellowstone and Denali he nailed them for trapping and shooting grizzly bear for the lucrative Far East market. The Koreans dished out thousands of dollars for a few ounces of grizzly gall. And in the Everglades, four years ago, he had busted an immense ring of exotic bird traders. Those bastards had been unscrupulous and armed. Only the size of his force, sixteen men toting automatic rifles, prevented an actual firefight. Lerario grinned. Today he finally had a shot at putting grave looters out of business. He cherished the moment. They rarely caught them in the act.

"Five minutes to the LZ!" a deep voice rose over the rotors' racket.

Lerario gave the pilot a thumbs-up and checked once more that each ranger's rifle held a thirty-round clip. Overwhelming force for such a mission! But it was all in the perception.

Santa Rosa loomed large before them, though the coastline remained shrouded in thick mists. They would soon begin their descent to the landing zone at the mouth of the canyon. He pulled out a Cuban Consuegra and savored its aroma. He'd light it up when the handcuffs snapped shut.

Their eyes met. The gunman's were hard and cold. Liam shivered with intuition. *This man shot Patrick.* He wondered whether he'd spend the coming night in a morgue. Should he yell for help? No! That seemed pathetic and cowardly. There was no one in sight anyway, as the grounds were uncommonly deserted. He could dart sideways, dive into the lake and swim till his lungs forced him up. He might still catch a bullet in the back of his head, but the guy would think twice before shooting such a distance. He too had to leave through the front entrance located on the opposite side of the lake.

The man rose and, surprisingly, shoved his gun in a pocket. *Why the hell did he do that?* Liam didn't know what to make of it. *He's about my size. Should I risk a fight?* They stared at each other for a small eternity as Liam weighed the pros and cons of tackling a man with a gun. Finally the stranger spoke.

"Where did you get the dagger?"

Liam hesitated. "I can't tell you that."

The guy sunk his hand in his jacket and stood there, a weird glint in his eyes. Liam clenched his fists and felt his entire body stiffen in preparation of what may come.

"It's a good day for you." The man's unexpected words stunned him. "Thank your lucky star." A hint of resignation had crawled into his voice. "This is a bad place to do what I came for, but I promise we will meet again. Then you will give me the name of the island and the exact place you found the dagger. Or it will not be such a good day again."

Liam didn't know what to say. Only a moment ago he had expected a bullet. And now the stranger didn't even seem like such a terrible guy. A stray thought surged through his mind. Of course! This was an once-in-a-lifetime chance, and it called for action. He beckoned the gunman and started walking.

"Come. I'm going to show you something." He still couldn't get over the way the cards had changed.

The odd couple circled clockwise around the lake until Liam stopped at the lawn of the World Peace Memorial. His shadow halted a few steps behind him and waited, his expression that of a man utterly incredulous at his actions. Liam pointed at the magnificent marble sarcophagus.

"It predates Columbus by five centuries. Inside lies the only portion of Gandhi's ashes outside India. Millions worldwide hold sacred the soil you're standing on." He let it sink in. "Perhaps that answers your questions about this being a bad place to carry out your plans."

Kuyam stared at the memorial for a long time in silence. Then he gave a short, almost imperceptible nod and shifted his weight. Suddenly he looked vulnerable.

"I . . . I can not undo the past." He hesitated. "I'm sorry." And he turned and swiftly walked away.

Liam, resisting an initial urge to call out to him, watched Kuyam's hand retrieve something from his jacket. With a quick, fluid motion he flung it far into the lake, where the gun sank with a splash. He never looked back and hurried along the path until the vegetation swallowed him.

Liam sat down on the thick grass, lightheaded. A profound and completely novel feeling of joy enveloped him. He no longer wished Patrick's assailant any harm. The break-in, even the shooting seemed no more relevant now than a violent scene in an action flick. Patrick's condition was improving, and there had been no permanent damage. To the contrary, today the Lake Shrine had worked a small miracle.

For a while Liam gazed at the peaceful waters and recounted all that had transpired since he first camped on Santa Rosa. Finding that dagger had set in motion forces that somehow defied physical science, and he knew in his soul that the locomotive of his life was inexorably steaming toward a crucial turning point.

He rose and marched along the path past the gift store and to the parking lot. No sign of the guy. He saw only a gardener and a banged-up wheelbarrow, a mother with twins in a stroller, and a monk in a long ocher robe.

Cob Rash had joined his brother early Wednesday, taking a personal day. Since morning both men were feverishly digging in the ground. A femur had followed the skull, and Dave recovered a pelvic girdle and the crushed remnant of what probably had been a foot. The entire excavation site ran fifteen yards long and averaged six feet in width.

It was an unlikely spot for a human burial ground. The creek must have deposited the bones from upstream and subsequently buried them below a layer of silt and sand. A couple inches of fine-grained silt had covered the pelvic girdle and foot. The skull fortunately had protruded above ground, the familiar shape of the cranium with its suture lines having attracted Dave's attention to the spot in the first place.

Cob pulled up his shovel, stood erect, and cocked his head. An eerie, distant whooping flowed from the mists. Then it was gone, but only for a second, and his ears registered the unmistakable whipping of air from a helicopter's rotor blades.

"A damn chopper," he shouted, racing for a blanket to throw over their tools.

Dave tossed his spade into the stream and flung two towels at its edge. He plopped down on one like a sack of potatoes and stuck his feet in the water. A moment later Cob dropped beside him, doing likewise. Picture perfect, they'd pass for happy campers soaking their sore feet in the cool waters after a long hike.

"It's probably a supply bird for the oil rigs," Dave said with indifference.

"Better safe than sorry. I don't remember a single chopper since we've started work here. This area is not in their usual flight path."

Dave had spent much more time in the canyon. "No, it ain't, but you know how it is. Every once in a while one of 'em will come close. The pilots like to go sightseeing." He chortled. "If they only knew what they're missing."

The Blackhawks swooped from the ridge, banked into a tight curve over the water, and touched down on the beach. They immediately disgorged twelve rangers and bounced back into the sky mere seconds after the last man hit the ground. The rangers had grouped in two teams before the sand stopped flying.

"Move out!" their commander barked. Team A sloshed through the stream to the far bank and formed an inverted

"V." Its point man, John Lerario, headed upstream without delay. His father led Team B on the near bank.

"That sure sounded like two or maybe even three of them, don't you think?" Cob snarled, his face filled with apprehension.

"So what? They're gone. Let's get back to work."

"There's never more than one bird. I don't like it." Cob hesitated. "We should wait. They could be circling around."

"I doubt it. It costs the oil companies bundles of cash to supply the rigs. It's one thing to take a turn here or there and check out stuff, but they ain't gonna let their pilots fly all over the islands just for the fun—"

"Shut up!" Cob's eyes widened with disbelief. Was he hallucinating? A man looking like a soldier stood on the other side of the stream. An automatic rifle rested comfortably in his arms, its muzzle pointing in their direction.

"Remain as you are!"

The crisp voice and appearance of five more men convinced Cob he was not imagining things. More commotion behind his back made him turn.

Dave paled, and his face twitched with an expression of despair. Cob began chewing his lips. They were in deep shit. How could they possibly talk their way out of this one? Everything stacked up against them—the tools, the bones, all of it. These guys' timing had been impeccable. That damn history professor and his friends must have ratted.

Dave made an effort to get to his feet.

"Get the hell back down," Cob hissed as discreetly as possible. "Don't muck this up and keep quiet. I'll do the talking."

His brother obeyed while the rangers swarmed them. "What exactly is this supposed to mean?" he snapped arrogantly as he rose, striving to lend firmness to his voice. "Whoever is in charge of this ludicrous war game, tell your men to stop pointing their weapons at us! This is an outrage."

The one who seemed in charge ignored him and watched one of his men pull off the blanket. Shovels, measuring tapes, trowels, a pickax, and a number of other obvious digging tools spelled volumes. The commander turned and stepped up to the Rashes, his face uncompromising.

"How cute! A genuine family business, huh? It seems we nailed your asses during regular business hours, didn't we?" He paused, measuring Cob with unveiled disgust. "Some fine high school principal you are! Now, *that's* an outrage. But tell me one thing. Are you the type who sings parents songs about all the wonderful things you're doing for their children while really you screw everyone who crosses your path?"

Cob's throat felt parched. This impudent son-of-a-bitch was way out of line running his mouth to him like that, but they'd caught them at the worst possible time. Some light still glimmered at the end of the tunnel, though. Those men had no hard evidence. Cob prepared to make a juicy reply when he heard the crumpling of a plastic sack, accompanied by subdued voices. His heart sank.

"Sir, I think you'll want to take a look at this."

One of the rangers dangled the bag with the bones before his superior's face. Cob broke out in a sweat, chewing his lips till they bled. His ugly scar glowed. He decided to keep his thoughts to himself and not say another word until he lined up a lawyer.

"They just picked them up," Deputy Keller announced, a broad smile on his round face.

"Good. That eliminates those thieves. Let's see what the Park Service can squeeze out of them. In the meantime, we will wait for our friends to make their move. Everyone play stupid and make it real obvious. I want our watches to leave every day before midnight, then return again by sunrise to both Malreaux's and Kindayr's houses. We'll dupe the fellows into believing they're not worth all that much attention."

Quint dropped a few mints into his mouth. "And I want two men at the harbor, around the clock. Who knows? They might fall for it."

* * *

The canoe had skirted the coast for one league when the familiar headland, shaped like the head of a horse, moved into Richard's line of sight. The steep western promontory, its base shielded from the pounding surf by slabs of bedrock that pierced the sea's surface, inexplicably caught his attention. The triangular, flat top high above the beach, with a broad ledge hanging over the abyss on the ocean side and a tongue-like extension connecting it to the backcountry, had a mysterious quality. Suddenly he saw Waspe, his head bent low, pounding down on some object. Then his hand went to his face. He was eating.

"John," he hailed the cook from afar, but got no response. He waited for the canoe to get closer and tried again. This time Waspe's head jerked up. He stared briefly before going back to cracking shells.

When they reached shallow water, Richard climbed over the gunwale. "I've come to take you to their village," he called out as he waded ashore.

Waspe scooped a hunk of clam onto his tongue and chewed happily. When Richard walked up, he swallowed and finally looked him in the face. "That's good of you." His cold tone betrayed his feelings.

Not again, Richard thought, shooting back, "You *chose* to stay."

He nodded very slowly, as though thinking hard on a matter of grave importance. "Yes, I did. Because we planned to reach Panama, with a cargo for which we killed."

This was too much. Richard boiled over. "You expect us to build a boat without ever leaving this canyon, despite the

Indians knowing we're here? That aside, call me a thief, or a deserter, but I'm no damn murderer."

Waspe's eyes bulged, and the veins on his temples pulsated as he thrust his face forward. His breath reeked of raw shellfish. "No? What about Smythe? I don't reckon it's possible you already forgot that swine. So, since you want a share of the gold, I don't approve wiping your hands clean of his death."

Richard wanted to punch his teeth out, but he stepped back past the reach of the clammy stench rising from Waspe's stomach. "*You* slit his throat! *You* made that decision. I've *never* laid hands on an unarmed man."

"Oh my, how sweet! You can sing that song to the magistrate." The cook laughed derisively, an evil grin distorting his face. "Trust me, if they catch us, you'll hang right next to me."

Guilt began to gnaw at Richard. *I shouldn't have let him kill Smythe.* For the first time he truly wished they had never met. Taking the gold hadn't seemed like such a bad deed initially. The greedy Dons had wrested it from the Indians over a mountain of corpses. Then the General and his officers, like a bunch of greedy jackals, sailed into the Pacific to raid the Spanish Main. England and Spain were not even at war. Besides, why should the noblemen get the lion's share of the booty and throw the sailors a mere pittance? Especially when they stood idle and grew fat, while the men before the mast worked their hides raw. He sighed. Things had gone so dreadfully wrong since Smythe discovered them. As much as Richard had loathed that sick ghoul, the killing did scar his conscience.

He scanned the beach. "Where is the gold anyhow? Where did you put it?"

Waspe ogled him. "Let's just say it's in a place no savage will suspect, not till long after we help ourselves to one of those boats." He tilted his head toward the canoe.

This repulsed Richard. "You're a bastard! These people have given us food and shelter, and your first response is to steal from them. I won't allow it."

"Oh, is that so?" in a mocking voice. "And what if I disregard your orders?"

"Then you're a bigger fool than I imagined. If you want to get back to Europe alive you need me. Sail alone and you'll die. So, for as long as we're on this island—"

"Island!" Waspe exclaimed. "Are you crazy? This is no island."

Richard chuckled gleefully. "Oh, yes! At least ten leagues lie between us and the mainland."

Waspe stared open-mouthed. Then something seemed to come to his mind. "Aye, I remember now. Cabrillo wrote of a nick in the coastline, but I always figured he meant some bay. We sailed too far offshore aboard the *Golden Hind*. That's why the General missed it."

Richard shrugged his shoulders. "It doesn't matter. What's important is that the Indians remain our friends. From the looks of it, the island is too small for them to war, and as long as they don't quarrel with mainland tribes we ought to be safe."

Waspe's relief showed in his softened demeanor and tone. "We may yet save our skins. What else have you learned?"

Richard could finally share all the exciting news and could hardly catch his breath between words. "They took me fishing. You won't believe how their canoes fly." He turned to point at his, where the Indians waited patiently. "Extremely sturdy and made of planks. They caulk them with tar. If we can build a similar one, make a sail, and rig ourselves a mast, we'll have a better chance of reaching Panama than we did before. And while we're here we can learn how to make bows and arrows, and anything else we need. We can hunt and fish and dry the meat. Of course it'll take time. But we've got plenty. The way I see it, wrecking here may work to our advantage. By the time we'll depart, the General is bound to be half-way across the Pacific, and the Spaniards will have given up on us."

Waspe nodded slowly. "Maybe, but you can't count on that."

~24~

Julia measured Alex coldly. "You look as though you're about to have a nervous breakdown. Life can't be treating you that badly." She paused. "At least I wouldn't think so."

They sat inside the cabin of the *Helen* as Joe Fox, de-facto captain of the luxury yacht, led them out of the harbor into the open sea.

Alex avoided her eyes and ignored the insinuation. "I've been thinking about those guys they caught looting Indian graves. I wonder what they'll get." He withheld that he had anonymously tipped off the Park Service.

"I'd love to see them in jail, but that probably won't happen. Most people couldn't care less about Chumash history. The court will slap their hands and attend to more pressing business. At least the principal's career should be finished."

"You know," she continued when he said nothing. "You too may get yourself in a lot of trouble. In my opinion, you're rushing it, especially with this weather forecast. You might consider waiting till Liam gets well. The two of you can watch each other's back. But then again, why should I really be concerned?"

He fleetingly admired her trim body. The dark sweater outlined her breasts beautifully, and the tight jeans clung to her long legs. He graced her with his nicest smile, but when she remained totally aloof, he dropped the facade. Since the incident with Rachel in the closet, she'd been remote and completely into herself. He feared she'd decide to ask for a divorce, which would ruin him economically and probably push him over the brink professionally. *I can't blame her. But I also can't let that happen. She has to stay with me.*

"I must take that risk. We can't afford to waste more time. Liam says so himself." Alex had deceived her, telling her that Liam had the flu. And he told Liam that he had to take leave from the university and fly to New York to meet his publisher. "The weather actually is a plus. No one will be out there till it clears up."

She studied him intensely. "You must know what's best, particularly since you insist on leaving at such an ungodly hour."

It was barely five a.m., and the sun hadn't come up. He had told her nothing of the police surveillance, which for some strange reason excluded the nights.

"I do think you're making another big mistake," she stabbed.

Alright. Let it pass. Stay cool. "The wind won't pick up for a while, and a little rain won't hurt me."

Meteorologists forecasted a Pineapple Express, a huge low-pressure cell moving in from the tropical Pacific. This usually meant more than 'a little rain.' The clouds might release torrents, with high winds driving the rain hard. Already, a heavily overcast sky kept the pre-dawn horizon pitch black. But where the rain might not threaten Alex directly, he discounted the danger of the land itself. A narrow valley bisected by a stream promised trouble during a powerful Express. These storms could generate devastating flashfloods, and the amounts of water drawn from the abnormally heated eastern Pacific had the potential for a tremendous tempest.

Alex had to find the source of the gold at all costs. Time was on his side only temporarily, which dictated action now. The Park Service almost certainly would shun the canyon for the duration of the coming storm, the Rashes were history, and he'd even neutralized Liam. With the cops dumb enough to let him slip through the net under cover of dark, the moment belonged to him—Alex Malreaux. He even brought his pistol, just in case. *I don't want to run unprepared into another looter or that pawnshop freak.* Of course he wouldn't shoot anyone, but he also had no desire to become a defenseless target. There was no use following in Patrick's footsteps. A bit of luck, and he'd return a rich man in a day or two. He'd tell his publisher there was a change in plans and that she could expect a different type of manuscript in due time. As far as the university was concerned, if he didn't get tenure, then they could kiss his ass. And that parched old dinosaur, Alfred Van Haik, could wait for his galley till hell froze over. Julia and her parents—*well, I'm going to straighten that out too.*

"I'm going up. I want to take a look at the sea."

Waves raced across the ocean from all directions, and the strengthening gusts foreshadowed worse. Alex looked at the hissing, foaming mass beating up on the hull. Fortunately, the waves were still relatively small. After they passed through the Santa Cruz Channel and approached the canyon, Fox spoke with a skeptical expression on his face.

"I don't know, Mr. Malreaux. You're sure you want to land? I doubt I'll be able to pick you up as planned. It's gonna get real wet and windy, and there's a good chance the swell will keep you from launching the zodiac for some time."

This irritated Alex. "I'm quite aware of that, Joe, but I do need to complete my research. I simply can't afford to push it off any longer, especially because another storm may follow on the heels of this one. I've got more deadlines than you want to hear about."

Fox smirked, as if he didn't believe such deadlines could exist for a professor, which irritated Alex even more. But the skipper's expression grew serious again. "You've heard of those guys they grabbed digging up Indian graves? Is that related to your work?"

He'd anticipated Fox asking such a question and had rehearsed his answer a dozen times. "Yes, indirectly. The book I've worked on for the past three years is a history of the coastal Indians between Malibu and San Luis Obispo. In the course of my research I've discovered several Chumash sites. Stupidly, I made no secret of it, and in the process attracted the wrong kind of people to the island. Now, with all this publicity, I'm forced to tie up loose ends before the Park Service in its federal wisdom decides to bar entry to the area. I haven't even told the Superintendent that I'm going back."

"That's bureaucracy for you," Fox interjected.

"It sure is," Alex replied. "Not that the Superintendent would mind, but if his superiors found out, they'd pull the plug. And that's precisely what I can't afford. It would push publication back even further, killing my deal with the publisher. Three years of work down the tubes, just like that."

The skipper nodded and looked up at the sky, still not looking too thrilled. "Well, let's get you there before it's too late."

* * *

Months had passed, and although the autumn had already progressed past its peak, the air never cooled. The hot days of July and August flowed into the withering weeks of September and October. Though morning mists brought some welcome hours of relief from the sameness, they inevitably burned off to reveal clear sky and a merciless sun that parched the land. Even the Indians remarked on the heat's intensity, and only the eldest remembered a season so scorching.

Richard and Waspe frittered away another afternoon by the creek, which had shrunk to such a trickle that the men could no longer launch their canoes from the village. They kept them near the marsh instead. Children frolicked in the last of the deeper pools that still dotted the channel and wrestled each other.

Waspe sat up and flung a rock into the creek. "Never thought I'd come to hate the damn sun. All my life I've waited for summer. Now I'd trade some of our gold for icy air and a mighty downpour. Ah, what I wouldn't give for a week of blustering storms."

Richard lazily got up on an elbow. "I don't care if I ever feel another drop of rain. There's nothing like a blue sky. God, sometimes I don't even want to return to England." He sank back down. "Think of it, there's everything a man could desire—plenty of wholesome food, decent people, no orders, a good woman, and the chance to roam the land as freely as an earl. I'm no one's slave here. In truth, I never felt so alive."

Waspe eyed him with a mixture of anxiety and contempt. "You've had too much sun. It's making you sick in the head." He watched Mónoy playing with the children in one of the pools, her firm breasts visible. "As far as good women go, you did find one."

Richard wondered whether he'd heard right. Did Waspe really say a positive thing about an Indian? Even though annoyed at the cook's lusty stare, Richard jumped on the unusual opportunity and tried to encourage him. "Why don't you take one? There are enough without husbands."

"Hell, no! Too bony. Besides, the women here have shown no more fondness for me than have those up north." He snorted, still staring at Mónoy. "Now, if this one wasn't yours, I'd think more on it."

"But you've come too late. Mónoy is mine, and we are made for each other," Richard fired back.

The cook snickered derisively. "There isn't no one this side of the River Styx that's made for each other. You wait. A woman belongs to herself. That one, she's damn sure got a head of her own, and it won't be long 'fore she'll use it too. Don't fool yourself. If we ever get back across the sea in one piece, a whole new world will open to her. Fresh sights, strange sounds, delicious smells—she'll want to take a bite of everything." He chuckled. "Now, you're a rich man. For some time that ought to keep her happy. But one day she'll know the language and make acquaintances. She'll learn the meaning of a title, of influence, and she'll resent that you have neither. You must always hide how you came to your gold. With her beauty sure to be highly prized by any man who casts his gaze upon her, some day you may wake to a cold blanket."

"This is crazy." Richard defended her. "It's your kind of women you describe. Mónoy is pure and untainted."

Waspe now burst out laughing, shaking his head. Mónoy and the youngsters stopped their game and looked over. "You've got a child's mind. Take a look at her! Those tits! She'll have more suitors than there are pebbles in this creek. They'll stalk her like randy dogs, foaming from their mouths till—"

The fist smashed the bridge of his nose, and he never finished his sentence. The impact knocked him over, and when he sat up to inspect the damage, blood stained his fingers. A thin line ran from the nostrils and dripped off his upper lip. Scowling at Richard, he licked it clean. "You'll pay for this," the cook whispered through tightly pressed lips, his words barely audible.

"In the future, keep your filthy mouth shut."

One of the bigger boys ran off, and his sudden motion detracted Richard. In this moment Waspe dove at him and brought him crashing to the ground. Richard pulled up his leg with lightning speed to deflect a thrust to his groin, and the cook's hard knee struck the thigh muscle instead. Trying to ignore the sharp pain, Richard's fists started hammering Waspe, who fell as Richard scrambled to his feet. But Waspe had had enough. Throwing him a hate-filled glance, he crawled backward. It was over, for now.

If there had been any doubt in Richard's mind, he was now convinced. Waspe had a rotten core. *He doesn't deserve my friendship. Why should I even leave this island?* Without the cook and his command of Spanish to get them aboard a ship bound for Europe, he had no chance anyway. Their whole plan surely had been a fantasy from its conception. No, he shouldn't continue this lunatic scheme, especially not with a man like Waspe.

*   *   *

Alex stood in the rearing zodiac, grabbed his backpack, and stored it near the bow. Then Julia made her move and started descending the ladder. She jumped the last two rungs. Alex whirled around. His jaw dropped.

"What are you doing?" he cried, gawking at Fox holding her backpack. Julia ignored him, reaching for her gear. Fox smiled uneasily. Obviously he disliked his assigned role.

"What is this?" Alex hissed through pressed lips as she stored her pack. "Why didn't you ask me?"

"Why should I?" She watched him struggle with his emotions. He was up to no good. *Well, he better start letting me in on his secret, because there's no way I'm staying out any longer.*

"Come on, I . . . I need to do this alone."

"Is that why Liam isn't here? You lied to me about that too, didn't you?" Another swell passed beneath them and the zodiac rose three feet.

"Of course not. He's sick. I told you."

He looked sheepish and complicit as can be. *Did he really believe he had her fooled?*

"You need to cast off," Fox yelled. "The wind keeps picking up."

Julia pulled the engine chord. "We're ready."

Fox painstakingly avoided eye contact with Alex as he untied the rope latching the zodiac to the cruiser. Amused, Julia found he looked like a priest who was told to resolve an argument between a pimp and a prostitute. Never did a man look more anxious to be elsewhere.

"Give me a call when you're done," he hollered. "I'll return as soon as the sea permits."

"Wait!" Alex barked. "She shouldn't be staying. Take her back."

"Shut up," Julia asserted with a tone that preempted any discussion. "And don't you ever again tell me what I can do. Besides, the *Helen* is *my* father's property, in case you forgot."

The heavy rope fell into the zodiac with a thud, and a gap of water opened between the small inflatable and the yacht's gleaming hull. "Good luck," Fox shouted. He waved once before his face disappeared.

*   *   *

Since the fight there had been no more incidents. Waspe pretended nothing ever happened, but he stayed to himself and seldom addressed Richard. They never spoke of the gold. Only once, during a rare moment of talkativeness, did Waspe share that the barrels were safe and Richard needn't worry about them until they could finally get themselves a boat and leave the island.

Much of the increasing tension, Richard knew, stemmed less from the fight than the fact that they made no progress in the construction of a canoe. A few weeks after arriving, Waspe had wanted to cut down one of the massive trees growing near the village. Wi'yapak wouldn't have it. He insisted Richard and Waspe await the arrival of the big logs that washed ashore during the stormy season. The Indians built all their canoes from these, a reddish wood of the highest quality. Also, the chief advised against travel so late in the year. By the time they could finish a canoe, the first rains would come, and the winter winds could whip the sea into a deadly opponent. Wi'yapak had invited them to stay as long as they liked, which caused even greater friction between them.

Richard knew his indifference to the delay galled the cook. While Waspe hated everything about the island and its people, and complained bitterly, Richard more and more enjoyed his adopted surroundings. He soaked up new knowledge, learning about the Indians' techniques of hunting and fishing, how to preserve food, the identification of edible plants, how to make weapons from obsidian, and their language. In effect, he was becoming one of them. Whereas Waspe isolated himself, Richard made friends and commanded respect throughout the village. He had to admit that he loved this life. Strangely, though, his attitude seemed to put distance between him and Mónoy. But that was minor. *The pregnancy is wearing on her.*

One morning in mid-December, as Richard and Mónoy chatted with Tuqan, Waspe strolled up and squatted down. "We need to secure the casks."

Richard, astonished as much at the cook's friendly demeanor as by his mentioning the gold, blurted out. "Why?"

"Winter is near, and from what his father says," Waspe tilted his head at Tuqan, "we must expect a violent sea. I stored the barrels well above the high tide line, but that may change with the onset of storms."

Richard sipped his steaming fennel tea. "You want to bring them here?"

To his surprise Waspe nodded. "That's probably best. Will you ask Wi'yapak for a canoe?"

*   *   *

They erected the dome tent in the shadow of an outcrop that would afford some protection from wind and rain. Alex organized his equipment inside the tent while Julia drove pegs into the ground. When the last one stuck tight she went inside, wondering whether he would stop sulking. They had hardly exchanged a word since landing.

He was rummaging through their gear but quickly slid something into his parka pocket when she entered. "What was that?"

"A flashlight."

It didn't look like one, but she let it pass. "So, what's your program?" she asked, trying to sound perfectly carefree. His behavior started getting on her nerves.

He turned and looked at her for a long moment. "Well, since I was stupid enough not to see through you when you insisted on making the crossing, and since I can't send you back, you may as well make yourself useful and come up the creek with me till we find the source of the gold. We'll start where Kindayr and I left off."

He showed her where they found the dagger, coin, and cross. She carefully examined the entire area, drawing on what she remembered from Stanford. Majoring in anthropology, she had also taken several geology courses. She could still hear Professor Cullen bubbling forth with that unbridled and contagious love for his subject, his discourses on stratigraphy and erosion, fossil fish and trilobites.

Julia ran through the possibilities and quickly eliminated all but two. First, no one in his right mind, even centuries ago, would be dumb enough to bury gold on a stream bank, unless he had to hide his booty in a hurry and never had a chance to return. *Had there been a shipwreck? Or a mutiny?* Whatever the case, the gold would have washed out many years ago, since the coin dated from the 1500s. The second possibility seemed more probable. Santa Rosa, like all the Channel Islands, had witnessed plenty of tectonic activity, which can affect the water flow regime. In all likelihood the elements hadn't gotten to the gold until recently—after the ground had shifted. Considering the physical nature of the rock layers, this scenario suggested the existence of some sort of cave.

Julia sized up the canyon walls, scrutinizing every square inch. She searched for a ledge, a cranny, or any sign of an anomaly in the topography. "Alex, where does this creek emerge from the ground?"

"I don't know." Strangely, he seemed surprised at this simple question.

"I figure we should explore the canyon only as far as the water's source instead of turning over every single stone."

He made a strange face. "You're right. I don't know why I didn't think of it myself."

They headed upstream, past the Rash site, and across the remaining debris of a recent slide. A cone-shaped swath of completely stripped surface scarred the hillside. Alex scaled a mound ten yards ahead when Julia, her focus on the devastated slope, stumbled over a shallow ditch. The soil still glistened, as though water had flowed here not long ago. Her gaze traced the dry rivulet as it meandered across a bank cluttered with loose rocks and roots dug up by a flood. She looked up. But the hill had no channel, and only a long ledge protruded from the cliff about eight feet high. *A spring?* she wondered.

Again her eyes followed the rivulet's course, this time to the base of the slope where the toppled trunk of an ancient tree spread its last branches skyward like the gnarled fingers of a dying man. The ledge jutted out directly above this tree, whose enormous root system lay exposed. Oddly, more secondary plant growth from the adjacent soil clung to those roots farthest from ground level, whereas those closest seemed washed relatively clean. The little gulch at Julia's feet led to the tree's skeleton, passing right underneath it. Intrigued, she crawled over the trunk and slid down on the other side into a space so tight between the tree and slope, she hardly had room to maneuver.

Her heart skipped a beat. A small crevasse, measuring no more than four square feet, yawned in the cliff. The surface of the surrounding rock wall was rippled like a wrung-out rag. With her back straight as a washboard, Julia got down on her knees to peek in, but she couldn't pierce the black void. Her legs turned damp. *Shit! No wonder!* She was kneeling smack in the center of the gulch where a small puddle had formed.

This tiny channel disappeared into the mountain. By now, Julia's heart pumped rapidly. She re-crossed the trunk and hurried along the ditch back across the bank toward the creek, examining everything like a hawk. *Too bad. No sign of any gold. But I think this is the place!*

"Alex, Alex!" The offshore storm had intensified, with a strong wind funneling into the canyon. She had to call twice more before he finally turned.

"I believe I found it," she shouted, waving and gesturing frantically at the ground.

He came running like a bloodhound, his head low as though he'd picked up an enticing scent. "Show me!" he demanded, nearly bouncing into her.

Julia triumphantly pointed down, beaming with pride. "Follow it to the other side of that trunk. It goes into the mountain."

He looked at the slope, and then shook his head. "How could I miss this?" he mumbled.

When he reached the trunk, he stared up at the steep wall with a reverent expression, as if he expected the sandstone to melt and expose the glittering vision of a long-lost treasure. "This is it," he said, his voice shaking. "I can feel it. The object of my search is here."

Julia got back on the trunk and slid down the other side. "It's large enough for one person, but it might get tight. I'll check it out. Hand me the flashlight."

He frowned and lost his poise for a brief moment. "I left it in the tent. Wait, I'll be quick."

Didn't he say he put it in his pocket? Julia wondered.

He returned in a hurry. "Be careful. Much of this rock is quite brittle. We don't need you getting crushed, or lost in some labyrinth. If you hit any fork, turn back at once."

"Since when do you care?" she said, reaching for the light. He made no reply. "Okay. I'm going in."

She got on her stomach and crawled forward. As she felt first her torso then her legs being swallowed by the mountain, her imagination ran wild with what might await her on the inside.

~25~

Tuqan cast uneasy glances at his father when it became clear that Waspe guided the canoe toward the cliff. Richard, intrigued, turned his eyes on Wi'yapak, who stood stoically in the aft and gave his son a mechanical nod. The chief then bent forward to tap Richard on the shoulder and point at the beach, repeating a phrase several times.

"What's he saying?" Waspe inquired anxiously.

Richard looked through the transparent water at the entrance to the sea cave. "Something in the canyon. I think it has to do with your discovery. Unless I'm mistaken, there's another way in."

Waspe stared in bewilderment. "If they touched the barrels, I swear, I'll kill them." He started pulling off his shirt.

Richard grew concerned. What should he do? Had Waspe entered a forbidden place? *We might both suffer serious consequences.*

Wi'yapak had a brief exchange with Tuqan, who abruptly stripped and dove into the water. Waspe tore off his ragged shirt and jumped in right after him. When the two Indians with the paddles looked questioningly from each other to Wi'yapak and the men in the water, Richard realized they knew nothing of this cave. *It must be some sort of private retreat for the chief and his son.* But he had little time to dwell on these thoughts, for Waspe already followed Tuqan through the dark opening.

Everyone aboard waited patiently. After a few minutes, the two divers came back out and shot to the surface. Grinning from ear to ear now, Waspe wiped the water off his eyes.

"All there! Dry and ready for transfer. No one meddled with the gold."

Richard only half-listened. An agitated Tuqan explained the facts to his father, who remained stone-faced. At last he ordered his son and Waspe to return to the cave and wait there for him and Richard.

"Did you get that?" Richard asked the cook.

"He wants us to get the barrels?"

"No. He expects you to go in and wait for us. Apparently there exists a second entrance, and I think it must lead here. He wants me to follow him along that route." Richard hesitated, his mind racing. "Be careful. I don't know if we violated a sacred place. There could be problems."

They walked briskly up the canyon until Wi'yapak crossed the bone-dry streambed and picked up the trail on the opposite side. Richard followed the silent Indian to a steep slope, where he halted in front of a tangle of rushes and vines creeping up the bedrock. The man slowly pulled apart the thorny vines and revealed a gaping hole five feet tall and comfortably wide for a man to pass through. The right edge of this passageway stuck out further from the slope and bent slightly to the left, so that at first glance it appeared narrower than it actually was. The rock surface bore strange curves and angles, as if a giant had kneaded a lump of dough. A sturdy young tree grew here. At some point in the distant future, it might obscure this entrance to the mountain.

Wi'yapak stooped and busied himself with some pieces of dry wood until he struck sparks. He rose holding a lit torch, waited a few moments until the flame burned strong, then ducked his head and vanished. Richard followed in his footsteps.

With his fingertips sliding over the cold, grainy rock, he inched his way into the void, kept his head low, and made sure his hands maintained contact. Total darkness swallowed him, tempting him to stop. *Where in the hell is Wi'yapak with his torch?* But Richard didn't want to fall behind and shuffled along as fast as he could. His fingers traced the wall and indicated that the cave turned right, away from the dry creek bed. An instant later he breathed more easily, for the dim glow of the torch just ahead promised an end to the oppressive dark.

Like a night moth, he hastened toward the light when the low ceiling increasingly gave way and shot up twenty feet. He stumbled into a broad chamber, too deep even for the tar-flame to fully illuminate. The scene presenting itself stopped Richard in mid-stride. Dozens of pictographs adorned the sandstone wall, and Wi'yapak, the image of pure pride incarnate, swayed his torch back and forth in a languid arc.

Three types of paintings covered the wall. There were concentric layers of circles of different designs, always with a point in the center, and sometimes with jagged lines. These circles, mostly red and orange, had black or purple centers. Curve-shaped figures with forked ends were interspersed with the circles. These figures had been painted in many colors. Then there was a collection of rectangles with one side missing. They were all either black or white, and they frequently overlapped where they had been painted over.

Richard spied a hidden recess in the wall, which was the storage place for a collection of abalone shells and concave rocks used for the pigments. They were neatly lined up on the floor next to a pile of eggshell remains, tightly woven plants, and the tails of animals.

The distorted, eerie shadows of their bodies flickered along the wall as they moved deeper into the cave, which terminated in a narrow, uninviting crack. Richard became apprehensive. The chief had made no threatening gestures, and his face betrayed no ill feelings, but it was clear that this place had a special meaning for him. Did he and his son consider Waspe's invasion of the cave a punishable offense?

* * *

Julia dragged herself over cold bedrock, cutting a path through loose stones and wet dirt. Ten feet in, the cave roof gave way enough to allow her to get up and crawl on all fours. The beam of the flashlight revealed a sloping ceiling that, several feet farther in, allowed her to stand. Then the tunnel hooked right, and the walls diverged. Julia came to the threshold of a large cavern so deep that the weak light did not penetrate to the far wall. The cave's floor tilted up and away.

She stepped into the great chamber with its high, vaulted ceiling and let the beam wander randomly. When it struck the wall, she stared, transfixed. Faded paintings covered the rock, extending along a wide band from knee to head level. Many-pointed stars, stick figures, concentric circles, geometric lines—everywhere. She assumed the paintings had to be the work of Chumash artists, and they probably dated to before the time when the Spaniards showed up in the late 1700s to establish their missions. Disease and the Spanish friars' enslavement of most Indians depopulated the countryside rapidly. Therefore, it was less likely these paintings post-dated the colonists.

Julia put the light on the opposite wall, which illuminated countless more images. *What was that?* Something shone in the beam. She pointed the flashlight down. A debris mound ran half the length of the chamber. She froze, and something akin to a wolf's yelp slipped off her tongue. There! A coin, like the one Liam found, poked out of the base of the mound.

She took a few steps, picked it up with trembling hands, and wiped off the dirt. An almost perfect replica of Alex's, it bore the rounded square on one side, head and upper torso on the other. She could read the letters "H I L I P" below the head. *PHILIP! Of course! The first letter must be a "P." Philip, king of Spain.*

She stuffed the coin in her pocket and scanned the cave floor for more. This time it momentarily took her breath away, and she burst out laughing with child-like joy. A half dozen pieces—gems, coins, jewelry—lay along the side of the mound. A score still partially buried in the dirt were all screaming her name. "Come Julia! Take us! Don't be shy!" It was incredible. *Here I am, in the center of a treasure chamber!*

This only came once in a lifetime. She wanted to take it in slowly, feel it, remember the smell and taste of the musky air, and live the moment to the fullest. She sank to her knees and reached for a magnificent jewel-studded necklace draped over a piece of whitish wood stuck in the soil. When she pulled on the necklace the wood came with it. What an odd shape, she thought. She looked more closely. Then her heart, overflowing with pure bliss only a second before, suddenly felt wrenched from its cavity and dipped in ice water. The necklace was wrapped around a bone—a human hand with its fingers still attached.

Julia jerked back in horror and let go of the ghastly discovery, dropping the flashlight. Total darkness pressed in on her. *Oh my God! Please don't let it be broken!* Frantically she searched for the light, praying fervently. She'd never felt so vulnerable.

Her hands found it, and she pushed the switch. Nothing! She tried again and pushed the other way. *Light! Thank you, Lord! Okay, keep calm. The bone has been here as long as the gold. No animal will grab me from the dark.* She relaxed her muscles and waited for her system to return to normal. With the adrenaline rush at last subdued, she detached the necklace from the bone, careful not to touch it.

Stunning pink and blue gems graced an intricately worked gold frame of heavy links. Julia wanted to put it around her neck, but the thought of the bony fingers quickly extinguished that desire. Then she spotted a flower-shaped golden brooch. What happened here? She wondered. Had there been a fight, or disease? Maybe the guy starved. *I'll probably never know.*

She studied the mound. Water had obviously eroded its side. It all made sense now. The ground water changed course and began eating into the dirt. It washed out the closest pieces, carried them through the hole in the cliff, and dumped them in the stream. This must have started with the record rains of the past two years.

Julia checked her watch. Seventeen minutes! She had totally forgotten Alex. Though she couldn't wait to break the news to him, she also needed to get to the tent and her cell phone. *Fox has to turn around and get his ass out here. No way is Alex cleaning out this cave behind Liam's back. No way in hell!*

After a final glance at the wondrous scene, she retraced her steps. The low ceiling forced her back down on her knees. Suddenly she sensed a muffled noise a bit like radio static. She moved forward on her stomach. The static steadily grew louder, and when Julia entered the last stretch she recognized the sound — rain.

She squeezed through the opening and stood up, staying as close to the canyon walls as possible. Gale-force winds drove a torrential downpour horizontally. Fortunately, the cliff's natural curvature and the tree trunk sheltered her somewhat. Alex, however, had disappeared.

*   *   *

A terrible attack of claustrophobia overwhelmed Richard when Wi'yapak climbed into the hole without further ado. Dreading to be left alone in the dark, and pushing aside any ideas of the chief turning on him, he faced his fears and followed him into a low tunnel. To make matters worse, the ceiling soon dropped precipitously, forcing them into a duck waddle that eventually became a stomach creep.

The terror of constricted spaces descended on him, which was exacerbated by the noxious mix of the torch's fumes mingling with the earthy odor of the rock and the men's sweat. Richard wanted to go back, but the possibility of passing for a coward kept him in check. They went forward until suddenly he heard the sweetest thing of his life—Waspe's hollow voice bouncing off the walls.

"Over here," it echoed. "This way."

Richard's heart throbbed with joy. He'd never yearned to get anywhere so badly, as out of this hellish tube. He almost succumbed to the urge to crawl over Wi'yapak, the sole obstacle between him and the sea cave. But already the tunnel's ceiling rose and they stood up. They passed the barrels and arrived in the little grotto. Waspe looked them over curiously. Tuqan took no note of their presence, squatting on the ledge with his eyes averted, a world unto himself.

"So?" Waspe inquired. "What way do we go?"

Richard waved at the tunnel entrance. "This leads to an enormous chamber with walls full of paintings." He caught his breath. "It's where they come to paint, which they probably did the day we landed."

Waspe snorted. "Why the hell spend all that time marching here from the village if they can take a canoe? It's foolish."

"What does it matter? We came here to get the barrels."

Waspe cast a long glance at the hioh, who crouched by his son. Both talked with hushed voices. "Yes, that's what I had planned, but now I wonder whether any of the other savages know of these tunnels. Tuqan has sulked since we parted. I know he's not happy about all this." He stared at Richard. "I'd just as soon keep the gold out of the village and in that chamber. That way the rest of 'em may never find out."

Richard laughed with contempt. "Why shouldn't they? You can't expect Wi'yapak and Tuqan to keep quiet. And you have no idea how many Indians are involved in painting."

"You didn't see the two others when we got here. I swear they knew nothing of this cave." He nodded toward the chief and his son. "They will keep it to themselves. Take my word."

Wi'yapak led Richard, and Tuqan brought up the rear behind Waspe. The heavy barrels rumbled over the rocky floor as the men crawled forward, struggling to push them.

Wi'yapak, even with holding the torch, had it easiest. Though he tried his best to help the others, he could not keep the tunnel lit around the bends. Waspe, and especially Tuqan, often crept through darkness. The cook cursed bitterly each time he hit his elbow or smashed his cask against the wall. Richard ignored him, trying to neutralize his fears and not think of the earthy taste in his mouth. *It's not that far. Every inch brings us closer.*

When they finally spilled out of the tunnel, he almost wanted to do it again, if only to prove it to himself. "Here we are!" he called out.

The cook glanced at the paintings with indifference. After a brief survey of the chamber he walked off forty paces and planted his feet. "This place is as good as any."

Tuqan ogled him in silence, his expression a combination of intense displeasure and barely controlled hatred.

* * *

Julia zipped up her Goretex and pulled the hood over her head. She tried to get on top of the tree trunk, but slipped and fell on her wrist. *You idiot!* she berated herself, massaging the hand and retreating from the monsoon-like rain. *Where is Alex?*

She took out the necklace and admired the brilliance of the sapphires and heavy gold. But her peripheral vision soon picked up movement, and she stuffed her trophy away. Someone in a forest-green rain suit came upstream. *Damned! A ranger!* Alex's jacket was tan. Hadn't she warned him? This looked like trouble, but before she could duck out of sight, the stranger turned his hooded head toward her. She recognized Liam at once.

Half-dead in bed with a terrible flu? Alex *did* lie to her. He must have fed Liam some half-truth to keep him off the island. Then he probably had seen him come up the canyon and hid like a rabbit. *Disgusting!* Mental images of that lewd bitch he'd screwed in the closet haunted her, for the hundredth time. Just what strange bug had wiggled its way into her head and made her marry him?

"Liam, Liam! Over here!" she yelled through the pounding rain, waving her arms. He stopped dead and stared at her with a baffled look.

Finally he found his voice and came to her. "Julia! I didn't expect to see you here. What are you doing behind that tree?"

She crossed over to his side, careful not to fall again. "Can't say I expected you either. I thought you'd be sipping a cup of hot tea, snuggled under a warm blanket."

He gave her a crooked smile. "Are you joking?"

"I was told you had the flu."

He rubbed his cheeks. "I see. I had a hunch New York was fiction. He wants the treasure for himself."

"Bravo, bravo. I must concede it was a lousy excuse," the professor's mocking voice startled them through the downpour.

Alex had been perched on the trunk, perfectly camouflaged behind a gnarly mass of twisted branches and vines twenty-five feet away. With legs pulled to his chest and the tan parka zipped to the nose, he blended with the surroundings. He jumped on the ground and sauntered toward them.

"You better explain yourself," Julia demanded icily.

He didn't try to hide his irritation. "You really have a way of getting under people's skin when you want to. Now will you please let me see what you discovered?" Her face changed drastically. After her initial haughty demand, she suddenly seemed on the defensive. He savored the moment.

"What are you talking about?" she defied him.

The first signs of extreme displeasure were beginning to sour his mood, and he knew she could see it in his face. "Just empty your pocket!"

When she countered with a furious "Screw you!" he lunged, thrust his hand into her jacket, and yanked out the necklace.

Liam, who had reached out to restrain him, stopped midway and ogled it in amazement. "Where did you get that?"

"What she does is really none of your business," Alex answered for her.

Liam grabbed Alex's arm. "What the hell is your problem? Ever since I showed you that dagger, you've become a royal jerk."

No one ever *gets physical with Alex Malreaux!* He automatically shook off Liam's hand. In the process he slammed his elbow hard in Liam's jaw. The artist stumbled back, holding his chin with an expression of shock that soon gave way to a thirst for revenge. Then he came for him.

Rage now took hold of Alex, paralyzing his mental faculties and blocking whatever reasonable course of action he could have taken to deal with this strange situation. It was a condition he feared, for he knew he was losing control and in danger of taking irreversible steps he'd regret. But he couldn't help it, and in that split-second a flood of thoughts surged through Alex's mind. He realized that Liam would have no difficulty administering a serious beating. He also believed that Liam had probably tried to take advantage of Julia's marital crisis, and had trailed them to the island to challenge him for the gold.

Alex did something he'd only done once before, when his father savagely punched his mother after too much whiskey. He pulled out the pistol he'd brought for self defense in case he'd run into another potentially violent grave looter, and he pointed it at someone in anger. Now, as before, it felt oddly good. Powerful.

Liam came to a dead stop and stared at the weapon, aghast. Julia found her voice first. "Have you gone crazy?" she gasped. "Put that away!"

Then Liam stirred and laughed with contempt. "I think you better see a shrink."

This so offended Alex that he had a murderous desire to pump the artist full of holes. Julia, staring at him as though he belonged in a nuthouse, and Liam—*Yeah, he must have had her*—laughing at him. What gall! Alex's mind went blank, his animal instincts taking control. He yanked his arm and squeezed the trigger twice.

The shots rang out and the bullets whistled into the sky. "You find this funny too? Now shut the fuck up!"

Liam's eyes glowed like charcoal and he didn't move. But the gunfire had wiped the stupid grin off his face. Julia looked mortified. Alex relished the rush and brushed aside the nagging voice in his head trying to call him to his senses. "Back inside!" he commanded Julia, keeping his attention on Liam. "You go in after her."

"It's an extremely narrow tunnel," she tried. "I don't know. You guys might get stuck."

Dammit! Alex thought. He really hated tight spaces and dreaded nothing more than earthquakes and the possibility of being buried alive under the rubble of a collapsing building. This damn phobia had haunted him as long as he could remember. Suddenly, he felt he had made a complete mess of his life by pulling out that weapon.

For an instant he almost gave in and even considered throwing away the pistol. His true self attempted to reassert itself through the haze of uncontrolled emotion and put an end to this idiocy. But he ignored it. There was no going back now. Too much hung in the balance. All he needed to do was continue with this charade for a couple of hours. The future would take care of itself. The marriage was finished, but she'd forgive him. As would Liam.

Alex looked at him. "He's bigger. If he gets through, so will I. If he doesn't, we all come back. Now go."

They wormed into the mountain like disjointed centipedes, with Julia illuminating the way and Alex keeping his flashlight on Liam. *This is not so bad,* he thought. He was already crawling. Soon he could stand upright.

"Alright. Take us to where you found the necklace. And you," he forced himself to wave the gun in Liam's general direction, "keep behind her."

When they entered the chamber, he snapped his next command. "Move!"

Liam and Julia shuffled to the side. "Put your flashlight on the floor so that it shines on both of you," he ordered her. He tried to keep his voice firm while attempting to mask the sinking feeling he got as he realized with each passing moment what deep shit he was in. He pointed the beam of light at the wall paintings, but the art bored him. *Child's work.*

Then he saw the reflection, the mound, and the sparkle. He grinned from ear to ear, despite the situation. But his smile quickly faltered. "What the hell . . ."

Julia had waited for precisely this instant. With Alex's attention riveted on the ancient hand, she inconspicuously inched toward the exit. *Do it! Now!* She darted off into the dark, wondering whether her husband really had gone completely insane and would send a bullet her way.

~26~

Though winter brought the long hoped-for rains, they didn't relent from December through the end of January. Richard had never seen it come down like this. The water played drums on the hut's roof, bent on stripping it off by sheer persistence. It did so for hours at a time, and once for two full days without letting up. Even the elders could not remember a wetter year with such intense deluges and terrible winds. People had grown irritable, and tempers flared daily. Waspe, who had complained so bitterly of the merciless sun, had become insufferable.

Richard could no longer tolerate the cook's horrible moods and avoided him. They hadn't exchanged a single word for many days. While Waspe had only poison for everyone and everything, Richard remained grateful for Wi'yapak's life-saving counsel not to sail until spring, and for the shelter and friendship the Indians provided. He kept dry and warm and had plenty to eat. Only, he struggled with the changes that accompanied Mónoy's pregnancy.

She often was withdrawn and impatient, probably on account of the nausea she still experienced so late in the pregnancy. They had fought twice, and neither time could he recall the reasons for doing so. In her sixth month now, her belly had lost its shape, and he noticed new bulges around her thighs and frequent fatigue in her face. Despite these changes, she looked healthy and beautiful. Not much longer, he reminded himself each morning, remembering the passion she fanned with a mere look only a few months ago.

There remained another source of friction that concerned him. He had never taken any interest in the growth of the fetus and understood little of the subtle changes taking place in the mind and body of a woman carrying a child. He sensed she craved greater demonstrations of affection and some signal that he cared, though this did not seem to be the norm in her culture. But as hard as he tried, he just couldn't feel much for a baby not yet born. So he decided to stay out of the whole affair until the birth, which would not only make him a proud father, but return to him the wonderful woman he met on that northern shore. Conveniently, the nature of Indian society made this easy.

Men and women performed mostly distinct functions. If a woman didn't gather roots or greens, she made one of the rugged baskets ubiquitous in each household, tended to the children, mended clothes, prepared food, or saw to a dozen other duties. The men worked on their canoes, fashioned new bows and arrows, or hunted and fished. During the day the sexes didn't mingle much, which allowed Richard to steer clear of Mónoy's accusations. In fact, he took so well to Indian life that, except for his complexion, few would have guessed that he'd ever lived anywhere but on this island. He thought less and less of returning to England, always evaded the subject, and blamed his lack of planning on the weather.

Waspe had become a virtual outcast and retreated into his own little world. Though always welcome to sleep in Umasikh's sister's hut, he had built himself a primitive lean-to on the village periphery. He stayed there, unless the wind blew so hard that it threatened to destroy his simple shelter. He never hunted or fished with the other men but went alone instead. At least, when he returned with the carcass of one of the small foxes that roamed the island, or a fat salmon, he shared with his host family. It was his only contribution to the welfare of the tribe.

Waspe had begun to make one exception to his self-imposed isolation—Mónoy.

*   *   *

Alex whirled around and for a long moment had a ridiculously easy shot. But he was fully in control of himself again, and, of course, he could never harm her, or Liam, or anyone. But he needed Liam, and the best way to ensure his help was to continue acting like he'd gone over the edge. So he pretended to take careful aim until she almost slipped from sight. Then, biting his lips and closing his eyes, and remembering to take off the safety, he fired well off to her side, almost deafening them all inside the cave's confines. She kept running. *Very impressive! I never knew she had such guts. Well, she has no place to go.*

Now they knew he meant business. Fox was long gone. Whoever set Liam ashore, probably his fisherman friend, couldn't risk anchoring offshore in such weather. Julia would hide somewhere in the canyon and get soaked.

In the meantime he would enslave Liam, have him dig out what remained of the treasure, and force him to lug it to the zodiac while he arranged for the *Helen*. Then he would chase him away. No! He'd take him back into the cave and tie him up. Next, he'd wait for Fox and lure him off the yacht. *Yeah, Julia got lost in the canyon, and I hurt my back. I need you to find her.* Then it would be bye-bye. He'd deny everything to the authorities and accuse Liam and Julia of having an affair. Deny, deny, deny! Hell, hadn't Göbbels said something like "a lie repeated often enough becomes the truth?" But how could he explain Liam being found tied up? Alex pondered with a sinking feeling. He forced his mind into a different direction. He'd worry about that with a lawyer. Deny, deny, deny!

It was a poor plan, but he had to see this through. No alternatives existed. His marriage was finito and his long-promised book flawed beyond repair. He'd been much too lax in his research and had played instead of worked. The reviewers would call his bluff and make mince meat of him. He'd never get tenure and might as well kiss UCSB good-bye. He'd hit a dead end professionally, personally, and financially. The gold would at least salvage the financial dilemma. Liam, Julia, and Fox surely would get him into trouble with the law, but he'd deal with that. Eventually he'd move on and buy himself a pleasant life in the Caribbean.

"It doesn't matter," he said, trying to sound cold-hearted.

"You sure?" Liam smiled contemptuously.

"Yes, as sure as that this cave will make my fortunes. And I'm rather pleased you've volunteered your assistance."

Liam looked immensely disgusted. "What do you even care? You have everything a man could want."

This cracked Alex up. "For your information, all you see belongs to Julia's parents—the house, the investments, the cars, everything. My salary hardly pays for the wine. Her wonderful mother didn't trust me from day one. Certain I married Julia for the money, she convinced her husband to keep the goodies in their name."

"A very perceptive woman, don't you agree?"

"Fuck you!" The heat came back to Alex's head, and he wondered if he could actually shoot a man if he had to. "Get your ass over here and start making a pile, the loose pieces first."

Liam obeyed, his cockiness apparently evaporated. Alex had to smile to himself, watching him get down on his knees to gather the coins and jewelry. A little humility served the artist well. Then Alex stopped smiling because Liam pulled an unexpected object from the dirt—a human skull.

* * *

The crisis struck without warning. After a week of intermittent rain and high winds the clouds had parted and the sea calmed. Wi'yapak had asked Richard and Waspe to come on a trading mission to Helo, a marsh village on the mainland. Waspe naturally declined the offer. Richard didn't think twice.

The chief and his band had spent two days exchanging otter skins, exquisitely crafted olivella shell bead money, chert blades, and sea lion meat for goods the island lacked. These included hematite for making red paint, antelope skins, pine nuts, and deer antlers that the men fashioned into various tools.

On the morning of their return to Wi'ma, as the Indians called their island, a dark mass of clouds gathered on the hazy horizon. They must get across the channel in a hurry, Richard surmised. The oppressive, humid air sapped his energy and made him indifferent and irritable. Even the birds refrained from their usual chitchat, and not the slightest hint of a breeze stirred the calm sea.

The three canoes of the trading party, heavily loaded with material conquests, made an easy crossing, only to struggle up the rain-swollen creek toward the village. When they reached the first cluster of huts, Richard immediately sensed something negative and insidious. Why didn't the children greet their returning fathers with the customary high-pitched banter? And how come the adults said nothing? They didn't even bother to wave. The men in the canoe had also become dead silent. He turned to Wi'yapak, who tried his best to avoid eye contact. That's when it hit Richard, and his body spun around. He didn't see Mónoy anywhere.

He looked frantically and finally discovered Umasikh and two of Mónoy's friends, but not her. It thundered inside his head and pounded at his temples. *She has lost the child!* His heart racing, he threw his legs over the side and slid into the current. He half-swam, half-thrashed his way ashore and stormed to Wi'yapak's dwelling. Empty! He darted from hut to hut, breaking into a cold sweat, shaking miserably. His knees felt like jellyfish. Nightmarish thoughts haunted him. *Something terrible happened! Dead! Mónoy has died!* Then he realized that Waspe was not among the crowd either.

Richard looked in the direction of the cook's lean-to, but saw no sign of life. Had he gone hunting or fishing? No!

Intuition told him Waspe's and Mónoy's absence were connected, which explained why the hole damn village tried not to look at him. He marched over to Umasikh.

"Mónoy. Where is she? And where is Waspe?"

When she pointed east, at the ridge, Richard required no further explanation. He had an ugly premonition the cook might try to deceive her, or set her against him. That's why he'd been so friendly to her. They would have to settle this once and for all.

Checking for the knife in his belt, he raced to the hut and grabbed his bow. He slung a quiver filled with arrows over his shoulder and filled a pouch with water. Tuqan suddenly stood beside him, his own bow and quiver in hand. Richard shook his head and patted his friend on the back.

"If he did anything to her, it is between me and him." He ran off in the direction of the canyon.

*   *   *

Liam wanted to let go of it, but couldn't. The second skull found on the island bore a peculiar deformity above the eye sockets. The brow ridge protruded like a small ledge over the face. Liam felt very cold inside.

Alex came up behind him. "What the hell is going on here?" he whispered, his voice unsure.

In that instant Liam experienced the most powerful déjà vu of his life. Unable to talk or to move, he forgot Alex. He forgot the ghastly find and all the events of the last few weeks. *Fate! Fate! Fate!* The realization surged through his consciousness like a mantra or a repetitious radio broadcast. Today was no accident, no random event. The Divine Architect had drawn the blueprint to this long ago, inexorably leading them into this mysterious cave.

After what seemed like hours, he finally returned to the present, the pistol's steel muzzle pressing into his spine.

"Now! Do it!" an infuriated and seemingly mad Alex shouted in his ear. "Keep working."

Shudders went through Liam as he dropped the skull. He bent forward and with trembling hands began to scrape free a growing pile of gold coins. *What was that?* An odd sound, like something being scoured, caused him to stop.

"What the fuck are you doing?" Alex barked.

"Don't you hear that?"

When Alex paused to listen, Liam grabbed the skull by the jaws, spun with lightning speed, and blindly swung his weapon in a tight arc. It slammed into Alex's elbow, and he screamed out in pain. The pistol landed with a loud clang somewhere out of sight.

*   *   *

As fast as he could, driven by dread of bad things in the making, Richard ran through tall grasses, bounded over freshly carved gullies still muddy from the rains, and plunged into thickets. When he reached the plateau he slowed to catch his breath. Dark clouds sailed in from the southeast, and whitecaps foretold another storm. Richard didn't care. He felt detached from everything, as though he were in a dream.

By the time he crossed into the canyon, the sun began its descent, casting his way in long shadows. How dead the land seemed, with no birdsong and no movement. It exuded an utterly unreal quality. The earth had even swallowed the omnipresent lizards. The only sounds to lend the island any life were Richard's footsteps on the muddy path and the roar of the bloated stream.

The rains had left the trail relatively unscathed, except for a five-yard-long strip. Remembering how nervous the steep mountain path had made him that day last summer, this time he felt perfectly at ease and climbed around the wash-out without giving it another thought. When he made it to the canyon floor, he began to move more cautiously. Only fragments of the stream bank had survived the winter's fury, with most of the vegetation ripped out. Richard made his way through the denuded wasteland. They were here. He knew it.

When he came within sight of the cave's entrance, he took cover behind a boulder. He saw no sign of either Mónoy or Waspe. *Check the beach first. It'll only take a couple of minutes.* Crouched low to avoid detection, he advanced. When he rounded the next bend, a fierce gust slammed into him unexpectedly and almost toppled him. Raindrops exploded on his face. The storm started to unleash. Twilight came on with an eerie suddenness. *Hurry,* he thought. *It will get dark shortly.*

When he arrived at the beach, a shocking sight made him cringe. The spectacle sucked the air from his lungs, and he dropped his bow. Mónoy was scaling the western headland, wearing only her deerskin skirt. *Where the hell is her thick winter cape?* Then Richard saw a heavy necklace around her neck, which must have come from the casks. But worst of all, less than six feet separated her from Waspe, who scrambled after her.

Straining to control his emotions and calm his nerves, Richard picked up his bow and pulled an arrow from the quiver. *Get him between the shoulder blades. Just drop him before he gets to her!* He hesitated. What if he missed? The arrow might startle Mónoy. A fall from that height would kill the baby, and probably her, too. His hands started shaking again. What should he do?

Frantically he surveyed the headland, which towered at least seventy feet above the beach. It came to a narrow overhang jutting seaward. Massive slabs of bedrock rising from the ocean floor broke the surface directly below this overhang. That approach was out of the question. Richard finally spotted a narrow, horizontal ledge about seven feet above ground, which was hidden from Waspe's and Mónoy's view. Thankfully, the landward face of the headland rose much less steeply than the other side. He might ascend to the top unseen. Richard laid down the bow and quiver and, waiting for Waspe to pull himself higher, made a dash for the slope.

His hands latched onto the slippery ledge and he pulled himself up. The steadily increasing rain had turned everything slick. He examined the rock face for solid footholds and found plenty. *Easy going! I'll get there before them.*

He rapidly gained height. Only once, after a brittle rock crumbled under his foot, did he slide several feet. He paused, concentrated on the task, and squinted into the rain. One more tough stretch and he could almost walk to the top. He regained the lost ground and a few seconds later pulled himself over the edge, just as Waspe started yelling.

Richard's head jerked up, and he saw Mónoy precariously perched at the far edge. Waspe shouted something and ran toward her, gesturing wildly. She spied Richard and looked straight into his eyes with an expression of utter despair and shame that burned itself into his mind. Suddenly she slipped and fell backwards. She reached out and valiantly struggled to grab something to hold onto. The next moment Mónoy was gone, leaving only a terrible shriek that trailed off to nothingness.

~27~

Richard's stomach knotted. With trembling legs he staggered to the edge of the cliff. He thought his palpitating heart would burst from his heaving chest.

"What have you done?" he gasped. Since the cook ignored him he repeated the question. Waspe didn't stir. When a third try still failed to evoke any response, he realized that his vocal cords had produced nothing but a miserable rattle.

"You killed her!" he finally yelled over the staccato spatter of the driving rain. Waspe spun around, an expression of fathomless shock disfiguring his face.

Richard drew his knife. "Out of my way," he demanded.

Waspe stepped aside. "She . . . she fell," he stuttered, fear-stricken. Richard waved him back before stepping to the slippery edge. He mustered all his courage and glanced down.

Her body sprawled on a flat rock at the base of the cliff. The rain had already begun to smear the dark stain surrounding her head and right shoulder. Richard felt an all-consuming rage rise from his core. He no longer cared for anything and wanted only justice for the death of Mónoy. He grabbed his knife and flung himself at shifty-eyed Waspe, who deflected the knife just short of his throat.

The blade tore a long gash from chin to temple, and thick blood poured down the side of his face. Waspe kicked at him but missed. Physically weaker and unarmed, the odds didn't favor the cook. *He's finished!* Richard realized. But he failed to react when his enemy bolted to the edge of the cliff, took one short glance, and leapt off. Richard ran to the edge and heard a great splash. Then he saw Waspe's head jabbing through the surface. The cook looked up and raced to shore.

Richard was stunned, and furious with himself. Waspe would run off and lose himself somewhere on the island. The wretch would get away with his musket and lie in wait to strike on his own terms. The only solution presented itself in stark reality.

Richard's nerves quivered. He was a lousy swimmer, and he'd never jumped from anything higher than a tree branch. His knees now shook like pudding and his stomach cramped. Then he remembered Mónoy's lifeless body. He shut his eyes tightly and jumped into the abyss.

After an eternity in the air, his body made impact and sank rapidly toward the sea floor. *Open your arms!* a voice inside his head warned, and he obeyed just in time to avoid shattering his legs on the rocky bottom. He fought his way back up. There! He could see Waspe already running into the canyon. Richard worked his way ashore as fast as he could.

Catching Waspe would be child's play. On solid ground Richard had the advantage, and he gave it his best. The distance between them shrank with each bound. The cook looked over his shoulder twice, then slipped and fell. By the time he got up, Richard closed the gap and dove for his legs. Both men crashed to the wet ground. Richard quickly pulled his knife and took a wild stab. The blade hit Waspe's arm, cutting skin, tendons, and muscle before it hit bone.

Waspe screamed and smashed his fist into Richard's teeth with a force that sent him reeling. Struggling to ignore the terrible pain that now set his mouth afire, he made another thrust at Waspe's throat, but the cook swiftly countered with an elbow to Richard's wrist, which sent the knife flying through the air. Then Waspe rained down a hail of blows on his back, neck, and head. He had gone berserk.

Richard ended the onslaught with a heel deep into Waspe's ribs, and the cook fell back and rolled out of range. Suddenly he jumped up and took flight. Where was the knife? Richard searched frantically. He needed a weapon before Waspe got to his musket. Finally he saw it in the mud, ran over to retrieve it, and the chase continued.

The wind howled furiously through the canyon, and the downpour soaked the earth. The area was no longer safe, since a flashflood could sweep down from the higher elevations any moment. Waspe dove far into the creek and swam to the other side like a fish, even though the swollen current pushed him two feet downstream for every one he gained. Back on dry land, with Richard just entering the water, he grabbed several rocks. The first two, thrown in haste, missed their target. The third grazed Richard's head. Then Waspe ran for the thicket by the cave entrance and disappeared into the mountain.

When Richard squeezed through the tight opening, darkness immediately enveloped him. The pounding rain, reduced to a muffled spatter, no longer beat into his face. He stabbed at the black void in case Waspe had set a trap. Then he stopped to listen and give his eyes a chance to adjust and tried to remember the cave's lay-out. He started forward as silently as possible, kicking and stabbing into space. His nose detected the familiar scent of a tar flame.

He inched along the wall as his eyes began to penetrate the black. Suddenly he reached the chamber. A torch rammed into a crevasse high above the floor illuminated much of the cavern. The barrels stood where they had left them and hadn't been touched, except for the one closest to Richard. Its lid, covered with several pieces of jewelry, lay on the ground.

"And now what?"

Richard flinched. The voice came from somewhere in the rear of the cave, where shadows held sway. Or was Waspe hiding close by, projecting his voice away to confuse him? "You have destroyed us." He needed to buy time because Waspe's musket was surely aimed at his stomach.

"How so? I am still alive." A pause, pregnant with meaning. "And so are you." Waspe stepped from a hidden recess behind the casks. He had no musket, only the dagger—the Spaniard's dagger.

"You understand," he probed, "that neither of us will leave this hellhole, unless we go together."

Richard didn't believe his ears. "You dragged her here, then killed her and my child!" He shook from despair, recalling the horrific sight of Mónoy's lifeless body.

"Dragged her?" Waspe laughed uneasily. "She came of her own accord."

"Don't take me for an idiot," Richard exploded, clenching the knife so strongly that his knuckles throbbed. However, a terrible suspicion began to poison his mind.

Waspe shook his head in despise and nodded toward the casks. "She wanted to see, but you never took her. It's your own fault." He stooped and picked up a bejeweled necklace from the lid. He wrapped it around his wrist, admired it for a moment, and then held up his arm to show it off.

Richard felt increasingly unsure. Could it be? Was it possible?

"You still don't get it?" Waspe continued without mercy. "You're blind. Mónoy didn't want to stay here, but all you've had on your mind is to become one of the savages. In all truth, I don't recognize you. Look at yourself. You're like them already." He spat on the ground before continuing.

"She feared you would never leave, and today she came to my hut. She would have sailed with me if I had a boat. Do you understand? She wanted to come with me."

Richard closed his eyes, mentally banishing the possibility it might be true. Could he really have been so blind? No, he couldn't have! A pregnant woman doesn't leave her man for another. The cook was lying! Richard suddenly sensed movement and opened his eyes. Waspe, who had snuck up to within ten feet, charged like a bull.

Richard felt the dagger slit his scalp while his own blade plunged into Waspe's side. Their motion separated them and tore the knife from his hand. It remained buried in Waspe, who grunted with pain. Richard, now almost blinded in one eye by the blood gushing from his skull, hurled himself at Waspe. They tumbled to the hard stone floor, where a vicious kicking and punching ensued. Richard tried to break the wrist holding the dagger. Suddenly he smelled the warm breath of the struggling cook, whose sharp teeth closed around his ear. He felt an awful, wrenching pain, and instinctively let go of the wrist. He knew instantly he'd made a mistake. With one powerful jab, Waspe drove the dagger deep into his back.

His inside on fire, his lacerated head squirting blood from his scalp and where the ear had been torn, Richard lost control of his body. He could not move a single limb. Their eyes met one last time. Waspe's showed no remorse, no sorrow, only the fierce glow of a man who had prevailed against the odds. Tiny black dots danced before Richard's eyes, and he could feel the blood fill his lungs. His breath gave out, and even the black dots were already beginning to fade as he drifted into a mysterious tunnel.

His final conscious perception stemmed from a vibration in his legs that seemed to come from the cave floor. He heard a distant rumble. Then all went dark as his soul vacated his body.

*   *   *

Malreaux's knife struck his shoulder and, because he twisted to the side, remained embedded there. Liam had never known such pain or fury. He reached for the handle, pulled it without hesitation, and moaned as the blade slipped out.

Kill! was his first thought, and he backed the professor into the wall. *Why hasn't he flicked the flashlight?* It would have given Malreaux a fighting chance. For some inexplicable reason, the idea never seemed to have crossed his mind. He only crouched there, defiantly, his face distorted with malice.

Liam gripped the knife tightly and aimed for the solar plexus. Then he heard that strange noise again. Louder this time, it reminded of a tranquil brook, or someone scraping the wall.

Suddenly he had the sensation of getting a punch to the head, or of hitting a wall of glass. Peculiarly, he no longer needed to breathe, his respiratory system seemingly having become superfluous. Bereft of all sense of time and space, he stood immobile. A flood of confused pictures flashed powerfully through his head, the present dissolving . . .

*

Planted aboard a wooden ship, Liam gazed at a starlit sky, listening to some fellow trying to convince him to make a decision that would have grave consequences. Liam couldn't quite see the whole face but recognized the voice. He knew this man. The vision faded into another, in which Liam handed white cloth to a beautiful woman. *Her* face was crystal clear. She had Julia's eyes but Asian features. Strangely, the expression in her eyes gave Liam severe pangs of guilt. A third image showed the same woman hiking up a narrow mountain path with two powerful men wearing animal skins. More phantoms kept floating across his mental screen. He saw a man of dark complexion in a handsome uniform crouched over a wooden barrel and blood trickling from his throat, a makeshift grave that made him cringe, and a huge fin coming at him. Finally the two most powerful scenes of this macabre picture show appeared.

Liam actually felt himself climbing over the edge of a cliff to behold the same dark-haired woman to whom he'd given the cloth. Driving rain soaked him. Again, her eyes glowed like an exact copy of Julia's. And this time, when their gaze met, he knew she *was* Julia. As he made this realization, her image faded into that of a male whose heavy brow ridge bulged over his eyes. This person, inside some dark and confined place, drove a dagger deep into Liam's back . . .

*

324

A second sharp punch to the head! Liam recognized the place. *I'm here, now, in the present—as is the one responsible for that mortal thrust into my body!*

His thirst for vengeance collapsed like a deck of cards. It was replaced by an equally strong yearning for freedom from the natural human impulse to plunge the knife into his enemy. The ego, though, hates to lose, and it bombarded Liam's mind with a dozen reasons why the professor must die.

His grip on the handle tightened again, but only briefly. With an indescribable joy unlike anything he had ever experienced, he burst the shackles of this impulse and tossed the knife far into the dark corners of the cave. His breath returned in force, as though someone had thrown a switch. Reveling in an overpowering sense of liberation, he resolved never again to feel enmity toward Alex Malreaux. He knew he'd broken the karmic cycle. *You poor soul,* he thought of the professor, feeling the kind of pity one might for a person slowly succumbing to a terminal disease. Their eyes met.

"Keep it. The gold is yours. I want no part of it." And Liam stumbled away and into the dark tunnel. Half way in he heard an explosion.

A deafening roar emanated from the cave. *Water!* Liam realized with a sinking feeling. It was the unmistakable roar of swiftly flowing water. Fear forced him on. *Get out!* But an inner voice prevented him, and he turned back for Alex. He anxiously retraced his steps into the current, which was already rushing past him and soaking his feet. *Are you crazy?* he kept thinking, remembering that long-ago day when he had fallen into the Colorado. Filled with dread, he continued through this subterranean nightmare, tapping his way along the wall as the icy water steadily rose. When a hard piece of debris hit him in the leg, he lost balance. The flood swept him away.

Blinded by the total absence of light, he tried to make himself as compact as possible and shielded his head with his arms. His shoulder and feet crashed into the cave's rock wall, and he flung his hands out in search of something to grasp. He found nothing. Terrified at the evil roar of the surging water, and shivering miserably from the cold, he sent a fervent prayer to the heavens.

*   *   *

The dead weight of Richard's corpse trapped Waspe. Too exhausted to free himself, and struggling to fill his lungs with air, he could do nothing to stem the warm blood from Richard's skull flowing on his face. Fighting the urge to vomit, he heard the low rumbling an instant before the first jolt hit.

There had been quakes over the last months, most too small to notice. Displacement along secondary faults had caused these smaller tremors. But the present one released three centuries of deadlock along the island's major fault. The seismic shock waves, felt by peoples a hundred miles distant, shook the crust both horizontally and vertically.

Waspe never had a chance. The floor flung him like a toy. Total terror filled him as he witnessed the solid rock of the cave walls come alive, vibrating and pulsating like a creature arisen from the underworld. A sharp blow to the back of his head distracted him from this frightful image. His body had hit the floor. At least Richard no longer pinned him down and lay at his side instead.

Stay calm! Waspe admonished himself. *It'll be over in a moment.* He immediately recognized his error when another jolt catapulted him four feet straight up. Suspended in midair beside him hung Richard, with his head dangling listlessly. The dagger's hilt protruded grotesquely from his back. When gravity reasserted its claim, Waspe got such a devastating blow to his body that he began to cry from hopelessness. Something deep inside felt broken beyond repair.

THE SPANIARD'S DAGGER

Fate spared Waspe the agony of lying paralyzed on the cold stone floor and slowly starving to death. The shaking had undermined the cave's structural integrity, and a section of the ceiling burst open. A river of rock poured from the hole and spread laterally. The debris claimed Richard's corpse first, tugging at the inanimate form at the same time that it covered it. Semi-conscious, Waspe watched from the corner of his eyes, for he could not move his head or anything else. The heaving mass advanced steadily. When a slab of sandstone cracked his jaw, he closed his eyes and prayed.

But the rock respected no prayers. It washed over him as it had over Richard and slid on until it met the opposite wall. There it rose vertically as many more tons of rock and dirt poured from above.

With the settling dust all movement ceased, except for the flickering flame of the torch.

The village weathered the calamity well, though no one had recollections of such violent shaking. Even the Indians' oral tradition made no mention of a quake so powerful it knocked down huts. Fortunately, no one suffered anything more serious than a broken foot, and they could easily rebuild the damaged huts.

On the second morning after the quake, when the clouds and rain finally blew toward the northeast, Wi'yapak organized a group of scouts. He dispatched Tuqan with four strong men and insisted they take their bows. He directed them to find the three and offer to return them to the village. Tuqan must not take sides in case the men had fought. Wi'yapak, who loved Richard like a son, regretted having to remain neutral. But he could not permit a quarrel over a woman to bring discord to his people, for Mónoy had gone with Waspe of her own free will.

The Indians searched the plateau, the thickets, the valleys, and the hilltops. They found no sign of the missing trio.

Tuqan then did what he had tried to avoid and led them to the canyon. The secret of the sacred chamber would die. Two of the four men knew nothing. The others had seen the sea cave the day he and his father helped move those strange wooden containers, but both swore never to speak of it.

Tuqan had recorded his dreams and visions in the cave as long as he could remember. His father had done so before him. They were the only ones who came there, till the arrival of the three strangers.

He smelled death the moment he saw the warped cave entrance and the pile of rock and dirt behind the vines. He sent one of his men to search the beach. Sadness filled his heart as he tried unsuccessfully to push into the tunnel. No man would ever fit through here again. He gave up, lost in thought. Richard and Waspe fought! His feelings never betrayed him. But what about Mónoy? Was she trapped inside? He'd have to enter from the sea. He jumped up and motioned his staring companions to follow him to the shore. Just then shouts rang out. The man he'd sent ahead came running.

From afar she resembled a hunk of driftwood. A massive gull ringed by dozens of smaller ones who maintained a deferential distance, sunk its beak into her skull. It pulled and twisted and shook its head sideways, finally severing a long strand of dark tissue. The Indians, waving and yelling, scared off the brazen birds. But the big one resisted and defended its meal until Tuqan flung a rock. The gulls scattered to just beyond the reach of Tuqan's rock-throwing orbit. A sharp stench fouled the air.

Mónoy's once sparkling eyes were gone. The gulls had already plucked them. Their beaks had ravaged both cheeks down to the jawbones and hammered a hole into the forehead. A huge, beautifully fashioned necklace clung to her neck. It bore shiny yellow stone and the same colorful bits of the smooth red rock like those on Waspe's knife. Tuqan held his breath because of the odor and tore free the necklace. The animals would devour her, leaving a heap of bones for the next storm to scatter. He handed the jewelry to one of his men, signaled them all to wait for him, and ran into the surf.

He dove into the cave and climbed onto the ledge. Debris covered much of the tunnel entrance. He tried to crawl over it, but the lose rock had sealed the passage. Tuqan sat down for a long time and meditated on death. Finally, when he no longer had the need for solitude, he slipped into the pool for the last time and rejoined his friends. The small band left the canyon.

* * *

Liam regained consciousness two days after the cold water engulfed him. Ironically, he woke in the same hospital room they'd put him after the burglary. He sat up straight, examining his body. Arms and hands moved well and his toes wiggled. He turned over without problems. *Good. Nothing's broken.* He put his hand between his legs and smiled with relief. Everything was in place.

The first one to visit, Julia stormed in and seemed delighted to see him. "How are you?" she demanded.

She bit her lips, anxiety clouding her otherwise beautiful face. It brought back ancient memories. *I've seen that look before, many, many years ago—on the edge of a sea cliff.*

"Like a reborn," he assured her in a calm voice. "In the true sense of the word."

She gazed at him, askance. "They said you had a severe concussion. I, I thought . . ." her voice broke.

"I'm okay. I feel fine." He looked at her, marveling at the strange vision inside the cave. The questions of his life had been answered. Now he knew. He smiled. Perhaps they'd have a second chance. Then he remembered.

"Is he . . .?"

Tears streaked down her cheeks. "They found him yesterday, a mile offshore. They caught you before you reached the sea."

He held her to comfort her. "They?"

She dried her face and blew her nose. "After I escaped I ran to the tent. I wanted to call Fox, or the police, but couldn't find my phone. I think Alex took it. So I hid behind a boulder, not knowing what to do." She squeezed his hand. "Suddenly a bunch of Coast Guard guys and cops led by a Sheriff Quint showed up. They came by helicopter."

Liam nodded. He wasn't surprised. They'd fooled themselves into thinking they'd outsmart the law. "What exactly happened? All I remember is a loud explosion and the cave filling with water."

"One of the officers said the creek breached the canyon wall about a quarter mile from where we went in. It must have blown through a weak spot in the rock and followed the tunnels already there."

"And the gold?"

"I don't think anyone knows about it yet. But I doubt it matters. That creek will flow strongly for a long time. It was a torrent. I fear there won't be a thing left inside that cave when it finally does dry up." She looked down. "I still can't believe how you made it."

He took her hand. "Julia, there is something, ah, well, about us I have to tell you." He searched for words. "It will seem . . . you know, strange. Very strange, especially after I supposedly suffered a concussion. I don't want you to think I lost my mind."

She stared at him, apparently taken aback. "This is too soon, Liam."

"It's not what you think." He grinned. "Tell me, do you believe in life after death?"

She took a step back and looked at him with fresh concern. "Life after death? I don't know. My parents always taught me to believe in what I can see and explain."

He thought of the day when he led the pawnshop owner around the lake to the Mahatma Gandhi World Peace Memorial. "How would you like to accompany me to a shrine that is very dear to me in Pacific Palisades?"

She eyed him suspiciously. "It sounds intriguing. But this won't lead to another treasure hunt, will it?"

He smiled mysteriously. "That depends entirely on you."

EPILOGUE

Police officers and National Park Service rangers could not enter the denuded cave until twelve days after Santa Barbara's biggest recorded storm. The Park Service is presently developing plans to preserve the remnants of the cave paintings.

The Rash brothers found a sympathetic lawyer. Loopholes in the law, the brothers' blatant lies, and a general lack of legal teeth in the laws to prosecute poachers and looters almost made a mockery of the rangers' work.

Michael Kuyam's store on Anapamu Street no longer exists.

Glen Lerario will soon retire from the Park Service.

Patrick still serves in the military, and is currently in Afghanistan.

Liam and Julia married the following summer at the Lake Shrine in Pacific Palisades. His work is on exhibit at a gallery in greater San Francisco. Julia breeds horses and gets involved in local archeological projects. They make their home in Marin County, not very far from where they first met.

In 1903 a man from Monterey purchased Mónoy's necklace from a Chumash Indian in Santa Barbara. The piece was part of a private family collection for over a century, until Julia acquired it. One day each year it goes on display at the gallery.